DREAMWEAVER

C. S. FRIEDMAN

DREAMWEAVER

Book Three of
The Dreamwalker Chronicles

DAW BOOKS, INC.

DONALD A. WOLLHEIM, FOUNDER

375 Hudson Street, New York, NY 10014

**ELIZABETH R. WOLLHEIM
SHEILA E. GILBERT
PUBLISHERS**

www.dawbooks.com

For Carmen

Acknowledgments

Special thanks to Gary Varner, whose exhaustive knowledge of southwestern symbology was both informative and inspiring.

Thanks to Kim Dobson, whose early plot suggestions played a major part in the conclusion of this trilogy.

And thanks to the *Dreamweaver* beta team: Carl Cipra, Jennifer Hina, Zsuzsy Sanford, Erin Warren, and David Williams. I don't think I've ever worked on a book where my beta's insights were so important. This book is what it is because of you guys.

PROLOGUE

O N THE WORLD that has no name,
        Atop a mountain of black stone,
    The skeleton waits.

Its bones are granite and mortar, scoured clean by the wind and sun. Its ribs are tall, vaulted windows, their glass long gone, their peaked arches crumbling. Amidst the ruins a single narrow tower stands, rising from the black earth as if the arm of some long-buried creature is struggling to reach the sun. Its turrets are jagged and broken, and where there are breaches in the walls one can see that the interior is streaked with soot from an ancient fire.

Surrounding the ruins is a field of tall crimson grass, and beyond that a thick black hedge twice as tall as a man, whose branches are so closely intertwined that not even light can pass between them. There are animals present: one can hear predators moving through the grass in search of prey and catch a glimpse of birds amidst the tangled branches, dodging thorns as long as a man's hand. But there is little life on the

black mountain itself. A few patches of moss cling to the base
of the broken walls. A single foolhardy vine has managed to
climb halfway up the tower, and its leaves stir in the breeze,
giving the tower the illusion of breath. As if the ancient fortress that once stood here is just asleep, rather than dead.

A shadow passes in front of the sun.

A three-headed dog looks up from its hiding place in the
tall grass, suddenly alert. A lizard with the wings of a bat
crawls out upon a thorned branch so it can see well. A cluster
of rats with tails knotted together peers out from a burrow, a
hundred eyes moving in unison as they nervously scan the sky.

The shadow is growing larger now, though there are no
clouds in the sky to explain its existence. The leaves of the ivy
curl in upon themselves, as if trying to draw away from it. The
surrounding sky begins to lose its color, fading from bright
blue to a more muted shade.

One of the dog's three heads whimpers.

The shadow starts to coalesce over the tower, taking on the
shape of a man. Its body is not made of flesh, but of a darkness
so absolute that all light and heat from the surrounding landscape are sucked into it. The sky surrounding it turns grey.
The leaves of the ivy begin to fall. Frost forms along the ancient turrets.

The winged lizard hisses in terror and disappears into the
hollow of a tree. The rats dart back into their burrow, tripping
over each other in their flight.

Another shadow begins to take form, identical to the first.
It is followed by another. Seven wraiths appear in all, their
substance darker than the blackest night, and the tower grows
dim as they circle it restlessly, as if searching for something.
Then the first one begins to howl. It is a cry of anguish and
fury commingled, and one by one the other shadowy wraiths
join in. The unnatural sound resonates across the landscape,
awakening memories of loss in all who hear it. The three-

headed dog remembers the mournful night its mate was killed. The lizard relives that terrible day when it returned to its nest to find that its eggs had been devoured. The king rat recalls what it was like to run free in the fields, alone and unencumbered, and whimpers.

And then, as suddenly as it began, the unnatural howling ceases. The shadows circle a few minutes longer in silence, then begin to dissipate. One after another they fade into the greyness of the sky, until they can no longer be seen. The first to arrive is the last to leave.

Not until the last one is completely gone does color return to the world.

1

MANASSAS
VIRGINIA

JESSE

THE SOUND OF SOMEONE SCREAMING woke me up.

For a moment I had no clue where I was. I just lay there staring at an unfamiliar ceiling, struggling to get my bearings. Then, slowly, the memories associated with my new home situation sank in. I remembered how we'd moved back to Manassas so Mom could return to work, which required renting an apartment that was way too small for our family. It was the best we could do on a monthly lease, Mom said; she didn't want to commit to more than that while the insurance for our fire-ravaged family home was still being settled. Having only two bedrooms meant that someone would have to share sleeping accommodations, and Tommy and I had agreed that Mom needed her privacy, so we'd worked out a time-sharing arrangement for the second bedroom. During the day either of us could use the room, but at night Tommy bunked on the fold-out couch in the living room. Hopefully, we'd soon be moving to a place where such a complicated dance wasn't necessary.

All of which was no help at all in figuring out where the scream came from. I strained my senses to the utmost, listening for any more disturbances but heard only the dim murmur of neighbors through the paper-thin walls, arguing or making love or watching TV.

Then I heard another cry—lower than the first, more of a moan this time—and realized it was coming from Mom's room. She wasn't in the habit of screaming in her sleep, so I threw off my blanket as quickly as I could and sprinted across the room, nearly tripping over one of Tommy's board games along the way. As I ran out into the claustrophobically narrow hallway I saw Tommy stirring on the couch—though whether he'd heard Mom's cry, or I'd woken him up when the bedroom door slammed open, was anyone's guess.

I found Mom huddled on her bed, her arms wrapped tightly around her knees, staring into the darkness with fearful eyes. I looked around the room for any sign of immediate danger, but didn't see anything. That meant little, of course. There were creatures in the universe that could move unseen through the night, and some of them knew my name.

"Mom? You okay?" I moved to the edge of the bed and sat down, reaching out to put a hand on her arm. She was shaking like a leaf. "What happened?"

"I saw it," she whispered. "In my dream. It . . . it attacked me."

"What did?"

"All darkness and cold. What did you call it? A reaper." Her voice was hoarse with fear. "It sucked in all the color . . . just like you described. Devouring everything. Then it saw me. It had no eyes, but I knew somehow that it was looking at me." She drew in a shaky breath. "I started to run. It followed me, and I couldn't run fast enough to get away."

"Shit," Tommy muttered from behind my right shoulder. I hadn't heard him come in, so his sudden voice made me jump.

I squeezed Mom's arm reassuringly, but inside I was anything but calm. Of all the things that Tommy and I had feared might happen after I came home, a reaper attacking Mom wasn't even on the list. She wasn't a Dreamwalker, so why would one of them go after her?

"I had no idea that I was dreaming at first," Mom went on. "It all seemed so real." She looked at me. "But then I remembered our talk, and what you said about them, and suddenly I understood what was really happening and was able to wake myself up."

"I don't get it," Tommy began. "Why would a reaper—"

I elbowed him in his side to shut him up. "You'll be fine," I told my mother. "What Tommy's trying to say is, the reapers have no reason to hurt you. They were created to hunt Dreamwalkers, and you're not one. So it must have been some kind of mistake. Identity confusion." I shot Tommy a look that I hoped would drive home how important it was for us to focus on calming Mom down, and discuss the larger implications of this later. He nodded his understanding but didn't look happy about it. He'd been there back when I woke up from my first confrontation with a reaper, and he was probably thinking about the bloody gash it had given me, that was still on my arm in the waking world. I could remember the horror of that discovery as if it had just happened, and I could see in his eyes that he did, too. If a reaper attacked Mom in a dream, did that mean it could hurt her in the same way?

I'd never told my mother about that wound, though with summer clothing it had taken some effort to keep it covered. It had seemed the right choice to make, giving her less to worry about. But now? If reapers were starting to show up in her dreams, maybe she should know the full measure of their power.

But that still left the question of why one of them had attacked her in the first place. Back when Isaac had researched them in the Shadowlords' archives, he'd discovered they were created during an ancient war between the Shadowlords and the Dreamwalkers, and were trained to sniff out and destroy anyone who possessed the dreamer's Gift. So every time I entered another person's dream there was a chance the reapers would find me. But Mom wasn't a Dreamwalker, so why on earth would a reaper attack her? Isaac might be able to answer that, or at least point me in the right direction to find answers on my own, but we were on different worlds now, and the only way I could contact him was to use the same power that would draw the reapers to me. Catch 22.

There was always a chance that Mom's assailant wasn't real. Tommy and I had told her about the reapers less than a week ago, so that conversation was still fresh in her memory; maybe my description had taken root in her mind and prompted a normal—albeit terrifying—nightmare. God, how I wanted to believe that! But the screaming suggested otherwise. Mom didn't do that with regular nightmares.

She brushed a hand across her face, wiping tears from her eyes. Then she mumbled something about freshening up, and I gave her room to slide off the bed. She seemed to be pulling herself together. As she walked to the apartment's one bathroom I felt a sense of relief that Tommy and I would have a few minutes alone to process all this.

Mom never told us exactly what she'd experienced when the Fleshcrafter repaired her brain after my last return from Terra Prime, but we soon figured out that she hadn't just been asleep during all that. Did she spend the time dreaming of other worlds, witnessing shadows of the truth? Or was she physically frozen but awake, conscious enough to sense what was being done to her, and to hear what we were saying? In the days following she never volunteered any information about that night, and Tommy and I respected her desire not to talk about it. But now and then I would catch her staring at herself in the mirror in a disturbing way, studying her face as if its shape was unfamiliar. And when Tommy and I finally decided to tell her the truth about our recent travels, she didn't discount our story like Dr. Tilford had, coming up with theories about false memories or shared delusions, but instead took it all in with an eerie calm. Like she'd known for some time that there were alien forces at work in our family, and had just lacked the details needed to give them a name. I knew in that moment that whatever she had experienced during her fleshcrafting, she understood on a visceral level that the Gift that was used on her was not of this world.

I'd warned her about the reapers so that if I ever wanted to visit her dreams I could do so safely, because she would know to wake herself up if one appeared. Thank God I'd done that. Tonight she had learned why I was so afraid to use the Gift that was in my blood.

"You're going to have to deal with them," Tommy muttered.

Through the window I could see the streets of Manassas, maybe not the exact location where I'd grown up, but close enough that I felt like I belonged there. Sometimes at night I would lay awake, staring into the Manassas darkness, breathing in the Manassas air, thinking about how our house was being rebuilt, how soon I would be back with old friends and familiar teachers, painting art that no one understood, doing normal teenage stuff. The concept was appealing.

Never mind that it was all a lie. Never mind that I'd been born on another world and possessed a Gift—or perhaps a curse—that might, in time, drive me insane. Never mind that I was being hunted by fearsome wraiths created by undead necromancers and that the odds of my returning to school in September like a normal kid were only slightly lower than being hit by lightning. Now reapers were showing up in the dreams of people I loved. What the hell did that mean?

Tomorrow. That was what I told myself each morning when I woke up. Tomorrow I would deal with the Gift that threatened to destroy my sanity. Tomorrow I would find a way to escape the reapers. Tomorrow I would seek a way to free myself from the frightening path I'd been sucked into, in which every possible choice seemed to lead to more fear, more destruction.

In the distance I could hear my mother washing up, calming down. Normal. So normal.

"Yeah," I whispered to Tommy. "I know."

I had run out of tomorrows.

2

DEVON'S TEXT CAME while I was busy searching the internet for necromancers. Or, more accurately, searching the internet for information on how to search the internet for necromancers. My best efforts hadn't yet turned up any search term that would weed through the forest of fakes, wannabes, and plain old delusional folks who were out there, and for once even Tommy had drawn a blank. If there was someone on my own world, Terra Colonna, who had the power to banish reapers, damn if I knew how to find him.

Isaac was the one who'd told me that there were probably real necromancers on our world, though not powerful ones. Since the most promising infants were habitually stolen away by the Shadows to be raised on Terra Prime, the only necromancers I was likely to find here were ones so weak that the Shadows weren't interested in them. But what choice did I have? The reapers weren't going to go away on their own. Isaac believed that someone with a trace of his necromantic Gift might be able to banish them, but he wasn't here to help, so I had to search for that someone on my own.

With a sigh I picked up my phone, grateful for the interruption. But when I saw Devon's text my good mood vanished.

Erase all texts from me. And from Rita. And emails, to and from. Tell Tommy.

My breath caught in my throat. *What's wrong?* I typed. *Are you OK?*

Seyer's number 2, he texted. *Delete it. Delete anything about other worlds.*

Whats this about?

Just do it. Trust me. After a pause he added, *Text me when you're done.*

I sent him another plea for information, but all I got back was, *Later.* And no response after that.

Damn.

I went to find Tommy, to show him the texts.

"Shit," he muttered. "That's not good."

Shaking my head in frustration—not to mention annoyance at Devon's melodrama—I brought up my contact list and scrolled down to Miriam Seyer's name. Devon wouldn't have given me instructions like that unless it was pretty important, and I clearly wasn't going to get an explanation until we did what he wanted. So we might as well get started.

All in all it took Tommy and me more than an hour to delete all relevant data from our devices. The stuff on our phones and computers was easy enough to deal with, but our internet provider still had copies of all our emails, so we had to go online and deal with that as well, rooting through every corner of their system where copies might be hiding, double-deleting the trash. Then Tommy checked the online forums where I'd once talked to other changelings, and did what he could to remove my past postings. Meanwhile I tried not to obsess about how pointless all this was. We'd both watched enough police procedurals to know that if anyone *really* wanted to find our stuff, copies were still out there somewhere. Neither Tommy nor I had the tech expertise required to make our internet history disappear from all servers for good. I hoped to God that the superficial cleansing we were able to manage would address whatever Devon was concerned about.

When we were finally finished I picked up my phone again to text him, but it took me a moment to figure out how to communicate what we'd just done without—well, without telling him what we'd just done.

Finished with chores, I typed at last.

The answer came so quickly it must have been typed on his phone already, waiting for him to hit the send button. *Got the car for the day. Grab lunch? Maybe the place we met, Red Robin off 28?*

I stared at the message, not knowing how to respond.

"What?" Tommy asked. "What is it?"

In answer I handed him the phone. He squinted at it. "I thought you guys met at IHOP?"

"We did meet at IHOP."

Tommy whistled softly under his breath as he handed the phone back to me. "That's pretty paranoid, Jess."

It was. And the paranoia was coming from a guy who was notoriously well grounded, so I had to assume he had a good reason for it. Did he really think someone might be spying on our conversation right now? Or was he just trying to be as thorough in this as he was with everything else?

Or what if it wasn't Devon at all? Someone else could have gotten hold of his phone. But I had no way to find out if that was true without showing up.

I stared at the phone for a minute, then typed. *Sure. Same time as last?*

Y. 1 pm. Meet u there.

Slowly I put down the phone. Devon and I had met at noon, not at one. So that was another lie, offered up for the consumption of unseen observers. I was feeling more and more uneasy about the situation.

"You gonna be okay?" Tommy asked. After a pause he added, "Am *I* gonna be okay?"

I don't know, I thought. Who did Devon think was spying on us? Local people? Gifted aliens? Ghosts? The fact that this was happening so soon after the reaper's visit to my mom was deeply disturbing. Were the two events connected? "I'm sure Devon will explain everything," I said. "And once we know what's going on, I'm sure we'll be able to deal with it."

It was another lie. And Tommy knew it was a lie. But the words were comforting, so we both let them stand.

iiiiiiiiiiiii

I watched the IHOP from a distance before approaching, but didn't see any overt signs of trouble, so I finally headed inside and sat at the same table where Devon, Rita and I had held our first conversation. I remembered how he had walked into the restaurant that day, tall and attractive and oh so confident. I'd relied upon that confidence during our first trip to Terra Prime, drawing strength from him in the midst of all the alien craziness. The fact that he wasn't the kind of guy who panicked easily made his recent texts seem ten times more ominous.

I ordered lemonade and played with the straw while I waited for him. Déjà vu. He arrived soon after and looked around the restaurant before approaching me, like Rita had done when she'd first arrived. Checking to see where the exits were. A knot formed in my gut.

"Hey." He slid into the booth opposite me.

"Hey."

The IHOP was full, but it was a lunch crowd, and everyone was busy with conversations of their own. Devon looked around the room again, searching for . . . what? Men in black suits and dark glasses guarding the doorways? Someone pointing a parabolic microphone at us? He was making me very nervous. It didn't help that we hadn't talked much lately. Devon's dad had decided that I was responsible for his son's delusions about alien worlds, not to mention his sudden illness in Berkeley Springs, and had been doing everything possible to keep us apart. Since we lived far enough from each other that a car was required for a visit, it was hard to get around that.

Would the reapers go after Devon as well? The sudden thought was unnerving.

"Do you still have the fetter lamp?" he asked me.

We'd given the lamp to his father for a brief time to study. Our hope was that once he confirmed its technology wasn't from Earth—our Earth—he'd be open to believing the rest of our story. But we'd underestimated the power of his denial, and once it was clear the artifact wasn't going to convince him that our story was real, I had decided to hold on to it. "Yeah," I told Devon. "But it's out of power now."

"Thank God." The tension in his shoulders eased a tiny bit. "Thank God."

It seemed an odd reaction. "You want to tell me what all this is about?"

"You remember Chen?" he asked, lowering his voice to a near-whisper.

I shook my head.

"The changeling in Taiwan," he prompted.

I remembered that during our first IHOP meeting, Devon had talked about a changeling in Taiwan, but I'd been hit with so much new information that day that it was hard to remember all the details. Was Chen the one who had been stung to death by bees? Or the one who had surfed in a hurricane? So many changelings had died that week, in strange and terrible ways, it was hard to keep them straight. "Just pretend I don't remember anything and take it from there," I told him.

So he reminded me about the changeling in Taiwan whose father had been a geneticist. It was through Chen that we'd learned changelings lacked genetic markers which normal human beings were supposed to have. Now, of course, we knew the reason for that. We'd all been born on another world, one where people looked human and acted human most of the time, but differed in ways that scientists could detect. And Chen's father was a scientist. He'd taken Chen's DNA to a lab, where he and his fellow scientists said they were going to study the matter further. Chen had promised to cut off all contact with us if things started getting dicey.

Then he had cut off all contact with us.

"My father kept tabs on their efforts," Devon said, "as much as was possible, given how secretive the whole operation was. He's got international connections who were feeding him information." He paused. "Key word there is, *were.*"

I felt a cold knot forming in my stomach. "They stopped?"

His face was grim as he nodded.

"Shit. That's not good."

"Dad worked for the government once, and he still has some friends in high places. One of them passed on a warning to him. He didn't tell me exactly what they said, but he told me it would be good if details of our Terra Prime story weren't part of the public record. And if any *unusual artifacts* we had weren't easy to find. Those were his exact words."

"I thought he didn't believe our story."

Following our return to Terra Colonna we'd convinced police investigators that we'd been drugged by fictitious kidnappers, so that our memories were effectively useless. It had proven a successful tactic for bringing the victim testimony portion of the kidnapping investigation to an early close. But the plan had backfired later when we tried to come clean with Devon's dad. We'd been drugged. We'd imagined things that weren't there. Wherever the fetter lamp came from, it wasn't from an alien world. End of story.

Devon shrugged. There was weariness in the motion. His relationship with his father had been strained since that phony confession, I knew. I ached to comfort him.

"I don't know what he believes anymore," he said. "But his suggestion makes sense. If we're going to pretend that what happened to us was a mundane crime, we should get rid of anything that would cause people to question that."

"Well, like I said, the lamp doesn't work anymore."

"But it's still got the sigil of the Weaver's Guild on it. Who's to say where else that might show up? We're all on the government's radar thanks to Chen. We can't afford to have anything around that would raise more questions. Destroy the thing, Jesse. Crush it to dust and scatter it on the wind."

His intensity unnerved me. "I will, I promise."

"And anything else that links us to Terra Prime. Or to other changelings. Or . . . any of it." He sighed. "If they really put their minds to it, we can't keep them from finding our data. Not without wiping dozens of servers clean. But my dad's right, let's at least make things less obvious. Maybe after a cursory survey they'll decide we're not worth the time and energy needed to dig deeper. After all, we're just kids, right?"

I reached out and took his hand. "The Gate we travelled through is buried under hundreds of tons of earth," I reminded him. "And asking us questions is pointless because of our supposed memory loss. We'll be fine."

"That's *our* trail, but what about all the others? Every changeling on Terra Colonna was brought here through a Gate. Each of them was exchanged for a baby born on this world, so hospital records had to be altered. You said that your own footprint matched the one on your birth certificate. Was that kind of thing managed perfectly every time? What about security cameras? Did the Greys in charge of baby exchanges never make a mistake?" He shook his head. "There's evidence of the truth out there, Jesse, it's waiting to be found, and someday someone will follow the right trail, and find out about the Gates. How do you think the Guilds will respond to that?"

I hadn't even thought about the Guilds. For a moment I couldn't speak.

"You see the problem," he said.

The Guilds of Terra Prime considered genocide an acceptable strategy for safeguarding their interests, I knew. And what greater Guild interest was there than preventing a world like ours from

finding out about the Gates? The last thing they wanted was for people from Terra Colonna to cross into their world without sanction,
armed with hi-tech weapons and bad attitude. If our government
started nosing around the places where Gates were hidden, the
Guilds' response to that might get ugly. They'd destroyed worlds for
less.

"What can we do?" I asked.

"Nothing. We can't do anything. Just get rid of all the obvious evidence and pray they never find what they're looking for. What else is
possible?"

Our food arrived then, temporarily halting our conversation. The
waitress attempted to make small talk with us but realized pretty
quickly that we weren't in the mood, so she left. The brief interruption at least dispersed some of the negative tension. It was hard to
think about genocide when someone was smiling and talking about
the beautiful summer weather.

When she was gone we talked about other things. Safer things. I
told him how my mom appeared to have accepted the truth of our
Terra Prime story, probably because of something the Fleshcrafter
had done to her. He said I was lucky. He said he would give anything
to have his father believe us, the way Mom did.

I might have been dating him by now, if not for his dad. We certainly would have been closer than we were, confiding in each other
on a daily basis rather than sneaking in a few moments during clan-
destine lunch dates. I always felt an ache of regret when I talked to
him, about what might have been.

We called for the check at 12:55, and were well on our way home
before anyone waiting for us at Red Robin would realize we weren't
showing up.

ıııııııııııı

On the top shelf of my bedroom closet were several boxed war games.
The three on top of the pile were Tommy's. The one on the bottom
wasn't.

I shut the blinds, pulled out the bottom box, and set it on the desk. It was well worn, with faded pictures of armed robots and hostile aliens all over it. I removed the cover and set it aside, followed by the loose pieces inside the box. Cards and dice and tiny models of robots, all well used. Last came the board itself, a heavy cardboard piece folded into quarters. It didn't unfold by itself, thanks to the paper-thin strip of putty I'd stuck inside it, but a fingernail inserted between the layers was enough to pry it open.

Inside were several papers. The first was a large sheet folded into eighths; I smoothed it open, revealing the map of Terra Prime that Sebastian had given us back when he brought us to Shadowcrest. *The United Colonies of New Britannia* were east of the Mississippi and *The Badlands* far west, with French-named provinces in between. I stared at it for a minute, considering, then opened the desk drawer and took out a red pen. *B+* I wrote in the upper left corner, slanting the handwriting so it wouldn't look like my own. *Good start, but needs more detail.* Next to a city in what would normally be Oklahoma, I wrote, *Why French?* Then I circled the area labeled "Badlands" and drew an arrow pointing north. *Badlands should be here,* I wrote.

There. Class project. No one would think twice about it.

Next came three round trip transfer tickets I'd bought before leaving Terra Prime, in case I ever needed to go back there. They had my Terra Prime passport code on them and a few other alphanumeric sequences I didn't recognize, but nothing that screamed "alien artifact." They looked like fancy raffle tickets. I folded them up and put them in my back pocket.

Then came the smoking gun.

Before leaving Terra Prime I'd gotten a list of Gates from the Fleshcrafters, along with the contact info needed to access them. I'd figured that if I ever wanted to go back to Terra Prime I shouldn't have to sell my soul to Alia Morgana to do so. My fingers trembled slightly as I touched the names and phone numbers of the Greys who controlled the Gates, sensing the power coiled within that data. If the wrong people got hold of this list they would be able to identify Terra Prime agents and locate the Gates they guarded. Maybe they would even visit one under the cover of legitimate business. And the fate of my world would be sealed.

I took out a small sketchbook and began to draw, quickly penciling in designs with fractal waves that cascaded in rhythmic sequences, like in a Hokusai print. Each curving crest broke up again and again as it descended, in seemingly random array. Only it wasn't random. Encoded in those waves were the phone numbers I needed, information I couldn't afford to lose.

The last item in the secret stash was my Terra Prime passport. It was made out to Jennifer Dolan, but the picture in it was unmistakably of me. After what Devon had told me, I was no longer comfortable leaving it in our apartment, so I decided to keep it on my person until a better hiding place presented itself. I put it in my pocket also, closed up the game box, returned that to the closet, and then retrieved the fetter lamp from behind my bed. A mere glass marble now, drained of its magic.

In the kitchen I set fire to the contact list, dropping it into the sink to let it burn itself out. When the last glowing edges died I tore the resulting fragments of charred paper into tiny bits, then lit them again. And again. In the end, all that remained was a pile of black ash, which I crushed to dust between my fingertips, mixed in with some leftovers, and sent down the garbage disposal. Then I put a bowl of water in the microwave, and turned the small glass marble over in my hand as I waited for the liquid to boil, tracing the Weaver's mark with my finger. I remembered how we had depended upon the tiny lamp to light our way through an alien and terrifying world. I remembered the other fetters I had seen there, the plates of metal with the life-essence of young children bound to them, including the essence of a Dreamwalker. I remembered the mysterious tower I had seen through his eyes, whose form changed every time I looked at it, whose every window revealed a different view. The girl who invaded my dreams had fled to that tower. The reaper who attacked me knew about it.

There were ancient secrets bound to that place, and perhaps the information I needed to survive might be found there. But was the tower real, or just a shared illusion? How do you search for a place without knowing the answer to that?

When the water finally boiled I took the bowl out of the microwave and dropped the fetter lamp into it. The glass ball fractured without breaking apart, turning into a jewel-like sphere riddled with glittering fault lines. Easy to smash. Easy to flush down the toilet.

Would that the memories it conjured could be flushed away so easily.

3

LURAY
VIRGINIA PRIME

ALIA MORGANA

IN DEFERENCE TO THE SHADOWS, the Council of Guilds always met at night. So when the reigning Shadowlord didn't show up for a scheduled meeting, it was more than a little annoying.

Morgana looked around the large chamber, noting how many of her allies were present. More and more members of her Consortium were rising in rank and no longer needed to wield power through back channels; several now ruled their Guilds openly. It had been an unexpected benefit of their conspiracy. Once they had agreed they were willing to share sensitive information to undermine the Shadows, using that information for personal gain was a natural next step. Morgana had leveraged that advantage to take control of her own Guild, and now others were doing the same. Among the thirteen Major Guild representatives seated around the Council table, Morgana and her allies controlled five votes directly, and they had measurable influence over others. It wasn't a rock-solid majority yet, but soon it would be.

All for hatred of the Shadows, Morgana mused. Perhaps she should thank the necromancers.

The power that filled the chamber was a sweet elixir, and Morgana shut her eyes for a moment to savor it. Luray's position as a major trade hub drew the most ambitious men and women from across the region, and many of the Guildmasters in Luray still had allies and agents in the cities they'd left behind. Some of the Guildmasters were said to have sway in the halls of the National Guild Council, and it was rumored that one even had agents in Buckingham Palace. In the shadows of Guild halls it was whispered: *As the politics of Luray go, so go the politics of the British Empire.*

Gazing at Virilian's empty chair across from her, Morgana wondered about the Shadowlord's absence. The undead were uniquely complex creatures, difficult even for a Seer to analyze. The fact that the *umbrae majae* absorbed souls of dead Shadowlords meant that at any moment some fragment of ancient memory might surface, sparking a long-forgotten passion or long-buried enmity. Without knowing the history of each soul a Shadowlord had devoured, one could not hope to untangle his motives.

The Shadowlords don't really devour souls, she reminded herself. *They absorb the memories of their predecessors.* But if a man's soul was shaped by his memories, wasn't that a mere technicality?

A chill wind suddenly swept into the room, raising the hairs along the back of Morgana's neck. Though she could not hear ghosts herself, she could sense them reflected in the mind of the Shadowlord Virilian, who was now approaching: whispery cries, tormented moans, a symphony of suffering. Morgana had never understood why spirits would gather around the Shadowlords if it caused them so much pain. Were they bound to the undead by some necromantic ritual, unable to leave their master's side? Or did the Shadows' Gift just draw them naturally, like a flame drew insects? As Morgana heard the Shadowlord approach she braced herself to ignore the pitiful moaning, as well as any other bit of undead activity that might echo in his mind. Virilian must never suspect how much of the Shadows' world she was able to observe through him.

Suddenly Augustus Virilian himself was standing in the doorway . . .

or maybe not. Though the body looked like Virilian's, something about him had been altered, dramatically enough that Morgana's Gift had no trouble detecting it. She had observed enough similar changes down through the years to guess at the cause. Virilian had undergone Communion again, absorbing the memories of yet another ancient Shadowlord into himself. If so, that would make him uniquely unstable tonight. Not that Shadowlords were ever truly stable.

Virilian looked around the room as if seeing it for the first time, which confirmed her suspicions. As his gaze fell upon each Guildmaster he paused, as if taking a moment to remember who he or she was. But when his eyes met Morgana's, recognition was immediate. His expression hardened, and hatred resonated in his aura. It was so surprising that it took all Morgana's self-control not to respond to it, to just smile and nod politely as if she didn't sense anything wrong. But God in Heaven, where was that coming from? She had never sensed emotion that intense in Virilian before, and certainly never hatred toward her. Clearly, whatever new soul he had devoured had no love for Seers. She dropped her hands into her lap so she could clench and unclench them without his seeing, bleeding off some of her tension.

"Forgive my lateness," Virilian said. There was an unusual cadence to his voice, Morgana noted, almost a trace of an accent. As he moved toward his chair the nearest Guildmasters edged away, a move that seemed more instinctive than conscious. That, too, was interesting. The Greys and the Soulriders were accustomed to dealing with Virilian, but even they seemed disturbed by his new aspect.

The Domitor was serving as Council Arbiter this month, and after watching the awkward ballet for a few moments, he picked up his gavel and struck it on the table. "The Greater Guild Council of Luray is hereby called to order." He looked at Virilian. "As you are the one who requested this meeting, the floor is yours."

"I thank you," Virilian said. He looked around the table. "Fellow Guildmasters, our Guilds joined forces centuries ago to do battle with an enemy that threatened our world, and though many of our people died in that conflict, or were driven mad—for such is the price of confronting this particular enemy. In the end we thought ourselves victorious. We believed our enemy destroyed, and that all we must do to guard against its resurrection was to weed out the seeds of its Gift whenever it appeared anew." He paused. "Perhaps we overestimated our victory at that time. Or perhaps we failed in our duty afterward, allowing the seeds of corruption to take root among us. The one thing that is certain now is that our ancient enemy was not destroyed, and is in fact returning. If we do not deal with it swiftly and mercilessly, all the human worlds will be at risk."

"And the name of this enemy?" the Farspeaker asked.

"I speak of the Dreamwalkers." The cries of ghostly suffering rose in intensity as Virilian's black eyes fixed on Morgana. Was there a hidden accusation in their depths? Morgana kept her face carefully neutral, but her mind was racing. Had Jessica slipped up and revealed herself to the Shadows? Or had Virilian perhaps caught wind of the game Morgana was playing? Thank God Morgana hadn't told her allies about Jessica's Gift yet. They couldn't betray secrets they didn't know.

"The Dreamwalkers are gone," the Domitor challenged Virilian. "The original ones were destroyed, and new ones are killed in their infancy. If one of them manages to slip through our net, then we catch him when his curse begins to manifest. It's not a subtle Gift, you know. And there are Seers trained to detect it."

"Yes," Virilian said quietly. His eyes were still fixed on Morgana. "There are such Seers, aren't there?"

There was nothing safe to say, so Morgana said nothing.

The Farspeaker said, "Is there any hard evidence that they're back? Or is this just speculation?"

Virilian's voice was like ice. "A Dreamwalker attempted to enter the mind of a Shadowlord. The effort failed, but only because our Guild has sentinels to guard against such things. The fact that those sentinels were activated is proof enough that one exists."

The Healer asked, "Why would a Dreamwalker target one of your people?"

"Who can say why they do what they do? Perhaps he was just practicing his art, testing his limits. Perhaps there was a darker agenda. Does it matter? One fully manifested Dreamwalker can awaken others. We can't afford to let the cycle begin anew."

There was rage building inside Virilian now, and it was unlike anything Morgana had ever sensed in an *umbra maja* before. The Shadowlords believed that passion hampered their ability to control the dead, so it was rare to see any of them give in to primitive emotions. But this was different. There was a cauldron of seething passion inside Virilian that threatened to break through to the surface at any moment. Dark passion, bloody passion, hatred and fury and a hunger for killing that bordered on madness. It was almost too much for her to absorb.

"How easy it is to discount a threat that you've never seen!" Virilian snapped. "It's little more than a legend to all of you, but I've witnessed what the dreamer's curse can do. I've seen grown men frothing at the mouth as they struggled to awaken themselves from sleep, trapped in dreams so terrifying that their sanity was destroyed forever. I've seen children running desperately through the streets, screaming as they fled from imaginary monsters, unable to distinguish between nightmare and reality. I've seen an entire city go mad as the paranoid fantasies of *a single Dreamwalker* poured into the heads of each man, woman and child, infecting every thought, corrupting every emotion. And if you think that the Gifted would be spared this fate, you are mistaken. The Seers suffered more than any others in those times, for their Gift made them uniquely vulnerable." He looked pointedly at Morgana. "In the end, there were so many suicides that bodies had to be piled on carts like those of plague victims. The Euphrates was so thick with corpses you could cross from one shore to the other by walking on them. That was the work of *one* Dreamwalker. One! So I ask you, how many must there be before this Council is willing to act? How many cities must we lose to them while waiting?" He paused. "How many *Gifted* must we lose?"

The room fell silent. Virilian's eyes were still fixed on Morgana, and the challenge in them was unmistakable. Did he suspect that she was involved with the Dreamwalkers? Or was there some other reason he was focusing on her? "How do you propose we fight these creatures?" she asked.

Lips tight, Virilian nodded his approval; Morgana had the sense that she had just passed some kind of test. "First, we must offer them neither sympathy nor mercy. They will tell you their intentions are benign, but that means nothing. Dreamwalkers do not *choose* to spread chaos; it is a symptom of their insanity, as natural to them as eating and breathing. Any promises they make while they're sane become irrelevant once their madness manifests. Our ancestors understood that, which is why they were ruthless in eradicating them. So we must be again. Anyone who would argue for mercy must be suspect. Any who would shelter a Dreamwalker must be punished harshly. And any world that harbors them must be Cleansed."

The Potter's eyes narrowed. "That seems . . . extreme."

"The threat is extreme," Virilian assured him. "Half-measures will not do."

"Do you have a particular world in mind?" the Domitor asked. "Or are we just theorizing?"

Virilian nodded. "I have reason to believe there is a Dreamwalker active on Terra Colonna."

The Healer stiffened. The Farspeaker cursed under his breath. The Grey said, "Terra Colonna and Terra Prime are in the same reality cluster. A Cleansing of their world would adversely affect our own."

"Then that's a risk we must take," the Shadowlord said. "Unless, of course, your Guild can manage to find the Dreamwalker." His tone was acid. "Then there would be no need for extreme measures."

The Grey didn't respond, but Morgana saw his jawline twitch. His Guild had no clue why they had failed to find Terra Colonna's Dreamwalker, but Morgana knew. It was Jessica's dreams that had originally alerted them to the possibility that one might exist, but since Jessica's brother was the one who had used them as inspiration for his online games, and had claimed creative credit for them, attention had focused on him. Once it was confirmed that he was not a Dreamwalker, the Greys started seeking out the original source for his stories. The problem was, she didn't exist. Tommy had created her, breathing life into a fictitious identity with the help of his gaming associates, seeding hints of fake activity in a thousand different forums. It was an impressive feat for such a young boy, and it had successfully turned the Grey's attention away from his family. But now it looked like Tommy's plan was about to backfire. By making his counterfeit Dreamwalker seem so real, Tommy had convinced the Greys there was an active threat they weren't able to find. And now the Shadows were involved. By protecting his family, Morgana thought, Tommy Drake might have doomed his world.

As for her own plans, they were in no better shape. She'd planned to tell her allies about Jessica when the girl was properly prepared to serve them, but now that Virilian had presented his tale of death and destruction to the Council, they weren't likely to handle the news well. Indeed, the discovery that Morgana had secretly been protecting a Dreamwalker all along could fracture their conspiracy.

Well played, she thought dryly.

What if Virilian was right? All Morgana's actions thus far had been based upon her belief that the ancient reports must be wrong, that the infamous Dreamwalker madness was never more than a legend. But what if she was wrong, and it was real? What if Jessica did have the seed of a monster inside her, and it was growing because Morgana had nurtured it? Morgana would be the one responsible for returning a deadly threat to Terra Prime.

No. My research was sound. My conclusions are sound. Virilian— or whoever was inside Virilian, using his body like a puppet—clearly had a vested interest in casting the Dreamwalkers as enemies. But why? The bloodthirst she sensed in him when he talked about them was unnerving in its intensity. If he knew that they weren't really a threat—to the point where he was making up stories to turn others against them—then why was it so important to him that they be killed? What made them so threatening to the Shadows that they merited the destruction of an entire world? She had her suspicions, but as of yet, no proof.

"I am sure I can count on the Seers for that," Virilian said acidly.

Morgana realized that her mind had wandered away from the conversation at hand, and that she had no idea what he was referring to. Usually she wasn't that careless. "My Guild understands the issues involved," she said coldly, hoping that would cover whatever she'd been asked. "We'll help in whatever way we can."

Will you? The challenge burning in his eyes was unmistakable. *Will you really?*

The Domitor broke in. "It is agreed, then. The Greys will prepare a contamination assessment for the Cleansing of Terra Colonna, and we'll resume this conversation when it's ready. Is that acceptable to everyone?"

A contamination assessment. That would explore how the destruction of Terra Colonna might affect Terra Prime. In a universe where dreams could bleed from one world into the next, such a study was a necessary precursor to any Cleansing. The request for genocide would not be approved until the Greys verified that any negative influence would be within acceptable parameters.

Genocide.

Jessica must leave Terra Colonna soon. If she didn't do it on her own, Morgana would have to send her Domitor back to prod her again. And perhaps it was time to recall Rita as well, just to be on the safe side. The game Morgana had played for so long was changing, and not for the better. If she didn't adapt quickly she could lose everything.

As soon as the crack of the Domitor's gavel sounded, ending the meeting, Virilian rose from his chair and moved toward the door. Ripples of ghostly misery echoed in his wake. On a sudden impulse Morgana reached out with her Gift to taste his essence. Normally she would never do that with one of the undead, but she needed to understand the change that had taken place in him, and the cause of his new obsession. A wave of raw emotion flooded her mind: Ice and fire, hunger and hate, and blood. So much blood. Death was wrapped around every thought, blood dripping from every emotion. The sensation left her breathless, and though she closed her mind immediately, she could not shut it out.

He had reached the doorway.

"Your Grace," she said.

He turned back to her. His expression was unreadable. Was this really Virilian? "By what name should we call you?" she challenged him. His emotions might reveal the truth, even if his words did not.

For a moment there was silence, and a fleeting hint of a cold smile. "Augustus Virilian." A lie, and also not a lie. "That's the current custom, is it not?"

Then he was gone, and the ghosts were gone, and only the silence remained.

4

MANASSAS
VIRGINIA

JESSE

MOM CAME HOME FROM WORK with her first paycheck in hand and announced that were going out to dinner to celebrate. The paycheck wasn't huge, so we had to eat cheaply, but it wasn't like we had a tradition of steak and caviar. We decided to forego fast food options and have a real sit-down meal at Denny's, a quarter of a mile down the road. Close enough to walk.

The weather was pleasant—unusually cool for a summer afternoon—and under normal circumstances I would have enjoyed it, but in the wake of Devon's warning it was hard to enjoy anything. Denny's, by contrast, was crowded and noisy, which normally would have been annoying, but if we kept our voices low we could talk without anyone overhearing, and that was good. As I settled down into our booth I saw Tommy looking at me over the menu. *Tell her,* he mouthed. But I shook my head and mouthed back, *food first.* Because once I told Mom what was going on she would start asking all kinds of questions, and after that we'd be too busy to eat.

I must have looked as disturbed as I felt, because at one point she asked if I was all right, but I just mumbled something vaguely reassuring. Finally I was done eating, and I pushed my plate away and braced myself. Mom looked at me curiously, then put her fork down.

It's now or never, I thought.

Telling her was harder than I'd expected. Mom knew the basic story of our travels, of course, but explaining to her that our whole world was now in danger, and there was nothing anyone could do about it—and oh yeah, the government might be watching us—was another thing entirely.

The waitress showed up with our desserts just as I finished, and Mom nodded absently to her as the woman put down the plates. That's when I knew how much my words had shaken her. Normally she went out of her way to be friendly to servers.

When the waitress left, Mom looked down at her slice of layer cake and pushed it aside. My news had spoiled her appetite. "Assuming Devon's father is right," she said quietly, "what can we do?"

"I don't know. Keep our heads down. Be careful what we post or text. Or talk about on the phone, even."

"You've all got a good cover story."

We did, thanks to Tommy. But it would only protect us so long as we kept playing our parts perfectly. If someone ever heard us talking about our kidnapping in a rational, knowledgeable way, the story about us being drugged wouldn't hold water.

"I could make up a game," Tommy suggested. "Write some rules for a role-playing adventure, with parallel worlds and dream-wraiths and all sorts of other stuff that we might want to talk about. So if anyone ever *did* overhear us, we could always claim it was that."

"That's not half bad," my mother said.

"So long as you don't post it online," I warned him.

Tommy glared. "I'm not stupid."

Mom patted his hand. "No. You're not stupid. And the suggestion's a good one. You should start work on it as soon as we get home."

But now he was too excited to wait, so he started telling us how his new game would be structured, and what kinds of characters he would design, and what random generation system he would use . . .

we let him ramble on, nodding at intervals in the way we had learned to do long ago, enjoying the normalcy of the moment. Little in our life seemed normal, these days.

||||||||||||

The sun was setting when we finally headed home, and the trees cast deep grey shadows across the street, lending the whole world a dream-like aspect.

"Whoa!" Tommy stopped short in the middle of the street. I almost ran into him.

"What's wrong?" Mom asked.

But his attention was elsewhere, his eyes staring into the distance as if he was straining to see something. Or perhaps he was straining to hear something. "Don't go home," he murmured. Almost a chant. "Don't go home, don't go home, people are coming." He looked at me. "I can understand them!" There was wonder in his eyes, but also fear.

"Understand whom?" my mother demanded.

"What people are coming?" I asked.

Tommy'd never told our mother about how he sometimes heard ghosts. Maybe because he was worried that she wouldn't believe him, but more likely because he was afraid that she would feel obligated to help him if she knew. And how could she do that? Send him to a child psychiatrist? Better to just keep it to himself for now, he'd told me. In hindsight, maybe not the best choice.

"Hide!" Tommy whispered suddenly. His pupils were so dilated that his irises were barely visible. "They're coming. Hide!"

I looked around, but the only things that we could hide behind were a few parked cars, and that wouldn't do any good if we didn't know what direction the danger was coming from. Then I saw that Mom's car was only a few spaces down, and pointed toward it. Tommy started running that way immediately, but Mom hesitated, so I grabbed her by the arm to start her moving. As we sprinted toward the car she pulled her keys out of her pocket and I heard the doors unlock. Tommy pulled the front door open, I grabbed the back door, and somehow we all managed to fall inside and close the doors behind us before anyone—or anything—showed up.

Breathless, we crouched down below the windows. Tommy tucked himself under the dashboard until all I could see of him were two glistening eyes. Mom reached out a hand to reassure him. She was giving him the benefit of the doubt right now, treating his warning seriously, but I could see concern in her eyes. What if her son was crazy? I wanted to reassure her, but what could I say? *Don't worry, your son's not crazy, he's just hearing ghosts.* Somehow I didn't think that would help.

We waited in silence. Every second seemed like an eternity. Then Tommy whispered frantically, "Now! Now!"

Carefully I raised up my head just far enough to peek out the window. At first I saw nothing other than an empty street. Then, deep in the shadows behind our house, I saw movement. My mother, who was now peeking out the front window, drew in a sharp breath; clearly she'd seen it, too.

There were two men exiting out of the back of our building. They were dressed in dark clothing and keeping to the shadows, but the brief flash of a street light reflecting off a cell phone gave their position away, and once we knew where they were they were easier to see. The taller one spoke on the phone for a few seconds, then gestured for his companion to follow him to the rear yard of a neighboring house. We lost sight of them after that, but a few moments later we heard a motor starting, and a sleek black sedan pulled out of that driveway. Not until it was gone did I realize I'd been holding my breath.

"It's okay," Tommy whispered. He sounded exhausted. "They're gone now."

We were silent. Mom said nothing. I could hear my own heart pounding as I waited to see how she would react to all this. The concept that strange men might have been waiting to ambush us didn't frighten me half as much as the thought of what could happen to our family if the next few minutes didn't go well.

"We shouldn't discuss this here," she said at last, starting the car. "Get up in the seat," she ordered Tommy. "And both of you, put on your seat belts."

Like Gollum crawling out of a cave, Tommy slowly extracted himself from under the dash, settled himself into the seat, and pulled the belt across his chest. His eyes never left Mom. Even as she began to drive, taking us to some unnamed place, his eyes never left her.

The lot where our house once stood looked eerie in the dying light of day's end. The last time I was there the ground had been covered in black ash and the aroma of stale smoke had clung to the place like a shroud. Now all evidence of the fire had been cleared away, and what little grass survived had been beaten down into the mud by the shoes of countless police detectives, insurance adjustors, and, most recently, construction workers. There were stacks of wooden planks piled everywhere, sorted by size, and several pallets of bricks blocked the driveway, forcing Mom to park on the street. A few items were covered by blue protective tarps, and as we got out of the car the breeze caused them to flap weakly, like tired birds.

For a moment the three of us just stood there, trying to come to terms with the recent changes in our lives. The destruction of our house felt strangely permanent now, in a way it hadn't before. I wondered if Tommy and my mother found the clean, orderly landscape as disturbing as I did. Then Mom pointed to several stacks of wood in what had once been the back yard and led us there. They were the right height to offer convenient seating, and she settled down on one of them, with Tommy and I taking up places opposite her. The wood creaked beneath our weight.

She sighed deeply and looked at Tommy. "Now. Tell me all about the voices."

He did, and this time he held nothing back. He told her about the soul shards that had surrounded him while he was in Shadowcrest—spirits so fractured by the trauma of death that they could barely be called sentient—and how they had talked to him constantly while he was a prisoner in the Shadowlords' dungeon. He told her that since coming home he'd heard the same kind of voices in our world, but not until tonight had he been able to make out what they were saying. And he told her that he was terrified this was all happening because the Shadows had done something terrible to his mind. That last bit was something he hadn't even confided in me. Now I knew the truth. Mom knew the truth. The sense of relief in him was visible, like some terrible weight had been lifted from his shoulders. Whatever happened after this moment, at least our whole family would be facing it together.

Mom said nothing while he talked, just listened. I thought her expression was strangely distant. When my brother was finally done he looked at her expectantly, and when she didn't respond right away, added, "I'm not crazy, am I?" Of course, *he* knew that he wasn't crazy, and *I* knew that he wasn't crazy. The question wasn't about his sanity but about our mother's acceptance of him.

At that point Mom seemed to come back to us, and she reached out, took his hand, and squeezed it. "No, Tommy, you're not crazy." Mom's tone was gentle. "There was a time when I might have thought that. But now that I understand more about how the world works, what kinds of creatures are in it, and what the two of you went through, I'm not so quick to judge." Her voice caught in her throat for a second. "I just . . . I'm sorry you and Jesse had to face all that alone. But you're not alone anymore." She looked at me. "You are so strong," she whispered. "Both of you . . . so strong . . ." Her words trailed off into silence. Her eyes seemed to lose focus again.

"Mom?" I asked. "You okay?" I'd never seen her like this.

She closed her eyes for a moment. "I guess this is the time for sharing secrets, yes? So I have something to tell you as well. Something that maybe we should have talked about a long time ago . . . But I hoped it would never become an issue. Now, apparently, it is."

"What?" Tommy asked, anxiety creeping back into his voice.

"Your father." She sighed. "Something happened to him when he was young. Apparently . . . he heard voices, too, Tommy. It happened many years before we met, and he never really wanted to talk about it, so I don't know all the details—"

"Dad heard *ghosts*?" Tommy interjected. His eyes were wide. "Seriously?"

"Back when he was a teenager. I'm not sure exactly when; like I said, he never wanted to talk about it. All I know is that he told his parents he was hearing voices, so they sent him for a psychiatric evaluation. They were concerned about the possibility of mental illness—specifically, schizophrenia. No one was even thinking about ghosts back then. Then the voices suddenly stopped, and they never came back. The doctors observed him for a while, but eventually concluded that they didn't have a clue what had caused the problem, but it seemed to be gone now. Since there weren't any other symptoms of concern, they gave him a clean bill of health. Only now, with all you've told me . . ." She hesitated.

"You're thinking the voices didn't go away," I said quietly. "That he stopped telling other people about them so the psychiatrists would leave him alone, but he kept on hearing them."

"Maybe," she murmured. A breeze blew a few strands of hair across her face; she pushed them back behind one ear. "It would explain a lot, wouldn't it? Maybe he started drinking to drown out the voices that everyone insisted weren't real. Or maybe he drank to deal with the stress of living a lie, of hiding such a terrible secret from his own family." She wiped a hand across her face to deal with the tears that were forming there. "Dear God. I want to say that if he'd only trusted me with the truth, everything would have been all right. We could have dealt with it together. But the truth is, I never would have believed that his voices were real. And I certainly never would have imagined they were ghosts! I would have just thought that he needed help, and convinced him to go back to his doctors—or to some other doctors—and then where would that have led? They would never have been able to identify the cause of his delusion, because it wasn't a delusion. So, what then? Drugs? Committed to a mental hospital?

You can't make voices in someone's head go away if they're real. But they would have kept trying." She sighed heavily. "Maybe it was best he never told me."

"You think that Dad was hearing the dead?" Tommy asked. "That I inherited this power from him?"

"It's possible," she allowed. I noticed that she didn't correct his use of the word *power*.

"Jeez." He looked at me. "You think maybe it's some kind of Gift? They run in families, don't they?"

I tried to remember all I knew about the subject. "Isaac told me that Guild families would arrange marriages to increase the odds of having Gifted kids. So that means that yeah, there's some kind of genetic component. But if you had any power worth speaking of, they'd have detected it when you were being interrogated in Shadowcrest. Or way before that, when you were first born. They'd have been watching the whole family—"

I stopped myself, but not in time. Biting my lip, I looked at Mom.

"I know that they took my first child away because she was Gifted, which allowed them to leave you in her place." There was a haunting sadness in her voice. "And if these powers run in families, they would probably have kept an eye on us after that, to see if any of my other children were born Gifted. Is that what you're trying to say?"

I nodded.

She looked at Tommy. "But you're still here." She forced a smile to her face. "So that answers the big question, doesn't it? At any rate, you can't spend your whole life at the mercy of ghostly voices." *Lest you go down the same path your father did.* The words weren't spoken aloud, but I heard them clearly nonetheless. "We have to find a way to silence them."

"Don't you think I've been *trying*?" Tommy demanded. "There's reams and reams of information online, but it's all bullshit. Spells by wannabee necromancers, discussions from the fantasy gaming crowd, nothing real! The people who have real necromancy aren't just out there, waiting for me to find them!" He spread his hands wide. "So what do we do? How do we weed through all that crap to find the one person who knows what he's talking about? And could we trust him even if we did? If he's Gifted, then Terra Prime probably has its claws in him. What are the odds I could get help without the Shadows finding out about it?"

I shut my eyes for a moment, fearing what I knew I had to say. "There's someone who might be able to help. But contacting him won't be easy." *Or safe*, I thought.

"Someone on Terra Prime?" Tommy asked.

I nodded.

"Sebastian?"

"No. We need someone who knows how the Shadows' Gift actually works. Someone who could tell you how to control it."

"You mean Isaac?"

My mother asked, "The boy who helped you escape from Shadowcrest?"

I nodded.

"Jeez," Tommy said. "You're thinking about dreamwalking? To Terra Prime?"

"Do you have a better idea?"

"What about the reapers? Aren't you afraid of them?"

Damn right I am. "They didn't show up when I dreamwalked with Mom, so we know it's possible to sneak a brief trip by them. And Isaac would know to wake himself up if they appeared. That worked in your dream, remember? That said . . ." I sighed. "Yeah, it's risky as hell. But I don't see any alternative."

Tommy stared at me. The intensity of emotion in his gaze shook me to my core. "Have I told you that you're the most awesome sister ever?"

Despite the seriousness of the conversation, I couldn't help but smile. "Not recently."

"Isn't this boy Isaac a Shadow?" my mother asked. "Do you know you can trust him?"

Did I? I bit my lip, considering the question. Yes, Isaac had helped us escape from Shadowcrest, but that had been a very different situation.

By then the Shadows had figured out that Tommy wasn't the Dream-walker they'd been searching for, and the rest of us were just intruders who needed to be dispatched. We were irritants, not threats. This time it would be different. If I told Isaac that someone outside the Guild was manifesting the Shadow's Gift, would he be honor bound to report it? What if he thought the information could be used to get him back in favor with his family? That would be one hell of a temptation for anyone.

"I don't know," I admitted. "I'd have to feel him out."

"You really want to do this?" my mother said. "You think it's worth the risk?"

I looked into Tommy's eyes. "Yeah. I do."

"Okay." She leaned back a bit, the planks of wood shifting audibly beneath her. "Then figure out how to do it as safely as possible, and we'll help you."

"Ask him about the electricity," Tommy interjected.

I blinked. "Say what?"

"Ask him why their world has no electricity. They visit other worlds all the time, so they know about it. And it isn't like it's hard to generate. Two wires and a potato will run a light bulb. So ask him why they don't use electricity on Terra Prime."

"I seriously doubt we're going to have that kind of conversation," I said. "But I'll bear the request in mind."

"Cause if you go back there, you might need to know."

"Go back?" Mom said sharply. "Go back where?"

Inwardly, I cursed Tommy. I shouldn't have let him know about the tickets I'd bought. "Nothing, Mom. We were just throwing ideas around. I'd never do anything like that without talking to you first."

"It's a mother's job to protect her children," she murmured. "Not the other way around."

"I know, Mom." I reached out and squeezed her hand. "It's okay."

She gazed into my eyes. I felt strangely naked, as though she was reading my mind. Then she nodded. "Come on," she said. "Let's go home and see if our apartment is still there."

She headed toward the car. I slid down from my perch and started to follow her, but Tommy reached out and grabbed me by the arm. He waited a few seconds until Mom was safely out of hearing, then he whispered to me, "If the Shadow's Gift runs in our family, then that's what the mom's original child would have had. The one they switched out for you. She'd be a Shadow, Jess."

I froze for a moment, then pulled my arm away from him. "Don't call her that," I muttered. "Don't ever call her that. Jessica is my name, not hers."

I headed off after Mom before he could say anything more. I didn't want him to see how much his words had shaken me. I shouldn't care if Mom's first child was a Shadow, or a Seer, or anything else. It shouldn't bother me what she was.

But it did.

||||||||||||||

Our apartment was still there, and at first glance it looked undisturbed. But there were a few little things that were off. I thought the socks in my drawer might have been arranged a little differently. And the items I had hidden in Tommy's game box were still there, but I thought I had positioned the map slightly differently. Both those differences were so subtle that I couldn't be sure they meant anything, but I had a gut feeling that they did.

As we gathered in the living room to compare notes, I reached into my pocket to make sure the Gate tickets were still there. It was a good thing I had kept them with me, and destroyed the original Grey info and the glow lamp. I shuddered to think of what might have happened to us if someone found those. Thank God Devon had warned us in time.

Tommy confidently told us the place wasn't bugged. He knew that because the ghosts said so. Apparently they were watching over him now.

I guess there were worse things than having the dead protect you.

5

LURAY
VIRGINIA PRIME

ISAAC

THE HOUSE WAS SILENT.

The street was silent.

The breaking of glass was sudden and loud, and it resonated in the darkness, filling the world with sound. For a moment Isaac stood frozen at the back door of the house, as wary of the approach of neighbors as a deer would be of predators. But either the locals hadn't heard the noise, or they didn't care. Good enough.

Wrapping his arm in a stolen shirt, he reached in through the broken window on the door, released the guard chain, and opened the deadlock. The knob itself wasn't locked.

And he was in.

He took a moment to breathe deeply, steadying his nerves. Not that he lacked for experience in petty theft; in the two years he'd lived on his own, he'd learned to lift what he needed from unsuspecting marks as casually and callously as one plucked an apple from a tree. And once he'd joined the gang in the Warrens he was expected to contribute to the common good, so he'd become adept at lifting goods from a vendor's cart without drawing the eye, or snatching purses in broad daylight from people so distracted that they didn't even know what happened until he was long gone. He'd had a few close calls, true, but had never been caught. Now, however, the Guild's mark of shame changed everything. He was far too conspicuous to lose himself in a crowd, before or after a crime. And if word reached the Shadows that a pale, thin teenager with their mark emblazoned on his forehead was causing trouble, they might rethink their decision to spare his life.

So now he was a true shadow, a thief who struck in the depths of night, claiming for his booty things that no other thief would value, with a few expensive items thrown in to muddy the trail.

He strained his necromantic senses to see if the ghost of Jacob was still with him. Of course it was. The broken spirit was bound to him now, though whether by its own choice or the Shadows' misapplied ritual, Isaac didn't know. And he didn't care. The fragmented wraith, invisible to mortal eyes, was a constant companion. Sometimes Isaac thought Jacob's company was the only thing that kept him sane.

"Keep watch?" he whispered.

He sensed, rather than heard, the affirmation. *Yes.*

The first room he came to was the kitchen, which was his main objective. He opened his backpack on the counter and then began to rummage through shelves and cabinets, seeking whatever nonperishable goods he could find. As usual, he didn't take everything. From a row of canned vegetables he chose half a dozen items; from a collection of canned fruit preserves, half a dozen more. There was dried fruit in wax paper bags, so he claimed a few of those, and packages of nuts as well. He never took an item that there was only one of, since the family would be likely to detect such a loss sooner. He wanted the pantry to look as normal as possible, so that while the owners of the house might sense that something was amiss, the exact pattern of his predation wouldn't be obvious.

Perhaps that was a pointless conceit. Perhaps if his Guild heard that there was someone stealing food from residential neighborhoods, they wouldn't care who was behind it. Or maybe they would even be pleased if they knew. Maybe they would laugh into the sleeves of their long grey robes, knowing that the mark of humiliation they had branded him with had turned him into a desperate scavenger. Regardless, if news got out that local houses were being burglarized for food, people might start locking their pantries, and while that wouldn't keep him out, it would certainly slow him down. Something to be avoided if at all possible.

Quietly he padded up the stairs to the bedrooms. He'd watched the owners leave the house earlier, from the cover of a wooded area behind the property, so he knew that he had time to look around. In one bedroom he found clothing that was approximately his size, so he took a few items, including a rare and precious find: a down-filled winter jacket. He checked that one off his mental list of things he had to find before the weather turned cold. Then he took some jewelry from the master bedroom, and a pair of silver candlesticks as well. Such valuables were of little use to him—even the local fences would shun a boy with the mark of shame branded on his forehead—but they would help make his visit look like a normal robbery.

As if that matters to anyone, he thought bitterly. Was pragmatism his true motive, or just pride? Stealing silver was a respectable pastime for thieves, while stealing common food was just . . . well, pitiful.

It was while he was heading toward the last room upstairs that he heard—or rather, *felt*—Jacob's alarm. He turned back just in time to see a dark, four legged shape racing up the staircase toward him. It was sleek and black and silent, a true hunter, not barking in rage like a common house dog would do, but with a guard dog's perfect clarity of purpose, giving its prey no warning. How had Isaac missed its presence when he'd first cased the house? Stumbling backward, he fumbled to open the nearest door, and for one terrifying moment thought he wouldn't reach cover in time. But then Jacob's chill presence manifested in front of him and the dog pulled up short, growling low in its throat. All animals instinctively feared the dead, but some were more resistant to that fear than others; this one, tasked to guard its master's territory, quickly regained focus. Even as Isaac backed into a bedroom it leapt through the space that Jacob occupied, coming straight for him.

Isaac slammed the door shut just in time. The dog hit the barrier so hard that the two small shelves flanking the door were shaken, and the glass animals on them went tumbling to the floor. As they shattered on the hardwood the dog began to bark furiously. Isaac looked desperately around the room for a weapon, but he had taken shelter in a little girl's room, and saw only plush stuffed animals and small toys. Nothing that would help him fend off an animal as large and as vicious as this one. And there were only two exits: the door he had come in through and a small window over the dresser. He had no way to fight, and nowhere to run.

What? Jacob asked. The ghost was in the room now, and the tang of its fear was so sharp in the air that Isaac could taste it. *Whatwhatwhat?*

Barking wildly, the dog threw itself at the door again and again and again. Surely neighbors would hear the ruckus soon. Surely there would come a point at which someone in a neighboring house would look out their window to see what was going on. If Isaac tried to climb down from the window now he would be plainly visible in the moonlight.

But what other option did he have?

Opening the window, he stuck his head out to take stock of his situation. The drop to the ground was formidable, but there was a drain pipe nearby, affixed to the house with metal braces; if he could swing over to it he might be able to work his way down safely.

Another glass figurine fell and shattered.

As he climbed through the small window, his backpack got stuck. He knew that he should leave it behind at that point, but he couldn't bring himself to abandon the precious supplies inside. So with a heave of his shoulder he jerked it through. The sudden shift in weight threw him off balance, and he grabbed hold of the drain pipe just in time to save himself from a nasty fall. The thin metal tubing swayed ominously as he shifted his full weight to one of its braces, pressing his toes against the edge of the metal strap that fastened the pipe to the building.

People! The ghost's frantic tone cut through the crisp night air like a razor. *Danger!*

Heat pounding, Isaac tried to swallow his fear and focus on the task at hand. Now that the window was open the dog's barking could be heard throughout the neighborhood, and between its barks Isaac could hear human voices approaching, as locals responded to the disturbance. *Focus. Focus.* He gripped the drainpipe between his knees and tried to slide himself down as he would a fireman's pole, grasping at any protrusions he could use to control the descent. But then his hand slipped from a brace and he fell back, the ground rushing furiously up at him as he tried to twist his body in midair to get his feet under him. But it was too late, there was too little space, too little time—

He landed on his back; the pain of the impact was blinding. For a moment he just lay there, afraid to try to move, lest he find out that he couldn't. But the voices were rapidly growing louder, and he didn't have the luxury of a leisurely recovery. With a groan he tried to roll over, and to his relief found that his body still worked, though it hurt like hell. The stolen jacket, stuffed into his backpack like a bolster, had saved him from crippling injury, but not from the bruising edges of the cans and candlesticks packed beneath it. He got to his feet and started to lope toward the nearest cover, a thickly forested strip between two rows of houses. He'd scoped it out before attempting the break-in, and knew that it led to a place of safety—assuming he could get there in time.

He could hear people behind him now, their voices rising as they spotted him and began the chase in earnest. Limping slightly as he ran—he must have twisted his ankle during the fall—he felt a raw and terrible fear grip his heart. The mark on his forehead set him apart from the laws that would protect a normal thief; if these people caught him they could do anything they wanted to him, with no fear of legal ramification. He was the outsider, the alien, the reject.

He was prey.

He made it to the cover of the trees before they caught up with him, but with barely yards to spare. Even as he stumbled into the shadows he could hear men breaking through the brush behind him. His only hope lay in getting to the Warrens before they caught him, to lose himself in the twisting network of tunnels where none of them would know how to navigate. He'd cased the route before, so he knew how to get there. But it was getting harder and harder to stay ahead of the pursuit. Each step jarred his back and ankle, fostering fresh waves of pain. Maybe he had broken something.

"Can you do anything?" he gasped. "Anything!"

He couldn't hear ghosts while he was focused on other things, so he had no idea if Jacob responded. But a moment later, a cold, unnatural wind swept past him. The trees overhead began to rustle, and he heard an animal screech in terror. He stumbled into a gully and fresh pain shot up his wounded leg, but he had to keep going. Had to. A deer bounded out from cover on one side of him and went running toward his pursuers. Birds launched themselves from nests on all sides of him, filling the air behind him with panicked wings. A wave of skunk-stink filled the air, so putrid and powerful that it nearly felled him; only being upwind of it saved him. Every living thing in the wooded area seemed to be running or flying or scuttling or slithering or leaping, driven by primitive instinct to flee the presence of the ghost that had manifested in front of them. And they were being driven right into the pack of angry humans that was following Isaac.

He could hear people cursing behind him as they tried to dodge the tsunami of wildlife, branches snapping as some of them lost their footing and fell. With newfound energy Isaac bolted the last few yards to the end of the wooded strip, ignoring the fire of pain in his flesh, fighting to gain enough ground to be able to reach a place of safety. Then the trees gave way to a dirt path that led him to a narrow passage flanked by storage sheds, then to an alley between houses. People were still following, but it sounded like they were no longer right on his heels. If they lost sight of him he might be able to escape.

He ducked under a poorly balanced pile of abandoned construction materials, crawling on his elbows through a tunnel of rotting planks and rusted pipes, where hopefully no one would think to look for him. He had to shrug off his backpack to make it through, but he dragged it behind him, even though he knew it would slow him down. The pack had protected him when he fell, and it was a lucky token now. When he reached the other end he loped down a short alley, to emerge in a narrow street lined with shuttered shops. Normally he would have stopped to check for observers before heading out into the open, but what difference would it make if anyone was watching? If he hesitated now he was as good as dead.

Limping more severely now—his injured ankle was threatening to give out completely—he made it to the nearest manhole, knelt down, and managed to pry up the heavy cover. Down into the darkness went the backpack; he heard it land with a splash far below. Quickly he followed it, lowering himself far enough on the utility ladder that he could pull the cover back in place, praying that no one was watching. Then he grasped both sides of the ladder and slid the rest of the way down. At the bottom he hit six inches of water covering a layer of slime and stone, and he slipped and went down hard, pain lancing through his injured back again. For a moment he just sat there in the pitch blackness, filthy water rushing around him on its way to someplace even deeper underground. After two years of living in the Warrens, the setting was strangely comforting.

Suddenly overhead he heard the muffled sound of feet pounding on earth, then yelling. Someone must have seen him come this way. He should move. He should really move. They might think to look down into the manhole. He shouldn't stay in this spot, where they would be able to see him. But the fear and pain had taken their toll, and he just sat with his back against the slime-covered wall, his hand on his precious backpack, taking comfort in the sense that Jacob was still with him. That battered, broken soul might just have saved his life.

Drawing in a deep breath, he thanked the god of thieves and Guild rejects for letting him survive this night. One single night, in an endless stream of deadly nights. This was his life now. This was his forever.

||||||||||||||

The world is lifeless, colorless, devoid of any landmarks that might lend it identity. Grey sky bleeds into grey earth, the frigid wind moaning a dirge as it sweeps across fields of stark rock littered with broken bones. The smell of blood is in the air: old blood, stale blood. There's snow in the distance, not yet visible but nonetheless apparent, as real as the frost on the ground. The warmth of summer is alien to this place, as is the warmth of life.

Isaac walks. Bone shards crunch beneath his feet as he moves. He's heading nowhere, leaving nowhere.

Suddenly he realizes there is a person in the distance.

No one else belongs in this place. He knows that instinctively, though he doesn't know the reason for it, and a cold dread overtakes him as the figure approaches. But then the person gets close enough for him to make out who it is, and with that knowledge comes understanding. He's dreaming. That means the dismal world surrounding him is a thing of his own creation, not real. But the person in front of him is very real, and as he recognizes her his soul is flooded with fear and despair and hope and loneliness and hunger. So much hunger! Is that because of who she is, or would any human presence stir the same response at this point? He's starved for the company of his own kind.

Jessica.

She calls out his name as she approaches, but he can't bring himself to respond, afraid to make a sound lest the fragile dream shatter like glass. As she approaches he straightens his shoulders and does his best to keep his expression from revealing the storm of emotion inside him. He longs to touch her, to drink in the vibrancy of her life, to draw fresh strength from her soul to replace his own lost vitality. But he doesn't want her to see that. He doesn't want her to know how weak he has become, or to realize how much others were able to hurt him. It's his final fragment of pride.

"Jeez." She looks around the landscape as she comes up to him. "You're not into happy dreams, are you?"

He forces a half-smile to his face. It feels strained and unnatural. "You only show up for the bad ones." The words feel strange on his tongue; casual human conversation is an alien thing these days. "Just before this I was hanging out on a tropical beach. Sunlight, surfboards, piña coladas. You would have liked it."

"So, who's that, then?" She points to something past his left shoulder. "A cabana boy?"

Startled, he turns to look behind him, and sees Jacob standing there. The dead boy's flesh is as white as chalk, his eyes are black pits of nothingness, and streamers of blood are slowly trickling down his arms, face, and bare torso. Other than that he is motionless, still as only the dead can be still, since they have neither pulse nor living breath to move them.

"That's Jacob," he says, turning back to her. "He's a soul shard."

"Soul shard?"

"Damaged ghost." He draws in a deep breath to steady himself, trying not to think about exactly how the boy was damaged. "Parts of his psyche are missing."

"Is that what he really looks like?"

Is it? Isaac's Gift isn't strong enough for him to see the dead clearly; what she's looking at is the product of his imagination, nothing more. "It's what he looked like when he died." Memories of the Shadows' ritual suddenly surge into his head, and he sees Jacob lying on the stone slab again, his terrified eyes fixed on Isaac as he begs silently for help. Isaac curls his hands into fists at his side as he struggles to set those memories aside, to remain in the current moment. *Concentrate on*

Jessica, he tells himself. *If you lose focus now, the dream might end and you'll lose her again . . . perhaps forever.* "I guess it's how I picture him," he manages.

"And this?" She points to her forehead. "What's that about?"

It takes him a moment to realize what she's asking. Is the mark of the Guild still on his forehead? If so, does that mean it's so much a part of his identity now that even in his dreams he can't envision himself without it? Or did the ritual that applied it do something to his mind, so that even in dreaming he can't banish it? Either concept is deeply disturbing. "It's a Guild mark." He says it quietly, casually, trying to make it sound like it isn't really important, but he can see from her expression that she isn't fooled. "What about the reapers?" he asks, changing the subject. "Are they gone? I can't imagine you'd come here if they were still hunting you."

For an instant her mask of confidence slips, and he can see the fear that lies beneath it. "Still around. Apparently it's harder to find a good necromancer than you'd think." She looks around the dreamscape, studying the grey land, the grey sky, the grey-on-grey horizon. "Not sure I could see the warning signs in this place. So if it suddenly looks as if this whole dream is getting sucked into a black hole, you need to wake yourself up, okay? For both our sakes."

He nods.

She's studying him now. He feels strangely naked.

"You all right?" she asks at last.

It takes him a moment to find his voice. "Yeah. I'm all right." If she suspects that he's lying, she doesn't challenge him on it. "Why are you here? I mean, it's great to see you again, but I know how dangerous dreamwalking is for you right now. You wouldn't have come to me if there wasn't a pretty important reason."

"I need information," she says quietly. "And yeah, it's pretty important."

Not about the Shadows, he prays. *Please, let it not be about the Shadows.* The one time he was ordered to reveal Guild secrets, to test the mental binding that a Domitor had placed upon him, the results were unpleasant enough that he had no desire to test its limits again. "What is it you need?"

She glances at the sky again. Looking for wraithly invaders? "When someone is born with a Gift, does it always have a . . . a type? Back at the fair we saw a little girl playing with fire. Was she born with that particular talent, or could she have done something else with her Gift if she wanted to?"

"Depends on the person. Some people are born with the ability to apply their mental energy in a particular way. Others may take years to develop a focus. That's why the Guilds exist, to help people specialize. The more focused a mind is, the more powerful it can become." He looks at her closely. "What's wrong, Jessica? You know I'll help you if I can."

But he can see that she's hesitant to speak. Is she wondering about his loyalties? Is she worried that even though he helped her before, he's still a Shadow, apprentice to the undead, and that if she shares the wrong secret with him he may have to reveal it to his Guild? The irony of that makes him want to laugh. Or cry.

With a heavy sigh he puts a hand to his forehead, where the mark of shame is. The transformed skin feels slick and cold beneath his fingertips. "Jessica, this mark means I've been cast out of my Guild, and can never join another one. I'm an outsider, now, politically and socially. No duties, no loyalties, no allies. No friends. If I showed up at the door of Shadowcrest with all the secrets of the universe in hand, they'd slam the door in my face. So whatever you want to say, it's just between us. I swear it."

Her eyes grow wide. "You're being *shunned*?"

Biting his lip, he nods.

"Jeez, that's pretty extreme—"

"It is what it is," he says sharply. "I'll survive."

"What about your parents? Are they okay with this?"

See now, this is why I didn't want to talk about it. "Just ask what you came to ask, okay?"

"All right." She draws in a deep breath. "My brother is hearing voices, Isaac. He thinks they're spirits of the dead, like he heard in Shadowcrest. And I just found out that my father used to hear voices, too. I . . . I don't know what to make of all that."

"You're worried that Tommy's becoming a Shadow?"

"Is that possible?" she asks.

"Sensitivity does run in families. The original Jessica Drake was harvested because she was Gifted—" He pauses. "You know about that, right?"

Quietly she says, "I know."

"So it wouldn't be unreasonable to think her blood relatives might manifest the same talent. But if the Seers thought Tommy was truly Gifted, they would have harvested him, too. So whatever ability he's got must be minimal."

"But why *that* Gift? Doesn't it stretch the bounds of coincidence?" She spreads her hands wide. "I mean, why on earth would someone hide a Dreamwalker in a household full of necromancers? It doesn't make any sense."

"Unless Tommy didn't start out as a Shadow. Wasn't that your original question?"

"He hears the dead," she points out. "As did my father, apparently." A shadow of pain passes over her face.

"You said that your father heard *voices*," he reminds her. "There are plenty of Gifts which can manifest like that. Seers and Farspeakers, to name just two." He shakes his head. "Tommy was emotionally vulnerable when he was a prisoner in Shadowcrest. He was surrounded by wraiths that may have mocked or even threatened him. It's possible that survival instinct kicked in, molding whatever little talent he had into a useful form."

Her brow furrows. "Is that kind of thing common?"

"No. But it's not unheard of. We call it imprinting."

"Is it permanent?"

"I'm afraid so."

She exhales noisily. "So my little brother's turning into a necromancer? Great."

He smiles slightly. "Hearing the whispers of the dead isn't the same thing as forcing spirits to do your bidding. At best he'll become what your world calls a medium, able to sense the presence of ghosts and sometimes understand them, but no more than that. Mind you, most of what the dead have to say, you don't want to hear anyway. Few of the spirits who cling to this world are sane."

"Can *you* do that?" she asks suddenly. "Force spirits to do your bidding?"

His heart skips a beat as he realizes what she's really asking. He chooses his words carefully. "Had I completed my apprenticeship, I might have mastered that art. But without proper training, without knowledge of the necessary rituals, I doubt I could do more than voice an emphatic request."

"But you might be able to do more than that someday?"

"Maybe." He says it quietly. "But not as soon as you would need me to."

There is silence. It's all out on the table now. All his secrets. All her need.

"I have to find answers," she says. "About what I am, what I'm going to become. Most of all, about how to kill the reapers before they kill me. There's a place where I think I can find those answers, but I'm going to have to search for it. And once I get there, the reapers might be waiting." She holds out a hand toward him. "Come with me, Isaac."

For a moment his throat is so dry he can't force words out. "I . . . I . . . that's not possible . . ."

"Why? Is there somewhere else you have to be?" A corner of her mouth twitches slightly.

"The Greys will never let me pass through a Gate with this mark on my face. And even if they would . . ." He hesitates. "I can't hold the reapers at bay for you. And I don't know how to destroy them."

"But you understand their nature. So you can help me find someone else who knows how to destroy them. Someone who doesn't answer to the Shadowlords. Or maybe find rituals you can use yourself."

He turns away from her. He's trembling now, partly from fear, partly from the desperate hunger to have purpose again. That's what she's really offering him: hope. "You don't understand," he whispers. "I'm marked. You couldn't travel discreetly if I was with you."

"So hide the mark."

"How? A hat won't cover all of it. Or a scarf."

"Makeup."

"Tried it. Doesn't stick. At least, not anything I've been able to steal." He laughs weakly. "It's not like I can walk into a beauty salon and ask for help."

"But if we could find a way to make it work," she pressed, "Would you help me?"

He wraps his arms around himself. He wants purpose so badly. He wants hope. He wants her. "If I could help you destroy the reapers, I would. You know that."

"Yes," she says quietly. "I do." There is a pause, then a soft chuckle. "I guess I should go back and tell my kid brother he's turning into a necromancer. And a shitty necromancer, at that."

He turns back to look at her. He wants to reach out and touch her, but he doesn't know how. So he just stares at her, praying it's not pity that he sees in her eyes.

"Take care of yourself," she whispers.

And then she's gone.

Suddenly his legs feel weak. He wishes there was some-where to sit down that didn't involve piles of bones, but there isn't, so he just stands where he is, staring at the space she occupied. Trying to imagine her still there.

"Are you sure this is wise?" Jacob's sudden speech from behind startles him. The dead boy is talking in Isaac's voice, expressing Isaac's thoughts. "If the Shadows find out you're helping her, they may rethink their decision to let you live."

No, he thinks, *it isn't wise. Does that make a difference?*

In the distance, along the horizon, a hint of color begins to seep into the sky.

6

THE BLACK PLAIN TREMBLES beneath my feet, its surface rippling like water as I walk. Unsolid. The feeling that I might fall through it at any moment is terrifying, but I force myself to keep walking. I must keep walking. The doors nearest my entrance point hold no answers for me, I know that, and so I must risk a longer journey, trusting that the black water surface of my inner mind will not betray me.

Is the new instability my fault? Is my dream vista reflecting my own fears back at me? Or is there some external cause? How I ache to find a teacher who could explain these things to me! How tired I am of guessing, soul-weary of stumbling blindly through dreamscape after dreamscape, figuring out the rules of my Gift by trial and error. I starve for guidance.

The doors surrounding me were jagged arches when I first arrived, but I have transformed them into gleaming Arabian arches, like the ones that were there when the avatar invader appeared in my dreams. Will that make it easier to find her? Maybe. Once more, I am guessing.

I don't think the reapers can come here—their previous appearances have all been within other people's dreams—but if they do, I'm ready. Worlds away, my mother is holding my hand, her finger pressed against the pulse in my wrist. The minute I experience any major agitation she'll know it, and she'll call me back.

That much I have learned, at least.

I walk past dozens of arches. Hundreds of arches. Though the images behind them are only dreams, I know now, each one reflects the mind of the person who created it, and it echoes that person's world like a warped mirror. The nearer arches will lead me to worlds not unlike my own, created by people not unlike myself. Since those won't help me find the one I seek, I keep walking.

What will her reaction be if I do find her? The last time I saw her she tried to attack me, and if not for the sudden appearance of the reaper she might have succeeded. If I do manage to locate her, will she attack me again? Or will the fact that we're both Dreamwalkers allow me to establish some kind of camaraderie, so that she'll be willing to share information with me?

She knows where the changing tower is. More to the point, she knows *what* it is. One moment a cathedral, the next a ziggurat, or a vaulted tomb. Is it just a dream symbol, or does the building really exist somewhere? The boy in the Weaver's camp had seen it, and the reaper who attacked me had been there, so its significance is beyond question. Can I find the answers I seek within those inconstant walls? Or at least an indication of where I should search for them? All instinct insists that I can. But what if instinct can't be trusted, if I'm so desperate for enlightenment that my mind will grasp any hope it is offered?

Stopping for a moment, I shut my eyes and breathe deeply, turning my focus inward. *Concentrate, Jesse. Concentrate.* I'm going to try to find my dream invader the same way I once found Sebastian, by focusing my mind on her and letting instinct guide my steps. But my connection to Sebastian was much stronger, and I don't have an artifact to guide me. All I can do is create an image of her in my mind and hope it will be enough. I force myself to see her: slender, youthful, androgynous, with the spiked black hair and impossibly wide eyes of an anime character, and strange golden patterns swirling around her body. I have no idea what she really looks like, so I focus on the image she has presented to me in dreams, hoping it can connect me to its creator.

Golden patterns begin to flicker inside my eyelids, gone too quickly for me to remember them. Strains of music accompany them, exotic alien melodies that resonate within my flesh, as if their source were inside me. The patterns are similar to some I've drawn myself, tracing my journeys through the dreamscape. Are they maps? If I follow the right one, will it lead me to the avatar? I concentrate on those patterns with all my might, trying to sense if one is more important than the others. But to no avail. And then they all fade from my mind, and the music gives way to silence. I mutter a curse under my breath and open my eyes, meaning to resume my search.

The avatar girl is there.

She's standing a good distance away, her hand resting on one of the arches as if she is ready to flee through it at any moment. She looks much the same as I remember her, except that now her hair is arranged in a kind of mullet, with short spikes on top and a long, thickly plaited braid hanging down over one shoulder. There is a small striped feather fixed to the end of the braid. Golden patterns twitch across her body like spastic spiders, and I realize suddenly that they are bits of the mystical maps that reveal the paths one must follow to get from world to world. The girl's a living atlas.

For a moment we just stare at each other. I'm afraid to

move, afraid to speak, lest any change in the situation might cause her to turn and run, like she did the last time. But then I remind myself that she came here of her own volition. I called to her, and she came. That's a powerful statement of intent.

"I'm not an enemy." I say it slowly, spreading my hands wide, as if to show her that I'm not holding a weapon. She continues to look wary, and says nothing. "The reaper attacked me," I remind her. "It's my enemy as well as yours. We're on the same side."

Still she doesn't respond. Does she not understand English? She's never said a word to me, so I don't have a clue. But then, very slowly, she lowers her hand from the arch. She still looks like a deer about to bolt for cover, but the message of the movement seems clear. We've passed our first hurdle.

"I'm a Dreamwalker," I tell her. "Like you." I'm watching her closely for reaction as I speak, trying to read her. Though she doesn't nod, something in the way she looks at me confirms that yes, I'm really standing in front of another Dreamwalker, one who knows how our shared Gift works. A sense of relief washes over me, followed by wonder. There's so much I want to ask her, to learn from her! But we're not there yet, not by a long shot.

Slowly I walk toward her, and though she looks nervous, she doesn't back away. Soon we are only a few yards apart, and I can now see that her skin is unnaturally smooth, her eyelashes spaced so perfectly that they look like they've been painted on. According to Tommy, what I'm looking at is an avatar, an image that this person designed to represent herself. Its creator could be an alien from Mars for all I know. Or from any other planet where people think sticking feathers in mullets is a good idea.

What matters is that she's a Dreamwalker. I'm not alone any more. The sudden shift in mindset is dizzying, and my lips feel so dry I have to wet them with my tongue before speaking. "The tower," I manage at last. "The one in our dream." *Our* dream—our shared dream—what a wondrous concept! "It's important, isn't it? Some kind of fortress? Or meeting place?" I sketch the shape of the tower with my hands, just in case she doesn't understand what I'm saying.

A flicker of pain comes into her eyes, but she says nothing.

"Where is it?" I press. "How can I find it? At least tell me that much." *Tell me anything!* I want to scream. *Don't leave me in ignorance!*

Slowly she reaches out toward me. Her hand is curled into a fist as if she's holding something. Does she want me to take it from her? She's standing too far away for an easy transfer, so I just wait for some clear indication of what she wants me to do. Then she loosens her grip slightly and sand begins to trickle out from between her fingers: golden sand, the same color as the map-designs on her body. It cascades to the ground in a thin, glimmering waterfall, and as she moves her hand a pattern takes shape on the ground between us. Intricate, delicate in its detail, hauntingly familiar. As more and more details are drawn with sand-trickles, I suddenly recognize where I know it from. Parts of it are from the design that I once saw a Shadow invoke in Mystic Caverns, before passing through that Gate—the pattern that led to Terra Prime. But there is more to this one, and I find myself mesmerized as the design on the floor grows larger and larger, until its outermost details almost reach my feet. A strange music fills the air, alien in melody, unbearably beautiful; it seeps into my skin, my flesh, my soul. I am the music. I am the pattern. I am the pathway between two worlds, which leads to a place that has no name. I am the gateway.

And then, suddenly, the music is gone. The design in front of me grows dim, its magic extinguished. I look around for the avatar girl, but all that I see is the feather from her hair, lying in the center of the sand pattern. As I lean down to pick it up my movement stirs a breeze that scatters the sand, erasing the pattern. Now there is nothing left of her but the feather in my hand. I don't know what it signifies, but the message of the sand painting seems clear. Either the tower that I seek is on Terra Prime, or there is a path there that will lead me to it. To find the changing tower, I must return to the world of my birth. The world of my enemies.

||||||||||||

I lay motionless on the couch, eyes half open, struggling to transition back to the waking world. Details of the room filtered into my awareness in a jumbled manner, mixing in with the horror of that final revelation. The feel of the couch beneath me. The glare of the floor lamp across the room. My mother's face, tense with concern, as she leaned over me and said, "Jesse? You all right?"

"I'm fine," I whispered. The act of speech felt alien. Everything about this world felt alien. It was as if half my soul was still trapped in the dreamscape, struggling to process what it had just learned. I looked down at my hand and saw that it was empty, but what did I expect? That the feather would return to this world with me?

Terra Prime. The road to the tower began there. If the avatar girl was right (and if I was interpreting her meaning correctly) I would have to travel back to that cursed hellhole to find it.

Shit.

"Did you find her?" Tommy asked from his perch on the arm of the couch.

I drew in a deep breath and tried to steady myself, so that they would not see how shaken I was. "She found me." I pushed myself up to a sitting position with some difficulty; my muscles ached as if I'd been running for hours. Mom reached out to help me, but I waved her off. "I'm good. I'm good. I just need to draw before I talk."

I knew from experience that the memory of my dream would fade quickly, so I took up the pad and pencil that were waiting on the side table and began to sketch as quickly I could. I started with the sand pattern, blocking in the major shapes and then filling in the finer details around the edges. But the vision in my mind was already fading, and soon I realized that I was sketching and erasing the same lines over and over. I could sense that they weren't right, but I no longer had a clear enough memory of the design to know how to fix them. Damn. This wasn't something that usually happened to me.

With a sigh, I accepted that no further effort was going to improve the drawing, so I turned to the next page and began to sketch the avatar's feather. That, at least, went well. God alone knew if the design of the feather was significant, but at least I had a good picture to work from in figuring that out.

Finally, I had drawn as much as I could. I leaned back and stared at my sketches in silent frustration, angry at myself for failing to draw the avatar's design perfectly. Usually, I did better than this. Mom reached over and took the pad gently from my hands so that she could look more closely at the sand design; Tommy peered at it over her arm. "What is it?"

"Some kind of map, I think. Or the key to unlocking a Gate. I'm not sure." I put down the pencil and stretched my drawing hand, working the muscles loose. "When I asked her how to get to the tower, she drew that design. In sand, on the ground." I hesitated. "The Shadows used a pattern like that when they activated the Luray Gate, to take us to Terra Prime."

Her eyes narrowed. "You're thinking . . . what? That she was telling you to go back there?"

Fear rose up in my throat; I had to swallow it back to force words out. "I can't think of any other reason why she would show it to me."

"But do *you* believe you need to go back there?"

I wanted to say no. I wanted to tell them that there was some other way to find out how to fight the reapers. But the lie would be so obvious neither of them would buy it. "I need to go somewhere to find answers, and right now, that looks like the only option. I can't just sit around waiting for more clues. The next time the reaper comes for me you may not be around to wake me up. And then it'll all be over. No second chances. So if you have a better plan—any plan—then tell me, I'm listening. Because I can't think of anything."

She looked at my sketch in silence for a moment. Then: "You're sure that finding this tower will help?"

I sighed. "I'm not sure of anything. All I know is that dream-wraiths are trying to kill me, and without knowing what they really are I can't figure out how to defend myself." I rubbed a hand across my face, wiping away the first hint of tears. "That tower is where reaper history and Dreamwalker history intersect. If the information I need is anywhere, it'll be there."

"That's all well and good," Mom said, "but you need to have a plan."

I blinked. "A plan?"

"You can't just go over there and hope that clues will come to you."

I stared at her in disbelief. "You . . . you would let me go?"

"Seriously?" Tommy asked.

A corner of her mouth twitched slightly. "I think we're beyond the point of my 'letting you go,' Jesse. You've already run away from home twice without asking my permission. What am I supposed to do to prevent it from happening again? Lock you in your room for the next ten years? Put a tracking bracelet on you? Or maybe spend every wak-ing moment wondering when you'll disappear again without telling me, and I'll never know where you went, or if you'll ever come back?"

I felt my cheeks flush. "I'm sorry, Mom."

"Don't think that means I'm letting you just run off on your own. I want to hear a plan from you first. Where you're going. How you're getting there. Who you intend to travel with. It's no less than I would expect if you were planning a trip on *this* world, Jesse. So you will give me that much, or God help me, I *will* lock you in your room for the next ten years, I swear it."

"I understand," I murmured. The threat was strangely soothing. Going to Terra Prime was no less frightening a concept than it had been ten minutes ago, but at least now I wouldn't have to lie to my family. Or make up stories to divert them when I left home.

This is all theoretical, I warned myself. *I can't just go to Terra Prime and ask if anyone has seen a shapeshifting building. I have to narrow down the search area somehow.* I took the drawing back from my mother and stared at the avatar's design. Was there another clue hidden in it? Something that would tell me exactly where I had to go? If so, I couldn't see it.

I will figure it out, I told myself stubbornly. *One way or another.*

Then I looked at my mother and brother and corrected myself: *We will figure it out.*

⸻ IIIIIIIIIIII ⸻

I stood on the back stoop looking up at the moon, resting my eyes. All I could see after hours of computer research were lines connecting the craters on that satellite, like a giant connect-the-dots game.

The avatar girl had shown me a pattern. Part of it was familiar to me and revealed that the path to the Dreamwalker tower led through Terra Prime. So maybe some other tangle of forked lines or angled fragments was meant to tell me *where* on Terra Prime I was supposed to go. If that was the case, wouldn't the information be coded in a way that I could understand? What sense would it make for her to give me a message if there was no hope of my reading it?

Following that logic, I had scoured the internet, searching for any pattern on Earth (my Earth) that could help me interpret what I'd seen. Tommy downloaded an image recognition program and set it loose on the internet, which netted us a lot of fantasy art but nothing that looked useful. The three of us spent hours searching, each glued to his or her laptop screen, scrolling through endless galleries of pre-historic maze carvings, Buddhist mandalas, and even Australian dream paintings, until our eyes were red and mental exhaustion was setting in. All to no avail.

Now, staring at the moon, I wondered if something in Morgana's collection of Dreamwalker art could help me. But no, I would never beg for that woman's aid again. Better to die at a reaper's hands—or whatever alien appendages it had in the place of hands. With a sigh I headed back up to the apartment, bracing myself to resume the fruitless search. Until we thought of a better way to approach the problem, it was a choice between more searching and giving up, and I wasn't ready to give up.

But as soon as I walked in the door I knew that something had happened. Mom's reddened eyes were sparkling and Tommy grinned as he announced, "I found it!" He was veritably glowing with smugness, which I guess one should expect from a kid who had just proven himself more useful than the all the adults in his family. He turned his laptop toward me and waved me over to have a look at it.

What he'd found wasn't a new design, but an article on sand painting. Apparently the technique that the avatar had used for drawing her mystical map was traditional in several cultures. That was interesting, but I wasn't sure why Tommy believed it would help decipher the avatar's message. I scrolled down the page to skim the main details of the article—

And then I saw the picture at the bottom. I stopped scrolling.

"See?" Tommy grinned. "I told you."

It was a 19th century photo, grainy and faded, that showed a Native American man in traditional dress. He was kneeling on the ground with one hand held out in front of him. A thin stream of sand trickled from between his fingers, and though the sand itself looked blurry, the way he positioned his hand to control the flow of sand mirrored the avatar's performance exactly. Beneath the photo was a caption that explained sand painting was practiced in the American southwest, in Australia, and among the Buddhists in Tibet—which just happened to be three locations where I'd found the closest matches to the avatar's design.

There are places where the wall between the worlds grows thin, Sebastian had told me. *Where dreams, and sometimes people, can cross from one world to another. Seers will seek insight there. . . .* Had seers from those three locations experienced the same visions?

Had they been inspired by the same alien source, or perhaps inspired each other? If so, then the avatar's choice of artistic method was itself a message. She had told me where I must go to find the tower, not in spoken language, but in the language of dreams.

The only problem was, she was directing me to a place no sane person would choose to visit.

"Jesse?"

Without speaking, I headed toward the bedroom. I retrieved the map of Terra Prime that Sebastian had given me and brought it back to the living room, where I unfolded it on the coffee table. And there was the area marked *Badlands*, exactly in the part of the Southwestern U.S. that Tommy's article said was associated with sand painting.

"Shit," Tommy muttered.

"Badlands?" my mother asked. "What are those?"

"It's a no-man's land." I tried to keep my voice steady as I described it. "People who go there are never seen again. At least not sane." If that was where the tower was, it might fill in a piece of the Dreamwalker puzzle, albeit in a terrifying way. Supposedly my Gift drove its users insane, and their madness then infected everyone surrounding them. So if enough insane Dreamwalkers gathered in one place, might their state of mind impact the entire region? Could they taint the very land with their madness, so that long after they were dead and buried, those who came to the area were still affected, driven insane if they tried to enter it? My fingers trembled on the map as I considered the implications of that.

Calm, Jesse. Stay calm. Focus on what you know. When I had told Sebastian about what happened at the Weaver's camp when the reaper appeared, he said he'd heard stories of similar events at the edge of the Badlands. Bloody rain. Insects gone mad. Trees that cycled between life and death in the blink of an eye. They were the kinds of things that could easily drive you mad if you weren't mad to start with. But they didn't necessarily have anything to do with my Gift.

The path to the Dreamwalker tower was in the Badlands. I'd only suspected it before, but now I was certain. Which meant that if I wanted to learn how to fight the reapers, I would have to go there. I would have to walk into the heart of that region's insanity and embrace it. And I would have to do that alone, because no one on this world or any other would be crazy enough to go with me.

Mom reached out to take my hand. I jumped at the touch. "We'll find another way," she assured me.

There is no other way, I thought. *The avatar girl would have shown it to me if there was.*

I had a choice between two roads, and both ended in darkness. If I stayed at home the reapers would continue to attack my family, and eventually devour us all. If I went to the Badlands I would have to confront the source of the madness that had consumed so many, and perhaps succumb to it myself. Or maybe I would go crazy anyway, since that was supposed to be the final stage of my Gift. Where was the safe path between those obstacles? How was I supposed to choose my way, with so little information to go on?

That night the reaper came to Tommy. My little brother knew the warning signs and was able to wake himself up before it fully manifested, but he was badly shaken. So was I. There was an atmosphere of fear in the house now, and for as long as I stayed there, I knew it was going to keep getting worse. It was a special kind of madness to watch your loved ones suffer, knowing that you were responsible. Surely it was better to brave the unknown and take one's chances than to live like that.

At least once I left Terra Colonna my family would be safe. That would be a kind of victory, wouldn't it?

iiiiiiiiiiii

We drove to the Gate in Front Royal, the closest one to Luray. That was after a shopping trip where Mom spent the last of her paycheck buying me every supply that she or Tommy or I could think of, including some specialty cosmetic items I thought might help Isaac. I felt guilty as I saw all that precious money draining away like sand between her fingers, but she said she was investing in her daughter's survival and nothing mattered more than that. How could I argue with her? She gave me a few pieces of jewelry she had, mostly semi-precious, to pawn once I crossed over, so I could have local currency. I told her I still had a little money left from the last trip, but it was a token protest. I didn't know what a cross-country trip would cost on Terra Prime, but it probably wasn't cheap.

And then we drove to Front Royal. It was about an hour's trip, and we didn't talk much in the car. If things went south this might be the last time we ever saw each other, and on the one hand that made you want to cry your eyes out and hug everyone and try to say profoundly meaningful things that would be remembered, while on the other it stopped up your throat so no words would come out. The latter seemed to win out for all three of us.

The Gate in Front Royal was in the basement of a movie theater that was closed for renovations. Mom parked outside the building, and for a long while the three of us just stared at it.

"You have your tickets?" she said at last.

I pulled them halfway out of my purse to show her. "Check."

"Passport?"

"Check."

"Tablet?"

I peeked into my bag. "Check. Check."

"Money? Pawn supplies?"

I took her hand. "It's all there, Mom."

She squeezed my hand so hard it almost hurt. "I shouldn't let you go," she whispered.

"But you've seen the reaper, and you know why I have to." My eyes were getting wet now; I reached up to wipe my face with my free hand. "Thank you for believing in me." I turned back to Tommy. "And you . . . you are the best little brother any girl ever had. Even if you do drive me crazy sometimes."

He wiped his nose on his sleeve. "You'd better come back. I'll never forgive you if you don't."

"I will," I whispered. "I promise."

"I'll never forgive you either," my mother said softly.

It's hard to hug people in a compact car, especially from the front to the back seat, but the Grey I had spoken to on the phone to arrange this trip had told me that no "departure behavior" should take place in public view, so we managed somehow. Then I reached for the car door, but Mom put a hand on my arm to stop me. "One more thing."

I turned back to her. She was holding out a small box. "What is it?"

"Look inside."

I took the box and opened it. Inside were two gold rings, one with a diamond in it. I hadn't seen them in so many years that it took me a minute to realize what they were. "Oh, Mom, I can't."

"In case you need real money. I don't know what the gold is worth, but the stone is a good one. Don't let them cheat you."

"I can't take your wedding ring—"

She took my hand in hers, folding it over the box. "It's not something I'm ever going to wear again," she said firmly. "And you mean more to me than a piece of jewelry."

Now there were real tears in my eyes. "Oh Mom, I love you."

"Shhhh." She took a tissue from the console and wiped my eyes. "No departure behavior, remember? Now put them where they won't get lost and go to your Gate before they leave without you."

I turned back to look at Tommy. He quickly held up a hand to fend off anything maudlin I might say. "Just bring me back a cool souvenir. Okay?"

"Okay," I whispered.

And that was it. My last words to my family. I got out of the car and said goodbye to them from the street in a casual way, like they were just dropping me off to see a movie or something, because the Grey had asked me to do that. Then I shouldered my bag and headed to the door that I'd been told to use, a windowless steel one off to one side of the theater. Jessica Drake, interworld traveler.

As the steel door closed behind me I heard my mom drive away.

7

VICTORIA FOREST
VIRGINIA PRIME

SEBASTIAN HAYES

S EBASTIAN WAS CLEANING his musket when the call came. Not that the gun needed cleaning, but the familiar ritual was soothing. At times like this it helped ground him. The little pterodactyl, perched on his shoulder as he worked, periodically tried to nip at the stock, and he swatted it away so often that eventually it flew off to find some other amusement.

Another exile, like himself. In some ways he had more in common with the small creature than he did with the humans on this world.

Running his fingers along the thick steel barrel transported him back to a time when life had been simpler. He could smell the sweetness of baking bread as if it were real, and if he shut his eyes he could hear the laughter of his daughter as she chased butterflies in the yard, his wife singing as she cooked. The echoes of past happiness filled his heart for a short time, and Terra Prime faded from his awareness. But then the peaceful images gave way to memories of war, and once more he was surrounded by the chaos of battle. The stink of blood and death and sulfur filled his nostrils, while chokingly thick clouds of gunpowder smoke hid both friend and enemy from view. He remembered the

madness that had driven them all to keep fighting even when the tide
of the war turned against them, frozen mud slogging their march to a
crawl in winter, dwindling supplies turning them into ghosts of their
former selves. Because they had to win. There was no other choice.
They would never have picked up their guns in the first place if they
had believed there was any other option.

On Terra Prime, however, that same effort had failed. Mere guns
and human courage could not prevail against an Empire whose Gifted
generals commanded the very elements. When Elementals could split
the ground open beneath the colonists' feet and Stormbringers could
summon fist-sized hailstones to rain down upon them, guns were almost superfluous. Wars on Terra Prime were won by whoever had the
most powerful Gifts at their disposal, and the British Empire had devoted centuries to making sure that it did . . . even if that meant kidnapping infants from neighboring worlds.

Sometimes, when Sebastian gave himself over to the past, he suffered visions so painful that the horrors of war paled by comparison.
He would relive that terrible day when he returned home to find his
wife and his daughter dead, murdered in his absence. If he'd been
home he could have protected them, but instead he'd been trapped
on Terra Prime, fighting a pointless war with the Shadows while the
people he loved most in the universe were dying. God's blood, how he
hated this wretched world! How he hated the Shadows! If there was a
way to destroy them all in one blow he would do it without hesitation,
even if that meant being lost in the darkness between the worlds for
eternity. Not just to avenge his family, but to redeem himself for having failed them.

Suddenly a low buzzing from across the cave drew him back to
the present moment. It took him a moment to realize that it was coming from his coat, currently slung over a chair near the entrance. Putting his musket carefully aside, he went to investigate. None of the
protective fetters pinned to the coat's lapel would make a noise like
that, but there was one in the pocket that he was betting was responsible. Indeed, as he found it and drew it out he could feel it vibrating

rhythmically against his palm. A thin slab of quartz crystal in a silver frame: it was unmarked, but there was little doubt about what its purpose was. Farspeakers used such crystals for their fetters because the unique pattern of flaws shared by adjacent slices helped them resonate in unison across great distances. Or so the Farspeakers claimed.

Morgana had given him this fetter, dropping it into his hand when she returned all his other ones after their last meeting. He hadn't even realized he had it until much later, while he was pinning his other fetters back onto his coat. He had almost thrown it over the edge of a cliff. He didn't want anything of Morgana's on his person, least of all a fetter that would connect the two of them. Merely having the thing in his pocket made him shudder.

But he had agreed to serve her, and that was a contract he dared not breach. She was the only thing standing between him and the Shadows right now, and unless she demanded something so abhorrent that he would rather face death than obey her, this was the game he was stuck playing.

The fetter buzzed softly in his palm. He hesitated, then closed his fingers over it, willing it to activate. The crystal warmed as Morgana's image took shape before him, translucent and ghostly.

"Your Grace." He bowed his head respectfully. The image was of minimal quality, he noted. That was good. If she couldn't see him clearly she wouldn't be able to read him as easily.

"Private Hayes. You are well?"

He shrugged. "I'm alive, and no man's prisoner. Given what else I might be, I suppose that qualifies as *well*."

A faint smile twitched her lips. "Good enough, then. As time is short, I will be direct. I have a task I wish you to perform."

His stomach clenched. *Of course you do.* "I am your Ladyship's servant."

She dismissed the thought with a graceful sweep of her hand. "Please. Not a servant, Private Hayes. More like . . . an ally."

He was glad that she couldn't see his expression clearly. "What is it you wish of me?"

"What you do best, of course. Information collecting. There's someone who will be returning to Terra Prime soon, who I believe will seek you out. I wish to know her business. That's all."

"Who is this person?"

"She currently travels under the name Jennifer Dolan. I believe you know her as Jessica Drake."

He tried to keep his expression blank, so that she wouldn't guess at the knot of dread suddenly forming in his gut. Thank God he wasn't in her physical presence; a Master Seer like Morgana could read a man's emotions like a book. "I remember the name."

"You travelled together for a while, yes?"

He shrugged. "For a while. We parted company after a few days." *Beneath the looming tower of Shadowcrest.* "Am I to gather from your words she made it home safely?"

"Her welfare is of interest to you?"

Choose your words carefully, Sebastian. "She's from my home world. All things of Terra Colonna are of interest to me." He paused. "I'm surprised she would come back here."

"Indeed. I think she was surprised as well. Sometimes fate directs us along a path we would not have chosen on our own. Don't you think so, Private Hayes?"

Beneath the fetter's visual field, where she could not see, his hand tightened around the fetter. "We are judged by how we travel that road, your Grace. Wherever it may take us."

"Indeed." The image of Morgana nodded sagely. "I do think we understand each other."

"What is it you want, exactly?"

"To know where she goes. Whom she travels with. What she seeks. She trusts you as she trusts few other people in this world and will come to you for counsel. I suspect it will take very little urging on your part to get her to share her current business."

His mouth tightened. "And you wish to know all of it."

The Guildmistress smiled coldly. "I'm sure you will be able to pick out the parts that interest me."

He hesitated. *Be smart, Sebastian. End the conversation now. The more she tells you, the more you will owe her.* But he had to ask one more thing. Even if the odds of her answering him honestly were close to zero, he had to try. "What is it you want with her?"

A corner of her mouth twitched. "This, from the man who sells Guild secrets to the highest bidder?"

"If you know my reputation as well as you claim, you know that isn't how I operate. Others have entrusted me with their secrets, and I've guarded those with my life."

"Yes," Her eyes narrowed slightly. "I do know that."

"I can serve you better if I know what you're looking for. Doesn't that make sense? Help me to understand why you have such interest in her, and I'll get you all the information you need."

There was a moment of silence. Sebastian held his breath.

"You don't want to know my business," she said at last. "For your own safety. Trust me in this."

Her image vanished.

Slowly Sebastian opened his hand; his fingernails had left sharp dents in his palm, but he didn't feel them. His flesh was numb. His soul was numb. In his mind's eye he could see the grave of the last young girl he had failed to protect—his daughter.

Don't come here Jessica. Don't offer me your secrets. If Morgana ever asks about you while I'm in her presence she'll know how much I'm hiding from her, and she has ways to get it from me. I know too much about you already for either of us to survive the consequences of that.

8

THE WARRENS
VIRGINIA PRIME

JESSE

I N SCHOOL WE WERE TAUGHT the story of Theseus, who descended into the Labyrinth to battle the Minotaur. He brought along a spool of string that he unwound as he went, leaving behind a trail he could follow later to escape that dismal place.

It sounded good in theory, but as with so many things we were taught in school, it was not quite as easy as it seemed.

Getting to the entrance of the Warrens was harder than I'd expected. Oh, I remembered where to find the storm cellar entrance that Isaac had showed us, and just beyond that lay the hidden door that would give me access to the network of utility tunnels, storm drains, and sewers that extended under most of Luray. But the storm doors were securely locked, and I had no clue how to open them from the outside. For a brief moment I wished Rita was with me; she could have picked the rusted lock with ease. But I was on my own now, and since I couldn't force the doors open without making enough noise to alert the entire neighborhood, I walked around the property searching for another entrance. Finally I found a small basement window that I was able to pry open, giving me access to the musty, debris-filled cellar

I remembered. Working by the light of a single thin beam trickling in through the filthy glass, I shoved trash out of the way to reveal the hidden trap door that would give me access to the Warrens proper.

I had brought along chalk to mark my way, and even a reel of string, just case I wanted to do the Greek mythical thing. So in theory my descent should have been safe enough. But I was acutely aware of the fact that I'd only come this way once before, and then it had been with a guide. The thought of being alone in that filthy darkness scared me more than I wanted to admit. But Isaac was down there. I knew it in my bones. And if he was avoiding the aboveground world because of the mark on his forehead, as I suspected, then my waiting for him to emerge on his own would be a waste of time. This was the haven he was familiar with, the one safe shelter where no one from home could find him, and if he wanted to escape from everyone and everything that had caused him pain, this was where he would go.

With a sigh I eased through the narrow door, bracing myself on the rusty steel ladder just inside it. I took out my flashlight and a thick piece of chalk, drew in a deep breath, and shut the door behind me, committing myself to Theseus's nightmare. The ladder was less stable than I remembered, and the air seemed ten times more humid; the sweat of my palms slicked the metal rungs, making descent difficult. But I managed to reach the floor of the first utility tunnel without losing my grip, and after a moment's consideration, I set off in the direction that looked most familiar. It wasn't long before the stale smell of the Warrens came wafting up to me, and the further I went, the worse it got. By the time I reached the storm drain system, my stomach was lurching and my nostrils were stinging. But the last time I was here I'd had to wade through a river of putrid filth, so today was a veritable health spa compared to that.

I marked my way as I went. Oh, how thoroughly I marked my way! Future visitors might wonder what madwoman had scored the walls with so many stripes and arrows of neon-colored chalk, but I was damned if I was going to take the smallest chance of being trapped down there. I even tucked some small marbles into the muck of the floor at key intersections, my personal version of bread crumbs. So if some malevolent being should come along and erase all my chalk lines, I would still be able to find my way out.

Soon I was feeling my way through the narrow tunnels that a tribe of abandoned children had once called home. A few weeks ago there would have been residents watching me from every shadow, but now all those shadows were empty. The Lord Governor's men had raided the place thoroughly, capturing or killing all those children, and, apparently, they had destroyed many things along the way. When I came to where lamps had once been hung, I found only shattered glass and pools of glistening oil. When I came to where supplies had once been stored, I found only smashed cans, broken jars, and trails of rat droppings. As I picked my way past all those messes I couldn't help but think of Moth, the brave little girl I'd rescued from the Weavers' experimental lab. She'd told me about other refugees who'd been sold to brothels, or maybe worse. Their ghosts seemed to surround me as I travelled, and I let the memory of their voices guide me, choosing at every intersection the direction which echoed most loudly with the shouts and laughter of those poor doomed children.

But finally I had gone as far as memory could take me. I was standing at the juncture of four narrow tunnels, and I had no idea which one to follow next. Finally, with a sigh of frustration, I marked my entrance point with chalk, used the tip of my shoe to push a marble into the muck, and stood there for a moment considering my options. Theseus hadn't known where he was going either, I reminded myself, and eventually he found what he was looking for. Then again, he'd invaded the Minotaur's turf; probably the monster came to him.

Good enough.

Raising up my head, I yelled out, "Isaac!" My voice echoed through the tunnels with startling volume. "It's me, Jesse!" I couldn't have followed such echoes to their source, but Isaac was a creature of the Warrens, and knew how to navigate in the darkness better than I did. I held my breath as the echoes faded, each one weaker than the last, until the tunnels were silent once more, with only the distant sound of dripping water to compromise their terrible emptiness.

What if he wasn't here after all, I wondered suddenly. What would I do then? The only other way I had to find him was dreamwalking, and that would be ten times more dangerous on Terra Prime than it was back home. This was the home world of the reapers, the domain of the Shadowlord whose dream I'd invaded. Not a good place for me to be drawing attention to myself, in the dream world or out of it.

"Isaac!" I yelled again. Maybe there was a bit more desperation in my voice this time. *Come on, Isaac, I know you can hear me. Come out from the shadows so I can talk to you.*

Suddenly a voice from behind me said, "You'll wake the dead yelling like that."

Whipping around, I found Isaac standing behind me, framed by the mouth of a tunnel I had just passed. His face was even paler than I remembered, his cheeks were hollow, and just before he raised up a hand to shield his eyes from my flashlight's beam I saw they were underscored by deep shadows of exhaustion. He'd lost weight since last I saw him, and his clothing hung loosely about his frame. On his forehead was the same mark I'd noticed in our dream, but now, in the thin beam from my flashlight, it glistened unnaturally, as if a slug had left a blood-colored slime trail running down his face. It was hard not to stare.

"Is this a dream?" he asked hoarsely. "Or are you really here?"

"Really here," I assured him. Suddenly all the things I had intended to say to him were gone from my brain, and the best I could manage was, "Are you okay?"

A corner of his mouth twitched slightly. "My standards for 'okay' are a bit lower than they used to be. But I'm surviving. That's something, I guess."

He walked slowly toward me, his pale, strained face like that of a ghost. When he got within arm's length he hesitated, and I thought that maybe he wanted to reach out and touch me, to reassure himself that I was real flesh and blood, not just another dream. But though his hand twitched slightly, he just stood there, staring at me. "You shouldn't have come here," he said at last.

"Probably not," I agreed.

"The risk for you—"

"Is pretty serious. Let's not talk about that, okay?"

What hunger there was, in his eyes! What loneliness! Every fiber in my soul urged me to step forward and hug him, to offer him the comfort of a physical connection. But there was a defensiveness about him like Tommy once had, and I thought that he might not be able to handle it. So I kept my distance.

"Why are you here?" He nodded toward the tunnels surrounding us. "I'm guessing not for the five-star accommodations."

Despite the mood of the place, I smiled slightly. "I'm looking for information about the reapers. It turns out that it may be here, on Terra Prime. You said you would help me if you could, and since this is your home world, I figured I'd ask if you want to come along."

He sighed. "Jesse, you know what the problem is—"

"Let's say that I could make that problem go away." I raised up a hand to cut short his objection. "Just hypothetically, okay? Would you come with me then? Help me navigate my way across your world, maybe scare off a few ghosts along the way? I'm going to ask Sebastian also, but honestly, I think the chances of him leaving this region are pretty slim. There are people here who owe him favors, local information he's collected, a network of political influence that he's spent years cultivating . . . he'll lose all that if he travels too far. So it may just be you and me."

"Where you want to go . . . it's far from here?"

I nodded.

"How far?"

I drew in a deep breath. "The Badlands."

He stared at me like I'd gone mad. "Are you *serious*?"

"I'm afraid so."

"People die there, Jesse. *Everyone* dies there."

"Or goes insane," I corrected him. "And as a Dreamwalker I'm supposed to do that anyway, so I figure I've got nothing to lose. As for you," I looked around, "well, you'd have to leave this cheery place."

"Jesus." He shook his head in disbelief. "I'm not sure if you're brave, or just plain crazy."

"Both brave and crazy. I'm also desperate. A reaper attacked my mother a few nights ago, and she barely woke up in time to save herself. Last night one went after my brother. I can't just wait around until it gets them."

His eyes narrowed slightly. "What do you mean, a reaper attacked your mother?"

"It came to her in a dream. She realized what was happening and was able to wake herself up, but barely in time." Isaac was looking at me so strangely I said, "What? What's wrong?"

"Your mother and brother aren't Dreamwalkers, are they?"

"Not that I know of. Tommy hears voices, but you're the one who told me that's not necessarily a sign of my Gift. And I'm not really related to either of them anyway, so there's no reason they'd share my talent." I paused. "Why do you ask?"

"Because the reapers were created to hunt Dreamwalkers. Why would they go after your family like that? It doesn't make any sense."

"Maybe to manipulate me?"

He shook his head sharply. "Wraiths are simpleminded creatures. If they were commanded to perform a task—like killing you—they would do it as quickly and as directly as possible. The dead don't conspire and manipulate like the living do; they just act."

I spread my hands wide. "Now, there, you see? This is why I need you. To tell me things like that." When he didn't respond I pressed. "Necromancy is in your blood like dreamwalking is in mine, Isaac. We both hunger for the same answers. Come with me. Help me find them."

He looked away from me. For a moment I thought he was considering my request, but then I realized he was listening to something. Was his ghost talking to him? Giving him counsel? All I could hear was dripping water. I remembered the bloody figure that had stood behind Isaac in his dream, and shuddered at the thought that Jacob had been watching our whole conversation.

Finally Isaac said, "What would you need, to work this magic of yours? So that I could travel with you?"

I felt like I'd just crossed the finish line of a marathon. "Good lighting. Enough to see what I'm doing. Take me to where I can have that, and I'll show you the rest."

"You understand, all the rest of this discussion is pointless, unless you can actually change my situation. Which—for the record—I don't necessarily believe you can do."

"Of course," I said.

He sighed heavily. "The Badlands, eh? Can't be too much worse than this place, I suppose." He gestured toward one of the tunnels. "Come on. I'll take you to where there's sunlight." A weak smile appeared. "I think I still remember what that looks like."

⁙⁙⁙⁙⁙⁙⁙⁙

He led me to the tunnel where we'd first met Sebastian, where the water from the storm drains gushed into the North River. The rusty iron grate that had once blocked our way was still there, but the lock had been pried off; apparently Isaac had invested time in making sure all possible exits from the Warrens were open. We squeezed past the grate and used some tree roots to swing ourselves around the opening of the tunnel, onto solid ground. Soon we were sitting on the embankment, our backs to Luray, invisible to anyone coming toward us from the city. People passing by in boats might spot us, but a thin screen of brush between us and the water meant they wouldn't be able to make out any details. It was as private as any sunlit place was likely to get.

I opened my backpack and unloaded the cosmetic products Mom and I had bought for this trip. We'd packed a bit of everything, from regular makeup to hardcore theatrical supplies; hopefully something in that collection would work. Isaac watched with interest as I rummaged through the supplies, but he didn't seem very hopeful. I remembered what he'd told me about how makeup wouldn't stay on his transformed skin, so I tried not to get my own hopes up. But so much was riding on this, I had to make it work.

The first thing I tried was some tattoo cover cream. It went on smoothly enough, and hid nearly all of the mark's deep bloody color—for about thirty seconds. Then it began to slough off. "See?" Isaac said. The defeat in his voice was painful to hear. "I told you." The flexing of his forehead as he spoke dislodged the rest of the cream; it fell from his face in a lump, like a dead slug.

"That was just the first experiment." I tried to sound more confident than I felt. "Lots to try here."

But none of the other cosmetic products performed any better than the first. The worst was heavy greasepaint designed to cover bald caps; that one didn't even last long enough for me to sit back and take a look at it. With a sigh I took up the rag I was using to wipe my hands clean—now streaked with ten different tones of flesh color—and reached out to wipe his forehead clean. His skin was turning red from all the chemicals, and I could see in his eyes that the tiny bit of hope he'd entertained was rapidly fading.

"I guess I'm not coming with you after all," he said dejectedly.

"Not done yet," I told him. I had one product left to try, a bit of a long shot, but everything else had failed, so what the hell. I took out the bottle of white fluid and shook it for a few second, then removed the cap. The liquid inside smelled sharply of ammonia. Isaac winced. "That's going on my face?"

"Unless you think drinking it would help." I gestured toward the ground. "Lie down, please."

He raised an eyebrow, but did as he was told. I made him lie on his back, face up, then knelt by his head and dipped my finger into the thick white fluid. It smelled even worse as it left the bottle. "You should probably close your eyes," I told him. He looked like he was about to ask a question, then bit his lip and just obeyed. I began to smooth the liquid latex across his forehead, working in long strokes, covering not only the scar itself but a good bit of surrounding skin. I tried to work quickly, as the stuff was likely to start coming off pretty quickly. If it didn't form a skin before that happened, this experiment too would fail.

Finally his forehead was coated in white. I leaned down to blow on the stuff, to speed its drying. It was an oddly intimate moment, and Isaac opened his eyes and looked at me, startled by the touch of my breath across his forehead. *Come on,* I thought to the liquid latex, trying to stay focused on that and not on him. *Dry fast!*

Then, finally, the white liquid began to turn clear. "Hold still!" I told him. I kept blowing. Patch by patch the whiteness was disappearing, and I had to fight back a surge of elation. *We're not out of the woods yet,* I cautioned myself.

Finally I sat back on my heels to inspect my handiwork. His forehead looked like it had been smeared with Elmer's glue. "Try moving," I said. He furrowed his brow a bit, and though the latex layer wasn't adhering to the mark, it looked firmly stuck on everywhere else. I'd successfully tented over the miserable thing.

"What?" he asked, trying to read my expression. "Did it work?"

Without answering, I took up the greasepaint again and began to smooth it over the dried latex. The result didn't look anything like real skin, and the center of his forehead had a long, thin bubble that looked like a blister, but now I had a surface in place that would accept makeup. Soon the red mark was completely covered over. He looked like his face was covered in scar tissue, but it was flesh-colored scar tissue, and from a distance you might not even notice it.

I gestured for him to sit up, and I took out of my backpack a visored cap I'd bought for him. When I put it on his head and pulled the visor low, it shadowed the affected area enough to mask some of its textural oddity. He looked almost normal now.

I took out a mirror and gave it to him. The look on his face when he saw his reflection was something I would never forget. There was still pain in his eyes, but there was also awe, and maybe even a spark of hope. It was overwhelming to see.

Then he reached out and embraced me. The motion was so sudden, so unexpected, that for a moment I couldn't even respond. His

arms closed tightly around me, and as I put my arms around him in
return I could feel his shoulders trembling. He might have been
weeping—it certainly felt that way—but if so, he did it quietly, probably not wanting me to know. So I just held him as he trembled, and
maybe tears trickled unseen down his face, carrying with them some
of his despair. Washing it away. I hoped that was the case.

Somewhere on the river bank, a blood-streaked ghost watched us
in silence.

9

SHADOWCREST
VIRGINIA PRIME

LEONID ANTONIN

THE DEAD WERE RESTLESS TONIGHT.

Isaac's father could hear cries of anguish echoing in the hallway as he walked toward the Guildmaster's study; not the usual moans and whispers that accompanied any Shadowlord but sharper, more strident cries, with more intense emotion behind them. Frustration. Fear. Fury. Mere soul shards didn't experience emotion that intensely, which suggested that these ghosts were not the normal fragments, but creatures more complex. More sentient. Since the voices were getting louder as Antonin approached the study, it was reasonable to assume that they were associated with Virilian. Perhaps spirits that the Guildmaster had claimed since his last Communion? The memories Virilian had absorbed in that ritual were said to come from one of the greatest necromancers the Guild had ever known. If anyone could enslave spirits so thoroughly that centuries later another man might lay claim to them in his name, it would have been Shekarchiyandar. Such spirits would have been free agents for centuries, suddenly snatched from their freedom and reduced to slavery once more. That would certainly explain their foul mood.

Lord Antonin remembered the black spirits that Virilian had summoned at the end of his Communion ritual—horrific wraiths who trailed raw hatred in their wake. To gaze upon them was to taste the malevolence of Hell, and even the most seasoned Shadowlords in the room had struggled to maintain composure when the reapers were summoned. All had managed it, of course. The undead were proud creatures, and most would rather die the true death than display weakness in front of rivals.

The servant standing guard at the door of the study opened it as he approached, and a chill wind swept out from the room. Antonin's own flesh was equally cold, so he took little notice of it as he entered.

"Your Grace." Antonin bowed respectfully to the Guildmaster as a servant shut the door behind him. "You wished to see me?"

Virilian was seated in a high-backed leather chair whose size and shape gave it the aspect of a throne. He waved for Antonin to come closer. "Have a seat, Lord Antonin." He indicated a chair directly opposite him. It was closer than Antonin would have preferred, but moving it further away might be read as an insult, so he sat. He did not relax, however. He never relaxed around Virilian.

Several of Antonin's ghosts began to murmur in distress, which was very odd. They had been around Virilian before and had never done that. Could they sense some trouble that he could not?

"Your service to the Guild has been exemplary," the Guildmaster said. "But I would expect no less from such a prestigious bloodline."

"You do me great honor." Was Virilian speaking with a slight accent? If so, that was odd as well. The parts of the brain that affected speech and movement shouldn't be affected by Communion.

"Your support for our traditions sets an excellent example for our apprentices," Virilian continued. "As does your willingness to make personal sacrifices for the Guild's welfare."

Antonin stiffened slightly. Was he referring to the recent incident with Isaac? If so, the statement might not be intended as praise, but as a reminder of Antonin's failure to control his family properly. He kept his voice carefully neutral as he said, "I am my Guild's servant."

"Your wife's Communion is scheduled soon, is it not?"

"We're in the planning phase. There's no date set yet." Definitely there was a trace of an accent. And Virilian's movements were subtly different than in previous meetings. Someone who didn't know him well would probably not even notice the change, but Antonin did.

"A woman from such an illustrious family should have a Communion that honors her heritage," Virilian continued. "Let me know when the time comes to choose her first soul, I will make sure it is worthy of her."

Normally it was the Guild elders who decided which set of memories a new Shadowlord would receive, but Virilian was offering to oversee the choice himself. It was a tremendous honor, but one that Antonin was suspicious of. Why would Virilian single them out for special favor like that? When the fiasco with Isaac had taken place, Antonin had assumed that just the opposite would happen, and that his family would have to work twice as hard to earn back the trust and respect that Isaac had cost them. It was hard for him to accept this kind of gesture without wondering what game the Guildmaster was playing. "I am grateful for your favor, Your Grace, as I am sure she will be."

"We are entering a period of unique challenges, Lord Antonin. The destruction of the Luray Gate weakened us, and our rivals in the city plot to take advantage of that. Meanwhile, enemies that we thought long defeated are stirring again. I will need a strong right hand in the coming nights, someone who is respected by our Guild, who will not be challenged when he wields my authority. Someone whose loyalty and sense of sacrifice are beyond question." Eyes black as ink fixed on him. "I want you to serve as my Secundus, Lord Antonin."

The offer was so unexpected that Antonin didn't know how to respond. For as long as Virilian had been in charge of the Guild there had been no second-in-command; the man was too suspicious of his own Guild elders to place one of them so close to his throne. Why would he change course now, after so many years? Given the shame House Antonin had just suffered because of Isaac, it made no sense.

When Antonin did not respond immediately, the Guildmaster asked, "The offer doesn't please you?"

"It pleases me," he said quietly.

"Few *umbrae majae* would be granted such an honor."

"I understand that, Your Grace."

There was no denying that the offer was tempting. Not only would it raise Antonin up above all the other elders, but it would bolster the status of his entire family, granting them a unique position in Shadowlord society. And it would wipe out any shame that might still cling to their name after Isaac's banishment. It would be the culmination of all that Lord Antonin had worked for, all that he had sacrificed for years to achieve. How much did Virilian's motives really matter, in the face of that? Surely any storm that came of this, House Antonin could weather.

Still he hesitated.

"And your answer?"

If he didn't accept, the Guildmaster would assign someone else to the position. Which meant that a rival family would be elevated above his own. That was unthinkable. "As you see fit to offer me such an honor," he said carefully, "It is my duty to accept." *There. It is done.*

"Good. I will see that your change in status is announced immediately. Later tonight, you and I can sit down and discuss your new duties. For now," he paused, "there is a special project I want you to oversee."

Of course there is. "I am your Lordship's servant."

The Guildmaster leaned back in his chair; his ink-black gaze was a bottomless abyss. "I will have need of new servants soon. You will help me obtain the raw material for them."

"You mean bound spirits?"

"Exactly."

Antonin's eyes narrowed. Binding a spirit was bloody business; only by murdering a man could one gain perfect control over his ghost. "How many would you require?"

"Let us say, for now, a hundred. I don't care what manner of life they lived, only that they are suitable for binding."

"A *hundred*?"

"For now."

He didn't dare protest. He couldn't ask Virilian to give the job to someone else. His acceptance of the Secundus position had removed those options from the table. Check and mate.

"The city will notice if a hundred people go missing," he said quietly.

"The Lord Governor is a practical man. I am sure there are criminals in his custody that he would rather be rid of. Life sentences do nothing but drain a city of its resources. Tell him our Guild will take responsibility for the worst murderers he's got, in return for their help in digging out the Gate. He'll think that we're doing him a favor. And look up the name of the flesh broker who collected those children from the Warrens; some of them might still be available. Just make sure they're old enough to become suitable servants. I have serious work for them to perform, and the fragmented ghost of a six-year-old child won't be able to contribute much." A corner of his mouth twitched. "I am sure my new Secundus can find other creative sources of supply."

A hundred murders. The Guildmaster might be the one to order those deaths, but he, Leonid Antonin, would be the one the Lord Governor questioned when prisoners did not return to jail, the one the child buyers whispered rumors about, the one that other Guilds watched, setting spies upon him, wondering what the hell he was up to. Whatever nastiness might result from this, it would land squarely on his shoulders.

He had walked into the trap of his own free will. That was the part that rankled most. "May I ask why you need so many bound servants?"

"They will search for Dreamwalkers, Lord Antonin. And hopefully find them before they come into their power, instead of afterward, as we've been doing."

"Isn't that the job of the Seers?"

Anger flashed in the depths of those black eyes. "The Seers have their own agenda, and only a fool would trust them. And they have failed. That's simple fact. There's at least one fully manifested Dreamwalker active right now, who they neither identified at birth nor detected later. How many others have they missed, that we don't know about? An army of the dead, capable of crossing between the worlds without assistance, undetectable by any normal means, acting in vast numbers, can do a proper search."

An army of the dead. Were Antonin fully alive, the image might have sent a chill down his spine. "Ghosts can't detect the presence of Gifts, your Grace, much less identify them. So how do you imagine these spirits will find Dreamwalkers, when the Seers, who are able to detect Gifts, have failed to do so?"

Virilian smiled. It was a cold expression, more predatory than human. "Do as you are commanded, Lord Antonin, and the rest will follow, I promise you." He paused. "Or should I say, *Secundus* Antonin."

He bowed his head in assent. What other option was there? "I will do my best," he promised.

As Secundus, he had no choice.

||||||||||||

The great black doors that led to the Chamber of Souls were carved with a thousand images, gracefully horrific. Demons and skeletons, dead men and dying men, accidents and slaughters: images from the Lost Worlds, depicting civilizations that had died because of the Shadowlords. Combined into one great mural, they served as a reminder of the awesome power the Guild wielded, and also of the responsibility that came with that power.

Tracing one of the black carvings with his finger, Lord Antonin remembered the day he had brought his son down here. He had hoped to inspire Isaac with the grandeur of a Shadow's heritage, to show his son that by joining the *umbrae majae* he would become part of something greater. Something eternal. But it was a mistake. He understood that now. One could not fit a square peg into a round hole by praising the nature of roundness. So which was more painful: the loss of his only son, or the fact that he had only himself to blame for driving the boy away? Remorse and guilt were both dangerous emotions for the undead, but they were hard to banish. Even as a Shadowlord, he was still half human.

Responsibility. That was the message of these doors. There was no room for impulse in the Shadowlords' world, nor for the kind of hot-blooded passion that drove living men to acts of desperation and folly. When you had the power to condemn an entire world to death, you could not allow yourself to be driven by emotion. So why did he get the sense that Virilian was doing just that?

With a whispered word he commanded one of the ghosts in attendance to help him unlock the doors, and he entered the Chamber of Souls.

No matter how many times he came here, he never failed to experience a sense of awe as he entered. In that moment before one's eyes adjusted, the tiny golden stars suspended in an endless black void seemed almost mystical, and one could imagine oneself standing in the center of the universe, surrounded by the music of a thousand worlds. Then other details took shape, and one could see pedestals with ancient books stored on them, topped by glass domes with tiny golden soul fetters suspended inside them. Each fetter contained the memories of a past Shadowlord, the imprint of a human soul, and the book stored beneath it contained the history of that soul.

Back when Virilian had first announced that he intended to Commune with a Dark fetter, Antonin had come here to research the Shadowlord the Guildmaster had chosen. But the biography of Shekarchiyandar had revealed very little, other than the fact that he was a key figure in the Dream Wars, renowned for his ability to root out and destroy Dreamwalkers. That was all. His real name was not even recorded, only the title he had been granted during that conflict, which translated to *Lord of Hunters*. Antonin knew there were additional tales in the Guild archives about Shekarchiyandar's exploits—fantastic tales—but those could not be trusted. The man was a legend, and the biographies of legends were notoriously unreliable.

But other Shadowlords had interacted with Shekarchiyandar during the Dream Wars, and their biographies must surely contain references to him. Which meant that somewhere in the thousands of handwritten volumes, Antonin might discover information about the dark fetter that Virilian had Communed with—and perhaps discover why all the other Shadowlords who had attempted to absorb Shekarchiyandar's memories had suffered the true death soon afterward. Hopefully he could accomplish that before the same thing happened to Virilian.

Or at least save his own family from the fallout.

10

LURAY
VIRGINIA PRIME

ISAAC

EYES. There were eyes everywhere. Isaac could feel them fixed on him no matter where he went, no matter how deep a shadow he hid in. Were people staring at the strange flesh-colored patch on his forehead, wondering what it was? Did some of them remember seeing him days earlier, when he was wandering lost through the city with his Guild's damning mark emblazoned across his forehead? Did they wonder if he had been forgiven by the Shadows, or had just found some way to dodge their justice?

He couldn't bring himself to go into the pawn shop with Jessica. He told her who to talk to, and how to deliver a message so it would be passed along to Sebastian, but more than that he couldn't do for her. The thought of going inside a shop and standing mere yards away from other people—maybe people he had once known—was more than he could handle.

So many eyes . . .

He watched from the shadowy alcove of a nearby townhouse entrance as she went inside, but the pawn shop's blinds were drawn, so he couldn't see her after that. The owner of the shop was the same contact the leader of the Warrens tribe had used to send a message to Sebastian back when Jesse and her friends had first arrived on Terra Prime. In theory Isaac knew how the process worked, though he'd never used it himself. *Go inside and ask for something in green. Say it's the only color you are interested in. Mention whatever information you wanted relayed, preferably in a cryptic form that only the Green Man will understand. Payment isn't required, but if you want to offer something, give him money to hold an item for you, and don't ask for a receipt.*

Back in his Warrens days Isaac had seen the pawnbroker get hold of Sebastian in record time, so he knew this message was likely to be delivered expediently. Hopefully when Sebastian got it he would come quickly. If he came at all, that was. Now that Isaac knew the Green Man's history, he understood that Sebastian hungered for news of his homeworld, and as soon as he had learned there were new visitors from Terra Colonna he had rushed to meet them. But this time things were different. He might not come.

The fact that Jessica spoke of Sebastian like he was a friend disturbed Isaac. The Green Man was a mercenary, and she would do well to remember that. The last time Sebastian had helped them, they'd paid him with artifacts from Jesse's world and one of Isaac's fetters. Not to mention other information Jessica might have given him, that Isaac didn't know about. So what would the price be this time? All the tales of the Green Man agreed on one point: he never did anything for free.

She comes from a more trusting world than mine. Here, everyone's motives are suspect.

Finally the door opened and Jesse emerged, holding a brown envelope in one hand. When she looked around for him he stepped into the light to wave her over, then fell back into shadow while she crossed the street to join him. When she reached the alcove she opened the envelope and tipped it forward so he could see the money inside it. "Not as much as I expected," she said. "But I guess that's the price you pay for a quick sale."

"Did you sell everything?"

She hesitated. "I kept the rings. I figure I can always sell them later if I need to."

He smiled slightly. The expression felt strangely alien, a memory from another life. "You're hoping to give them back to your mother when you get home."

She flushed. "Yeah." She put the envelope into her backpack and tied the latter securely shut. "*When you get home.* I like the sound of that. Not, *if you get home.*"

"Well, you know me," he said dryly. "I'm an optimistic sort of chap." He nodded toward the shop. "Will he pass on your message?"

"I think so. Hard to be sure, with no one saying anything directly."

"Did you pay him?"

She nodded. "There's a big tasteless ring he's supposedly holding for me." She settled the backpack onto her shoulder again. "So what now? We just wait?"

"Where did you ask Sebastian to meet you?"

"Same place as last time. Hopefully he'll realize I meant the docks. You said not to name anything directly—"

"Because we don't know how many people will be involved in relaying the message to him. Best to say nothing specific."

"I didn't realize he was so . . . organized."

"He has ears everywhere, Jessica. This city is full of people who owe him favors. That's how he managed to survive for so long." His mouth tightened. "He sells information. You understand that, right? Anything he learns from you, he may pass on to someone else if the price is right."

She said it quietly: "He won't sell my secrets."

"You don't know all his—"

"*He won't sell my secrets.*" She glared at him. "Drop it, okay?"

He sighed. "I'm just worried for you."

Her expression softened. "I know. I know." She sighed. "So what now? We go to the docks and wait for him to show up?"

"There's no guarantee," he warned her.

"He'll come," she said firmly. She hitched her pack up onto her shoulder. "He may not agree to help us, but he'll definitely want to know why I summoned him."

‧‧‧‧‧‧‧‧‧‧‧‧

They sat on a slatted bench facing the river, watching moonlight play over the water and eating food Jesse had bought from a street vendor earlier that evening. The fatty hamburgers and cold fries didn't sit well in Isaac's stomach after two weeks of near-starvation, and his legs still ached from the long walk across town, but he didn't complain. Even an ex-Shadow had his pride.

Hours had passed since they'd begun their vigil and still there was no sign of the Green Man. Jesse was becoming more and more anxious, but Isaac was unsurprised. He wondered if he should remind her that since they didn't know where Sebastian would be when he got her message—if he got it at all—they couldn't possibly predict how long it would take him to join them. Even if he did eventually come, they might be sitting on this bench for a quite a while.

Suddenly she stiffened; Isaac followed her gaze and saw a man walking along the boardwalk, heading toward them. He wasn't wearing a long coat bedecked with fetters this time, but a simple cotton jacket and jeans, casually unremarkable. His walk, however, was anything but casual, and when he saw the two of them sitting there his pace quickened. A gust of wind blew strands of a white ponytail over his shoulder, settling any doubt about who he was.

Jessica stood as Sebastian came closer, anxiety giving way to visible relief. But there was a hint of fear in the mix as well. If he refused to help, she and Isaac would have to go on to the Badlands alone. Clearly she wasn't as confident about that option as she had been pretending.

Sebastian stopped a few yards from them and for a moment just stood there, studying Jessica. Isaac apparently didn't exist in his universe. "I'm surprised you came back here." His voice sounded oddly strained.

"Yeah." She laughed shortly. "You and me both."

"Was it by your own free will?"

She nodded. "All my own idea." The fleeting smile faded. "I have business here."

His mouth tightened slightly. "Which I'm guessing you want my help with, else you wouldn't have summoned me." For the first time since arriving he looked directly at Isaac. That he didn't like him was obvious. "What about this one?"

"He's helping me."

Sebastian's eyes narrowed. "Are you sure that's wise, given his background?"

Annoyed at being discussed in the third person, Isaac said, "I'm not a Shadow anymore."

Sebastian nodded, but his expression didn't soften. "I heard about that."

"Is it a problem for you?"

"I rarely care what Guilds think. Least of all yours."

It's not my Guild anymore! Isaac wanted to protest. But if he started arguing about the technicalities of his exile, Sebastian might get annoyed enough to walk off and leave them on their own. And Jesse would never forgive him for that. So he swallowed his pride and muttered, "That makes two of us."

Jesse offered, "I couldn't have contacted you without his help."

There was a pause. "As you wish." It was clear from Sebastian's tone that he was less than happy about the situation. "So tell me why you summoned me."

"You remember the reapers?"

"It's hard to forget such dismal creatures."

"I think I know where I can find the information I need to destroy them."

Isaac watched Sebastian for reaction, but the man just said quietly, "Go on."

"The tower I've seen in my dreams, I think really exists. If not on Terra Prime, then somewhere I can access from here. It's connected to both the Dreamwalkers and the reapers."

"And you learned about its location . . . how?"

"A Dreamwalker told me."

Sebastian's eyes widened in surprise; Isaac was perversely pleased to see him taken off guard. "There's more than one of you?" he asked at last. "Fully manifested?"

"Well, I don't know how *manifested* she is, but yes, there's at least one more. She walks in dreams like I do—well, sort of like I do—and seems to know about our kind."

"Well." Sebastian stared off into the distance, as if remembering something. "That might explain about Virilian."

Isaac said, "What about Virilian?"

Sebastian looked at him. "Rumor has it he's decided to rid the entire universe of Dreamwalkers. Given that they were supposedly wiped out in the Dream Wars, some consider that a bit unhinged. I thought perhaps it might be a reaction to—" He hesitated, then looked back at Jesse. "To recent activity. But if there are other Dreamwalkers active, and he knows about them, then such a reaction would make sense. Perhaps he sees them as an ancient force returning to the world, one that his Guild swore to eradicate."

"But how would he even know about her?" Jesse asked. "I can't imagine the girl who contacted me would reveal herself to him. She didn't even trust me, at first."

He shrugged. "Who can say where a master necromancer gets his information? Maybe he learned something during his last Communion. It's rumored he submitted to that morbid ritual yet again, so now he has a new lifetime's worth of memories to work with. Maybe the last soul he consumed knew more about the Dreamwalkers than Virilian did." He glanced coldly at Isaac. "I don't suppose you heard anything about that."

Isaac bit back on the sharp retort that was his first impulse. "I haven't been keeping up with Guild news."

"If all that's true," Jessica said, "this trip just became ten times more dangerous."

"And not only for you," Sebastian muttered.

"What do you mean?"

He said nothing.

"Sebastian?" she asked. "What's wrong?"

"Where is this place you want to go? I'm guessing it's not local, since you wouldn't need me for that."

"It's in the Badlands."

A white eyebrow rose slightly. "God's love . . . you don't make things easy on yourself, do you girl?"

"Think of all you could learn there," she urged. "Legends put to the test. Hidden knowledge revealed. Think of how much *information* you could collect, once we figure out how to get in and out of there safely."

"I collect information because it helps me stay alive," he reminded her. "A goal not furthered by suicidal expeditions. What makes you think you can survive in that place, where so many others who have tried to explore it have failed?"

"Because it's a Dreamwalker who wants me to go there. Maybe she'll give me more instructions when we arrive. Or maybe I'll have to figure things out on my own, based on the clues I've already got. Either way, I'm willing to bet the other people who went there didn't have Dreamwalker help."

"And what if she's worried about the company you keep?" He looked pointedly at Isaac. "What if she would rather see you silenced before you can reveal too many Dreamwalker secrets, and having you disappear in a place where no one could find your body or enslave your spirit would be a perfect solution?"

Shaken, Jesse stared at him for moment; for the first time since her return, doubt was visible in her eyes. "Look, I only have two choices. I can follow this lead and hope it's legit, or I can go home and wait for the reapers to show up and kill everyone I love. Including me. There's no other option. So unless you have a better plan to offer, that means I'm going to the Badlands. And you and Isaac are the only two people I would trust to come with me."

Sebastian looked away. "Don't trust me. Don't trust anyone on this world. There are games being played behind the scenes that you know nothing about, games that will swallow you whole—"

"Then let's go where those games have no power." She put a hand on his arm. "Please, Sebastian." When he didn't respond she added, very softly, "I *need* you."

He shut his eyes for a moment, looking pained. "Ah, Jessica . . ." He sighed heavily. "I'll go with you as far as the border of the Badlands, and see what the situation is. Beyond that, I make no promises."

"Thank you," she murmured. "Thank you." Her hand fell away from his arm.

"Go find a place where the two of you can rest up, some place better than a park bench. You both look exhausted. I'll meet you back here at nine in the morning to finalize plans. After that . . ." His voice trailed off into silence. He turned away, but not before Isaac saw the turmoil in his eyes. This was not the Sebastian that Isaac remembered from their travels together. This version made Isaac much more wary.

"May God protect us," said Sebastian. And he walked off into the night without looking back.

11

LURAY
VIRGINIA PRIME

JESSE

WE DECIDED TO TAKE THE TRAIN. A zeppelin might have been nearly as fast, as it could travel in a straight line over geographical obstacles, but in the end we agreed that it lacked one important feature: our ability to jump out if there was unexpected trouble. Granted, that wouldn't be easy to do from a moving train either, but at least there was a chance of not dying in the process. Zeppelin travel was all-or-nothing.

It was sobering reflection on the nature of our journey that we had to plan for such things.

We booked passage on a train that would take us to the last station in the western provinces, after which we would have to find another means of travel. We were wary of spending too much money at the start of our journey, but we paid for six tickets in order to have a small sleeper cabin all to ourselves, figuring the privacy was worth it. The berths were shallow slots set high in the wall, accessed by built-in ladders, with curtains for privacy. I was reminded of the Edgar Allen Poe story *The Premature Burial*, where a man wakes up in a dark, enclosed space and thinks that he's been buried alive, only to discover that he's sleeping in a ship's berth. Other than that the train was pleasant enough, and its polished wood, brass, and leather decor re-minded me of movies I'd seen of the old Orient Express.

None of us relaxed until the train finally pulled out of the station, but once it started moving the tension bled out of everyone, and I slumped in my seat as if my bones were dissolving, my heart slowing to a normal pace for the first time in hours. No one had tried to stop us from leaving Luray, and the only threats we had to worry about now were those that were present on this one train. Our fears had become finite.

Soon the cities of the Shenandoah Valley (or whatever they called it here) faded into the distance, and the train began a gently twisting course through the mountains and valleys of Victoria Forest. Our cabin had a southern exposure, which meant it was awash with sun-light, so I took out my portable solar charger and set it up on the seat beside me, my backpack shielding it from the view of anyone passing by. I figured this was as good a time as any to harvest some sunshine.

"What are you doing?" Isaac demanded.

"Charging my stuff." I pulled out the e-reader I'd brought with me and plugged it in. Terra Prime might differ from Terra Colonna in the fine points of its history, but physically the two worlds were identi-cal, so I'd loaded the device with every map of the American south-west that I could find. Better safe than sorry.

But from the look on Isaac's face you'd have thought I was tortur-ing small animals. "Electrical?"

"Yes. Of course electrical. Why? Do you work for customs now?" I started to slide my e-reader into the charger's storage pocket, but to my surprise he reached over and yanked the plug out of its socket and pushed the device away.

"Hey!"

"You know the rules, Jesse."

"Who's going to see it?" I indicated the barrier I'd erected to block it from sight. "I was careful."

"You don't know who's on this train."

"No one looking in will know—"

"Jesse, there are people who can *sense* electromagnetic activity. And it's not impossible that one of them is on board."

"You didn't have an issue with my flashlight in the Warrens."

"Because no one was going to detect a brief spark of power down there. Or if they did, it was unlikely they'd crawl through filthy tunnels to find the source. But now we're on a cross country route, one of very few that goes as far as the western provinces. If someone wanted to ship contraband to that region, this train would be a great way to do it. Some of our fellow passengers might be customs agents assigned to watch for just that."

I remembered the e-reader I'd given Sebastian in Luray. He'd seemed happy enough with it at the time. Had he been unaware of the existence of electricity enforcers? Given how obsessive he was about collecting information, it seemed unlikely. But he was also a child of the eighteenth century, I reminded myself, not the twenty-first, and probably had no innate understanding of how electromagnetism worked, or the fact that the e-reader's subtle emanations could be detected through a closed door.

He understood it now. I could see it in his eyes.

"All right." I closed the solar charger and began to fold it up. "No charging. But now you have to explain to me why electricity is such an issue here. It's not like your people don't know what it can do, since they visit our world all the time. And it's not like it's hard to generate power." I remembered Tommy's comment, "Two wires and a potato and you're up and running. So what's the problem?"

I expected some long, convoluted explanation, with Gifted greed and/or Guild paranoia woven into it. Or maybe no explanation at all. But instead he simply said, "It inhibits Gifts." And I was totally taken aback, because damn, that made sense. I remembered Devon's dad telling us how our fetter lamp was triggered by the electromagnetic field of the human body. "So if I shine my flashlight on you, you won't be able to talk to the dead?"

"That's overstating it a bit. A device that small won't have any measureable effect. But on a world like yours, where the very air is teeming with electromagnetic energy, everything gets harder. Gifts are more difficult to invoke and less effective. Our world decided long ago that such technology isn't worth the price, and since it would be nearly impossible to control it once it was established, they banned it altogether."

Had dreamwalking been harder back home? I had so little experience with my Gift it was hard to be sure, but certainly it was possible. "By *they*, I assume you mean the Gifted."

Sebastian muttered, "Is there anyone else whose opinion matters?"

Isaac shot him a glare. "We have our own kind of tech here."

Yes, I thought, *but anyone on my world can buy a flashlight at Walmart. On your world, the equivalent tech would be a customized fetter from a Lightbringer, crafted by a Weaver, and I'll bet that's way more expensive than a tube of plastic and a couple of batteries. Thus you limit the amount of tech your lower classes can access, and give the Gifted upper class yet another way to control society. Don't tell me that wasn't a factor in their decision.*

Little wonder there were people who specialized in detecting electronic contraband. Gifted tourists from Terra Prime would have a vested interest in supporting the system, so they were unlikely to bring forbidden items back home. But with the unGifted, like Tommy said . . . two wires and a potato. If dreams could bleed from one world to the next, then surely some people on this world had seen visions of what electromagnetic energy could do to transform their lives. Surely some understood that electrical power could serve as an equalizer, lessening their dependence upon the ruling elite. Nipping those dreams in the bud must be a full time job.

I thought about the Fleshcrafter who had healed Mom. Would she have eaten fewer donuts if the air around her hadn't been buzzing with stray cellphone signals and electromagnetic bleed from the toaster oven? The thought was almost too bizarre to grasp. "All right, what about plastic, then? Why is that banned?"

Isaac and Sebastian looked at each other.

"What?" I asked. Their expressions made me feel like I'd stumbled into a mine field.

"Terra Fuentes," Sebastian's tone was unusually solemn, even for him. "Wasn't that the name of it?"

Isaac shook his head. "Phagia Fuentes, if you're referring to the source world. It was reclassified."

"Whoa!" I said. "In English, please?" Then I added, "*My* kind of English?"

Lips tight, Isaac nodded. "Terra Fuentes was a world like yours. A bit ahead of you in its technology, but following the same general pattern. By the middle of last century they'd dumped enough plastic into their oceans to kill off several species, and their environmentalists demanded a better solution than looking at pictures of dead turtles and feeling guilty. So they developed a bacteria that could digest polymers. They made it incapable of reproducing, so it couldn't spread on its own, and gave it a lifespan of only a few days, just long enough for the specimens they created in a lab to do their job."

"Jesus," I muttered. "Please tell me this story isn't heading where I think it is."

"The initial tests went well, so they took it out into the middle of the ocean and sprayed it on some floating junk. And it worked. Polymers in the ocean were digested, and harmless compounds were excreted. Ecological salvation was at hand."

"It mutated?"

"I don't know the exact science involved. In school we're taught that 'Nature defies restriction,' and Terra Fuentes is the prime example of what happens if you try to ignore that. By the time the altered bacteria got to shore, it was too late for anyone to stop it. Not that people didn't try. Desperately." He leaned forward in his seat. "Imagine what would happen to your world if all plastics suddenly disappeared. Devices dissolving in your hands, polymer adhesives disappearing—"

"Planes would fall from the sky," I murmured. "Communication would fail. Utter chaos."

"Terra Fuentes is a failed world now. And the bacteria that destroyed it is still active, and very contagious. It spread to half a dozen spheres in the Terran cluster before we could get an effective quarantine in place, and there are probably still reservoirs of the bacteria hidden on less travelled worlds. One person passing through an infected area could spread the plague to a hundred new locations."

"So is that what happened on Terra Prime?"

He shook his head. "No. It hasn't arrived here yet. But given how much our people travel, infection is inevitable. We went off the polymer standard decades ago, not only to protect ourselves, but to avoid infecting other spheres." He paused. "What? Why are you looking at me like that?"

I drew in a deep breath. "Because in all the time I've been here, that's the first time I've ever heard anyone express concern for the welfare of other worlds."

For a moment he just stared at me. There were emotions in his eyes I couldn't give a name to, but they were dark and pained, and I sensed they were rooted in memories I might not want to know about.

"Those who have the power of life and death over entire worlds don't take it lightly," he told me. And without further word Isaac got up and left the cabin.

IIIIIIIIIIIIII

Shadowcrest is empty.

I walk past abandoned buildings that stand tall in the darkness, like ghostly sentinels. Tonight there is no light coming from the windows. Tonight there are no workmen in the yard. I am alone.

I know that I'm dreaming, because these days I always know when I'm dreaming, but this scene lacks the sense of urgency that usually accompanies dreamwalking. It's just a simple dream, a natural vision, the kind of sleeping fantasy that other people have all the time and forget upon awakening. I probably have dreams like this every night, because the human

mind can't function without dreaming, but after all my dream-walking it feels . . . strange.

I find myself walking toward one of the abbie dormitories, where the Shadows' slave hominids are housed. Something important is inside it, I know. Something I have forgotten. As I walk, letting instinct guide me, I wonder if the reapers can find me here. One of them attacked my mother, and she wasn't dreamwalking, so that suggests they can enter normal dreams. But if that's true, why haven't they killed me yet? They've had enough chances. It's a paradox I don't know how to resolve.

The dormitory is cold and grey and nearly windowless, and sadness is draped over it like a shroud. This is where Devon and Rita and I came when we were trying to sneak into Shadowcrest through a service tunnel. Back then there were abbies in the building, and we had to take care not to be seen by them. Tonight there is only silence; no one exists in this universe but me. Again I have the sense that this dream *matters*, that something is here my sleeping mind wants me to see.

I walk to the common room and pause in the doorway. This is where the dream has been leading me, I realize. Opposite me is the mural the abbies created, an entire wall covered with lines and patterns and shapes and random bits of scenery, a mad scrambling together of images that seem to have nothing to do with each other. The image wavers in my vision as I stare at it, fading in and out of focus as my mind struggles to recall its details. I only spent a few minutes looking at it that night, and we were all pretty distracted, focused as we were on sneaking past the Shadows' security. I don't remember enough to conjure a clear image.

Something in that mural matters. It matters a lot. But I don't know why.

‖‖‖‖‖‖‖‖‖‖

My neck was sore when I woke up. Apparently I'd dozed off while slumped against the window, probably from sheer exhaustion. Thanks to the state of my nerves, it was the first sleep I'd gotten since leaving Luray.

"Are you all right?" Isaac whispered. He'd been keeping watch while Sebastian and I slept.

I reached up to try to rub the crick out of my neck. "Yeah. How long was I out?"

"Barely an hour." He nodded up toward the berths. "You should lie down and try for more."

I looked up and saw Sebastian sleeping, tucked into one of the crypt shelves with the curtain half open. Given that he was used to sleeping in caves it was probably comfortable enough for him, but it still looked pretty unappealing to me. I went over to the other bench seat and began to move our bags aside so I could stretch out a bit. My backpack and Isaac's still smelled a bit stale from the Warrens, so I moved them to the far side of the cabin. Next came Sebastian's bag, a long black canvas duffel with a worn bedroll tied to it. As I moved it I could feel a long, rigid object inside it. I'd noticed the bag's odd shape when he returned to the docks with it slung across his back, but I knew that he often hunted with a bow, so I figured he'd packed it for the trip. Or a hiking staff, maybe.

This was neither.

I hesitated, then glanced up at Sebastian. He was still sound asleep, and Isaac was busy reading a magazine he'd picked up in the dining car, something with a lead story about angry ghosts. I shut my eyes and asked myself if I really wanted to betray their trust by snooping through other people's luggage, but my curiosity was just too strong. I positioned myself with my back to them, so they couldn't see what I was doing, and eased the zipper of the duffel open just far enough to see what Sebastian had packed.

It was wrapped in protective cloth, but even so I had no problem identifying its shape. It was his musket.

I stared at it a moment, then asked, very quietly, "Hey, Isaac. Are there guns on your world?"

"Huh?" I heard Isaac put down his magazine. "Yes, of course. Not as many as on your world, I'd expect. Even the police rarely carry them." I could hear a smile in his voice as he added, "No plastic ones, of course."

Hand trembling slightly, I rezipped the bag and carefully put it aside. Why would Sebastian bring his musket with him? If he expected to have to shoot things on this trip, a modern rifle would be a much better choice. The musket was more about memories than firepower, a memento of the life Terra Prime had stolen from him. Why on earth would he bring it here, when we were facing such unknown dangers that he couldn't guarantee its safety?

He's not planning to go back to Luray, I realized. *Even if we survive this.*

For a moment all I could do was stare at the bag, wishing I hadn't opened it. Then, finally, I lay down on the bench, drawing up my legs so I could fit. It wasn't a comfortable position, but that was all right. I no longer felt like sleeping.

12

SHADOWCREST
VIRGINIA PRIME

AARON HARDT

THE HALLWAY LEADING TO Virilian's audience chamber seemed unusually dark tonight, but the Secundus of the Soulriders hadn't come to Shadowcrest recently, so perhaps his memory of it was skewed. He certainly didn't remember hearing the moaning of the dead last time he visited. Supposedly that was something only a Shadow could hear, though it was rumored that if the dead were numerous enough—and powerful enough—even the unGifted might become aware of them. The dead surrounding Virilian were both numerous and powerful, it seemed. And agitated.

He'd heard rumors that people were asking questions about the Shadowlord's mental state. Virilian had always been bloodthirsty—to a degree that often dismayed his fellow Guildmasters—but no one had ever questioned his sanity before. His plans might have been twisted, even perverse, but there was always a rational purpose at their core. And who expected a Shadowlord to be compassionate, anyway? But things were changing now. Rumors from inside Shadowcrest suggested that Virilian's own people were uneasy about his behavior.

Having heard about the Shadowlord's tirade against Dreamwalkers in the Guild Council, the Soulrider could understand why.

Maybe it would be better not to do this now. Maybe he should wait until things settled down within Shadowcrest before delivering his information to the Shadows' Guildmaster.

Things are moving swiftly now, he reminded himself. *If you delay your duty too long you may go down with Morgana.*

Morgana. Sometimes he was so frustrated with her he could barely contain himself. What good would it to do bring down the Shadows if there was no one to replace them? How would Terra Prime function if no one could arrange safe passage between the worlds? Where would new slave stock come from if the abbies' home-world could no longer be raided, and how would the Guilds strengthen their bloodlines if they couldn't steal promising babies from other worlds? Everything would fall to pieces.

We must lay the groundwork for change first, Morgana once told him. *Then we will have new options.* But the groundwork had been laid and no new options were in sight. A man had to protect himself as best he could.

When he reached the audience chamber there was a servant waiting for him. To his surprise, the servant led him away from the chamber, to another wing of Shadowcrest. Apparently Virilian had decided to meet with him in a less formal setting. That was good. It was hard to have a conversation with someone while he gazed down at you from a throne made of human bones, with ghosts moaning in the background.

He reached a heavy oak door. A servant knocked, and though the Hunter didn't hear a response, the man seemed to. He opened the door and ushered the visitor inside, announcing him as he entered: *Master Aaron Hardt, Secundus of the Guild of Soulriders.*

Augustus Virilian was an imposing man, the sort who intimidated others without even trying. But Hardt was accustomed to dealing with people who had absorbed the primitive instincts of the beasts they possessed, so he was not easily cowed. "Your Grace." The Hunter bowed his head very slightly: a token gesture, no more.

Seated behind a desk of polished ebony, Virilian was turning a letter over in his hand, studying the picture pinned to it. He motioned for Hardt to take a seat in the leather chair set opposite him. "Your news about the girl Morgana is watching intrigues me," he said quietly.

The Hunter nodded. "I thought it might." He gestured toward the letter. "Is she one of the ones who escaped from this place?"

A shadow of annoyance crossed Virilian's face. "I never saw that girl—in person—so I can't say. But others did" He shut his eyes for a moment, his left hand sketching out a pattern in the air in front of him. His lips moved slightly, as if he were whispering, but Hardt couldn't hear the words. A chill wind swept into the room a few seconds later, raising hairs along the back of his neck. Or maybe that was just his imagination.

Virilian opened his eyes and held up the photo, displaying it to empty space. "Is this one of the Colonnans you were watching?"

"I don't—" he began to respond. Then he realized that Virilian wasn't talking to him. Judging from the direction of the Shadowlord's gaze, there must be a spirit of the dead standing right next to him.

Finally Virilian turned his attention back to his guest. "It's her." He nodded a dismissal to empty air and then put the picture down in front of him. "You say Morgana is watching her?"

"More than watching, your Grace. She's intimately involved with the girl. I'm not sure what the game is, but I know she's asked a Domitor to help her, as well as encouraging my own Guild to keep its distance from her."

Virilian raised an eyebrow. "A Domitor? Do you know what that was about?"

"Apparently Morgana hired someone to give the girl's family nightmares." He paused. "I didn't know they could do that."

"They can implant a suggestion to make someone dream about something. Sometimes that's enough." He tapped a finger thoughtfully on the letter. "Morgana told us that the girl's brother was a Dreamwalker. He wasn't. That in itself was of no great concern to me; the Seer's Gift is notoriously fickle, and she could simply have been wrong. But she urged us to kill him, and I found that suspicious. Usually she's not that involved in our business." Lips tight, he leaned back in his chair. "Had we taken her advice, we would never have discovered our mistake. We would have declared ourselves victorious, congratulated ourselves on killing a Dreamwalker, and moved on to other business. Instead of continuing in our hunt for the one who inspired the girl's brother." He paused. "Killing Thomas Drake would have protected his sister from our scrutiny."

"I was told by my agent that Morgana has asked after the girl's dreams."

"And thus she reveals her true game." Virilian's jaw twitched. "I think it's time we interviewed this Colonnan girl."

"She's back on Terra Prime now, travelling under the name of Jennifer Dolan. I had someone watching her."

Virilian raised an eyebrow. "Had?"

"She and two companions booked a train cross-country. My agent followed it for a while, but eventually his host became exhausted and he had to return to his own body. I assume they're still heading west."

"Where to? Do you know?"

"They bought tickets to Rouelle."

The Shadowlord's indrawn breath was a hiss.

"You know what's there?"

"I know what she seeks," he said coldly. "She won't find it. At least not in a condition that will do her any good. Tell me about her two companions."

"An old man with long white hair and a pale young boy. Ghostly pale, my agent said." Seeing Virilian's expression harden, he asked, "You know them?"

He spoke very quietly. "If that boy is who I think he is, then he has made some foolish choices. Some *very* foolish choices." He nodded. "My Guild has an outpost in Rouelle. I'll ask the Shadows there to pick up the girl for me. May I count on your people to assist?"

He hesitated. "I'm not sure how many Soulriders are out there, but I'll advise his Grace to arrange it."

"Excellent. Do make sure they understand that I need the girl alive. Or if that isn't possible, that a Shadowlord must be present when she dies."

The Hunter tried not to think about what Shadowlords could do to the dying. "And the others?"

"Are of little concern to me. Though . . . perhaps we should make examples of those who stray, so that others don't follow in their footsteps. Let's bring the 'pale young boy' back alive as well." He smiled coldly. "I'm sure my own Secundus would be pleased to oversee the demonstration."

"I'll make sure they know that, your Grace."

"We are entering a dangerous time," Virilian warned him. "Your information will help both our Guilds get through it safely. But there are still many challenges to come, and we must be unified and alert in dealing with them."

"What about the Seers?" Hardt asked. Not daring to ask what he really wanted to know: *What about Morgana?*

For a moment there was silence.

"They, too, have made foolish choices," Virilian said. "And would also benefit from an example being made. But all things in their time, Secundus Hardt. Alia Morgana isn't going anywhere. Let's deal with the girl first."

13

ROUELLE
TERRA PRIME

JESSE

OUR FINAL STOP, a town named Rouelle, was as close to the Badlands as one could get without risking instant death or insanity. I expected it to be little more than a ghost town, a lonely outpost maintained for those few fools who were curious enough to want to visit such a cursed site. Who else would live so close to Chaos?

I had failed to take human nature into account.

As we crossed the Rockies our train was surprisingly full. Probably that should have tipped me off about what lay ahead of us, but by then I was too tired to think clearly. The trip had been way too long already, and since each time I managed to fall asleep I had nightmares that quickly woke me up, I'd been awake for most of the trip. Meanwhile Isaac and Sebastian had been giving me a crash course in Terra Prime 101, stuffing my head full of information about Guilds and Gates and every other interworld factoid they thought I might ever need, but after ten hours of that I felt like a kid who wasn't being allowed to leave the classroom at the end of the school day. God alone knew how much of it I would remember later.

Some of the information was not as alien to me as they thought.

For example, clusters. When worlds were similar in type, Isaac explained, they exerted a kind of emotional gravity on one another. Any event that was dramatic enough to affect many people in one sphere—or to affect a single person with unusual intensity—could bleed through to neighboring spheres in dreams and visions. A scientific discovery in one world might cause dreams that inspired the same discovery in others, while a tyrant committing genocide in one location could likewise spread dreams of bloodlust and power to others who were susceptible. Thus, though histories within a cluster might vary in minor details—like the failure of the American Revolution on Terra Prime—neighboring worlds were under constant pressure to adopt similar paths. For example, the Louisiana Purchase had never taken place on Terra Prime, but France had ceded the same territory to Britain at a later date.

Isaac thought the cluster concept would be hard for me to grasp, but actually it wasn't. The doors in my dreams had always been arranged in clusters, with similar visions being located near one another. And much of my art reflected the same kind of pattern. Without even realizing it I had tapped into reality's master plan.

In a town named Chanteaux we had to switch from our cross-country train to a smaller one that would carry us over the Rockies. The new one had no private cabins, so we were forced to sit in a public car along with all the other passengers. That meant we could no longer discuss sensitive topics, for fear someone would overhear us. After an eternity of talking to the same two people, however, I was grateful for the break.

Snow-capped mountains, forests of aspen, and cool, shadowy gorges flashed past us like a series of National Geographic photographs, lush and inviting. But soon those gave way to a region of sandy red plains punctuated by low mountain ridges and sandstone mesas. The view was impressive—land striped so perfectly you'd think someone had painted it, stone spires carved into bizarre shapes by the wind—but it wasn't exactly what you'd call welcoming. Some parts looked so dry and lifeless that I got thirsty just looking at them. Now and then we crossed a canyon that had water at the bottom, and you could see a thin ribbon of green slicing through the landscape, but that was only visible when we were right on top of it, after which we were back in the semi-barren landscape.

I took out the small wooden box I'd prepared back home and opened it, removing a feather and thin leather cord from inside. My companions watched curiously as I tied the feather to my hair, letting it hang down over one shoulder like the avatar girl had done. With strangers sitting so close they didn't dare ask any meaningful questions.

Finally Sebastian dared, "Wren?"

I hesitated. I'd wanted to get a real wren feather, but that turned out to be difficult to find on short notice, so I'd had to settle for buying a generic feather from the local crafts store and using textile paint to give it the right markings. The result must have been convincing enough, since Sebastian recognized the species, but I was uneasy about the forgery. If there was some mystical quality to a wren feather that might actually protect us, I doubted a cheap fake would qualify.

"Someone gave me a feather like this in a dream," I told him. That was true enough. God alone knew if my wearing it would help us in any way, but it seemed worth a try. Maybe if nothing else it would encourage the avatar to contact me again.

You have to stay asleep long enough for that to happen, I reminded myself.

Finally the train began to slow. Rows of houses were coming into view now, neatly aligned and surprisingly mundane. I guess I'd expected something more . . . well, *exotic.* Larger buildings followed, equally mundane, and we even passed a shopping mall that wouldn't have looked out of place back home, save for the giant cactuses flanking the main entrance. Everything had a strange reddish cast to it, as if I was looking at the world through tinted glasses, though that was probably just a trick of the light, reflecting from all that sandstone. Otherwise it was all quite unremarkable.

Finally the train stopped. As passengers gathered up their

belongings, I sensed a strange mix of energy in the air, part excitement and part fear. Or maybe that was just me.

This is it, I thought as I shouldered my backpack. *The place where my fate will be decided.*

When the train door opened a blast of dry heat hit me in the face, and I had to put up a hand to shield my eyes from the ruddy sunlight outside. We waited patiently while the first few passengers climbed down the train's narrow stairs and then stepped off onto a concrete platform, glancing west as they did so. I expected them to keep moving and was prepared to follow them, but to my surprise they all just stopped, as if something had frozen them in place. After a few seconds the people behind them started getting irritated and began to push forward, but as the new people disembarked and looked west, they also froze. A knot of dread began to form in my gut as I watched the strange ballet, and I wondered what could possibly be out there in the desert that was so disturbing that the mere sight of it was enough to incapacitate visitors. Finally it was my turn to climb down to the platform and step out into the ruddy sunlight. I drew in a deep breath and looked west myself, to see what all the fuss was about.

Holy shit.

It stretched from horizon to horizon, a massive cloud of red dust towering so high that its crest brushed against the clouds. Anchored to the ground perhaps a mile from where we were standing, it curled over our heads like a great wave, ready to come crashing down on us at any moment. The sight of it was terrifying, but it was also mesmerizing, and while part of me wanted to flee for my life—preferably screaming in fear as I did so—I couldn't bring myself to look away. It was the great wave of sand that was filtering the light of the sun, staining it crimson, making the entire town seem like it was washed in blood. The image reminded me of an Arabian sandstorm I had once seen pictures of—a *haboob*—but this surreal version was better suited to a Martian landscape than Earth. At least it didn't appear to be moving toward us.

"Keep a move on, folks." A transit officer on the platform was urging us along now, and I noticed that he showed no interest in the view. Was it possible to get so used to this bizarre landscape that you stopped noticing it? "El Malo won't hurt you unless you go walking right up to it, and you're all too smart for that, right? So let's clear the platform, please."

Numbly, I let myself be herded to the far end of the platform, along with everyone else, and down the short flight of stairs at its end. To leave the station we had to pass through the ticket office, and as we entered I saw a small counter at the far end, flanked by half a dozen paintings of the red wave. One of them looked like a depiction of Hell, with lost souls swirling in whirlwinds of red dust. Not exactly the kind of decor I would have chosen, but a powerful image nonetheless.

On the wall opposite the ticket counter, racks of colorful brochures were affixed to the wall. THE BEST OF THE BADLANDS, one proclaimed in bright red letters, while another declared WALK THE WAVE! There were restaurant brochures as well (GAZE UPON THE FACE OF DEATH WHILE YOU ENJOY OUR FIVE-STAR DINING), and bars (TRY OUR WORLD-FAMOUS HOUSE DRINK, THE BADLANDS BASTARD) as well as hotels (PAN-ORAMA WINDOWS IN THE HONEYMOON SUITE!).

Rouelle was a tourist town.

"Jesus," Isaac whispered.

We'd known that Rouelle served as a base of operations for people who wanted to get a look at the Badlands—that's why we'd come in the first place—but I got the impression that neither he nor Sebastian had expected such tacky exploitation. Sadly, on my world this kind of thing wasn't unusual.

The western wall of the ticket office was entirely glass, allowing for an unrestricted view of the blood-colored haboob, and as the other passengers continued on their way, I walked over to it. Looking at it through a pane of glass gave me a bit of emotional distance, like it was something on a movie screen rather than real. That helped calm my nerves but only a little. El Malo was something you feared in your gut, not your head.

Isaac and Sebastian took up positions next to me, one on each side, and for a while the three of us stared at El Malo in silence. *The Evil Thing*, locals had named it. Or perhaps, *the Evil Being*. Either name worked well.

Sebastian said quietly, "That's where you're talking about going."

I shut my eyes and shivered. Not just from fear, but from despair. The plan that had seemed so reasonable back in Manassas—and Luray—had been blown away like so much desert sand. What was I supposed to do now, just walk into that thing? Even if I survived the first few minutes, where was I supposed to go after that? I'd assumed that once I got out here and assessed the situation I would be able to come up with a plan, but now that I was here, and saw the nature of what I would be facing, I didn't have a clue how to start.

I turned away from Sebastian, not wanting him or Isaac to see how upset I was. I was the one who had brought them out here, so I had to be strong. But I didn't feel strong. I felt lost. Sebastian put his arm around me, drawing me gently to his chest, as a father might. A wave of exhaustion and despair broke over me, leaving me shaking.

Isaac said, "Maybe the Dreamwalker will contact you."

"Maybe," I whispered.

But what if Sebastian was right and the avatar girl wasn't a friend, but an enemy? He'd suggested she might be luring me to my death in order to silence me. So what was I supposed to do if she offered me advice—follow it, or do the opposite?

It was all overwhelming. If not for Sebastian's arm around me, providing an emotional anchor, I don't know how I would have held myself together.

"Where do you want go now?" Sebastian asked.

"Somewhere safe," I whispered. "Please."

But there was no safe place for me. Not here, not anywhere. If I didn't find a way to get rid of the reapers, there would never be a safe place for me again.

I let the two of them lead me out of the ticket office. A bird was circling overhead as we exited; was that something we needed to worry about? Or were there times a bird was just a bird?

God, how I hated this world.

ııııııııııı

We found a hotel far enough from the border that its rooms were reasonably priced, and Sebastian checked us in as a family so we could stay together. The place was structured like my hotel in Luray, with rooms accessed directly from the outside. Our suite had windows facing the front and back of the building, so once we made sure we knew how to open/smash the appropriate glass, we had exits available in both directions.

Not that we were paranoid or anything.

I'd already noticed that the population of Rouelle was much more diverse than in Luray—probably because of the tourist industry—so it wasn't surprising that the girl who checked us in was Native American, as were many of the people we passed on the street. Whatever quirk of parallel history had rendered the east coast so aggressively Anglo, this region was a melting pot by comparison.

The Native American girl took note of my feather as we checked in, giving me a long, narrow-eyed look before handing Sebastian a set of room keys. I wasn't sure if the wren feather meant something special to her, or she was just annoyed by my cultural appropriation. Or maybe she recognized it as a fake and was disdainful of my low standards. I looked away and saw a map of Rouelle on the wall, with areas blocked out in different colors and numbered. The hotel was in a blue area marked with the number two, while the western edge of town had mostly green threes and yellow fours, with higher numbers beyond that. Sebastian asked what then numbers meant.

"Risk factors for El Malo," she told him.

"Risk factors for what?" I asked.

She shrugged. "Strange mental effects, mostly. Some sensory distortion, often a sense of impending doom. El Malo shifts around, and

sometimes the outskirts of Rouelle are affected. But we're in a relatively safe zone here."

Relatively safe. Gee, that was comforting.

"We post each day's conditions," she continued, nodding toward a
bulletin board in the corner. "You should check it before you go
sightseeing."

Today's weather will be hot and dry, I thought, with 80% chance
of insanity or death.

We went out for dinner, not in a fancy place with panorama windows that would allow us to 'gaze upon the face of Death' while eating, but in a coffee shop down the street that had no view of anything.
Bison burgers and fries. It was close enough to American food that if I
closed my eyes I could imagine myself back home again. God, I
missed my family. I missed being in a world where I could take out a
phone and talk to them, could tell them how scared I was, how alone
I felt. Because as long as you were able to do that, you weren't really
alone.

It was dark by the time we finished eating. El Malo was reduced
to a dark cloud on the horizon, with only a faint tinge of red on a few
moonlit clouds hinting at its existence. As we walked back to our hotel
I felt the accumulated exhaustion of the entire trip adding weight to
my steps. By the time Sebastian opened the door I had no energy left.

I set up my charger before retiring, resting it on a table by the
window so that it would power up come dawn. Sebastian and Isaac
both protested, afraid that it might draw attention from the wrong
people, but that was a chance we were just going to have to take. I had
to have the geographical information that was loaded on my tablet,
and unless someone came up with a Gift that could read hard drives
directly, that meant I would have to turn it on.

"Don't worry," I told them. "This town has bigger things to worry
about than the electricity police."

God willing I would be able to get some sleep.

‖‖‖‖‖‖‖‖‖‖‖

Midnight, Rouelle time. Two in the morning as far as my body was concerned.

I sat on the top step of our hotel's external staircase, staring out over the city. I could sense El Malo's presence at the edge of my awareness, a kind of mental heaviness. The lower edge of the moon was hazy and reddish.

I heard footsteps approaching on the concrete walkway and looked up to see that Isaac had come outside. I slid over a bit to give him room to sit down. He hesitated, then joined me, our legs an inch apart.

For a while we just sat quietly together, staring out into the night. Finally he said, "Bad dreams?"

"Just restless." I sighed. "Can't stop worrying long enough to fall asleep."

"Any idea of what you want to do tomorrow?"

I shut my eyes for a moment. "What are my choices? Give up and go home? The whole reason I came out here was because the reapers are hunting me. Well, they're still hunting me. Going home and giving up would be a death sentence. But moving forward . . ." I looked to the west and shook my head. "What am I missing, Isaac? There's got to be something. Some clue, that when I find it I'll know what to do. Or am I just kidding myself?"

He shook his head. "I wish I could help you, Jesse."

"You do help me," I said softly. "More than you know."

How pale he looked, in the moonlight. I saw that the edge of his latex patch was starting to peel off, and I reached up to smooth it down. I'd reattached it several times for him, but the edge was starting to get ragged from handling and it no longer looked as natural. "We should replace this," I murmured.

He reached up and caught my hand in his. His eyes were as dark as the night sky; I could have lost myself in them with very little effort. "You'll be okay," he said.

"Yeah." I laughed softly. "Sure. Nothing to worry about."

"Listen to me." His hand tightened around mine. "You're strong,

Jesse. So strong. Whatever life throws at you, you just don't back down, ever. People like that . . . they can do amazing things if they want to." He drew in a deep breath. "I believe in you."

There was suddenly a lump in my throat. "Isaac . . . if I did decide to risk going into El Malo, would you come with me?"

"You know I would."

"Even knowing we might never come back?"

"Even knowing that." There was a hint of a dry smile. "It's not like I have that much to go back to."

I couldn't say anything more. The words were stuck in my throat.

He reached out and put his hand to my face. His palm was as warm as the desert sun, and I trembled as he ran his thumb along the edge of my lower lip. How alive he was tonight! How vital! This wasn't the tormented child of undead necromancers, or a lost little boy condemned by this world's most powerful Guild, but someone real, someone warm, someone who cared enough about me to walk into Hell by my side. Even if we never actually had to do that, the promise had power.

Slowly he leaned toward me. Or maybe I leaned toward him first. Our kiss was all hunger and fear and loneliness and desire, and it left me breathless. He slid his arms around my waist, pulling me close, I responded in kind, pressing myself so tightly against him that I could feel his heartbeat against my chest, while I ran my hand up into his hair. We had been lost, the two of us, adrift in a world beyond our control or understanding, but now we had found each other. When I kissed him there was no El Malo, no Guild of Shadows, no Morgana— only heat, and solace, and desire. And for the moment, that was enough.

‖‖‖‖‖‖‖‖‖

The air is dry. So very dry. As soon as sweat appears on my skin it's gone, but that doesn't cool me at all. Beneath my bare feet the ground is hot as burning coals, and I try to balance on

my toes as I stand at the edge of the canyon, minimizing contact. Ghostly voices are swirling around my head, and the wind
that whips at my face is full of sand, making it hard to see.
Each windborne grain is as sharp as broken glass, and each
gust leaves behind it streaks of blood on my skin. Now I am
red, like El Malo. ·

It would be madness to enter the Badlands. I understand
that now. No matter what I might say to Isaac—no matter what
I might try to tell myself—the place is impassable, and no
amount of determination on my part is going to change that.
Whatever secrets the Badlands guard, I will not be the one to
discover them.

The revelation is anguish.

Suddenly the ground begins to tremble, and I step back
from the canyon's edge quickly, not wanting to lose my footing.
The dust storm in front of me is starting to break up, coalesc-
ing into whirlwinds that sweep up and down the canyon. Between them I catch glimpses of the ground that was hidden
from my view before, and I can see it is littered with broken
bones. Human bones? I can't look at any of them long enough
to be sure.

The whirlwinds begin to draw back from me, gathering
north and south of my position. They form a canyon-like passage between them, and I see a carpet of sun-bleached bones
at the bottom. And yes, some of them look human. Am I supposed to go down there? Even in a dream that seems like a
really bad idea. I peer down the length of the wind-canyon,
trying to see how far it extends, and suddenly I realize that
there is someone standing at the far end, watching me.

The avatar girl.

Fear and elation rush over me. If she's dreamwalking, then
we're both in terrible danger, as neither of us have the power
to escape if a reaper appears. But she's here. I needed her, and

she has come to me. Tears of relief begin to gather in my eyes, but they evaporate in the dry air before they have a chance to run down my cheeks.

"Where should I go?" I cry out. The sound of rushing wind is loud; it takes effort to speak over it. "What am I supposed to do?" When she says nothing I beg, "Tell me!"

But she doesn't speak. She spreads her arms to both sides of her, as if inviting me to look, but all I see around her is dry earth and scraggly brush. Is that supposed to be an answer? I'm frustrated now, and starting to get angry; it takes all my self-control not to yell at her, *Stop playing games with me!* But if I do that she might leave me, and if she never comes back, where will I look for answers? Like it or not, I need her.

Then suddenly I realize what I'm looking at. She sees the stunned look on my face and nods. *Yes,* the gesture seems to say. *Now you understand.*

The whirlwinds close in again, red winds crashing and churning as the narrow passage between them disappears. I can't see the avatar girl any more. Nor can I see the land that surrounds her, hot and dry and spotted with brush. But I know that the landscape is there, and I think I understand why she showed it to me: El Malo doesn't affect the whole of the Badlands, just a narrow strip at the border. If we can find a way to cross it, we'll be safe on the other side.

It's not much to work with, but it's infinitely more than I had before this dream started.

"Thank you," I whisper. "Thank you."

The dream is still brightly colored when it ends.

14

LURAY
VIRGINIA PRIME

ALIA MORGANA

WHEN FRONT ROYAL'S Guildmaster of Domitors arrived, Morgana was sitting in the garden, going over a list of apprentices who were up for promotion. When she looked up and saw him a smile spread across her face, but there was also a flicker of concern in her eyes. The Domitor rarely came to Luray on casual business. "Russell. I didn't realize you were in town."

"I thought I would surprise you." He leaned down and air-kissed her cheek. "You look well."

She smiled slightly. "Stress must be good for my complexion."

He was a stocky man with broad Mediterranean features, a striking contrast to her own delicate paleness, and was dressed casually as always, with no hint of his rank. He didn't need hints. His Gift was strong enough that anyone within ten paces could sense it, and even if he wasn't actively giving them orders they sensed that he *could* give them orders if he wanted to, which they would then have to obey. In his youth it had made him unpopular at social events. "Have time for some serious business?" he asked.

The smile vanished. "Of course." She tucked her list into a front pocket and stood. "Walk with me."

She knew exactly how far from the Guildhouse she had to be to guarantee that no one could overhear them, and she led him to that place, butterflies scattering in their path as they walked. He admired a few flowers along the way. Small talk.

When they finally stopped he asked, "Do you remember Jennifer Dolan? The girl that you asked me to watch out for, and tell you if she passed through the Front Royal Gate?"

"Which you did. It was very helpful. Thank you."

"Who is she, Alia?"

Morgana's eyes narrowed slightly. "A young girl from Terra Colonna."

"You know what I mean. Why is she significant?"

"Why are you asking?"

"Because Virilian wants to know about her . . . and your connection to her. One of my people has been questioned. I'd like to know what's going on."

Her eyes narrowed slightly. "Who's been questioned?"

"The apprentice I sent to give her family nightmares. Or rather, to suggest that they have nightmares." He waved a hand. "Don't worry. He knows how to keep secrets. And even if he did slip up, he has no idea that you were the one behind that order." He paused. "What was all that about, anyway?"

She shrugged. "The girl was becoming too comfortable. I needed her to act before we all died of old age."

"Which brings us back to my original question."

"Virilian questioned your apprentice?"

"One of his people did. He's asking about Soulriders, too. Are any of them involved with this girl?"

Alia was silent for a moment. "I asked one for a favor."

"Aaron?"

She nodded.

"Well, that answers another question. Though it's not an answer

I'm happy about." Sighing heavily, he crossed his arms in front of his chest. "We have a leak, Alia."

"In the consortium?"

He nodded.

"You mean—"

"A spy. Someone who told Virilian about your business, and also told him Aaron was helping you." He paused. "Unless Aaron himself is the leak. We can't rule that out. At any rate . . ." His expression darkened. "Our consortium is useless now. Worse than useless. Whoever betrayed you knows all our names. This could go downhill very fast. So if your secret project is what's bringing enemies to our door, I'd like to know about it."

A delicately painted eyebrow arched upward. "You bring me news of betrayal and then ask for trust?"

"And I'm standing in front of you as I say that, knowing that you have the ability to sense a man's intentions. Good God, why else do you think I came all the way from Front Royal to tell you this in person? Do what you need to do as Seer to be sure of me, and then let's have a real conversation."

She looked at him for a moment, considering, then reached up and touched his temples gently, fingertips resting on his skin so lightly he would barely feel it. "Think about betraying me," she whispered. "Think about the Shadows." His emotion flowed into her fingers, suffused her flesh, and unfolded in her mind like a blossoming flower. She studied its form, tasted its quality, and at last nodded.

"So what's with the girl?" The Domitor said.

Morgana drew in a deep breath. She hadn't wanted to reveal her plans so soon, but circumstances were forcing her hand. *It's all moving too fast,* she thought. *Too uncontrolled.* "She's a Dreamwalker."

He took a step back. "Damn. Well, that would explain Virilian's recent tirade in your Council." He sighed. "Are you sure?"

"That she has the Gift in her blood? Yes. That it's manifesting?" She hesitated. "She's been very careful who she talks to about it. But all the signs are there."

"And what about the 'going insane' part? There was a reason all the Dreamwalkers were killed off, you know."

"There was a reason," she agreed. "But that may not be it."

His jaw twitched slightly. "*May* not?"

She spread her hands. "We're playing for high stakes here, Russell. Sometimes that means you have to take chances."

"So what's your end game? Why risk your reputation like this? And possibly your life, if the wrong people find out who you're protecting?"

Morgana looked away for a moment. She'd envisioned this conversation many times, and had figured that when the time came she'd be ready for it. But this was too early. Jesse was still a wild card, her Gift not fully understood, her role in Morgana's plans not yet established. Morgana needed more time to refine her plans before revealing them to others.

But if she'd been betrayed by an ally, there was no more time to be had. Virilian had made it clear in the Council meeting that he suspected her of something, and since he'd spent the whole meeting talking about Dreamwalkers . . . it was not good. She needed allies by her side who were fully informed, if she was to weather this. "I believe the ancient Dreamwalkers may have known how to communicate between worlds, without needing Shadows to assist them. Possibly they even knew how to travel between worlds on their own."

The Domitor's eyes widened. "If that was true, it would be . . ." He floundered for the right word. "Monumental."

She nodded. "And it might explain why the Dream Wars were launched in the first place."

"The Shadowlords wanted to destroy their only rivals? Because with the Dreamwalkers gone, they would have absolute control over passage between the worlds?"

Lips tight, Morgana nodded.

"That's *if* you're right in how you're reading all this."

"That goes without saying."

"What about all the other Guilds? The Shadows weren't the only ones hunting Dreamwalkers, back then. Surely the others wouldn't have joined in unless there was damn good reason for it."

"Or the illusion of damn good reason. Think about it, Russell. I used your Domitor to influence dreams. You could convince any man that he'd seen delusions, if you wanted to. A skilled Farspeaker could insert voices so close to someone's head that they would sound like they were coming from inside it. Madness isn't hard to fake. Or inspire."

"You think the whole insanity story was a setup? That the Shadows wanted to convince the other Guilds the Dreamwalkers were dangerous, so everyone would join in the killing?"

"That's my current theory."

"But even if it's true, you're only talking about one girl. No matter how powerful her Gift is, it won't be enough to bring the Dreamwalkers back."

"Won't it? There are hundreds of worlds that we know about, probably thousands more that we haven't discovered yet. What are the odds that we've tracked down every single person who has a trace of that Gift, on every human world? There must be others out there, Russell. You and I can't find them, but another Dreamwalker might be able to. That's what I've been waiting to see if Jessica would do."

"Does she know that's what you want?"

She shook her head. "I needed to test her first. To make sure that the stories of her Gift causing insanity weren't true. Because if she does go down that path, and she has knowledge of our business . . ."

"She can take us all down with her. I get that. But when you're satisfied about the insanity issue, then you'll fill her in?"

She laughed gracefully; it was a practiced sound. "What am I supposed to say to her? 'I'm so sorry that I arranged for you to be abandoned on an alien world and raised by strangers, then did all sorts of terrible things to awaken your Gift and test your sanity, but would you mind helping me out in a little political matter? Which will, as a side note, make every Shadow on this continent want you dead?' I'm sure that will go over well."

"I don't think you have a choice, Alia. If Virilian figures out what you're doing and gets hold of the girl, it'll be bad news. For all of us." He sighed. "You need to talk to her. Reveal the role you intend her to play, and see if she'll cooperate. If not, then cut your losses and end this, lest we all be dragged down with her."

Years of practice in hiding her emotions enabled Morgana to keep her expression blank, but it took effort. "I appreciate your counsel."

"Do you know where she is now?"

"She's travelling with someone who is carrying a fetter that I can trace, so as long as they're together, yes, I know where she is. But unless I miss my guess, they'll both be out of reach soon."

"Well, when they come back within reach, think about what I said." He shook his head. "Jesus, the stakes are high here. Be careful, Alia."

"Always," she promised, offering her cheek to be kissed before he left. *My personal stake in this is greater than you can imagine.*

15

ROUELLE
TERRA PRIME

JESSE

SUNLIGHT WOKE ME UP. Isaac and Sebastian were still sleeping, and for a moment I was torn between waking them up to tell them my news and checking on my tablet so I could gather more information first. The tablet won.

The sun must have just come up because the device didn't have much of a charge, but I was able to turn it on. I felt a wave of relief when the screen lit up, as if having a working tech device had healed some unseen wound in my soul. My files were all intact, and while I couldn't access Google Maps for obvious reasons, I'd copied so many images that I almost didn't miss it. That said, it took me forever to find our current location on Colonnan maps. None of the city names here were the same as on my world, state borders didn't exist, and even the forested areas seemed to be shaped differently. But at last I found a series of small canyons that reminded me of an area we'd passed through. From there I could trace our path down to the flat land surrounded Rouelle, and . . . yes. That's where we were. I could even see where El Malo probably began, which offered some possible insights into its nature.

"Jesse?"

It was Isaac. As he threw off his blanket the motion woke Sebastian, and then both of them were looking at me like eager puppy dogs waiting for breakfast. I smiled despite myself.

"Did you dream?" Isaac asked.

I turned off the tablet so it could devour more solar energy while I told them about my dream. They were less enthused than I'd expected, which frustrated me. Granted, it was only the first piece of our puzzle, but now that we had that much, surely we could figure the rest out!

When I was done, Sebastian was very still. "I'm sorry," he said at last, "I must ask. Is it possible it was just a dream?"

"What do you mean?"

"You do still have normal dreams, don't you? Dreams where your Gift is not involved?"

The question startled me. "I guess. Yeah."

"Because you didn't mention seeing doors, or any of the other signs that might indicate dreamwalking."

But I saw the other Dreamwalker! I wanted to protest. *Doesn't that mean something?*

But he was right. In my excitement, I'd forgotten that I was still capable of having normal dreams, without any special significance. My brain might simply have been processing all the data it had accumulated during my waking hours, venting my hopes and fears in an imaginary landscape while it figured out how to cope with everything. Like normal people. The fact that I sometimes was able to enter the dreams of other people didn't mean that I never needed REM sleep beyond that.

But it had felt so real, so significant! When I'd dreamed about the abbie building near Shadowcrest it had felt the same way. I'd sensed then that something, or someone, was guiding me toward important information, and last night had felt exactly the same. *But you don't know that the first dream really meant anything*, I reminded myself. Maybe there was nothing about the abbie mural that mattered. Maybe

I had dreamed about the avatar last night because I wanted so much to dream about the avatar, and there was nothing more to it. "She was there," I told Sebastian. But despite my defiant tone, I was no longer as sure of what I had seen.

My tablet had charged enough during my recitation that I could now bring it over to the sitting area to show them my topographical maps. I pointed out the place I'd found, just west of town, where elevation dropped off suddenly, marking a steep escarpment that cut across the map from north to south. Unless I missed my guess, that was where El Malo began. If so, might it not explain the presence of the haboob? Dry, dust-laden winds swept across the open desert until they hit a natural obstacle, then were forced upward. Why they never moved from that spot still begged for explanation, but it was reassuring to be able to apply science to the phenomenon. One tiny thing in this crazy world that made sense.

"If we climbed down the cliff face," I said, "we'd be on flat ground after that. Which wouldn't make El Malo any less dangerous, but at least we wouldn't be trapped at the bottom of a canyon or something."

"What was it you saw in your dream?" Sebastian asked. "Razor-sharp whirlwinds and a field of human bones? Refresh my memory."

"All right." I sighed. "Point taken."

"Dreams aren't enough for this," Isaac said. "We need to go take a look at the real thing up close, so we know what we're dealing with. Because if we're even thinking about going down there, I for one don't want to try it with no more information than what's in the tourist brochures." He looked at me. "But before we go anywhere we need to know that the message from the avatar was real. I'm sorry, Jesse, I hate to question you on this, but there's no point in going further without that."

"I understand," I said, and I did, but I was also getting frustrated. How the hell was I supposed to prove my dream information was accurate without checking out the site I'd dreamed about? I couldn't verify the abbie dream either without going back to Shadowcrest.

Suddenly I realized that I had a way to test the abbie dream. It would be risky, but what wasn't risky on this journey? And I'd get the answer to another question, which might prove equally important. "I have an idea. What time is it?" I asked.

Isaac looked over at the clock. "Seven thirty."

Still early. Allowing for time zone differences, the person I needed to contact was probably asleep. That seemed as clear an omen as any Dreamwalker could ask for.

"Okay," I said. "Who's on reaper watch this time?"

〰〰〰〰

Devon thinks: *Something is wrong.*

The street outside his home looks normal enough. The air is filled with the usual suburban smells: newly cut grass, rose bushes in bloom, a faint whiff of diesel from the main road. But there's a sense of wrongness that he can't give a name to, that makes him wary. At one point he might have ignored such a feeling, but after Terra Prime he tends to trust his instincts.

I should go inside, **he thinks.**

He turns back to the house and sees Jesse standing there. For a moment he's too surprised to speak. Tommy had told him about her going back to Terra Prime, so the last thing he expected was that she would show up on his doorstep.

"This is a dream," she says. "And we have very little time." Her voice has the suppressed energy of a tightly wound spring. "I need you to become aware."

Suddenly he has a dizzying sense of dual existence. He's still standing here talking to Jesse, but he's also lying in his bed asleep, and for a moment it's hard to sort out the conflicting input. He feels himself losing control of the dream, and the streets and trees and houses begins to fade around him.

"Stay with me!" Jesse says. "Forget your body. Focus on the dream. You can stay here if you want to."

He does his best to concentrate on his surroundings—on

her—and slowly the sense of duality fades. He knows that his body is still out there, but he's no longer aware of it.

"Okay," she says. "Listen carefully. If I tell you to wake yourself up, or you see anything that looks out of place, go back to your body *immediately*. Don't ask questions, don't try to understand what's going on, just end the dream as fast as you can. Got that?"

The sense of urgency in her voice is unnerving. "You're afraid reapers will come."

She nods. "I've been trying to stay under their radar by not dreamwalking, but I really need some information from you, and this is the only way I can get it."

And I have some information for you, too, he realizes suddenly. He hadn't expected to have a chance to talk to her, but now that she's here he needs to make sure she's fully updated. "What do you need from me?"

"You remember back at Shadowcrest, when we went through the abbie house, there was a mural on the wall?"

His brow furrows as thinks back to that journey. "Somewhat."

"Can you remember any of its details?"

"I didn't look at it very long. That was the whole point of taking a picture, so I could study it later."

"Try, Devon." There's an edge of desperation in her voice now. "I need you to try."

"Why? What's in the mural that's so important?"

"I'm honestly not sure. I sensed in a dream that it's significant, but I can't remember enough details to figure out why. You're the only one who paid any real attention to that thing, Devon. I know how organized your mind is. Try your best to recreate it for me. Any parts you can remember."

He nods and shuts his eyes, trying to envision the events of that day: sneaking through the abbie house, coming into the common room, seeing that the far wall was painted with random images. What a shock that had been—what a revelation!—to discover that the abbies had the same artistic drive as humans. Devon had promised himself while they stood in that room that he would help them.

But he hadn't. He'd come home and returned to his comfortable life, and now there is no way he can help them. His soul aches with guilt over his failure.

As he recalls that day, details of the mural start to surface in his memory. He opens his eyes and looks around for a flat surface to exhibit them on. The best candidate is the side of a nearby house, but it's covered in aluminum siding. Can he alter his own dream? He concentrates on that element of the dream, trying to take conscious control of it. After a few seconds the edges of the siding began to blur, eventually disappearing altogether. Now there's only a flat white expanse, like a movie screen.

"Good," Jesse approves. "You're getting it."

Focusing on the few details he does remember, he tries to make them appear on the wall. First a row of handprints along the bottom. A horse. A waterfall. Nothing seems like it's in the right place, but Jesse is staring at his work with an intensity that suggests he's giving her what she needs, so he keeps going. Clouds appear. A sunset. A few geometric scribblings. A building—

Jesse gasps.

Startled, he loses control of his creation; the images start to fade. "What is it?"

"Just keep going." Her voice is strained. "Give me everything you can remember."

He returns his full concentration to the task and tries to add details to the building, a tall conical tower with a spiral running around the outside. The coloring was so strange that it stuck in his memory, each window a different hue; he works to reproduce it for her. As he does so her eyes slowly grow wide. "They saw it," she whispers. "The Dreamwalker tower. One of the abbies saw it!" She points to it. "Every time I've seen it the windows have different views. That must be what the colors mean. This is what my dream was trying to show me!"

She closes the distance between them and hugs him. It takes him by surprise, but after a second he wraps his arms around her and holds her close. He feels her trembling against his chest and tightens his embrace. "Thank you," she whispers. "I knew you'd come through for me." Her hair smells sweet; he resists the urge to touch it.

After a few seconds she draws back from him. For the first time since the mural started taking shape, she checks the sky. "I need to leave before they find me."

He puts a hand on her arm. "Jesse, there's something else you need to know."

She looks at him.

"They're going down into Mystic Caverns."

Her eyes narrow. "What do you mean?"

"They think they can dig out enough of the debris to explore the place. They've got some high tech Israeli robot that's shaped like a snake, that's used in disaster rescue, and they're going to send it down to take pictures."

"I thought excavation was supposed to be too costly to attempt. Wasn't that why they gave up on it when we first came home?"

"Yeah, when all that was at stake was evidence in a mundane kidnapping. But now there are people in the government who know about the changelings—who know about *us*—and if they suspect there's some kind of global network connected to that site, they may be willing to spend the bucks needed to investigate. I don't know, maybe they think someone is tinkering with DNA, or there's a high-tech weapons lab down there. It doesn't matter what they think. We know what's down there, waiting to be found."

"Pieces of the Gate," she says hollowly. "And bodies. Maybe

no more than skeletons at this point, but they'll still be identifiable as bodies, and they've got those crazy toe tags on them."

"And think about what could happen if the portal's still active. Because it's a natural phenomenon, right? The Gate was just there to stabilize it. So if people were able to get down that far, they might be able to go through it."

"The Shadows would never let that happen. They'd—" She stops suddenly, eyes wide.

"What? What is it?"

"Go," she orders. "Now!"

He follows her gaze to the mural and discovers that half of it is gone. The images he worked so hard to create are bleeding down the wall like wet paint, colors diluting, bright blues and golds and reds transforming into lifeless gray. The trees and grass surrounding his canvas are also being sapped of color; the entire world seems to be fading.

He remembers her warning and tries to wake himself up. Nothing happens.

"End the dream, Devon!" There's panic in her voice now.

"I can't," he chokes out. He tries again—and again—but no matter what he does, he can't regain awareness of his sleeping body. It's as if everything outside the dream has ceased to exist.

The leaves of the rosebushes are turning brown now, curling back on themselves. Even the smell of diesel is fading. It's as if reality is being leached from the universe.

He hears a voice cry out Jesse's name, but he doesn't know where it's coming from. Clouds are beginning to gather overhead, congealing into a single black mass the size and shape of a man. The mere sight of it awakens a primitive fear in Devon, and every instinct screams for him to turn and run, as fast and as far as he possibly can. But where would he run to? If a reaper has taken control of his dream, he's got nowhere to go.

Jesse! He hears the voice again, louder than before. Jesse

hears it too this time, and seems to know where it's coming from. Someone must be trying to wake her up, he realizes. Her Gift is channeling his voice into the dream. It's clear from the way she's looking at him that she doesn't want to abandon him.

"Go," he says. The thought of being left alone with the reaper makes him feel sick, but if she stays for his sake she'll die. And maybe he'll die, too. "It's you they want, not me. Go!"

Suddenly the dream starts falling to pieces around him, reality shattering like broken glass, and then he's falling, falling, and somewhere at the bottom of the blackness his sleeping body waits, and the reaper vanishes like smoke as he surfaces—

||||||||||||

Awakening was a physical shock. For a moment it was all I could do to lay there and try to breathe steadily. I half expected a reaper to burst into the room at any moment.

"Your pulse was racing," Isaac said. "We took a chance on waking you."

"You did right," I told him. "Probably saved my life." *And maybe Devon's,* I thought. I had sensed him breaking free as I left the dream, so he was probably unharmed—albeit badly shaken—but the fact that he wasn't able to do that while I was present was pretty damn frightening.

As I raised myself to a sitting position, Sebastian offered me a glass of water. Drinking it made my throat less dry, but I still felt weak. "He couldn't wake up." My voice was shaking. "He tried, but he couldn't wake himself up." I shut my eyes for a moment, shivering as I remembered that moment. "They must have figured out how I was avoiding them and learned to compensate. Which means they're not just mindless hunters. They're learning. Adapting." I drew in a deep breath. "I can't rely on other people to end their dreams when reapers show up. We'd both be trapped."

Sebastian said quietly, "You shouldn't dreamwalk again until this is over."

"No shit." I stared down into my glass. "But that would take away the one advantage I have."

"It's not an advantage if it gets you killed."

I sighed. He was right. I hated him for being right.

Isaac asked, "Did you get what you went for? Or did we wake you up too soon for that?"

"I got it. Just in time. And no, you didn't wake me up too soon. A few seconds more in that dream and I might not have made it back." I looked at Isaac. "Do the abbies have Gifts?"

"What? No. Of course not."

"Are you sure?"

"What did you see?" Sebastian asked.

"Devon helped me recreate some abbie pictures I once saw. There were patterns that looked like . . . like a codex."

"Those patterns are visible when a Gate activates," Isaac said. "So any abbies who serve the Shadows or the Greys might have seen them."

Yes, I wanted to say, *but they would associate such patterns with their masters, and why would a slave want to decorate walls with his oppressors' designs?* But I couldn't say that without revealing that we'd discovered the mural while sneaking into Shadowcrest, and I wasn't comfortable revealing that to Isaac. No, he wasn't a Shadow any more, and should have no reason to care about Shadow business after what they did to him. But telling him that there were abbie secrets hidden in that Guild's stronghold just didn't seem right. They weren't my secrets to share. "There was a drawing that reminded me of the changing tower. I thought only Dreamwalkers could see that. Hence my question about the abbies."

"Their brains aren't as developed as ours," Isaac said. "And the abbies on Terra Prime were bred for servitude. Any that showed signs of Gift-like abilities would have been culled from stock before market."

Culled from stock before market. I tried not to resent him for using such dehumanizing references. It wasn't his fault. He'd been

raised to think of the abbies as little more than animals, and to take
their servitude for granted. But the place that I called home had out-
grown such arrogance long ago, and it was hard to stomach. "At any
rate," I said, "the significance of my first dream has been confirmed.
The abbie drawing was indeed important. So it seems likely the message of my second dream was equally meaningful, and not just a fig-
ment of my imagination." I glanced at Sebastian. "Which means El
Malo doesn't cover the whole of the Badlands. It's just at the border.
And I need to cross it."

I put my glass on the night stand and eased myself off the bed.
My legs felt a bit wobbly, but I was able to stand. After I ate something
I'd probably feel okay. Suddenly I felt sympathy for the Fleshcrafters
and their endless boxes of donuts. I would have given my soul for a
couple of those right now.

As I walked to the bathroom to freshen up I said, "It's time we
took a look at El Malo."

16

ROUELLE
TERRA PRIME

JESSE

WE PACKED ALL OUR BELONGINGS into our bags, along with a good supply of water, but left our bedrolls behind, the better to look like normal tourists. Sebastian dithered over what to do with his musket. He knew he couldn't play the tourist with a five foot gun slung across his back, but he didn't want to leave it in the room. Finally he decided to leave it with hotel security, so we stopped at the desk on the way out to take care of that.

The Native American woman who had checked us in was working the desk, and she assured Sebastian several times that his treasured possession would be well cared for. When he finally turned it over to her she handled it with the kind of care one would give a child, which seemed to soothe his fears a bit. Bless her for that.

When we turned to leave she said, "A brief question, if I may?"

We all turned back to look at her.

"A man came here last night asking after a Jennifer Dolan. Is that name known to any of you?"

"Doesn't sound familiar to me," Sebastian said quickly.

"Or me," Isaac said.

I shook my head, afraid that if I tried to speak the wrong words would come out. "He described her to me in some detail," she continued. "I imagine anyone who heard that description would have a pretty easy time recognizing her." Her eyes were on me now.

"Don't know her," I said. "Sorry."

I saw a brief smile as she turned back to her work.

Isaac had to press a hand to my back to get me to leave. My legs felt frozen. "Who's looking for me?" I muttered as the door closed behind us, my voice hardly louder than a whisper. There were a few people across the street, and though no one was paying attention to us I suddenly felt dreadfully exposed. "How did they know my name?"

"Do you want to leave this place?" Sebastian asked.

I considered it for a moment, then shook my head. "No, if they've checked here already and been turned away, it's safer here than elsewhere. And she did warn us. We may not get that courtesy at another hotel."

"That was odd," Isaac said. "She obviously knew who you were."

It *was* odd. I didn't know quite what to make of it. "Maybe she disliked the people who were asking. Or just doesn't approve of her hotel being used for manhunts." I remembered the way she had looked at my feather when we'd first arrived. Did this have something to do with that?

I sent Isaac into the first shop we passed to buy me a sunhat. I needed one anyway, and he bought one I could pull down low over my eyes to cast my face into shadow. Given that he was wearing his own cap equally low to hide his mark, together we looked like a pair of fashion-challenged *turistas*. On my world it would have gone unnoticed, but I wasn't so sure about Rouelle.

I wondered if the people who were asking about me knew that Sebastian and Isaac were with me.

We stopped at a small café for breakfast, and over eggs and toast decided to start our day with a tour of El Malo, to get a general overview of the situation. The tour service that operated closest to the Badlands border started some distance from town, but there was a tunnel we could use to get there, half underground, half open to the sky. It was comfortably cool thanks to the insulation of the surrounding sandstone, but the setup worried Sebastian. As we walked, he studied the walls intently, and I realized he was assessing our chances of climbing out if we had to. And it really was an ideal arrangement for an ambush. As we walked I grew anxious as well, and I kept turning back to see who was behind us. At one point Isaac drew close enough to whisper to me, "Jacob says there are bad spirits here." I knew from the tour brochures that anxiety was one of the effects of El Malo, but knowing didn't make it any easier to deal with. I was relieved when we finally reached the staircase at the end of the tunnel and could return to open ground; at least we would no longer feel so enclosed.

The stairs led to a vast, glass-walled chamber filled with ruddy light. One side of it faced El Malo, and we were so close to the great sand wave that it looked like it was about to break over our heads. I could see now that every inch of it was in motion—eddies and whirls of sand rippling across its surface, with spouts of dust vomited forth whenever they collided. Now and then a gust of sand-filled wind struck the glass and the tourists standing close to it gasped. Everyone seemed on edge, but in an excited, roller-coaster kind of way. They'd come to be scared.

At the other side of the room were a ticket counter and a small souvenir shop. I was tempted to buy Tommy a tacky postcard (well, he *had* asked for a souvenir) but Sebastian nudged me gently forward. Business first. We bought our tickets and were asked to sign waivers. They were similar to the ones I'd signed to go through the Gate, except this one had a much sterner warning, and a longer list of things that might go wrong. *I understand that El Malo is a natural phenomenon over which tour administrators have no control, and that by choosing to approach it I am accepting legal responsibility for any damages to my body or mind.* I started to sign as Jennifer Dolan, then hesitated, then started to sign it as Jessica Drake, then hesitated again, and finally just made up a name. Dana Adams.

A crowd of two dozen people had gathered by the western window, and we headed in that direction. Just as we got to the back of the group a brightly dressed man with VISTA MALA TOURS emblazoned across his shirt clapped his hands for attention. When everyone was looking at him he raised a hand toward the window and announced melodramatically, "Ladies and gentlemen, behold one of the most fearsome phenomena on this Earth, or on any Earth. The Badlands encompass nearly three hundred thousand square kilometers of territory, more than half of which is desert, and El Malo sits like a crown atop it, impassable to all human travelers. Some legends say it was created by spirits to guard a sacred location hidden deep in the desert, while others claim it is a gathering point for the ghosts of those who died defending this region against invaders. Whatever the cause, it is a truly terrifying phenomenon, and even its outermost effects are capable of driving a man mad—as you are soon to experience for yourselves.

"The red cloud you see before you is a secondary phenomenon, first noted by travelers in the early twentieth century. Frightening though it may appear, it actually serves a useful purpose by making the border of the Badlands clearly visible. Prior to its appearance, explorers or settlers might wander into the area by accident and never be seen again.

"My assistant will be offering you Elemental fetters to protect you from the sand. Twenty pounds rental for the hour. I strongly recommend them, especially for people with respiratory issues. Please stay on the marked paths at all times. El Malo can shift position without warning, and some people are more sensitive to its effect than others. If you start feeling odd, or have a sudden impulse to do something destructive—or self-destructive—please alert the tour guide so he can help you get back safely. We don't want to lose anyone." He gestured toward a rack of canteens by the door. "Remember, the air out here is very dry. It's easy to dehydrate without knowing it. Please take a canteen on your way out, and drink from it periodically during the tour. If you start to feel weak or dizzy, notify your guide immediately." He looked over the crowd. "Any questions?"

A woman in a bright floral shirt raised her hand. "Does El Malo affect animals?"

"Not in a mental sense, but they don't like the sandstorms any more than we do. Any others?" There were none. "Very well." He stepped back and gestured toward the door. "Have a good tour, folks, and don't forget to visit our souvenir shop on the way out!"

A young woman with medallions looped over her arm started moving through the crowd, exchanging fetters for cash. I gave her twenty pounds and received a large bronze disk with VISTA MALA TOURS on one side and a relief picture of the wave on the other. I put the cord around my neck as the crowd began to move forward, while Sebastian purchased his own. Isaac whispered reassurances into the air as he put his on; apparently Jacob was upset. I wasn't sure if that was because of El Malo's general effect or the bad spirits he'd mentioned, but I got the impression that Jacob was trying to get Isaac to go back to the hotel.

We kept to the back of the crowd, not wanting to be surrounded by strangers. Soon the door opened and a wave of heat swept inside, along with a gust of sand that set several people to coughing. I touched my fetter to activate it. There was no visible effect, but I didn't breathe in any sand, so apparently it was working.

Outside, both the sun and the heat were harsh, but it was the great sand wave that drew one's eye. Without the glass wall it appeared much closer, and it was hard to look up at it without cringing. Gusts of sand whipped in our direction, but they parted before they reached us. I remembered how the winds had parted for me in my dream, and I felt a rush of excitement. One omen, at least, was proving true.

Outside the welcome center was a stone path with a wind-scoured iron railing on one side, and I gripped the latter tightly as we followed the herd of tourists moving slowly toward the Badlands. El Malo invoked a fear that was primitive and visceral, impossible to deny; if not for the urgency of my mission I might not have been able to force myself to go forward. Indeed, I saw several people turn back, unable to tolerate the metaphysical assault. Isaac looked anxious but determined, but Sebastian . . . Jeez. He was gazing at the cloud in utter fascination, looking more curious than afraid. The loremaster in him had taken over, his hunger for knowledge counteracting El Malo's malevolent magic. It was exactly the reaction I'd hoped he would have, though I'd never imagined a trial quite this intense.

Step by step, we struggled toward the nightmare that was the Badlands. At one point I felt the railing beneath my hand fall away, and I cried out as I started to plummet into a bottomless abyss. Isaac grabbed me and held me until the fit passed. The railing was fine. I was fine. I took a few deep breaths and started walking again. Ahead of us I saw a young boy try to climb over the railing; his parents frantically pulled him back. Apparently sensory distortion wasn't the only weapon in El Malo's arsenal. I remembered the tour guide's warning about self-destructive impulses, and I shuddered. The thought that the Badlands could draw people to it against their conscious will was truly frightening.

The fifteen minutes that it took us to reach the first observation platform seemed to last an eternity. Now we were close enough that sand was swirling all around us. It wasn't sharp, like in my dream, but I was still glad that the fetter was keeping it away from me, so that I could see and breathe. I wouldn't want to be out here without one.

The three of us stood at the railing, side by side, and gazed into the face of Hell.

"That's where you want to go," Sebastian reminded me. "Into that."

I closed my eyes for a moment, but it did nothing to shut out the waves of malevolence that were pounding in my brain. "It's where I have to go." I could hear voices in the wind now, low moans, as if from dying animals. "There's no other choice."

"There are spirits in there," Isaac said. "I can sense them now."

"Malevolent?" Sebastian asked.

"No way to tell in this mess. Everything feels malevolent here. What?" He was silent for a moment. "Jacob says we're being watched.

I think he's trying to tell me . . . it's been happening since we left the tunnel."

I resisted my instinct to turn around quickly and try to catch someone in the act of staring at us. Instead I turned slowly, trying to make the motion look casual. But everyone else in the crowd looked like real tourists, and no one seemed to be paying attention to us.

"Look. Those are Soulriders." Isaac nodded toward a group at the far end of the platform. "And those." A group at the other end.

"How do you know?"

"They pick up animal mannerisms from their hosts. Shadows deal with them a lot, so I know the signs. That one uses birds." He was using his eyes to try to indicate someone, but I couldn't tell who he meant. They all looked pretty human to me. "This isn't good, Jesse."

Before I could say anything the crowd began to move again. We tried to bring up the rear, but one group of Soulriders was chatting at the railing, waiting for us to move ahead of them. My heart was pounding now, and not just because of El Malo. I feigned an issue with one of my shoelaces to gain a moment's time for thought, and knelt down to retie it. I took long enough that I guess the Soulriders felt it would blow their cover if they kept waiting, so they moved on ahead of us. For now.

There had to be a way out of this situation. Clearly the Soulriders weren't willing to attack us while there were so many witnesses around, or they would have done so already. Most likely they planned to target us on the way back. An ambush in the tunnel, maybe, or, if we avoided the tunnel, an assault on open ground. The land surrounding the tour center was flat and bare, with no nearby buildings for cover. Nothing to hide behind, no way to lose them. There were eight of them—maybe more that we didn't know about—and three of us. Not good.

I looked at El Malo. A lump rose in my throat.

Isaac said in a worried tone, "Jesse."

"They're here for me." I was speaking as quietly as I could, so that the Soulriders wouldn't hear us, but the sound of the wind made whispering impossible. "You heard the girl at the desk. They don't care about either of you."

"You don't know that," Sebastian said.

I looked at him. "Sooner or later I'm going to have to go in there." I nodded toward El Malo. "You know it. I know it. Even Jacob probably knows it. Yeah, I would have liked more prep time, but who's to say that would have changed anything? El Malo is what it is." I touched the fetter around my neck. "Right now I have this to protect me from the sand. I won't have it later."

Suddenly a voice rang out from ahead of us. "You people all right?"

I looked up and saw the tour guide staring at us. Everyone else appeared to have moved on.

"We're fine," Sebastian called back. "She just needs to get a rock out of her shoe."

I hobbled a few steps and winced.

"Okay. Just checking. I'll hold things up at the next platform so you can catch up." As he walked back to the other tourists sand blew between us, blurring his outline, making him seem more ghostly than real.

"It's only a border phenomenon," I said in a low voice. "If I can get through it, I'll be okay on the other side."

"If we get through it," Isaac corrected me. He took my hand.

I looked at Sebastian.

He stared at us for a moment like we were crazy people—which, by most people's standards, we were—then shook his head. "Age has robbed me of the resiliency of youth, Jessica. If I went with you I would only slow you down."

Firmly I said, "I'm willing to chance that."

I could see indecision in his eyes. He'd never promised to go into the Badlands with us, I reminded myself, only to come this far and consider it. Would he back out now, and leave us to go on alone? Finally he sighed. "God's blood. If you two disappear I'll be the only one left for the Soulriders to question. I suppose even El Malo is preferable to that." Despite his offhand tone, the message in his eyes was clear: *I will help protect you as long as I can, but even I have my limits.*

"Do you still have the stealth fetter?" Isaac asked. "That would help us get away from the tour group, at least."

"That expired some time ago, I'm afraid. Recent events have been . . . unusually demanding."

"All right," I said. "So we do it the old fashioned way." I looked around the observation platform to confirm that we were the only ones there. We were, but that was no guarantee one of the Soulriders wouldn't come back at any moment to see why their prey was lingering. I took a few deep breaths, muttered a quick prayer, and started to climb over the railing. Isaac followed suit. After a moment, Sebastian did as well.

Sorry, Tommy. Looks like you're not going to get that postcard after all.

17

EL MALO
TERRA PRIME

JESSE

WE MOVED AS QUICKLY AS WE COULD, anxious to get far enough that we could no longer be seen from the tour route. It was dangerous going. The closer we got to El Malo the worse visibility got, and since the last thing we wanted was to rush over the edge of the cliff in our haste, we were soon reduced to a snail's pace, edging forward step by step as we tested each stretch of ground before committing to it. The closer we got to the cliff's edge, the more loudly the wind roared, until talking at a normal volume was impossible. Periodically the delusional aspect of El Malo would make the ground seem like it was bucking and heaving, and no matter how much you told yourself that it was only an illusion, it felt so real you had to struggle to walk steadily. At one point I looked back and all that I could see was sand, which in a way was good; no one on the tour path would be able to see us anymore. As far as the Soulriders knew, we had just vanished. But I felt disconnected now, as if the world we'd left behind had ceased to exist. Our universe had been amputated.

We managed to find the edge of the escarpment safely, and stood on the very last bit of solid land, sand-laden winds whipping past our faces. The slope before us wasn't vertical, but it was hellishly steep, and I couldn't see more than ten feet down the face of it. We'd packed supplies to camp in the wild if we had to, so we had rope, but there was nothing to tie it onto; if we descended, we'd have to do so free style.

I looked at Isaac, and he nodded grimly. Sebastian mouthed, *Are you sure?* With a weak smile I shook my head: *No.*

I went first, lowering myself backward over the edge of the cliff, and Sebastian and Isaac did the same a few feet from me. There were horizontal ridges eroded into the sandstone that could be used as footholds, but they were shallow, and it took all my concentration to stay on them. I discovered it was nearly impossible for me to maintain a firm grip on the rock; my hands slid off as if it was slick with oil. With a sinking heart I realized the tour fetter was probably causing that problem, as it tried to keep my skin from coming in contact with any sand. I had to force my fingers into the rock, digging them into whatever small depressions I could find, fighting the effect of the fetter to maintain my grip.

Now that we were inside El Malo the wind was ten times as fierce, and the updraft along the cliff face threatened to tear us loose at any moment. My stomach scraped against the gritty slope as I inched slowly down it, trying not to let the wind get underneath me. The sound of the gale was so loud that I could not have heard my companions if they had screamed, and visibility was so bad that although I could still see them, everything else around me was just a red haze.

There was no going back now, whatever happened.

We climbed down for so long that my arms began to ache, my hands were scraped raw, and the roar of the wind in my ears made my head feel like it was going to explode. I remembered what Sebastian had said on the tour path, about his no longer having the resilience of youth, and I felt guilty that I had dragged him down here. But there was no stopping now. I tried to estimate how far we had to go, but though I knew the measurements of the slope from my topographical map, those numbers were an abstract thing, disconnected from reality. I had no idea how far we had come or how much further we had yet to go.

Suddenly I felt something strike the back of my hand. Startled, I looked down and saw a small red drop, like a spot of blood. Then, while I watched, another appeared beside it. And another. There were drops striking the back of my head now, and I remembered the viscous downpour in the Weaver's compound. That rain hadn't been real blood (we figured that out later from the stains it left behind) but this rain sure looked like it. I carefully lifted a hand to my mouth, hesitated a moment, then touched my tongue gingerly to one of the drops. It tasted like blood.

More drops were falling now, splattering down on the three of us, streaking the surrounding rock with crimson. If this rain started to come down with anything near the force of the Weavers' rain, descent would become infinitely more dangerous. I tried to move more quickly down the slope, but almost lost my footing as a result and had to force myself to keep to a more cautious pace. The slope was quickly becoming slick with blood, and rain splashed in my eyes, making it difficult to locate footholds. I had to feel around for support, but though my toes found a promising crack, I couldn't anchor a foot in it. As I struggled for balance my fingers began to slide from the rock; everything had become so slick that there was no traction to be had anywhere. To my horror, I felt myself slipping. Desperately I flattened myself against the slope, hands splayed out like a lizard's, fingers digging into every notch or groove they could find. But it wasn't enough. My right foot slid free of the rock, forcing me to shift my weight to the left, which in turn skewed my balance so that I lost that foothold, too. Suddenly I was sliding—then falling—ridges of rock buffeting my body as I grasped for any handhold that I could use to stop my fall, or at least slow it.

I could sense the ground rushing up at me though I could not see it, and when my legs finally hit bottom I tried to go with the impact and roll, rather than snap all the bones in my legs. Even so, I hit the ground so hard that the breath was knocked out of me. For a moment it was all I could do to lie there, praying that nothing was broken, sputtering as blood rained down on my face. A moment later a dark shape emerged from the sand cloud overhead, heading straight toward me; I managed to roll out of the way just in time. Isaac struck the ground with a gut-wrenching thump, then lay face down and silent. As I tried to rouse him I saw Sebastian descending; he alone had managed to maintain his grip.

"Isaac!" I called his name even though I knew it would do no good; it was impossible to hear anything over the wind. "Wake up!"

He coughed as he slowly lifted his head from a puddle of blood rain, then winced and grabbed his side. I prayed that he was just badly bruised and that nothing had been broken. Sebastian offered a hand to help me up, and I helped Isaac in turn, and somehow all three of us managed to make our way back to the slope, which we leaned against for support while trying to catch our breath.

No longer were we standing in a world that we recognized, but in a landscape so alien that the human mind could barely make sense of it. The crimson rain was falling in sheets now, and everything within sight was coated in it. A few meters ahead a stream was forming, and it grew broader and deeper as we watched, its viscous current flowing like syrup over the ground. Soon it might be too deep to cross.

This is only a border phenomenon, I reminded myself. Once we got past this, the terrain would be flat, with no more need for climbing. *We can do this.*

I looked at Isaac; with his hair soaked in blood and his hand gripping his side he looked like a gruesome accident victim, but he nodded. Whether he was really okay, or just understood that we had to keep moving even if he wasn't, I didn't know, and didn't want to know. Stopping was not an option.

Slowly we began to inch forward, moving directly away from the rock wall in order to head west. Every step was a test of balance on the slick ground, and when we got to the newborn river—now ankle deep—the current was strong enough to nearly knock us off our feet. Suddenly my foot shot out from under me, and I went down with a splash. A small red creature scuttled out of the water and across land, quickly disappearing from sight. A lizard? It was gone too fast for me to be sure. Then another appeared, and another. Now frogs were emerging, dozens of them. Hundreds of them. I got back up and we tried to keep moving, but the little creatures were all over us now, and I had to fight the reflex to swat at them each time they touched me, possessed by mankind's instinctive horror of small icky things.

We managed to get across the river somehow, and onto solid ground again. I looked back at the cliff to make sure we were still headed in the right direction, but it was already invisible, masked by a torrent of crimson rain. The fetters that protected us from the sand did nothing to protect us from the downpour, and I had to hold one hand over my eyes as we moved forward, to keep the blood rain from getting in them.

Suddenly I felt a stinging pain in my arm. I thought that maybe one of the lizards had bitten me, but when I looked down I saw a large wasp had landed on my sleeve. Another one landed right next to it and immediately stung me through my shirt. Shit. I shook my arm to throw them off, cursing, but there were more coming now, and they started settling on other parts of my body. We must have disturbed a nest somewhere nearby. Each sting was like fire injected into my veins, and I wondered how many I could endure before their venom overcame me. Sebastian and Isaac were similarly outnumbered, and since the swarm seemed to be coming from one particular direction, we started running the other way. They followed us, stinging us on every inch of our bodies as we ran, until my flesh felt like it was burning and my vision began to blur. I knew that this many stings could kill a person, but we had no way to defend ourselves, could only try to escape the swarm before the wasps pumped a lethal amount of venom into our veins. We splashed through thick red blood puddles until our lower limbs were soaked in the stuff, staggering in pain. Still the wasps kept coming; whatever we had done to piss them off, they were clearly not in a forgiving mood.

Finally, though, the cloud of angry insects thinned a bit. We staggered a few hundred feet more, and then they were gone. I fell to my knees in exhaustion, my head swimming. My body felt like it had been stabbed by red hot knives, and God alone knew what would happen when all that venom spread through my body. But for now, at least, I was alive, and the wasps were gone. I felt a nudge on my arm, and turned to find Isaac holding a canteen out to me. I took it and drank deeply, which made me feel a little steadier, but as I handed the canteen to Sebastian I saw that my exposed skin was covered in angry red boils. My companions were in no better shape, their faces covered in red pustules. But that was not the worst of it.

We didn't know where we were.

The realization seemed to come to all three of us simultaneously. In our wild flight from the wasps we'd lost all sense of direction, and now all we could see was crimson rain on every side. The ground was completely awash, so we didn't even have the bloody river to guide us; everything looked the same now, one featureless, directionless hell. I looked upward for guidance, hoping the position of the sun would tell us something useful, but what little light was seeping down through the storm was so diffuse that we had no hope of telling what direction it was coming from.

We were lost.

I saw Sebastian rummaging in his bag, and to my relief he pulled out a small compass. Cupping his hand over it to protect it from the rain, he waited for the needle to settle. But it never did, just kept circling. After a few seconds he shook it, and this time the needle stopped, but if he moved the compass it changed direction and then stopped again. He tried a few more times with increasing desperation, but each time the result was the same. The compass wasn't working. We were lost, hopelessly and irrevocably lost, with no way to figure out what direction we had to go in to escape this hell. And moving forward without that knowledge could bring us back to the cliff face, which we could never hope to climb in this deluge, or send us walking down the miles-long length of El Malo until sheer exhaustion claimed us.

I lowered my head, wiped the blood from my face, and tried not to let despair overwhelm me. There *had* to be a way out of here. The avatar girl wouldn't have shown me the way if there wasn't. Unless she was what Sebastian had once suggested—an adversary, not a friend— and her intent all along had been to lead me to my death. By causing me to die in this place, she guaranteed that the Shadows could not get hold of my corpse to use in their necromancy.

I'm sorry, I thought to the others. Guilt was a knife blade through my heart. *Sorry I brought you here to die.*

Suddenly something struck me on the head, hard. I reached up to feel the spot and was struck on my hand, then on my head again. It felt as if someone was raining down rocks on us. They were striking the ground on all sides of us, most disappearing with a splash into the crimson river, although a few landed in places shallow enough that I could see their upper surfaces gleaming whitely. Ice. They were ice. Glistening chunks of hail, with thin streaks of blood rain webbed across them, like the vessels in a human eye. The Badlands were stoning us to death.

Suddenly Isaac got to his feet. I looked up and saw him peering into the rain, his hands cupped over his eyes to protect them. He spoke a few words, but I couldn't hear what he was saying. Was he trying to talk to Jacob? The ghost had been so terrified of this place earlier that I'd assumed he'd stayed behind. Even if he was with us, I wasn't sure what he could do to help us.

Isaac looked at us, then pointed into the rain. Mustering what little strength I could, I struggled to my feet. Any direction was better than no direction. We staggered across the featureless landscape, flesh throbbing from all the wasp stings, poison surging through our veins. The hailstorm intensified, pelting us with lumps of ice so large that one of them nearly knocked me out. Isaac stopped us a few times and peered into the depths of the storm again before signaling us to move on. God alone knew where he was leading us, but if we didn't reach safety soon we weren't going to make it.

Suddenly I saw something so startling and wonderful that all other concerns were forgotten. A point of light was shining weakly through the rain, right ahead of us. What could it be but the sun? We began to stagger faster in that direction. At one point I fell and pain shot through my knee, but that didn't matter. Just ahead of us was an end to this nightmare, and all we had to do was get there before this place murdered us.

And then suddenly the rain was gone, the hail was gone, the wind was gone. I fell to the ground and found it solid beneath me, blissfully dry. I looked at my hands and there was no blood on them, no boils, no wasp stings, only the normal bruises and scrapes one would expect from a bad fall. It had all been an illusion, the madness of El Malo possessing our minds. I was so furious I wanted to scream, and so relieved I wanted to cry.

It really could have killed us, I told myself. If we'd given up hope and surrendered to the illusion, we all would have died. That much was real.

"Jessica." Sebastian's voice was tense. "Look up."

I did so, and saw six men on horseback arranged in a semicircle around us. They were wearing bleached animal skulls as masks and were pointing weapons at us, miniature crossbows that they held like pistols. I couldn't see their faces because of the skull masks, but from their posture I had the distinct impression they were not happy to see us. Very not happy. Like, *about-to-fire-their-crossbows-at-us* not happy.

Shit.

18

EL MALO
TERRA PRIME

JACOB

RED. RED. Everything was red. Red sky. Red ground. Red gale winds sweeping across a barren red landscape. Ripples of red pain vibrating through the air, echoing the last thoughts of everyone who had ever died here. Disembodied voices screaming in crimson agony.

Even by the standards of the dead, this was a terrible place.

Jacob could see that Isaac was growing weaker by the moment. The other humans didn't matter to him, but the thought of what would become of him if the young necromancer died filled him with terror. Right now Isaac was the only thing anchoring his ravaged spirit to the world of the living, allowing him to maintain some semblance of humanity. Without that anchor he would have nothing left to keep his identity intact. The few fragments of human memory he still possessed would be dispersed upon the wind like scattered leaves, and he would finally meet the fate that the Shadowlords had intended for him: total annihilation.

Don't die! He hovered over Isaac in panic, desperate to do something to help him. *Don't leave me!* But Isaac couldn't hear him in this terrible place, and Jacob could do nothing but watch in helpless misery as the three humans fled from dangers his dead eyes couldn't see, as they beat at their own bodies to drive off an unseen threat. Whatever nightmares the three of them were fleeing were invisible in the realm of the dead; how could Jacob help them if he didn't even know what they were running from?

Unless none of it was real.

The revelation was almost too complex for his shattered mind to process. What if the threats that the humans were fighting didn't really exist? What if the spirits of this place had placed lies in the humans' minds, in order to destroy them? That would explain why Jacob couldn't see any of it.

Lies! He screamed it as loudly as he could, trying to warn Isaac. The realm of the dead resonated with his desperation. *Fake! Don't believe!*

But Isaac couldn't hear him.

Desperately he looked around, seeking . . . what? What could possibly help him? It was nearly impossible for the broken fragments of his soul to think at all, much less deal with complicated speculation. All he could do was search his surroundings in the hope that something would come to him.

The humans had stopped moving. Isaac and the girl had both fallen to their knees. Jacob could sense the spirits of the Badlands drawing close to them like invisible vultures, hungry for death.

Suddenly he saw a faint light in the distance. He focused all his attention on it, struggling to figure out what it was. The effort was acutely painful; thoughts slipped from his mind as soon as he formed them. But just as his strength was nearly exhausted, he realized what he was looking at.

Sunlight.

Somewhere ahead of him the red winds were thinning out, enough that the sun could shine through. The travelers couldn't see it yet, blinded as they were by the illusions of this place, but in the realm of the dead it was visible as a lighthouse beacon. If only they went in the right direction, they might reach it before they collapsed.

HERE! Jacob screamed. He moved so that he was standing between Isaac and the sun; maybe if Isaac looked that way he would see
the light. *HERE!* But Isaac still couldn't hear him. Over and over
again Jacob repeated the cry, trying to drive that one word like a jack-
hammer into Isaac's brain. *Here here here here HERE HERE HERE!*

Suddenly Isaac looked up. He rose to his feet. He was listening.

HERE! Jacob screamed. *COME! BE SAFE!* He poured all his
strength into each word, drawing upon his few surviving memories
for fuel. Images from his lost life flared in his mind. The Shadowlords'
torture chamber. Stealing food from a street vendor. The agonizing
sweetness of Mae's smile. *COME!* he yelled. *HERE!* He was growing
weaker by the moment and couldn't keep this up much longer.
ESCAPE!

Then Isaac looked at him. Directly at him. He understood!

Struggling to hold himself together, Jacob slowly backed away,
moving toward the light. After a moment's hesitation, Isaac pointed
others in that direction and began to follow him. Relief swept over
the exhausted ghost. The others were coming, following Isaac's lead.
Jacob was going to save them after all.

But who was going to save him?

By the time the sun's light was visible to the humans, Jacob had
become so weak that it was difficult for him to think at all. He could
see how excited they were when they finally realized where he'd been
leading them, but their joy was a distant thing, as if viewed through
hazy glass. The few memories that remained to him were fading rapidly, brief sparks of hope, pain, fear, and despair swept away by the
red wind. Without them he was nothing.

Isaac was running toward the light now. They were all running
toward the light. All but Jacob.

He had saved them.

Then the winds swept that final thought away, and all that was
left was crimson.

19

BADLANDS
TERRA PRIME

JESSE

FOR AN ENDLESS MOMENT no one moved. The three of us crouched on the ground, waiting to see if they were going to shoot us, while the men with the skull masks remained on their horses, not shooting us. I told myself that delay was a good thing, and that every moment that passed without them killing us increased the odds that we were going to make it out of this situation alive. Whether that was true or not I didn't know, but it sounded good.

Suddenly Isaac broke the silence. "Jacob's not here." He looked back the way we had come. "He didn't make it through!"

As he began to scramble to his feet, one of the horsemen took aim at him. I grabbed Isaac by the arm to try to stop him, but he shook me off. "I'm not leaving Jacob in there!" Without looking at the mounted men, he limped toward El Malo. From the way he clutched one hand to his side it was clear his fall had hurt him pretty badly, but there was an air of defiance about him that seemed to say, *Shoot me if you have to, but nothing short of that will stop me.*

I held my breath, braced for the worst, but no one fired at him.

He staggered a few yards toward El Malo, and for a moment I was afraid he would try to go back into that death zone. If he did, I doubted either Sebastian or I was strong enough to rescue him, and I was pretty sure the horsemen weren't going to help. But then he stopped and spread his arms as if embracing the sandstorm, and he yelled into the howling winds, "Jacob! Can you hear me? Jacob!" He waited a moment and then yelled it again, this time with an edge of despair in his voice. I saw his body stiffen, and I guessed that he was trying to invoke the Gift that allowed him to speak to the dead. His fingers sketched patterns in the air. "Follow my voice!" he yelled. "Come to me!" The sand wave in front of him seemed to loom even higher and darker than before, and I wondered if there might not be spirits in there that were unhappy about necromantic rituals being performed on their doorstep.

After holding his rigid pose for several endless minutes, Isaac suddenly staggered back a few steps, as if he'd been struck. Then he found his balance again, and cried out in a voice hoarse from desperation, "Come to me!" Then he collapsed backward. Without a thought for the masked men I ran to him, Sebastian right behind me. Isaac lay face up on the ground, his pupils dilated, whispering words I couldn't hear. "Jesus," I said, "are you okay?" I put a hand on his chest; beneath my palm his heart was pounding wildly. I didn't know what else to do. Sebastian was on the other side of him, but he didn't seem to know what to do either. "Talk to me," I begged Isaac. "Please."

Slowly he turned his head to me. The pupils had returned to normal size but the whites of his eyes were an angry red. "Jacob's safe," he gasped. "Safe." He winced in pain and shut his eyes. "I gave him my strength."

"I didn't know you could do that," Sebastian said.

Isaac tried to laugh. The sound turned into coughing, and he rolled onto his side so he wouldn't choke. When the fit finally passed he gasped, "Neither did I." He looked a little better now, though he was still very weak. Sebastian and I helped him get to his feet. He couldn't walk unassisted, so we supported him, one on each side, as we slowly made our way back to the semi-circle of skull warriors, who had been waiting in silence through all this.

Judgment time.

If not for the stirring of their long black hair in the breeze, they might have been statues. Even the horses were still. Though it was hard to tell where they were looking with the skull masks casting shadows across their eyes, I got the impression they were studying Isaac. Finally one of them barked orders in a language I didn't understand, and his men lowered their crossbows. The wave of relief that came over me was dizzying.

He pointed to me and said something, but I didn't understand. After he jabbed his finger at me a few times, clearly frustrated by my stupidity, I realized that he was pointing to my canteen. I nodded and removed it from my belt, opened it, and held it to Isaac's lips. He was so dazed that it took him a few seconds to realize what was happening, but once he did, he grabbed the canteen and began to drink greedily, desperately, as if not only his flesh was parched, but his very soul. I had to stop him a few times to give his body a chance to absorb what it was taking in, and to keep him from choking. When he was finally done I took a deep drink myself and then passed the canteen to Sebastian. There was no point in rationing water now. If these skull warriors chose to spare our lives, I was sure they had enough supplies to go around.

Kicking his horse into motion, the leader rode toward us. I tried to pull Isaac out of the way in time but couldn't. He came up to Isaac and grabbed him by the back of his shirt, yanking him up and over the saddle, backpack and all. I heard Isaac cry out as he hit the horse stomach first, and I winced, but there was nothing I could say or do to improve the situation, so I bit my lip and kept my silence. A little rough treatment was still worlds better than being impaled on crossbow bolts.

To my surprise one of the other men now rode toward me, a riderless horse trailing obediently behind. Had I failed to notice the extra animal while staring at masks and crossbows, or had one of them fetched it while our attention was elsewhere? I was offered the reins, with clear invitation to ride the animal. Surprised, I looked back at Sebastian, who shrugged and then stepped forward to help me mount. Once I did that I wriggled out of my backpack and hung it from the horn at the front of the saddle so Sebastian would have room to squeeze on behind me. It wasn't comfortable, but it sure as hell beat walking.

And then we were headed away from El Malo and into the desert. I hoped Jacob could keep up with us, but even if he couldn't, at least he was safe now. We wouldn't be leaving him trapped in Hell.

We rode for perhaps half an hour. I was so exhausted that at times I nearly nodded off; only Sebastian's arms kept me anchored in place. At one point I saw Isaac begin to stir, and the leader stopped so that he could be transferred to another horse, in front of one of the other riders. Isaac had no strength to mount on his own, but had to be lifted up, and the man he was now riding with had to hold him upright as we started riding again. I wondered if he even knew where he was any more. But at least he was alive. That was the singular goal of today: staying alive.

Soon the bare red earth gave way to dry beige soil and scraggly brush. The horses carried us down into a granite-walled canyon, at the bottom of which was a narrow stream of water. God, what I wouldn't have given to dismount and lie down in it! Just for a few minutes. But we kept on riding. The sun was starting to set now, and the steep western wall of the canyon cast us into shadow, a premature night. We'd been on the move since morning, and at that point I wasn't sure how much longer I could make it without collapsing.

Then we came around a curve, and I saw a campsite spread out before us, with a large rectangular vehicle at one end. With canvas sheets for walls and beams at the front end that were obviously meant for harnessing horses, it looked like a cross between a covered wagon and a Winnebago. In front of it a single figure sat before a campfire, stirring something in a pot. She stood as we approached. Her hair was long and grey and dressed in two braids drawn forward over her shoulders, and around her neck she had a collection of silver necklaces and pendants on leather cords. For some reason the latter reminded me of Sebastian with all his fetters. Her clothing was long and loose, a blue cotton shirt tucked into a long skirt, and I envied how fresh the fabric looked. Even though the blood rain in El Malo had turned out to be an illusion, the sweat-caked dirt that clung to my clothing was unpleasantly real.

As the horses stopped the woman approached. She looked at me for a few seconds, and I had the odd impression she was not only studying my disheveled appearance, but trying to peer into my soul. Finally she stepped back and gestured toward the wagon/Winnebago. The skull warriors dismounted, and Sebastian and I followed suit. When Isaac was lifted down, the woman seemed unhappy about how he was being handled, and she snapped a few terse orders to the warriors in charge of that maneuver. Given how fearsome the men had seemed to us, it was nothing short of amazing to see how naturally they deferred to her.

Isaac was carried into the wagon, and Sebastian and I followed. The interior was strewn with colorful rugs and cushions, with carved bits of bone and wood and disks of engraved metal hanging from every support beam. There was a low cot against one wall, and the woman directed the men to put Isaac on it. Then she waved for them to leave. Once more I was struck by how naturally they obeyed her. Soon after, we heard the sounds of hoofbeats receding into the distance.

Without sparing a glance for Sebastian or me, the woman sat on the cot beside Isaac and eased his shirt open. The deep purple bruising all over his torso was worse than I'd expected, and when she saw it she shook her head sharply. "Fools," she muttered. It was our first hint that anyone here spoke English. She shut her eyes for a moment, breathed in deeply, then placed her hands on Isaac where the damage looked the worst, causing him to moan softly in pain. She touched a few different spots, then announced, "Nothing broken," in an accent I'd never heard before. "But he's bruised in many places. It'll hurt for a while." She reached over to a side table for a small glass bottle. "Drink this," she told him, and she lifted him up so he could do so. When the bottle was empty she lowered him gently, and he sank back limply into the cot, like a doll that had been emptied of all its stuffing.

"You're a Healer?" Sebastian asked.

"Among other things." She put the bottle back on the table and turned to us. Her skin was weathered and ruddy, her strong Native American features rimmed by fine lines. She could have been fifty or eighty or anything in between, but her gaze had a depth that was ageless. "Well." She looked me over from top to bottom. "So you're the one I was asked to protect."

My heart skipped a beat. "Why? Who asked you to do that?"

She nodded toward the entrance. "Go sit by the fire. I'll be there shortly."

We did as we were told. There was a small circle of rocks around the campfire, and as I sat down on one of them I felt the last of my strength leave me. If the skull warriors had returned with their crossbows at that moment and told me I had to get up or die, I couldn't have managed it. I saw a bowl of water with a ladle in it sitting off to one side, and I took the liberty of taking a drink. It was cooler than the water in our canteens, and it refreshed my spirit.

I looked at Sebastian. "Any idea what's going on?"

He glanced back at the wagon. "Tribal shaman, I'm guessing. But customs differ, so there's no telling what that means."

A few minutes later the woman came out, carrying two small bowls in one hand and several spoons in the other. She went to the campfire and stirred whatever was in the pot, then portioned out some of it and handed the bowls to us. The spoon she gave me was smoothly polished and mottled in color: horn, perhaps.

"Thank you," I murmured. The stew smelled of chili and black pepper and after I blew on a spoonful to cool it down, I found it delicious. A touch of heat settled in the back of my throat.

"You've come a long way," the woman said to me.

I laughed a bit. "Yeah. You could say that."

"There are closer portals. You could have covered some of the distance on your own world and then crossed over. It would have been faster."

The spoon stopped on its way to my mouth. "You know about my world?"

"I know a lot of things."

I nodded toward Sebastian. "I had friends I wanted to bring with me."

"Which cost you dearly."

"What do you mean?"

She reached over and touched the feather in my hair. "Because of this, my people knew to help you. The spirits knew to let you pass. All of that was arranged by the one who gave it to you, before you ever set foot on your journey. But then you showed up with outsiders." She glanced disapprovingly at Sebastian. "And one of them a necromancer. A boy who enslaves spirits, preventing them from moving on to the next world. There's nothing more deeply offensive to the spirits of El Malo."

Slowly I put my bowl down. "Are you telling me that all that hell we went through getting here was because Isaac was with us?"

"Not all of it. They would have tested anyone. That passage isn't meant to be easy. But I'm sure it was far worse because of him."

"God's love," Sebastian muttered, and I said, "Please don't tell him that."

She shrugged. "He's earned his redemption, at least in the eyes of the *azteca*. His willingness to give his life to save a wounded spirit proved him worthy. At least for now." She paused. "Though whether he'll be allowed to leave here is another thing."

Ignoring the implied threat, Sebastian asked, "Who are the *azteca*?"

"Descendants of those who sought refuge here when the Spanish invaded their homeland. Their warriors guard our border. Used to make their masks out of human skulls, but the Council put a stop to that. Desecration of the dead is never a wise move." She sipped from her cup. "Be glad you're out of their hands. They're the ones who in-voked the sandstorm for us, to block the sight of outsiders, and their methods for maintaining it are, let us say, somewhat bloody." She put down her cup and rose. "Enough for tonight. I have little but blankets to offer you, as I don't usually entertain company, but the night is clear and there's good earth around the campfire. Tomorrow I'll take you to the place you came to see." She looked at Sebastian for a moment, her eyes narrowing slightly. "You have healing on you. I don't know what form it's in, but I can sense its power. Come and give some to the boy."

"Wait!" I said. "You knew about the wren feather. That means you know who gave it to me. You know what I'm here for, don't you?"

She shook her head slightly. "The place you're searching for isn't in the Badlands, though there is a path here that may lead you to it. I'll take you there tomorrow morning. Beyond that, no one can help you. Not even *her*."

I opened my mouth to ask another question but she held up a hand to silence me. "Enough. Sleep now. We'll talk in the morning."

ıııııııııııı

The buzzing of Morgana's fetter woke Sebastian up.

For a moment he just lay there in the darkness, pretending the fetter didn't exist. Every joint in his body ached, and he had no desire to move one inch more than he had to. But then he realized there was a basic physical need he would soon have to take care of, so slowly, painfully, he unwrapped himself from his blankets and eased himself to his feet.

The night was cold—surprisingly so—and with the campfire re-duced to dying embers it was hard to see in the canyon's shadows. He picked his way carefully past a turn a few dozen meters from the camp site, which offered enough privacy for him to deal with his body's needs discreetly. After that was done, he leaned back against the rock, took out the com fetter, stared at it for a long while, and then finally activated it. "Be quiet," he whispered, as Morgana's image took shape in front of him. "Others are sleeping nearby."

"Have you any information for me?"

He respected her information network enough to assume that she knew where he was, if not the fine details of what was happening to him, so there was no point in lying to her about the basics. "I'm travelling with Jessica. She's looking for information that will help her get rid of some wraiths that are bothering her. Nothing has come of that yet. If we turn up any interesting information I'll be sure to contact you." There was an edge to his voice as he added, "As promised."

The face was too grainy for him to see Morgana's expression. "I have another task for you."

He sighed. He could remember a time in the not-so-distant past when no one had given him orders, or asked him for favors that he couldn't deny. It seemed a lifetime ago. "I'm listening," he said, resigned to the inevitable.

"I want you to arrange a meeting between Jessica and myself." She raised up a hand to forestall any objection. "Only when it becomes physically possible. I realize that's not the case right now."

So she does know where we are. "With all due respect, your Grace, I doubt that's ever going to happen."

"I need you to make it happen."

"I think you underestimate how much she distrusts you."

"Trust is a luxury. We can't always choose our allies, Private Hayes."

He raised an eyebrow. "Is that what you're offering her? Alliance?"

"I have information she needs. Nothing more. But its nature is such that I can't entrust it to messengers. Trust me, she wants it."

"She knows what you're capable of," he warned. "She knows how vulnerable she would be in your presence. And she's not a fool."

"Well then, let's be blunt, shall we? The Shadows are mobilizing against her, and other Guilds may soon join them. The last time her kind was hunted, none of them survived the holocaust. She needs allies in powerful places, or she won't survive the coming storm. The information I have can give her the upper hand against her enemies. Can she afford to forego it?"

The last time her kind was hunted. So the pretense was over. Morgana knew exactly what Jessica was, and probably always had known. *Unless she's bluffing,* he reminded himself, *and fishing for confirmation.* Dealing with Morgana was like dancing with a cobra. "And that's all you care about? Her survival?"

"It's not *all* I care about, no. But if the Shadows capture her nothing else really matters, does it?"

He remembered the Soulriders who had tried to encircle them in Rouelle. The hunt for Jessica already involved multiple Guilds. If those Soulriders knew what the girl was, as Morgana seemed to, they wouldn't let up until Jessica was dead.

"If you do this for me," Morgana said, "I will consider your debt to me settled. The moment she meets with me, you no longer owe me any manner of service or favor. It will be as if our previous conversation never happened."

His hand tightened around the fetter. He was glad she couldn't see his expression. "I can't raise the subject without her realizing we've been in contact."

"Then tell her the truth. Or whatever lie you need to. All I care about are results, Private Hayes; how you get them is your own business."

He winced slightly. "I'll pass on your message. That's the best I can do."

"Excellent. I look forward to hearing of your success."

Her image disappeared.

It was several minutes before he could bring himself to return to camp. When he did, Jesse was lying there with her eyes open, watching him. "You okay?" she asked.

"Had to piss." He smiled weakly. "Thought I'd spare you the sight."

He sat down on his blankets and stared into space. After a few minute she said, "Sebastian?"

He shut his eyes. *There's just the two of us here now,* he thought. *The setting won't get better than this.* "Alia Morgana wants to meet with you."

He heard a sharp intake of breath. "Seriously?"

He shrugged stiffly.

"She's not here, is she?"

"No. She means once you leave the Badlands." *If you leave the Badlands.* "She says she has information you could use to stay alive, but she'll only deliver it to you personally."

"How did you find this out?"

He hesitated, then threw the fetter over to her. It landed on her blanket. "She gave me that a while back in case I ever came across information I wanted to sell her. She just used it to reach out to me. Keep it. You can use it to contact her if you want." He paused. "I can't imagine any circumstances under which I would want to do that."

He sensed she was staring at him in the darkness, but he couldn't meet her eyes. At last she said, "Do you really think I should talk to her?"

He sighed. "My first instinct is to tell you that wherever she is, you should run in the other direction as fast and as far as you can and never stop running. But we're already three thousand kilos from home and Soulriders are hunting you. They're servants of the Shadows, so at least two Guilds are involved. Maybe more. Honestly, Jessica . . . I don't know if running away will accomplish anything."

She said it quietly: "You think I should meet with her."

"It's your choice to make. But remember, once you're in her presence you'll have no secrets left; I warned you about that before. A Seer can read your emotions like a book, and someone as skilled as Morgana can leverage that into what might as well be true mind reading. Not to mention she'll be able to detect your fears, your insecurities, your hungers, your needs . . . She's a deadly creature, Jessica. But only if you're in her physical presence." He shook his head. "Might that be a price worth paying for what she has to offer? I honestly don't know."

"Is that—" She hesitated. "Is that why you brought your musket with you? So you wouldn't have to risk being in her presence?"

He turned back and looked into her eyes. How like his daughter's eyes they seemed sometimes! It made his heart ache. "You entrusted me with your secrets. This was the only way I could think of to safeguard them. Hopefully someday it will no longer be necessary."

"I was so afraid you were expecting to die—"

He laughed. "Good God, no! Where did you get that idea? I've been fighting to survive on this miserable world for most of my life. I'm not going to abandon that struggle for Alia Morgana, or any other Gifted tyrant!"

Jessica smiled slightly, then looked down at the fetter, turning it over in her hand. "I don't have to decide right now, do I? The Badlands may kill us tomorrow. Or I may find what I'm looking for, and not need Morgana any more. Anything could happen."

"Since I doubt your enemies will follow you here—or could survive the crossing if they tried—you have some time. You should make a decision before leaving this place, though."

"Understood." She tucked the fetter into her pocket and looked at him. "Thank you for your honesty, Sebastian."

He lay back down on his blankets without responding.

20

BADLANDS
TERRA PRIME

ISAAC

SAAC DOESN'T KNOW where he is. He only knows that he's lying on his back and the ceiling above him is rippling. It's also glowing faintly, as if some light behind it is seeping through. The result isn't bright enough for him to make out details of the small space he's in, but sometimes when the ceiling ripples its light glints off small bits of metal and polished bone that seem to be hung everywhere. He can hear a soft murmuring, too, like voices of the dead, only much fainter, as if the spirits that once inhabited this place left their echoes behind. The murmurs are mostly peaceful, unlike the tormented cries of the dead in Shadowcrest, and are surprisingly soothing.

With a soft moan he rises to a sitting position. His body is still weak from the summoning he performed at El Malo, but he knows he's lucky to be alive at all. When he reached out to Jacob he was offering the very substance of his life, and while he knew it was a risky move—possibly a fatal one—he didn't care. The dead boy's spirit had been loyal to him, helping him survive those first few terrible days of his exile, and Isaac felt like he owed him loyalty in return.

His father would have derided that sentiment. *The spirits of the dead aren't people any longer*, he would have lectured, *only semi-conscious reflections of people who once existed. We owe them no more loyalty than we owe to rocks or trees.*

Isaac doesn't remember anything from after the summoning, only heat and pain and utter exhaustion. Nothing he sees now offers any enlightenment. After taking a few minutes to gather his strength, he gets up from the cot, intending to search for answers. He begins to look around the tent—and he sees his own body lying before him.

As a necromancer he knows what that means, and he panics. Did his effort to restore Jacob drain him of so much life energy that his flesh could no longer sustain itself? Is he no more than a ghost now, looking down upon his own corpse? He has so much left to live for! So much left to learn! He's not ready to die yet.

But then he realizes that his body is stirring gently, its chest rising up and down with each breath, the subtle tremor of a pulse visible along the neck. Trembling with relief, he sees that a small circular item has been tucked into the bandages that are wrapped around his chest. A fetter for healing? Or some other kind that has allowed his spirit to leave his body without his flesh being harmed? His fear is slowly being transformed into wonder. Nothing in his apprenticeship prepared him for an experience like this.

He finds a flap that allows him to exit the small room and discovers that in fact it's a covered wagon, parked at the base of a canyon wall. He can hear running water in the distance and smell fresh greenery all around him, but he sees no other people. Overhead the full moon is shining brightly, but that's wrong, isn't it? Last night the moon was a crescent. Has he slept for a whole week, or is there some other explanation?

A large bird flies across the face of the moon, black against the silvery backdrop. Isaac is familiar with the species commonly used by the Soulriders, so he's able to identify this one as a raven. He watches as it circles around where he is standing, seven times in all, then begins to coast down into the canyon. As it spreads its broad wings to check its flight Isaac realizes with a start that the bird isn't really black, as it appeared in silhouette. In fact its feathers are white—a glistening, ghostly white—with only a tiny bit of black on its forehead, right where his own mark of shame is located.

It lands on a rock a few meters away, then cocks its head, studying him. There is an intelligence in its eyes that is so far beyond that of a mere bird he wonders if a Soulrider has found him. But no Soulrider has ever looked at him like this, with a gaze that pierces his soul, dissecting his spirit, deconstructing his very essence.

Without warning it takes to the air again.

He follows.

The night air is cool on his wings, and he coasts in the draft of the raven's flight with ease, as if he's done this a thousand times before. Together they soar over a desert bathed in moonlight, stark and beautiful. *Where are you leading me?* he wonders, but of course the bird doesn't answer. After several minutes of flying they come to a canyon wider than anything Isaac would have imagined possible, and the raven swoops down into it. As Isaac follows, he can see that dwellings have been built into the canyon walls, some housed inside natural crevices, others in neatly excavated arches. So many dwellings! The canyon's entire interior is lined with terraces and walled gardens and staircases and windows and tile-framed doors, as if some vast apartment complex has sprung up organically from the earth. People are present, thousands upon thousands of them, and as Isaac and the raven fly over every type of human activity—celebrations and funerals, lessons and prayers, courting and conflict—the city seems to go on forever.

Finally they leave the great canyon and return to the desert. Now they are approaching the red wave of El Malo, and Isaac feels a tremor of fear. But this time there is no assault on his mind. As they cross the border he can sense the presence of the spirits who guard it, and he suddenly understands that they have no malevolent power of their own, but merely unleash the fears that each man carries within himself.

Now the raven is leading him past El Malo and over Rouelle, approaching a central complex that Isaac realizes must house the local Guilds. His confidence falters, and with it his wingstroke; he doesn't want to have to confront his Guild, even in a vision.

That is your weakness. The raven is speaking to him now, not in words but in the beat of its wings, the rippling of its feathers. *You can't master your Gift until you master yourself.*

Isaac sees Shadowlords wandering through dark halls. Each one is dragging bound figures behind him, dozens of writhing bodies struggling to break free. The chains that shackle them are wrapped around their masters as well, tangling their legs, adding a burden of weight to every step. He sees that as the necromancers perform their bloody rituals they are constantly struggling against that burden, though they are even not aware of it. Their own inhumanity is strangling their power.

Behold your Gift, the raven tells him. *Is this what you hunger to awaken?*

"Not like this," he whispers. "Never like this."

The raven turns its head back to look at him, and once more he feels those piercing eyes take the measure of his soul. Then, without warning, the white wings dissolve into moonlight. The city beneath him crumbles to sand and is swept away by the wind. He is spiraling downward . . .

||||||||||||

The wagon's interior was dark, so it took Isaac a moment to realize he was back there. There was no longer any glowing fabric, and if there were trinkets surrounding his cot, they were now invisible in the darkness. He pushed himself up to a sitting position, his mind still spinning from all that he had seen. Had the vision been no more than a dream produced by his fevered mind, or was there something more to it? He'd spent so much time with Jesse that he no longer took dreaming for granted.

He got to his feet and looked back at the cot. There was no body sleeping there now; Isaac Antonin was whole. Even more than that: he felt strong now, and the cuts and bruises on his body no longer hurt. It was as if he had just awakened from a long, refreshing sleep, in which both his flesh and his spirit had healed.

When he exited the wagon he saw the same canyon he had dreamed about, but this time there was a crescent moon overhead, and an old woman with long grey braids was sitting on a fallen tree trunk near the wagon, inhaling smoke from a clay pipe.

"So you're finally awake," she said.

It took him a moment to find his voice. "Where am I?"

"Somewhere safe. Your friends are over there." She used the pipe to point to an expired campfire a short distance away. Isaac saw that there were two mounds of blankets near it, one of which was snoring gently. Was Jacob here as well? Reaching out with his Gift to find the ghost, he located him nearby. The spirit, too, seemed to have recovered from their traumatic journey.

The old woman was watching him. In the moonlight her eyes glittered like gemstones. "Did you sleep well?"

Isaac wasn't sure how to answer. "I had a strange dream."

"Tell me."

"I saw a vast canyon with a city built into its walls. Is that true? Are there cities here?"

"There are. Though what world they belong to is another question.

You're in a place where that's not always so clear." She sucked on the pipe. "What else?"

"I saw El Malo. It was . . . not malign . . . it just echoed people's fears back at them."

She nodded. "Good."

"But if that's true, how does it explain what we saw? Are you saying that one of us was afraid of blood, or lizards, or hail?"

"A man carries two types of fear inside him," she said. "One is personal, and reflects the life he's lived. One is mythic, and reflects the life his people have lived. Such fears are communal." She reached into a leather pouch by her side and drew out a pinch of fragrant herbs. "What else?"

Isaac hesitated. He didn't want to tell anyone about the Shadows he had seen, least of all a total stranger. "Who are you?"

She held the herbs up to her nose, smelled them, and then added them to the bowl of her pipe. "None of you have earned the right to know my current name, but you can have the one I used when I last walked among the Anglos. Lydia Redwind. Doctor Lydia Redwind, if you prefer formality."

"You're a doctor?"

"I am, but that's not what the title refers to. I have a doctorate in Comparative History from Bonaparte University." She shrugged. "But that was another life. In this life, I rescue bands of weary travelers from the clutches of vengeful spirits and bloodthirsty *azteca*." She gestured toward the wagon. "It's late, necromancer. Go get some blankets and join your friends, so an old woman can reclaim her bed. There'll be time enough for questions in the morning. Though please note, I'm not promising I'll answer all of them."

Isaac hesitated a moment, then did as he was told, ducking back into the wagon to collect two of the blankets from the cot. When he emerged and headed over to the campfire, he saw that Jesse was sleeping on a thick bed of grass, while Sebastian was inside the circle of bare earth that surrounded the fire. Beyond that circle, the plants nearest him had withered, their leaves turning brown and brittle. Isaac wondered if the old woman had noticed.

He made his bed next to Jesse, moving as quietly as he could. The thick grass was surprisingly soft beneath his woolen blanket, and as a cool breeze whispered across his face, he shut his eyes, letting the strange, sweet smell of the old woman's pipe lull him to sleep.

This time there were no dreams.

21

BADLANDS
TERRA PRIME

JESSE

I WOKE TO FIND ISAAC sleeping next to me. Sebastian was nowhere to be seen, but I heard splashing in the distance, so I wasn't too worried. The air was still chill enough that when I threw off my blanket the breeze raised goose bumps on my arms, but after the relentless heat of the day before it was a welcome discomfort. As I got to my feet Isaac opened his eyes.

I asked, "You okay?" Last time I saw him he'd looked close to death.

"I . . . I think so." He seemed disoriented but his color was good, at least what little of it I could see through his sunburn. Even the SPF 50 I'd brought with me apparently wasn't strong enough to protect the son of a Shadowlord from this kind of environment. He reached up and rubbed his eyes, and when his hand came away the piece of latex from his forehead came with it. With all the sweat and physical stress of the day before, his disguise had become a lost cause. We both looked at it for a minute, and no doubt were thinking the same thing. *This doesn't matter now.* We were in a place where no one gave a damn about Guilds, and from what the old woman had said the night before, I suspected that she found Isaac worthy of more respect than all his former undead masters combined. Which meant that he was free here. *Really* free. Not hiding behind makeup, hoping no one would learn his true status, but free from the whole psychological burden. As that realization slowly sank in, his shoulders straightened a bit, and a spark came back into his eyes that I had not seen for some time.

The old woman emerged from her wagon, spared us a minimal glance, and walked over to the expired campfire. "There's a place behind the wagon where you can wash up." She arranged some dry brush on top of the dead ashes, then walked to where some segmented tree limbs had been stacked between two boulders and chose a few large pieces. The size of the stack suggested that people camped here pretty often. "I'll have coffee going by the time you're ready."

Isaac and I looked at each other, then he held out a fist, and I held out a fist, and we did rock-paper-scissors to see who would bathe first. Scissors won, so I grabbed my backpack and headed in the direction indicated, wondering if I should feel guilty that my brother the gaming junkie had schooled me in rock-paper-scissors strategy. Behind the wagon I discovered a natural pool surrounded by large, flat rocks. The water was shockingly cold, but the thought of being able to wash off all the sweat and the grime from the day before was so enticing that I didn't care. It didn't even matter that I was out in the open, with people only a few yards away. I took a moment to rest my little wren feather carefully in its case, then I unpacked my soap, stripped down completely, and immersed myself in the water. I scrubbed my skin till it looked as red as Isaac's, washed my hair until it squeaked beneath my fingers, then rinsed out the clothing I'd worn the day before and laid it on some of the rocks to dry. With fresh clothing, I felt almost human again. The last thing I did was return the feather to my hair. I wasn't sure I needed it any longer, but it felt lucky.

By the time I got back to the campfire Sebastian was there, gathering his long white hair back into its accustomed ponytail. I signaled Isaac to take his turn in the pool and worked on drying my own hair while the old woman finished preparing breakfast: some kind of burrito-like wrap with corn, beans, and peppers in it. I was burning with questions, but asking them while Isaac was absent seemed wrong, so I waited.

'Coffee' turned out to be an espresso-strength brew spiced with chili and cocoa. It definitely helped wake me up. When Isaac came back we finally did a round of introductions. The woman gave Isaac and Sebastian the name she'd used with me, then I gave her both of mine—real and fake—and Isaac offered his first name in a way that made it clear we shouldn't ask about his family name. Sebastian was the only one who offered a traditional introduction, which was ironic, given that most of his contacts never used his real name. Then our hostess surprised us by asking Isaac if he intended to introduce his other companion. Startled for a moment, he nodded and introduced Jacob. I wasn't sure if she could actually sense the wraith's presence, or just assumed he was somewhere around. Or maybe she was playing mind games with us; that was always a possibility.

When those ritual courtesies were concluded I put down my half-eaten burrito and took a deep breath. "You said someone asked you to help us?"

"Someone asked me to help *you*." She looked pointedly at me. "Hence the number of horses the *azteca* brought with them."

So they'd never intended to kill me . . . but they *had* originally intended to kill anyone who was with me. It was a sobering revelation. "Okay, then who wanted you to help *me*?"

Slowly she poured herself more coffee, then sat down again. The leisurely pace was maddening.

"A few miles west of here is a place that locals consider sacred ground. It's what Anglos call a Grand Portal—though that name's a bit misleading, since physical passage through it isn't possible. It's more like a grand shallow: a place where worlds are naturally so close to one another that dreams can easily bridge the gap."

My ears perked up at the mention of dreams. "Go on."

"Holy men visit the site for enlightenment, and young people go there for dream quests. Some seers claim they can see into the future there, which may well be true. When visions reveal to us what has already happened on parallel worlds, they show us where our own choices might lead." She sipped from her coffee. "Needless to say, we do all we can to protect such a precious natural resource."

"Is that what the *azteca* are for?"

"That, and dealing with any Anglos who manage to cross El Malo. Legends of death and madness are all that keep the British Empire from trying to claim this territory. They have to be maintained."

I remembered what she'd said about Isaac the night before—that he might never be allowed to leave here—and the same was probably true for Sebastian. Maybe even for myself. "So who wanted you to help me get here safely?"

"Someone who's appeared in the dreams and visions of many people. A young girl—or perhaps a very feminine boy—who seems to watch over this place. I don't know if she's alive or dead, since she has qualities of both states and never speaks. In most dreams she appears only as a fleeting presence, a ghost glimpsed in the shadows, but some of us who serve as guardians of the portal have interacted with her briefly. There are records of similar contact that go back centuries."

"What does she look like?"

"Young. Slender. Small of frame. Her skin is as red as the darkest sandstone, for which reason some believe she's a spirit of the desert. Her hair is as black as a starless night and hangs down as far as her ankles. Her flesh is without blemish, to the point of seeming unnatural. She wears no human clothing, but she's dressed in a fine golden web whose pattern shifts constantly—"

"That's her!" I had to put my cup down for fear I would spill coffee in my excitement. "I mean, that's not what she looked like when I saw her, but she can look like anything she wants, so that doesn't matter, right? But I've seen those patterns on her. It has to be the same girl who gave me the feather to wear!"

"Given what I was told to watch for, I'm certain it is. Regretfully, I can't tell you much more about her. She seems to be guarding something, but I'm not sure what. Perhaps the shallow itself. A few times she requested that I remove someone from the area whose presence disturbed it."

"I know what she's guarding."

For the first time since our arrival, she looked surprised.

"It's a tower," I said. "I'm not sure whether it's real or dream-bound, but I'm guessing this portal can be used to access it." I looked at my companions. "That's why she helped me get here. So I could find it."

Doctor Redwind nodded thoughtfully. "There are legends of a tower located halfway between the realm of dreams and the realm of the waking. Some have glimpsed it in visions. None know its name or its purpose. I have long thought she had some connection to it."

There were tears coming to my eyes now, but they were tears of joy. After so many days of confusion and doubt and fear—to suddenly have all my theories confirmed like this, and discover that the portal I had travelled across half a continent to find, was only a few miles away . . . it was pretty overwhelming.

"What is there that you need so badly?" she asked me.

"Information." I wiped a hand across my face. "About a number of things but mostly how to destroy some creatures who have been hunting me."

"And all that is in this tower?"

"Oh, God." I drew in a shaky breath. "It had better be. If not, I don't have a clue what to do next."

"Then let's hope for the best." She began to gather up our plates and utensils. "I was asked to bring you to the portal and show you how to access it. After that you must walk this path alone." She glanced at Isaac. "Though anyone who has managed to win over the *azteca* might win over a desert spirit as well. We'll see."

||||||||||||

We rode on horseback to the shallow. The first part of the journey followed the course of the canyon, but after that we were back on flat land, and it became increasingly hot and dry as each mile passed. Several times we dismounted to stretch our legs and water the horses (and ourselves) with supplies we'd brought along; I don't think my legs ever felt as stiff or as sore in my life.

I wanted to be able to sense the shallow as we approached. I wanted it to be the kind of phenomenon that you could apply your normal senses to, a breach in the wall of reality so obvious that you'd have to be an idiot to miss it. But this one wasn't any more obvious than the one I'd visited with Rita in the Blackridge Mountains. Apparently the average human mind couldn't detect a shallow unless that mind was freed from the shackles of everyday sensory expectations, as it was when dreaming.

Jacob was still with us, but Isaac told me that the ghost seemed agitated and was muttering things about how there were too many voices. Isaac had explained on the train that the dead could travel between worlds more easily than the living, so I wondered if Jacob might be hearing voices from other universes. Isaac seemed to be communicating with the ghost more easily now, and his confidence in general seemed improved. He looked more comfortable in his own skin.

We passed by landscape that looked so surreal, I felt as if we were riding through a Dali panting. Huge bowl-shaped depressions in the earth were painted in op-art patterns of swirling stripes, while the twisted pillars that towered over them looked like alien life forms. It was as if God had gotten bored with creating prosaic landscapes and decided to try His hand at abstract art. Eventually we came to a long sandstone ridge whose lower portion had eroded away, leaving an overhang that allowed us to ride in the shade for a while. Thank God. The midday heat was intense, and I would have sold my soul for ten minutes of air conditioning. Finally we came to a cavern that looked manmade, dug deep into the ridge, and Doctor Redwind directed us to dismount and go inside. There was one large room with rows of huge earthenware pots and other supplies stacked against one wall, chairs and a rough-hewn table against another, and folding cots stacked in the rear. While our Redwind hitched the horses to a rail just outside the entrance and poured some water into a narrow trough for them, I sank down stiffly on a small stool, grateful that the riding part of our journey was over. Soon she came in, opened one of the pots and scooped out some kind of loose grain, which she fed to the horses. Apparently this was the Badlands version of a highway pit stop.

When she rejoined us she suggested we eat lunch, so we did. She also suggested we drink a lot of water, so we did that, too. Somewhere in the course of the day we'd become as accustomed to following her orders as the *azteca* were. When our meal was over she directed us to a waste pit hidden in a nearby cleft of the ridge, and I pictured my mother giving me instructions before a field trip: *Go now, because you may not have a chance later.* So we did that, too, one after the other, shoveling gravel over our waste when we were done.

Then she said, "It's time." And to me: "Are you ready?"

How can a person possibly be ready for something like this? I thought. But I nodded.

She fetched a heavy bag from behind the pots and began to hoist it to her shoulder, but Sebastian approached to take it from her. She looked at him for a moment, then nodded and let him carry it. Then we left the cavern on foot, hiking into a land that was flatter and less colorful than the last stretch. Still I felt no tingling in my psyche, and I wondered if that should worry me. We were approaching the heart of one of the most powerful portals on the planet; shouldn't I feel *something?*

Eventually we came to a small structure, a sand-colored canopy stretched over a wooden frame, with thick wooden posts supporting the corners. A circular area beneath its center had been paved in stone the same color as the earth, with four large pottery bowls spaced evenly around its edge. Nothing else was within sight. As we passed by one of the support poles I saw that it was carved with stylized images, faces and animals and small abstract patterns. Some of the designs were highlighted with paint—red was on the pole nearest us, with yellow, white, and black on the others—and judging from the brightness of the colors, they must have been touched up recently. Isaac put a finger to one of the carvings as we passed, and I saw him shudder slightly, as if they stirred some unpleasant memory.

"I can open the canopy if you would rather expose yourself to the sun," Doctor Redwind offered. "Some like to test their flesh when they seek visions."

"No," I said quickly. "I'm good with my flesh being untested. Thanks, though."

She chuckled.

I walked to the paved circle and, after a moment's hesitation, stepped up onto it. The surface was perfectly smooth and as feature-less as the desert that surrounded us. I felt oddly disappointed. I wanted his place to be . . . I don't know . . . *more*.

Doctor Redwind took some bundles of dried herbs out of her bag. "This is the center of the shallow. But if you don't like this setting we can go somewhere else. You don't have to be in any one exact spot."

"This is fine," I said. The faces carved into the tent poles were all facing in, making me feel like I was being watched. But whatever spe-cial magic or atmosphere they were meant to invoke was part of what I had come here to find. "Just tell me what I need to do."

She nodded and began to place her herbs in the pottery bowls. It seemed to matter which herbs went where. "Did she show you the path to the tower?"

I hesitated. "She showed me a design. The wren feather—" Sud-denly something occurred to me. I looked down at my feet. "It was in the center of the pattern." I raised a hand to touch the feather in my hair. *As it is right now.* An eerie sense of significance came over me. I felt like a priestess preparing for some grand religious ritual. Or per-haps a sacrifice. Hand shaking slightly, I reached into my back pocket and dug out the drawing I had made back home. "I sketched this right after I woke up. I know some of the pattern's not right, though. And it's missing a lot of detail."

"A two dimensional drawing can never be more than a flawed re-flection anyway." She took it from me and looked at it, then passed it to the others. "It's a start. Either your Gift will fill in the rest, or . . ." she hesitated, then shrugged, "We'll get back home before dark."

A tightness lodged in the pit my stomach. To come all this way and then fail to find the tower would be devastating. "It will."

Isaac looked at the drawing. "This looks like the patterns that the Shadows use to control their Gates. We call them codexes."

"Those, too, are flawed reflections. The difference is that your Shadows don't have the Gift needed to perfect them, hence the dance of bodies you must perform to use them safely."

"They're not my Shadows," Isaac said sharply.

She looked at him for a minute before responding. "No. They're not. My apologies."

Sebastian took the drawing. "Are you saying that if one had a perfect codex, no exchange of living matter would be required?"

She removed a large pouch from her bag of supplies and placed it on the floor beside me. "Why does a spider not stick to its own web?"

There was a moment of silence as we all digested the sudden non-sequitur.

"It knows how to walk properly," Sebastian said at last. "And its feet are designed for the task."

"Not all the strands are sticky," I offered. "Isn't that right? I remember that from science class. The spider knows which ones it can walk on safely."

"Very good," Dr. Redwind approved. "Now tell me: What happens if a fly stumbles into the web?"

"It gets stuck," Isaac answered.

"Why?"

"For all the reasons we just said. It doesn't know what parts are safe, or how to walk on them. And nature didn't equip it to do that."

"Good. So it's stuck now. What happens?"

I felt oddly as if I was back in biology class. "It panics. It beats its wings in an attempt to get free, and that gets it stuck even worse."

Sebastian said very quietly, "It knows where it needs to go, but it has no idea how to get there safely."

A slight smile appeared. "And what happens because of that?"

"The web is broken." There was a haunted quality to his voice. "Its strength is compromised." He paused. "It must be repaired before it can serve his purpose."

She nodded as she started unloading objects from her bag, arranging them by my side. Three large leather pouches. A machete-like knife. "All the worlds that exist are bound together by a network as fine and as intricate as spider's web. All living things are a part of it." She opened the pouches, revealing a different color of sand in each one. "The Shadows are like flies, blundering into that web. They glimpse a bit of its overall pattern and they think that's enough to guide them, but they don't understand the true nature of the journey. They try to balance the stress of their passage by adding counter-weights, and to some degree that works. But no matter what they add, the web still gets damaged."

Isaac blinked. "Are you . . . are you saying . . . the only reason the Shadows have to balance crossings the way they do, sending people in both directions, is because they don't have the information they need to map the trip properly?"

She said it quietly: "Their Gift doesn't allow them to see the web. That can only be done in dreams, and the dead don't dream."

What about Sebastian? I thought suddenly. *If he obtained a perfect codex, could he go home safely?* From the look on his face, I guessed that he was thinking the same thing. His hand trembled slightly as he handed my drawing back to me. How small and insufficient it seemed, now. So much of it was missing, and what little information it contained was imperfect.

"It's a starting point," she said gently, responding to me as if I had spoken aloud. "And you're not trying to go anywhere in body, so the task isn't nearly as complicated as it is for them."

To my surprise, she reached into a pocket of her skirt and took out a small gun, which she put down beside the machete. Startled, I asked, "What's that for?"

"Protection from those who might follow you into the dream

world. Because returning from this journey might not be as easy as just waking up." She looked up at me. "It's not a perfect defense, but better than trying to fight them off with your hands. They attacked you physically in the past, so you know they have substance."

It took me a moment to find my voice. "I thought—I mean, I'm not going anywhere in body, right? I can't take a gun with me."

"You will exist in two worlds at once. Anything which is real in this world will be easier to create in the other. So copy these when you get there." She looked up at me. "Do you know how to use this?"

I swallowed and nodded, thanking God in my heart for the lessons Uncle Julian gave me. Though this promised to be a bit more harrowing than shooting soda cans off a fence.

The last thing the old woman unpacked was a set of three rods with metal bands at the ends, which she screwed together into one long rod. At the end was a pointed blade of black glass. This was all becoming frighteningly real.

"Are we allowed to go with her?" Isaac asked.

She raised an eyebrow as she looked at him. "What makes you think you would be able to?"

"She can come into our dreams. Or maybe bring us into hers, I don't know. But we've done it together." He looked at me. "Can you take us with you?"

I hesitated, then looked at Dr. Redwind, a question in my eyes. She shrugged. "Who knows? There is no handbook for this kind of thing. You can certainly try."

I looked at Sebastian; there were conflicting emotions in his eyes. "It's not safe for you," I said softly.

"It's not *safe* for any of you," Dr. Redwind pointed out. "But since your bodies won't actually be leaving this world, Mr. Hayes' issue shouldn't be a problem." She looked at Sebastian. "Yes, I saw the plants die around you."

I saw a faint flush of shame rise to his cheeks.

"Now sit," she ordered, pointing to the edge of the circle. "All three of you, if that's what you want."

I lowered myself to the ground. Isaac and Sebastian followed suit, one on each side of me. Dr. Redwind set fire to the herb bundles in each of the four bowls, her lips moving slightly as the herbs subsided to smoldering embers. She made no sound, so I couldn't tell what she was saying. Scented smoke filled the air beneath the canopy, with a different smell coming from each direction. Musky, spicy, floral, woodsy. When all the herb bundles were smoldering, she came back to where we were sitting and set the bags of sand in front of me. "This will help you focus," she said. "Reproduce the pattern you saw as well as you can."

I nodded.

As she stepped back I shifted position, so that I was kneeling. I put the drawing down where I could see it, then reached into the nearest pouch; blue-grey sand as fine as talc slipped between my fingers. A tremor of fear ran through me—or was it excitement? I looked up at her. "Do you want to come with us?"

"Someone needs to watch over your bodies," she said quietly. "Though bear in mind, I will have no power to call you back from this journey. If anything goes wrong, you have to deal with it on your own."

I nodded. Then, my hand trembling only slightly, I scooped up a bit of sand from the nearest pouch. I held it out the way the avatar had done, testing the texture of the sand between my fingertips, then let it trickle down to the ground in a thin stream. There was no magical glow this time, but it seemed that as each grain settled into position I could feel it connecting to all the others, and even to grains of sand that I couldn't see, that were somehow part of my pattern as well. Echoes in other worlds, perhaps. I reached for some more sand, hesitated, then took some from another pouch, whose contents were the color of pale coral. More lines. More connections. I didn't have to look at the sketch anymore; memory of the pattern was coming back to me, and I felt my hand mirroring the gestures the avatar girl had made, each grain of sand cascading down into exactly the same position she had placed it in. The lines were melodies, and as I drew more and more of them, adding in fine details I didn't even consciously remember, the air surrounding me became filled with music. Sound blended with the scent of herbs and the caress of desert heat on my face, and each note was perfect, each sensation exquisite. I reached for a handful of golden sand and began to lay down a new layer over the old, making my design three dimensional. To the others present it probably seemed I was muddying my pattern, but in my mind's eye all the layers were distinct, and I could rotate the whole construction in my mind as I willed, adding details wherever they were needed.

I wrapped the music around my companions, drawing them into my pattern, sharing my vision with them. The black plain opened up to us and my sand painting began to blaze with shimmering light, while the universe filled with music, every note of it in perfect balance. Somewhere in the distance my hand was still moving, spilling sand onto the desert floor, but I no longer needed that vehicle. My soul was the sand, my will was the desert, the blood running through my veins was the music—

I'm standing in a small circular clearing in the middle of a field of waist-high grass. Not green grass, like back home, but red as sandstone at its tips, deep crimson in its shadows. Isaac and Sebastian are both beside me, and they seem disoriented. They're not used to this dream stuff like I am. Overhead I see a swollen red sun hanging in a sickly yellow sky, and my heart skips a beat as I recognize it. *We're here. We made it.* We are no longer in the waking world, nor in the dreaming world, but somewhere in between, a special realm that the Dreamwalkers once called home. As I watch, the sky changes colors, the sun shifting to orange, and then to yellow, the sky shifting to green, then blue. Now we're standing beneath a sun and a sky that look like Terra Colonna's. This landscape is responding to me.

So far so good.

Focusing my attention on the ground, I create a trio of weapons to match those Dr. Redwind gave us. They're much

easier to bring into existence than expected, and I give silent thanks for her wisdom as I pick up the revolver. I check to make sure it's loaded, then create a holster for it. The last task requires more effort than creating the gun itself, a testament to her theory about copying items from the real world. Isaac picks up the machete, while Sebastian takes the spear, holding it in front of him as I imagine he once held his bayonetted musket. His obvious readiness to use it makes me feel a bit more secure.

With all the high grass around I figure we'll probably lose sight of our arrival point as soon as we start moving, so I create a flagpole with a white banner on top to serve as a landmark. Then, for the first time, I take a good look around. To the north and the west of us, judging direction from the sun, the field of red grass seems to go on forever. To the south there is some kind of tall black hedge extending as far as the eye can see. To the west I see a long, low hill, and I have an odd feeling of déjà vu. Suddenly I realize why it seems so familiar: it's the same length and proportion as the ridge we rode past in the Badlands . . . and also the hill the avatar girl ran to when I was chasing her. I know where I am!

If I'm right, the changing tower should be right behind that ridge.

I head in that direction, gesturing for the others to join me. The tall grass makes it hard to move quickly, so I concentrate and flatten a narrow strip to serve us as a road. Then I start running. I'm so close to my goal that impatience burns in my veins, but though I keep looking at the hill in hopes of seeing the tower's summit peeking over it, nothing is visible yet. *Soon*, I promise myself. *Soon.*

Suddenly something huge and black bursts out from the grass to my right and barrels straight into me. I'm slammed onto my back with stunning force, and when a massive jaw filled with razor-sharp teeth tries to snap shut like a bear trap on my head, I barely manage to twist out of the way in time. Whatever is trying to bite my head off is immense, and I'm pinned beneath its weight, barely able to breathe. Even as the creature lunges for my neck I feel something stab into my left arm, and all I can do it bring up my other arm to try to protect myself.

Then the massive weight shifts to the left momentarily, and I am able to draw a full breath. I struggle to pull myself out from under the beast, desperate to get free before it pins me down again, but it's thrashing in rage and snapping at something I can't see, making escape almost impossible. Finally I manage to get my body free, and I crawl away on my elbows like a soldier trying to stay below the field of fire, trying to get out of range of its massive jaws before it turns its attention back to me. Now I can see the reason it pulled back from me: Sebastian has speared it and is using the long weapon to hold it away from me as I make my escape. The animal is thrashing with such force that the ground shakes beneath me, but Sebastian leans into the spear with all his weight, pinning it to the ground. "Get behind me!" he yells. I somehow manage to get to my feet and sprint to where he's standing. Gasping for breath, I turn to see what attacked me.

It's a dog, only ten times larger than any natural dog, with fur as black as pitch and three massive heads. Sebastian has run his spear through its shoulder and into its upper chest, but he must have missed its vital organs, because the beast is still going strong. I see one of its heads turn toward the spear and I realize it's going to try to bite through the shaft. If those massive jaws split the wood, Sebastian will have no way to keep it from charging us.

But I do.

I pull out my revolver and aim it at the beast, gripping it in both hands like Uncle Julian taught me. But where am I supposed to shoot it? A shot to one of its heads is unlikely to stop it. But then its jaws close around the spear and there's no more time to strategize. I fire at that head, close to point blank range, the recoil nearly jerking the gun out of my hand. Blood splatters everywhere, but though the head jerks back the creature keeps on struggling. I shoot again and again, trying to hit the heart this time, or at least the place where I think its heart should be. One shot misses completely. Another barely grazes a leg. Then my fourth shot pierces its torso, and the beast howls in fury. I move back while it convulses, black blood pouring out of its chest, while Sebastian strains to hold it in place. The spear is beginning to bend from the stress, and I hold my breath, knowing that it if breaks we will all be in serious trouble. But the shaft holds, and after what seemed like an eternity the creature's movements finally begin to slow. The head that I shot is hanging limply, and it swings like a pendulum as the beast thrashes desperately, its other two heads still howling. Blood is pooling beneath the massive body, and its struggles are growing weaker by the moment. Then all movement ceases. The only sound left is ringing in my ears from the gunshots.

"Shit," I gasp. The ringing is so bad I can barely hear myself speak. "What *was* that thing?"

Sebastian tries to pull his spear out, but it's stuck in the beast. He walks up to the creature and puts a foot on its shoulder for leverage, to work the weapon free. "Cerberus, I think. Or something that looks a lot like it. Guardian of the underworld."

My left arm is throbbing. I look down and see a circle of puncture wounds with blood oozing from several of them. One of the heads must have bitten me. "What the hell is a Greek myth doing here?"

"This place created it," Isaac says. "It's pulling images from our minds and giving them life. El Malo works the same way."

"Great," I mutter. *Since when do you know so much about*

how El Malo works? "Just great." I concentrate on my punctures, trying to close them, but whatever power allowed me to create our weapons evidently won't allow me to heal my own wounds. So I create an antibiotic ointment and gauze to protect the wound, hoping that there isn't some mythical Greek bacteria inside me, that will resist modern treatment. Beyond that, I don't know what to do.

We start to move again, more cautiously this time, weapons at the ready. The slightest rustling in the grass makes me flinch, and I keep scanning the surrounding terrain for new threats. The black hedge running parallel to our path looks larger than before. Or is it my imagination? I stop for a moment to study it, and yes, it has definitely gotten larger, and it's also closer to us, enough so that I can see the black vines sprouting from it. Each one is studded with thorns as long as my hand, and they're moving in our direction. Some of them are snaking down into the depths of the grass, where they can't be seen. The whole field could be full of them by now.

We start to run, and I pray that we can reach the hill before the vines catch up with us. But we aren't fast enough. A vine whips out of the grass and wraps itself around Sebastian's ankle, sending him sprawling. Isaac rushes in and hacks off the end of it with his machete, and thank God, the whole thing stops moving. We help Sebastian to his feet and start running again, but he's limping now, and the end of the vine is trailing behind him. Another one appears, but this time Isaac is ready for it, and his response is swift and sure. Even as that one is severed, another comes. They're showing up so fast now that Isaac can barely keep up with them, but somehow we keep going. We literally have no other option.

Then the grass beneath my feet gives way to gravel, and I'm no longer on flat ground, but stumbling up a slope. We've reached the ridge! As I work my way uphill I glance behind me to make sure my companions are still with me. They are, and the vines seemed to have stopped at the foot of the slope. Elated, I turn my attention to climbing. Only a few yards more and I'll be at the spot where I stood in my earlier dream, gazing at the Dreamwalker tower for the first time. I feel the kind of dizzying elation that Edmund Hillary must surely have experienced when he approached the summit of Mount Everest. So much hope and fear have been invested in this journey! By the time I reach the top I'm breathless, and I straighten up to take my first look at the magical place I have come so far to find—

—and for a moment I can't even process what I'm looking at. My mind refuses to accept it.

The other two come up beside me, but I'm barely aware of them. All I can see is the scene spread out before me, more devastating than I could have imagined possible. Hope drains from my soul like blood from a mortal wound. *No. Please, God. No. Don't let it be like this.* I fall to my knees, and tears come to my eyes. I don't want to look at what's in front of me, but I can't bring myself to turn away.

Past the hill is a dry lake bed, riddled with cracks and littered with the aged skeletons of tiny fish. In its center is the same black mountain I saw in my dream, the place the avatar ran to for safety. And atop that is rubble. Just rubble. Endless mounds of rubble. Shattered bricks piled high in some places, cascading down the black slope in others. The only thing that is half intact is the broken skeleton of a tower, fire-blackened and hollow. There's nothing else left.

The Dreamwalker tower is gone.

22

THE TOWER

JESSE

THE UNIVERSE IS A BLACK SEA of hopelessness and I am drowning in it, with no land in sight.

"Jessica . . ."

The Dreamwalker tower is gone. What should I anchor my hopes to now? What quest or location can save me? I've exhausted all my options.

"We can't stay here," Isaac says.

"He's right." Sebastian's tone is gentle but firm. "We can go forward or back, whichever you want, but we can't stay here. Eventually the reapers will find us."

"What's the point?" I whisper. "They'll get me no matter where I go. It's just a question of when."

He takes my face in his hands, forcing me to look at him. "The *point* is that you can't give in to despair, because when you do that the battle is over and your enemies win. Is that what you want, Jessica? To let your enemies win?"

How much pain there is behind his words! This is a man who lost everything he once lived for, and still he survives.

Banished from his home world, displaced in time, trapped in a universe where the very plant life despises him, he has every reason to give up hope. And yet he's still here. Long after other men would have surrendered to despair, he's still here. Surely, if he can find the strength to keep fighting, so can I.

"No," I whisper weakly. "I don't want them to win."

"All right then." He releases my face. "Now, we have two choices. We can try to find a way to get home that doesn't involve immediate impalement, or we can go explore those ruins. Maybe you'll find something there that will point you to a new path. Or show you a way to deal with this one. I don't know. But we won't know the possibilities if we don't even look."

I glance back the way we came and see that the black vines have taken root at the base of the ridge. A new hedge is in the process of creation, and it's already taller than I am. Even if we wanted to retrace our steps, we couldn't. *It's as if it's herding us.* Deep in my heart I know that Sebastian's right; I've travelled across half a continent and braved the nightmare of El Malo to search for answers here, and I owe it to myself not to give up prematurely. "Okay." I nod toward the black mountain. "Ruins it is." After a moment I add softly, "Thanks."

While Isaac helps me to my feet, Sebastian reaches down to remove the vine that's wrapped around his ankle. One of the thorns has penetrated his boot, and when he pulls it out I see a dark red stain spreading on the leather. "Sebastian—"

"It's not deep," he says quickly. "When we're in a more sheltered place I'll tend to it."

I look up at the sky. It's still brightly colored, but any moment that could change. Is there any shelter here that would be meaningful if a reaper appeared? We came prepared to fight one if we had to, but that doesn't mean we'd win.

One thing at a time, Jesse. Stay focused.

We work our way carefully down the rocky slope, sometimes walking, sometimes sliding. Sebastian is having a hard time of it, and he uses the spear as a hiking staff to keep his balance. It's clear his ankle hurts, but he doesn't complain or ask us to slow down. Once we get to the bottom of the ridge, walking becomes easier, and soon we're hiking along the dried lake bed, slabs of mud interlocked like paving stones beneath our feet. I try to energize my spirit by imagining the freezing cold water that was here last time I came this way, picturing it sloshing over my feet as I walk. It helps a bit.

When we get to the black mountain we look for a good route of ascent, but there really isn't one, so we begin to climb. The damn thing is obsidian, so the going is anything but easy; more than once I slip on the smooth volcanic glass and nearly lose my footing. Is this how the avatar girl intended to reach the tower, when she was fleeing from the reaper? I doubt it. Probably there are stairs somewhere that we don't know about. Or maybe she had enough control over her dream to create some. I'm wary of straining my Gift by making so many alterations, but maybe I can try to make things a little easier for us. I create some shallow horizontal ridges on the slope, so we have something to brace our feet against. It helps us climb, but the effort leaves me dizzy and breathless.

Soon we see scattered bricks and have to pick our way around mounds of shattered stone. Who was responsible for all this destruction? I'm acutely aware of how little I know about the history of my kind, other than vague stories from Morgana that might or might not be true. Finally we reach the top, and I bend over for a moment to catch my breath, then look up at the part of the tower that's still standing. It seems much taller now, and the illusion of long black streaks on its surface gives it a doubly ominous aspect. From this close I can see that the face of the brickwork has actually been scoured clean by the elements, but the soot embedded in a thousand tiny pits and crevices gives it the illusion of recent scorching. Whatever fire left those marks burned out a long time ago.

"Do you think it really changed shape?" Isaac asks. "Before it was destroyed, I mean."

I put a hand on the wall of the tower, but it feels like you would expect stone to feel: gritty, solid, slightly cool to the touch. Then again, what is a shape-changing tower supposed to feel like? "I don't know. Maybe each dreamer sees it differently. In the avatar's dream it was still intact."

I step over some rubble to go through the main doorway. Rusted hinges scrape my shoulder, their wooden doors long gone. The interior is cooler and surprisingly free of stone debris; whatever force destroyed this place must have exploded from within, blowing most of the bricks away. There are mounds of blackened wood everywhere, from where walls and ceilings collapsed and burned. When I step on a broken plank the outer husk of charcoal breaks away to reveal an interior riddled with insect tunnels. Even in this place of death, life persists.

Looking upward, I have a clear view of the sky. It's still blue.

"No ghosts here." Isaac comes up beside me.

"Is that a problem?"

"It's surprising. A place that suffers this kind of destruction usually produces at least a few soul shards. It's hard to imagine all this happened without someone dying."

"Maybe the place was empty when it happened." I look at him. "Is Jacob with us?"

He shakes his head. "Didn't expect him to be. You aren't able to sense his presence, so how could you transport him?" He pauses. "I do admit, it feels odd not to have him here. Strange how you can get used to someone's presence in so little time." He looks around the devastated space. "Not much left, is there?"

I whisper it: "No."

"I'm guessing Shadows were responsible for this. I don't

know how, since our Gift doesn't give us the ability to manipulate dreams, but I remember reading in our archives that at the end of the Dream Wars a small band of Shadowlords followed the Dreamwalkers to their home base and destroyed it. This place seems to fit the bill."

I raise an eyebrow. "*Our* archives?"

He blushes. "Sorry. Force of habit."

I look around and sigh. All I see is centuries of accumulated rubble and decay. If there are clues here I'm missing them. "Whoever did this is long dead."

"That doesn't mean much among the Shadows. They Commune with the souls of their ancestors, remember? Whoever ordered this strike may still be walking the Earth, albeit in a new body."

"Jessica! Isaac!" Sebastian waves to us. "Over here!"

We pick our way over to where he's standing, next to a knee-high brick wall. Something of structural significance must have been here. "Take a look," he says, and he points to the ground by his feet. Or rather, to the lack of ground.

Stairs.

They go down quite a distance, following the shape of the tower as they curve to the left, but the bottom is lost in darkness, so there's no way to tell where they lead. I feel a flutter of excitement as I gaze down at them, even a spark of hope. Maybe whatever is underground escaped the explosion that destroyed the upper portion of the tower. If so, I might find answers there.

"We'll need light," Isaac says.

I create three flashlights and hand one to each of them, trying not to let them see how much that small effort weakens me; I'm reaching the end of my dreamwalking strength. I turn mine on and lead the way downstairs. It's good that there's a stone wall on one side of the staircase, because I need it to steady myself. *This Gift has its limits*, I remind myself as I focus on descending safely. The last time I tested those limits I got violently ill, and I can't afford for that to happen here.

The curving staircase leads us down into a vast circular chamber, but we have to keep our flashlights focused on the stairs as we descend, so not until I finally step onto the chamber's floor am I able to swing my light wide, sweeping from one side of the chamber to the other, trying to get a sense of the room's overall purpose. When I do, I am so stunned I nearly drop the flashlight. "Holy shit," I whisper.

There are shelves. On every wall. Shelves filled with books. This place is a *library*.

Trembling with excitement, I walked to the nearest set of shelves. Could this be the archive where the collected knowledge of the Dreamwalkers is stored? The shelves are black, all black, set far back into the stone wall, with rows of black books lined up neatly along each one. I hunger to touch the books, but I'm also afraid to, as if contact with human flesh might reveal that this whole room and everything in it are illusions. I have so much hope invested in this place . . .

Sebastian and Isaac come up beside me, and they add their light to my own so that we can take a better look at the books. They're all different sizes and shapes, some stacked vertically and some piled horizontally, all neatly arranged. There's no print on any of them, just identical black bindings in some kind of matte finish. Finally, still wary, I reach out to take one of the smaller books from the shelf.

It crumbles in my hand.

Startled, I stare at the pile of ash and charcoal in my palm, then turn my hand over to dump the debris on the floor. I try to remove a different book from a different shelf, but it, too, disintegrates as soon as I touch it. Shaken, I start to go around the room, peering at each shelf in turn but not touching anything, shining my flashlight into every nook and cranny. I'm desperately searching for something that looks like a readable book. I don't even care what's in it; I need confirmation that something here hasn't been reduced to ash. But all the books I look at are charred inside and out, so thoroughly that not a single page remains readable. All is black.

The truth of the situation is slowly sinking in, and as it does, the last precious bit of hope I've been clinging to fades within me.

"This wasn't a natural fire," Sebastian says, shining his flashlight between two stacks of books. "The destruction's too perfect. None of the covers are even warped. And every page is perfectly blackened, even in the center of the thickest volumes. Real fires don't work like that."

"You're thinking a pyromancer did this?" Isaac asks.

"Or someone with a pyromantic fetter. Either way, the fire was clearly set for the express purpose of destroying the library's contents." He looks at me and says softly, "I'm sorry, Jessica."

"It was all here," I mutter hoarsely. "All the knowledge of the Dreamwalkers. That's what this place must have been for. Rituals, history, maybe even catalogs of codexes, all stored in a secret library halfway between the waking and dreaming worlds, so that only a Dreamwalker could access it. It should have been safe." I gaze out at the endless rows of literary corpses. "Someone must have figured out another way to get here."

"Or maybe a Dreamwalker betrayed his own people," Isaac says quietly. I glare at him so fiercely he puts up his hands as if to guard himself from a blow. "I'm sorry, but if only a Dreamwalker can come here, that means that either one of them brought an enemy with him, or provided an enemy with the knowledge he needed to come here on his own. Either way . . ." He spreads his hands.

It's all overwhelming. I lower my head and rub my forehead, as if that could banish the pain of this discovery. Surely there must be something left here, some fragment of knowledge that can be salvaged! But even if there is, how are we supposed to find it? I look around the immense room, and I feel the sharp bite of despair once more. It would take weeks to inspect every volume here. Our physical bodies would die of thirst long before the job was finished. There must be another way.

Suddenly I realize what it is. I push myself away from the wall and walk over to Sebastian. "Spear, please?" I hold out my hand. He looks curious but gives the weapon to me.

I walk to the nearest bookcase, study it for a moment, then swing the spear at a row of books with all my might, back end first. The wooden shaft breaks through the charred volumes with little resistance, scattering ash and charcoal chips everywhere. When the dust settles there's nothing's left.

"Jesse?"

I can tell from Isaac's tone that my actions have alarmed him. Maybe he thinks the stress of this journey has finally proven too much for me, and I've snapped. But when I look back at Sebastian, he stares at me for a moment, then nods his approval. He's figured out what I'm doing.

I assault another row of books. And another. The fragile volumes disintegrate as soon as I hit them, filling the air with black snow. Even the shelves themselves, thick enough to have remained intact for centuries, give way before my assault, leaving only dust behind. Sebastian and Isaac are joining in now, and soon there's so much ash in the air that it's getting hard to breathe. If any portion of a book didn't burn completely, this course of action will reveal it. Of course, there's also a chance we'll damage any extant pages by this method, but that can't be helped. I can't leave this place until I've verified that no information survived the fire.

I'm starting on my fourth bookcase when Isaac calls from behind me, "Jesse!"

I turn and see him pointing to a shelf near the floor. With so much ash piled on top of everything it's hard to make out what he's pointing at, but as I swing my flashlight that way I see a glint of a reflection. Definitely not charcoal. I head across the room as quickly as I can in the near-darkness, tripping over the skeleton of a half-collapsed table. Like the books, it falls to pieces as soon as I touch it.

By the time I get to where Isaac is, he has pulled out the object in question—or, more accurately, the objects. There are ten in all, sheets of blank metal with holes running down one side.

"They were inside one of the books," Isaac says. "Totally invisible until I broke through the cover."

"The holes suggest they were bound together," Sebastian says as he joins us. He takes one of the metal sheets from me and studies it in the beam of his flashlight. "The cover is what burned."

"Which may be what saved them," I point out. "Whoever destroyed this place probably thought he got everything in it." I turn one of the sheets over in my hand. "But why metal? That's an odd material for a book."

"Well, it did survive the fire," Isaac says. "Maybe someone anticipated that."

"But there's nothing on them."

"Maybe someone planned to write on them later?"

Sebastian offers: "Maybe there's writing on it that we can't see."

His words prod something in my memory, but I can't pin it down. As I run my hand over the smooth metal surface I have a strange sense of déjà vu. Why do I have the sense that I've seen something like this before? Then I remember.

"They're fetters," I murmur. My fingers can still recall the feel of the metal plates in the Weaver's camp. Those had been blank sheets of metal just like this, with nothing on them but identification codes. Metal must be the Weavers' material of choice for binding Gifts.

I rest the plates in the crook of my left arm so that I can place my right hand flat on top of them, but Sebastian grasps my arm before I can make contact, stopping me. "Upstairs," he says. "In the light, with clean air, where we can see anything that comes at us."

"I don't think reapers will attack us here—or they would have done so already, don't you think?"

But he's right; this dark, dusty hole isn't a good place to be experimenting with unknown powers. I hold the fetters close to my chest as the three of us head back up the stairs.

The sun is dropping low in the west when we emerge, which means that we spent way more time in the library than I'd thought. Our real bodies are still in the desert, I remind myself, unable to drink or eat until we return. We need to go back soon, regardless of what we find here.

I settle myself on the ground with my back to a partially collapsed wall. Sebastian and Isaac remain standing, poised to move quickly if they have to. "You know this could be a trap," Isaac warns. "Maybe these were left behind after the tower was blown up, to take care of any survivors."

I nod. "I know."

I lay the ten metals sheets out in front of me, hesitate for a moment, then place my palm on the first one. I concentrate on my Gift like I did in the Weaver camp, trying to trigger whatever Dreamwalker essence might be attached to the thing. If it works like the Weaver fetter, only a Dreamwalker will be able to activate it. What more perfect communication method could there be for creating a book you don't want outsiders to read?

For a moment nothing happens. Then, suddenly, sounds fill my head. *Wood burning. Bricks falling. People screaming.* The noise is discordant, overwhelming. Reflexively, I start to remove my hand from the fetter to cover my ears, then force myself to hold my position.

I see the library again, this time not filled with ash and

rubble but with books. There are hexagonal crystals set in the ceiling that channel light down into the chamber, illuminating a table of polished ebony at its center. A woman stands before the table, turning the pages of a large book. Metal pages. These pages. She closes the book and walks to one of the bookshelves, where she tucks the volume in among the regular books. Her intent is clear: no one looking at that spot will see anything unusual.

We will all die soon. Her words fill my mind without her speaking them aloud. *Our name will die with us. We leave behind the knowledge of what has happened here. Forgive us that we do not have time to prepare more.*

The vision fades. I sit there in silence for a moment, trying to absorb what I have just seen. Isaac opens his mouth to speak but I wave him off. Then I turn the page, brace myself, and activate the next fetter.

I see a tower whose shape reflects the mind of each observer, whose windows look out upon a thousand worlds. I know that from within that tower I can touch all possible worlds and draw sleeping minds to me. This is a place where dreams intermingle, the realm that Dreamwalkers call home.

I see spirits of the dead assaulting the tower, and I know that shouldn't be possible. Ghosts can't enter the dreams of the living. How did they get here?

I see Dreamwalkers seeding the land around the tower with nightmares to defend against invasion. Among the mythical horrors they conjure I see a three headed dog, and I understand now that the creatures that attacked us were the last remnants of that fearsome strategy.

I see those monsters destroyed by faceless shadows. I see dreamers fall in battle, torn to pieces by ghosts. I see other Dreamwalkers captured and bound, then sacrificed in bloody rituals so that Shadowlords can claim their Gift. I hear dreamers scream as their talent is stripped from them, and they keep screaming long after they are dead, bound forever to their tormentors.

Now the enemy can see our designs. The mournful words are in the same voice as before. *Now they can hear our music.*

I see twelve Dreamwalkers brought to a man in brocade robes, who drinks their blood and claims their souls. I watch as he shatters their spirits, molding them into the perfect predators. He calls them *ruuh bal*, but I recognize the creatures I know as reapers. And I hear their cries of anguish as they are forced to kill their own kind, a sound so full of hatred and pain that the universe itself must surely weep in sympathy.

I see five of them die the true death in battle. I witness the ritual that is used to destroy them.

Then silence.

I am sitting with my hand upon a fetter, my face wet with tears, my breath coming in gasps. My mind still resonates with the pain of all those lost souls. I look down and realize it's the last fetter I'm touching; I must have turned the pages without realizing it. Sebastian and Isaac are watching me with obvious concern, and I can only imagine how much they must have wanted to pull the fetters away and summon me back from whatever vision was tormenting me. I'm pleased that they had enough faith in my strength to wait.

I look up at them slowly. "They're Dreamwalkers," I whisper.

Isaac's eyes narrow. "What do you mean?"

"The reapers. They're Dreamwalkers. Or they *were* Dreamwalkers." I lift an unsteady hand to wipe the wetness from my face. "That's why they can hunt people in dreams. Normal ghosts don't have that power. Shadows don't have that power. But Dreamwalkers do."

"Good God . . ." Sebastian mutters.

I wrap my arms around myself, shivering. "I've seen how to

destroy them. But how can I do that? They're just like me. Victims of the Shadows."

"But they'll *kill* you," Isaac says sharply. "It's what they were made for. They have no choice about it."

"I know," I whisper, lowering my head. "I know. It's kill-or-be-killed now . . . but what happens when you can't bring yourself to kill? Does that mean you have to die? There must be some other way. . . ." My words trail off into helpless silence.

"Come." Sebastian reaches out and takes the fetters from my hand, laying them aside. "You have what you came for. Let's go home. We can talk about this more in a safe place."

Soul numb, I nod. The whole world seems distant to me now, like a movie I'm watching, instead of something I'm part of. I look down at the fetters. "I can't bring these back with me."

"I'll put them back," Isaac says. He gathers them up and starts toward the staircase.

"Hide them," I call after him. "Under the ash." *So that enemies coming to this place won't find them*, I think. But does that really matter anymore?

I wonder where the avatar is. I wonder if she's watching us.

When Isaac returns I gesture for him and Sebastian to sit by my side like they did in the desert. I don't really have a clue if that's necessary, but since Dr. Redwind talked about how it would be easier to manipulate things in one world if they matched what was in the other, it seems a logical thing to try. We lay out the weapons on the floor in the same configuration as the ones that are lying next to our bodies, back in the desert, and I take their hands just to make sure they stay connected to me. Then I try to wake myself up.

Nothing happens.

A wave of exhaustion washes over me. I barely have enough energy left to think clearly, much less manipulate dreams. If I have to go through the whole sand-painting-pattern-conjuration thing again to get us home, I'm not sure I can manage it. But what's the alternative? Chopping our way through the vines to find our entry point? What other mythological monsters are still out there, waiting for us to try?

You have to do this, girl. They're counting on you.

I close my eyes and try to envision the real world, detail by detail, just as I last saw it. First I fix the desert in my mind, then I focus in on the canopy. Then the carved support poles. The circular platform. I picture our bodies as they were when we left them, trying to make them as real as possible in my mind. Then suddenly a whiff of scent drifts past me, and I re-member Dr. Redwind's incense. I bring to mind the four plumes of scented smoke, each with its own unique essence: Musky, spicy, floral, woodsy. I arrange the scents around us just as they were in the desert, using them to orient myself in space. Slowly the smells become stronger, more real. I squeeze the hands of my companions just to make sure they're still with me—they are—and give myself over to the perfume—

—And sickness welled up inside me. With a cry of pain I fell to my side, curled up in a ball, and started retching. There was nothing in my stomach to bring up—not even water—but that didn't stop my body from trying. Others moved toward me, anxious to help, and I could hear both male and female voices asking if I was okay. *I'm fine,* I wanted to tell them. *I know what this sickness means. I pushed my-self too hard in the dream world, and now my body is paying the price for it. This is normal. This is good.*

We were in the real world again.

23

TERRA COLONNA

PAGE COUNTY, VIRGINIA
SHENANDOAH JOURNAL, WEEKEND EDITION

MYSTIC CAVERNS TO BE RESTORED

When Mystic Caverns closed to the public in 2007 it was a disappointment to cave lovers everywhere, and damage from the June 2016 earthquake seemed to banish any hope of its ever opening again. But today its parking lots are full of vehicles as an excavation team prepares to assess the cavern's overall condition and decide how best to stabilize it.

Sadly, this is not happening because of the caverns' unique geological offerings, but for a more sobering reason. Ever since three kidnapped teens were rescued from the property in late June, law enforcement officials have suspected that illegal activities were being pursued deep underground, perhaps in the very chambers where bootleggers once hid their revels from Prohibition authorities. Up until now the prohibitive cost of excavation has made it impossible for local authorities to investigate the matter, but with the federal government now stepping in to finance the project, the caverns may soon be forced to reveal their darkest secrets.

One can only hope that after the official investigation is concluded, Mystic Caverns will be able to reclaim its status as one of the more popular tourist destinations in the Shenandoah Valley.

24

BADLANDS
TERRA PRIME

ISAAC

THEY'RE DREAMWALKERS.

The words resonated in Isaac's brain as he struggled to help Jesse. Even after her fit of retching ended she was so weak she could barely lift her head from the platform, so he gathered her gently into his arms, not knowing what else to do. At least that position kept her from seeing the dismay on his face. If what she had said about the reapers was true, it cast the Dream Wars in a whole new light . . . and the Shadows as well.

A few meters away, Dr. Redwind was inspecting Sebastian's injured ankle. Isaac couldn't see the wound itself, but she seemed worried about it. He watched as she took small bottle of ointment from her bag and applied a few drops to Sebastian's leg, then pressed some herbs over the wound and wrapped a strip of cloth around it. Her lips moved slightly as worked, perhaps in some kind of prayer or incantation? She had told them this site was considered sacred, so maybe she was trying to summon its power. Or maybe apologizing to the local spirits for Jesse vomiting on their altar.

What if everything he had been taught about the Dreamwalkers was a lie? What if they really hadn't been destroyed, but had been transformed into bound spirits? If it had been done to the twelve reapers it might well have been done to others. And if the bound spirit of a Dreamwalker retained a vestige of its living Gift. . . . The implications were staggering. And sickening.

Jesse raised her head slowly and looked at him. He forced a smile to his lips, trying to make it look convincing. "Welcome back."

"Hey." Her voice was barely audible.

"You all right?"

She hesitated, then nodded.

Sebastian joined them. "Apparently this is a natural consequence of dreamwalking."

"Only if I overexert myself," Jesse reminded him. She coughed weakly. "I do fine if I don't."

"You're like a runner who can't feel pain," Dr. Redwind observed. She put the leftover herbs back in their respective pouches and tucked them into her bag. "She may run until her muscles cramp and her joints cry out in agony, but since she can't feel the pain, she doesn't know to stop. So the damage gets worse. Like her, a dreamer is not aware of her body's needs, so she misses all the warning signs."

"Maybe the runner wouldn't stop even if she was in pain," Jesse said. "Maybe she really needs to get where she's going."

Redwind's aged skin crinkled around her eyes as she smiled. "Maybe."

Jesse tried to get to her feet, but she wasn't steady enough yet. "I'll get you some water," Isaac said. He helped her settle into a sitting position and went to fetch a canteen.

There was an unspoken code of ethics that all the Gifted followed, which forbade them from using their talents to attack each other. If Shadows really did enslave the souls of Dreamwalkers, commanding them to hunt down and kill their own kind, they had betrayed that code. If the other Guilds ever found out about that, there should rightfully be hell to pay. But would that really happen? The Shadows controlled all passage between the worlds. Any Guild that refused to deal with them would suffer more than it gained. For so long as the Shadows had no competition, they were effectively immune from punishment, and could break any rule they wanted.

He came back to Jesse and handed her the canteen. "Slowly," Sebastian warned as she began to drink. "Or it may all come back up."

If Jesse's vision was accurate, then the reapers were simply wraiths. Hellishly powerful wraiths because of their innate Gift—terrifying even to the undead—but no different in substance than any other ghost. A Master Shadow should be able to destroy them, without question. But was Isaac strong enough to do the same? Even more to the point, could he figure out how to do so without the archives of the Shadowlords to guide his research?

Dr. Redwind made them clean the sacred space before they left, scrubbing the platform until not a trace of Jesse's misery remained, and then scrubbing it again. All ash had to be removed from the pottery bowls and buried outside. The last thing she required was that they smooth the ground to erase all signs of their presence. By the time they stood at the edge of the canopy with their backpacks, ready to trek the desert again, the place looked like they had never been there.

No one talked much on the way back. Dr. Redwind had given Sebastian permission to use the spear as a walking staff, but even so, he was still limping slightly. Jesse was so weak that Isaac had to help support her, and it took all of their joint effort to keep moving. By the time they got back to the supply cave they were all on their last legs, and as Redwind saw to the horses, the three travelers collapsed onto the rough-hewn stools inside, totally exhausted. After a few minutes Jesse pulled over her backpack and dug out some things she called energy bars, which she unwrapped and passed around. They were sweet and nutty, but the small portion of food only reminded Isaac how ravenously hungry he was. He headed over to the storage area to see if there was any more substantive fare.

"We need to discuss our plans," Sebastian said.

Isaac looked back at them. "I think I understand how the reapers were made. If so, I may be able to figure out how a Shadow would destroy them."

Jessica said, "We're not going to do that."

They both looked at her.

"I told you. They're Dreamwalkers. *Just like me.* They were captured and mind-raped and turned into slaves." She looked at Isaac defiantly. "If Virilian did that to me, would you destroy me, too?"

"Jessica—" Sebastian began.

"They'll *kill* you," Isaac said sharply. "Do you understand that? The dead don't tire or lose focus. They'll never let up. For as long as you live you'll have to worry every time you go to sleep. And every time your family sleeps they'll be at risk, too."

She sighed. "I'm not saying I don't understand all that. I'm just saying that killing someone for something he was forced to do wouldn't be my first choice for a solution. So help me find another way? There's got to be one."

"They're not whole people," Isaac told her. "The ritual that makes them—" Suddenly he felt as if a knife had been plunged into his stomach. He doubled over in pain, struggling not to vomit.

"Isaac? What is it?"

"Nothing," he gasped. "Nothing. Give me a minute." He stayed doubled over, one hand on the wall to steady himself, trying to breathe deeply. He remembered the moment when Virilian had demonstrated the full power of the Domitor's security mesmerism, showing Isaac that if he tried to betray Guild secrets he would suffer dearly for it. Thus far, nothing Isaac had discussed with Sebastian or Jesse had fallen into that category, but apparently details of Shadowlord rituals crossed the line. *But if I can't even talk to them about Shadowlord rituals I certainly won't be able to perform one in front of them. So how the hell am I supposed to do anything about the reapers?*

Breathing was becoming easier. Slowly he straightened up. "I'm okay," he gasped.

"You sure?" Jesse didn't sound convinced.

"Yeah." He came back to where they were sitting and lowered

himself stiffly onto his stool. "What I was trying to say is, these reapers may have once been people, but the process they've been put through . . ." He felt a warning twinge in his gut. "They're just fragments of consciousness now. Not self-aware in the same way you and I are. They don't remember the past, or worry about what might happen in the future. They just exist. In this case, they exist for a specific purpose. It's all they know."

"A soul shard," Jesse said.

"Yes."

"Like Jacob?"

The question startled him. Yes, by every measure of classic necromancy Jacob was a soul shard, so damaged by the binding ritual that only fragments of his original identity remained. In theory he shouldn't be capable of anything but the most primitive level of functioning. Yet the damaged wraith had managed to guide them out of El Malo. In fact, he had risked his own existence to save Isaac. Was it possible for a spirit to regain his self-awareness over time? Or was the binding ritual not as effective as Isaac had been taught? If so, that was just one more area in which his teachers had failed him.

"Are you telling me they can't feel pain?" she pressed.

Isaac remembered how Jacob had begged him to contact Mae. The dead spirit's affection for his former sweetheart had survived a ritual meant to destroy all capacity for love. How many other wraiths might be more human than their masters suspected? "No," he said quietly. "I'm not going to tell you that."

Sebastian asked, "So what do you want to do? Because clearly we need to do something."

She shut her eyes for a moment, then said softy, "I want to free them."

Sebastian's eyes widened, and Isaac asked, "Free them how?"

"I'm not sure of the mechanics. You know that stuff better than I do. But the reason they're hunting me in the first place is because their master ordered them to. Right? So if his control over them could be broken, they would have no reason to come after me."

"There's no way to know that for sure."

"Isaac, I saw what they were before they were enslaved. Can all of that simply be erased?" She looked defiantly at him. "It wasn't with Jacob."

He chose his words carefully, wary of triggering the Domitor's safeguard again. "Jacob is a new wraith, freshly bound. The reapers have been around for centuries. In all that time they've known nothing but hate, and had no purpose other than killing Dreamwalkers. Even if they began their wraithly existence with some degree of humanity—which is debatable—wouldn't all those centuries have changed them? After serving as the embodiment of Death for so long, might a soul not lose sight of who and what it was before?"

"Maybe," she allowed. "But no one knows for sure, right? So just tell me: *could* it be done? Could they be freed?"

"I . . . I'm not sure. I mean, in theory, perhaps."

I was freed, Jacob reminded him.

Shhh, he thought.

"Can you figure out how to do it?" she pressed.

"Jesus, Jesse . . . I don't know." He shook his head. "I was only an apprentice when I left. The greater mysteries of our Gift hadn't been taught to me yet. I don't know if such a thing is even possible, much less how to go about doing it."

"Well, we're in a place where impossible things happen." Her eyes were pleading now. "Please, Isaac. Promise me you'll try."

"I . . ." He shook his head. "I'll try to come up with something." He wondered if that promise sounded as empty to her as it did to him. *We're stuck in the middle of nowhere, with no necromantic teachers and no research library. My Gift may not even be fully manifested yet. And even if I could figure out how Shadowlords normally handle this kind of thing, I can't perform one of their rituals in front of you. So how the hell am I supposed to help?*

"That's all I ask," Jesse said gratefully.

Suddenly Isaac realized there was a figure standing in the entrance. Dr. Redwind was leaning against one side of the stone archway, arms folded, watching them intently. How long had she been there? As Jesse and Sebastian followed his gaze and also saw her, he could see the same question in their eyes.

She might not take kindly to seven angry wraiths being set loose near her sacred ground, he thought.

But if their conversation had displeased her, she offered no sign of it. "We'll spend the night here." She walked across the room to the food stores and began to pry a container open. "It will give you time to rest before we head back. Which the three of you clearly need."

Her dark eyes fixed on Jesse for a moment. Her expression was unreadable. Then she turned away, took up a wooden scoop, and began to measure out supplies for their evening meal.

ıııııııııı

Night. Darkness. Silence.

Isaac's footsteps resonate in the desert, punctuating an otherwise eerie stillness. Behind him, on the other side of the ridge, his companions are still sleeping, surrounded by supplies, weapons, and fear. He is surrounded by fear also, but of a different kind.

He comes to a group of boulders and settles down on one of them, and for a while just gazes out at the desert in silence. Overhead there's no moon, only a sky full of stars, glimmering like tears.

What is he supposed to do? Try his amateur best to give Jesse what she wants, and maybe get all of them killed in the process? What she's asking for is so risky that even a master Shadow would be wary of trying it, and Isaac isn't that, not by a long stretch. And what if he did succeed in freeing the reapers from Shadowlord control? There was no guarantee they wouldn't go after Jesse anyway. And probably Isaac too, because once they were free they'd be able to choose their own prey. For centuries they had suffered at the hands of the Shadows, and now there would be a Shadow standing right in front

of them, the perfect vehicle for their vengeance. Hell, they might even go for him before they attacked Jesse.

There's only one thing he's sure of in this whole mess, and that is that he doesn't have the ritual knowledge or the strength of Gift that would be needed to fight off seven murderous wraiths.

Ritual knowledge. That's the key. His Gift is an innate power that even Virilian can't strip from him, but Shadowlords use rituals to focus and intensify their Gift. Back home there's a vast library full of such rituals, but the only ones Isaac ever learned were low level apprentice tricks. Definitely not the kind of thing he needs now.

Could he develop something on his own? Abandon Shadowlord tradition entirely, and seek his inspiration elsewhere? The idea is daunting. To even attempt it he would need information about ritual practices outside the Guild, non-Shadow necromancy, and that's not something apprentice Shadows are usually taught. Dr. Redwind probably has that kind of knowledge, but logic suggests that a woman who won't even give you her real name is unlikely to share her mystical secrets with you. Then again, there may be some general knowledge she can share, not in the category of secrets, to suggest ritual elements that he can use.

Whether he can come up with a combination of symbols and incantations, powerful enough to sever the ties of bondage imposed on the reapers by Shekarchiyandar, is another question entirely. But he has to try. Jesse is counting on him.

Suddenly he hears a sound behind him. He turns to find the raven sitting on a rock several yards away, watching him. Its feathers are as white as polished ivory, its eyes as black as the starless night sky overhead. For an endless moment they just stare at each other.

Finally Isaac says, "All those souls we saw." His throat is so dry it's hard to force words out. "Chained to their masters. Those were Dreamwalkers, weren't they?"

The raven says nothing.

"You can hear them suffering whenever a Shadowlord is around. I thought they were normal wraiths, and that the sounds of misery that always surround the *umbrae majae* were normal. But they're not, are they? Those are Gifted spirits who were enslaved, and because of Communion they can never break free. Each new Shadowlord claims the slaves of his predecessors." His hands grip the rock by his side with painful intensity. "They're the ones with the Gift. Not us. All those things that my father said I would experience after Communion— seeing the pathways between the worlds, hearing the music of the spheres—it's the Dreamwalkers who were meant to see and hear those things. Not us." He chokes out, "We stole their dreams."

The raven says nothing.

"Jesse wants to save seven of them. That's a good thing, isn't it? Maybe we can't help all the rest, but at least we can save those seven. And then pray that once they're free they won't turn on us." He laughs bitterly. "That's assuming I can figure out now to negate a ritual performed by one of our most powerful Shadowlords. Hell, I don't even know where to start."

The ground in front of him begins to stir. Startled, he backs away. Lines appear in the dirt, as if someone is etching them with a sharp stick. Letters are forming. Words. Sentences.

Respect what was disdained.

Return what was taken.

Provide what was denied.

He looks up to the raven again, but it's gone. Overhead he sees a brief flash of white wings, but then those are swallowed by the night, leaving only stars. When he looks down at the earth again the words are gone; the ground is as smooth as if it had never been disturbed. But that's all right. The lines that were once etched in dirt are now etched into his brain. Nothing short of death can erase them from his memory.

Now all he needs to do is figure out what they mean.

25

BADLANDS
TERRA PRIME

JESSE

WE GOT BACK to the canyon campsite in the late afternoon. I collapsed onto a patch of grass as soon as I dismounted, and swore I would never move again. Dr. Redwind fed and watered the horses, then gestured for Sebastian to join her in the wagon. By that time I felt recovered enough to get to my feet and head over to the bathing pool, meaning to dunk myself, clothes and all, in its cool, healing water. But I wound up just sitting on a rock by its edge instead, staring at my own reflection. The fact that it still looked like me was strangely disconcerting. With all that we'd been through, I felt like I should have changed somehow.

Isaac came and sat beside me, and for a while we stared at the water together.

"I do think I could destroy them," he said. "That's not to say it would be easy, but I understand the theory, and I could try."

Without looking up I said, "You know my answer to that."

"I know. I'm just checking to make sure you haven't changed your mind."

"I haven't."

"You'd really risk dying to save them?"

I gestured toward my reflection in the water. "Mom once told me that any time you faced a moral dilemma you should ask yourself, *if I do this, how will I feel when I look at myself in the mirror tomorrow? Will I like the person I see?* Part of me is doing this for them. Part is doing it for me."

"Your mother sounds like an insightful woman."

I shrugged. "She's honest, and decent, and does her best never to hurt anyone. Qualities that seem to be in short supply in this world."

He reached out and took my hand. "You have those things here, Jesse."

"Yeah." I squeezed his hand. "I know."

"If that's what you really want, I'll try to free them."

I looked at him. "Do you think you can?"

"In theory? Yes. In actual practice?" He stared out over the water again. "I'll need a ritual to provide focus, but there's nothing that says it has to be a Shadow ritual. I could come up with something completely different, on my own."

"Do you know how to do that?"

He laughed. "Not a clue."

Despite myself I smiled. "Guesswork seems to be the theme of our expedition."

"I'm hoping Dr. Redwind will help me. I know she wants no part of Shadow necromancy—she's made that clear enough—but she knows so much about spiritual symbology, maybe she can suggest some options. A ritual is just a collection of symbols and incantations used to focus the mind, but you have to choose the right combination of elements or the whole thing fails."

"Like weaving a web," I mused. "Has to be perfect."

"I suppose." His hand tightened around mine. "Jesse, you know, whatever happens tomorrow—"

"Hey." I pulled my hand away. "No final statements, okay? Don't jinx this."

"Okay," he murmured.

I heard footsteps coming down the wagon stairs; the rhythm of the limp made it clear whose they were. Sebastian came over to where we were sitting and said, "She wants to see you, Isaac."

As Isaac headed off toward the wagon, Sebastian eased himself down beside me with a soft groan. "How's he doing?"

"Pretty well, considering how scared he is. He's doing his best not to let it show."

"How are you doing?"

"Pretty much the same. And you? How's the leg?"

He stretched it out in front of him. The ankle of his boot was distended from all the bandages underneath it. "Still hurts like hell."

"Infected?"

"No," he said. A little too quickly. I looked at him suspiciously. "Jessica, there's a hole in a part of my body that isn't supposed to have a hole in it. It's going to hurt for a while. Don't worry about me."

"Okay," I said, unconvinced.

"I do have something I want to discuss with you privately." He glanced meaningfully toward the wagon. "Serendipity seems to have provided us with the opportunity for it."

Curious, I shifted position so that I faced him, tucking my legs underneath me. "What's up?"

"I've been thinking about what we know about your birth story. Some of it just doesn't add up right. I've come up with a theory about why."

"Like what?"

"You know that children on this world are tested by Seers soon after birth, to see if they have Gifted potential."

I nodded. "Isaac explained that to me when we first got here."

"We know you were born to a woman from Terra Prime, after which a Seer identified your Dreamwalker potential and communicated that to Morgana—who then hid you on Terra Colonna so the Shadows wouldn't find you. Correct?"

I nodded. "That's the story as I understand it."

"But what reason would she have given for taking you from your birth family? She couldn't declare you Gifted, because then the Greys wouldn't accept you for a changeling swap. But if you weren't Gifted, why would a Guildmaster take you from your home? And if a Seer realized you had Dreamwalker potential, why wouldn't she turn you over to the Greys for destruction, as has been the practice for centuries? The risk of not doing so would be immense, if it were discovered later."

My eyes narrowed slightly. "So what are you thinking?"

Glancing back at the wagon, he quieted his voice so that those inside wouldn't hear him. "Your mother was probably a Seer, Jessica. And a high ranking one. No one else could have pulled it off."

"How high?"

"Enough that only Morgana would know your secret."

It took me a moment to realize what he was suggesting. "Sebastian, please don't tell me you're saying what I think you are."

"It would explain a lot, wouldn't it?"

"You think Alia Morgana is my *birth mother*?"

"It's a possibility."

"But . . . but . . . shit!"

He raised a finger to his lips, warning me to keep my voice down.

"No," I said, more quietly this time. I felt as if someone had punched me in the gut. "That's just crazy."

But even as I protested, I had to admit that it would indeed explain a lot. Morgana could have assessed her own child without anyone asking questions. She could have sent it away without anyone knowing it was hers. And this would certainly explain her fixation on me. Oh, the Dreamwalker stuff was important to her, but her interest in my life clearly went beyond that. This would explain it all.

"It could have been Miriam Seyer," I offered, floundering for another viable option. "She's in on all Morgana's secrets. Morgana even used her to spy on me. So Miriam might have known what was going on."

"Jessica." Was it my imagination, or was there a spark of amusement in his eyes? "Seyer is Morgana's daughter."

For a moment I couldn't find my voice. "You . . . you *knew* that? And didn't tell me?"

"You never asked me about Seyer. And honestly, it never seemed relevant. How would it have changed anything if the two were related?"

"But they don't look that different in age—" Halfway through the sentence I realized what I was saying. "Fleshcrafters?"

"I would assume." A corner of his mouth twitched slightly. "No one has ever accused Morgana of lacking vanity."

"Jesus." My head was spinning. "That's why she trusted Seyer with everything. They're family." And so what was I? Morgana's child, or her grandchild? Did knowing my heritage mean I should hate the two of them less? More? It was all too much to process. My head was spinning.

"At any rate," he said quietly, "I thought you should know my suspicions before you contacted her. In case you ever decided to do that."

"Yeah" I muttered. "I appreciate it." *It might not be true,* I reminded myself. *He's just guessing. We're all just guessing.* But at least I now knew it was a possibility, which meant that Morgana couldn't use the information to surprise me. That was worth something, wasn't it?

Isaac spent a long time talking to Redwind in the wagon; I hoped it was a good omen. The light was beginning to fade when they finally emerged, and Redwind waved for us to join her at the campfire. She sat down on a boulder and for a moment just sat there, staring into the circle of ashes. We waited in respectful silence. Finally she looked up and said, "These spirits that you want to summon embody a corrupt and unclean power, and the kind of necromancy that created them is abhorrent to my people. Nonetheless, Isaac has asked permission to perform his ritual in the Badlands. My first instinct is to say no, out of concern for how the essence of this land might be affected by it. But he asked me for the protection of El Malo, saying that if you left the Badlands, it would be impossible to perform the ritual without your enemies finding you. I do believe this to be true. I also know that your ultimate intent is to perform an act of mercy, to save tormented spirits from suffering. Therefore I have agreed to allow it.

"In the morning I'll bring you to a suitable location and provide the supplies Isaac has asked for. Understand, neither I nor any other locals who might attend can help you against the reapers. I say this not because we are callous creatures who don't care what happens to you, but because our primary duty is to protect this land. If we were to engage the reapers it would give them a spiritual connection to us, and through us, to the people we're sworn to protect. So you must rise or fall in this on your own. Do you understand?"

We all assured her that we did.

"I can promise that if any of you die in this effort, I will do what I can to ease your spirits' journey into the next world. Now . . ." she got up and brushed off her skirt, "I'm going to make some dinner, and then you should try to get a good night's sleep. Your minds will need to be sharp tomorrow, as well as your reflexes."

"Might we speak for a moment?" I asked. "Privately?"

She looked at me curiously, then nodded and gestured for me to follow her back to the wagon. Once inside, she turned to me and waited.

"I have a favor to ask," I said.

A grey eyebrow lifted slightly. "You've been granted quite a few already."

I took a slip of paper out of my pocket and handed it to her. "This is contact information for my family on Terra Colonna. Sebastian promised that if anything happened to me he would get word to them, so at least they wouldn't keep wondering if I was ever coming home . . ." I had to stop for a moment to compose myself. "With what we're doing tomorrow—"

"He might not be able to," she said. "I understand."

"If that happens, please, would you send them a message? Just let them know what happened to me. They know about the reapers already. And the tower. They'll understand whatever you tell them." I took out the box that my mother had given me and offered it to her. "This should cover whatever the Greys charge you for delivery."

As she opened the box her eyes widened slightly. For a long moment she gazed at my mother's rings in silence. Finally she said, "This isn't necessary."

"Please. We've imposed on you so much already. At least let me cover the cost of what I'm asking." After a moment I added, "My mother would want you to have them."

Lips tight, she nodded solemnly, closed the box, and put it aside. "I'll hold it for you until your business with the reapers is done. And if that doesn't go as planned, I'll make sure your family is told something that will comfort them."

"Thank you," I whispered. "Not just for this, but for everything."

She sighed and shook her head. "Let's hope you still want to thank me when all this is over."

26

BADLANDS
TERRA PRIME

ISAAC

BY DAWN, Isaac had seven bodies ready to go. They were the size of small dolls, not fully grown people, and they weren't perfectly human in form, but when he had tried to shape them more realistically they always came out looking wrong. In the end he had taken Dr. Redwind's advice and focused on their essence rather than on physical appearance. Simulacra, she called them.

Looking down at his handiwork now, he was tired but pleased. His goal had been to create spiritual representations of human beings by weaving together items that symbolized different aspects of the human spirit: cloth, herbs, feathers, shells, and even mystical patterns inked on paper, all woven and wrapped and tied together to the accompaniment of appropriate incantations. It had amazed him at the start of this project how many such items Dr. Redwind had stored in her wagon, but at this point he would have been more surprised if they were absent. After hearing her explain the significance of hundreds of items in various cultures, Isaac was filled with a respect for her that bordered on awe. He had no idea what Gifts she possessed— her people didn't name their talents—but her knowledge of mystical symbology was truly daunting. He now understood why the *azteca* deferred to her like they did.

He knew from Jacob that the ritual that had severed the wraith from his undead mistress—and nearly destroyed him—had incorporated a fragment of bone from his corpse. It wasn't uncommon for Shadowlords to use relics of the dead to control their spirits, but Isaac had no access to the mortal bodies of the reapers. Hell, he didn't even know their living names. Hopefully these ritual objects could substitute for bodily relics, representing the flesh that the reapers had once called their own. If that didn't work . . . well then, he and Jesse and Sebastian were all going to die. He wasn't under any illusion about that. This project didn't allow for half measures.

"You should get some sleep," Dr. Redwind said. "If only for an hour."

"Can't sleep," he said, but he agreed to lie down for a few minutes and shut his eyes while she packed the supplies they would be taking with them.

His necromantic senses seemed to be growing sharper by the hour. Maybe it was because of all the practice he'd been getting recently, or maybe the special magic of this place was affecting him. They were still close enough to the Grand Portal that some of its effects could be felt; maybe that was having an impact on his Gift. He'd noticed that now, when Jacob spoke, it was much easier for Isaac to understand him.

I am afraid, the wraith said.

"We're all afraid," Isaac murmured.

He did try to sleep, but of course it was impossible. Never before had the lives of others been placed in his hands this way. He was terrified of failing them. And of failing *her.*

And of failing himself.

IIIIIIIIIIII

Dr. Redwind guided them to a site that was flat, desolate, and close enough to the northern border of the Badlands that El Malo loomed over them once more. Whether she wanted the guardian spirits of the border region to play some role in Isaac's ritual, or just wanted him to perform it as far as possible from the inhabited parts of the Badlands, he didn't know and didn't ask. His mind was so focused on the ritual now that there was no room in it for anything else.

Two of the *azteca* met them at the site, and the way they took up station on opposite sides of Dr. Redwind made it clear they were there to protect her. Not only had they brought full-sized crossbows with them but a collection of bladed weapons also, including obsidian-tipped spears similar to the one Sebastian had carried earlier. They had regular guns as well, but everyone was in agreement that if the reapers manifested in physical form, it was unlikely that bullets would stop them. The single most important thing was to be able to hold them at bay until the ritual was completed, for which spears were the best option. The *azteca* had brought extra weapons with them for the visitors to use; Sebastian gratefully accepted one of the spears and Isaac hung a long sheathed blade from his belt and positioned a spear within easy reach. Jesse wouldn't take anything.

"What if they manifest physically?" Sebastian pressed her. "You need to be able to protect yourself."

"We're trying to restore their Dreamwalker identities, so I need to approach them as kin. If I look like I want a fight, it will send exactly the wrong message." Sebastian tried his best to convince her to take one of the spears, but she was adamant. In the end the best he could do was convince her to accept a long blade with a leather-wrapped handle, which she said she would wear sheathed.

Isaac said nothing during all that. He had seen in Jesse's eyes a reflection of his own mindset: *It's all or nothing now. We must commit ourselves to this without reservation and without compromise. Anything less dooms us to certain failure.* He did convince Jesse to stand close enough to Sebastian that the ex-soldier could protect her.

Choosing a stretch of earth that was flat and bare, Isaac began to sketch patterns into the soil with a pointed stick. A great sun circle would contain all his other symbols and act as a focal point for the ritual. Since the undead were weakened by sunlight, he was hoping that would make it easier to banish Shekarchiyandar's necromancy. Every little bit helped, right?

When all his designs were in place, he walked to the small folding table he'd set up inside the circle, and took a moment to gather himself. The seven simulacra, now wrapped in strips of black cloth, were lined up neatly before him, and his other supplies were in small bowls along the far edge of the table. Beyond them, in the center of the sun circle, Sebastian had arranged a pyramid of tinder and started a fire. Its heat was anything but welcome beneath the blazing desert sun, but Isaac would need a fire for the end of his ritual and didn't want to have to worry about trying to get one started after he began.

He closed his eyes for a moment, turning inward, trying to still his nerves. When he finally felt ready, he looked at Jesse. "Call them."

She swallowed nervously, but nodded. The plan was for her to try to invoke her Gift without sleeping, creating a dream vision in her mind that mirrored what she saw in front of her. Thus she would be able to stay focused on what Isaac was doing, while still activating the power that would draw the reapers to her. That was the theory, anyway. All of this was just theory—him with his improvised necromancy, her with a Gift whose rules had been forgotten centuries ago. What a pair they made!

The first step was for him to invoke his own Gift, which he did by lighting the bundles of herbs he'd prepared under Redwind's guidance, offering the scented smoke at ritual locations around the circle. Four cardinal points, the center of the sun pattern, the sky overhead. At each location he focused his concentration, trying to attune himself to the spirit world. It seemed that the circle changed as he did so, the lines of his inscribed pattern giving off a subtle heat beneath his feet. His awareness of Jacob became sharper—crisper—until he could see the ghost almost as clearly as he could see a living man. When he was done, he placed the remaining herbs in the fire and glanced at Jesse. She seemed lost in her own world, and he could only hope that she had achieved the state of mind they needed. If she had, the dream realm was now resonating with her Gift, and the fearsome predators who hunted her kind would catch wind of that and follow it to its source.

Respect what was disdained, the raven said.

At the table, he began to unwrap the black bindings from each of his simulacra. The reapers' original bodies, lacerated during the binding ritual, would have been discarded like rotten meat afterward. He had made them new bodies, weaving together sacred materials to serve them as flesh. Now those bodies lay naked before him, empty of soul. Isaac didn't know who or what the reapers were before they died, so he couldn't invoke their original identities, but he could give them new ones, replacing what the Shadows had destroyed.

It seemed that the sky overhead was darkening slightly. Or was that his imagination? The entire world looked different to him now; it was hard to tell which parts were as they were supposed to be.

Focus, Isaac. Focus.

"For those whose names were taken, I give them new ones." He touched a drop of oil to the first simulacrum. "I christen you Ethan Antonin." It was perversely pleasurable to give the reapers his family name, and also an act of defiance. The Shadowlords had tried to take his name from him by casting him out of his family, but no mere words from a Guildmaster—or even his own father—could change who and what he was. He was an Antonin and had the right to adopt these lost souls into his line if he wanted to. "I christen you Sarah Antonin," he said as he anointed the second simulacrum. Next came Kurt. And June. And Seth. He had no idea what sex the original reapers were, but he figured making them half female and half male was a reasonable guess. And so he continued, naming them after the children of the Warrens, whose resilience and strength had so impressed him. They were good names to have, proud names to have, and the act served as a memorial to the fallen children. "I christen you Moth Antonin," he said as he anointed the final one.

The sky was definitely growing darker. Jesse had noticed it too, and he could see the fear in her eyes as she looked up to check it out.

But a moment later she forced her gaze back to the ritual, nodding to him as if to say, *Don't worry about me, I can do my part.*

Provide what was denied, the raven said.

In Shadowcrest, Isaac had been taught that a spirit of the dead was shaped by two things: who he was in life, and the manner of his dying. The Shadowlords staged traumatic deaths in order to shatter the souls of their victims, so that their spirits could be molded like clay afterward. Isaac was going to give the reapers the death they should have had, and provide the funeral rites they'd originally been denied. Normally that alone wouldn't be enough to counteract the necromancy of a Master Shadow, but the reapers had been created many centuries ago, and control of them had been passed down through numerous Communions. Each time that happened, memories were diluted and power degraded. Hopefully the original binding ritual had been weakened enough by now that Isaac could override it.

Murmuring a prayer for the dead under his breath, Isaac prepared the simulacra as he would bodies for a funeral pyre, wrapping each one gently in a white shroud, laying it respectfully upon a wooden framework he'd prepared the night before. Overhead the sky had grown dark, and black clouds were beginning to gather, swirling in a circular motion around the ritual site. But reapers had not yet appeared. Perhaps they were wary of the power he had raised and not yet sure how to deal with it. Or perhaps they were having trouble entering the waking world.

No matter. If anything was going to draw them out, his next action would.

Return to them what was taken.

Taking up a small knife from the table, Isaac held out both hands over the first simulacrum. "That which the Shadows took from you, I return." Wincing slightly, he slit his palm with the knife. Blood welled up in the wound and began to drip onto the white shroud. Shekarchiyandar had stolen the blood of Dreamwalkers and taken it into himself to shackle their spirits; Isaac now offered his own blood, the blood

of a Shadow, to unshackle them. It was the core of everything his ritual represented.

The clouds overhead started to swirl faster.

He moved to the second simulacrum and made the same offering.
The blood flowed more easily now, so he was able to move on quickly
to the third.

They're coming, Jacob warned. There was fear in the words.

Isaac turned to Jesse to warn her, but before he could say anything she said in a strained voice, "I know. Finish it."

He offered his blood to the next simulacrum. The earth surrounding him was taking on a greyish cast now, and even the color of his
blood was growing duller. *Keep going,* he told himself. *Don't get distracted.* His hands trembled slightly as he offered blood to the next
simulacrum. *You have to complete the whole ritual no matter what
happens, or it will all be wasted.*

Then he heard Jesse gasp. Reflexively he looked up and saw several figures in the sky, blacker than any normal creature could ever
be, emanating such unearthly cold that Isaac's eyes were chilled when
he looked at them. None of Jesse's descriptions had done them justice,
but that was to be expected; she lacked the ability to see them for
what they really were. But Isaac could see them. To his eyes they were
corruption incarnate, creatures that should never exist in any realm,
piecemeal monsters constructed from broken bits of humanity reas-
sembled into a new configuration. If there was a Dreamwalker at the
heart of such a creature he could not see it. If there was anything
human there he could not see it.

Finish the ritual! an inner voice cried. *It's your only hope.*

He forced himself to look away, but his hands were shaking so
badly now it was hard to direct the blood sacrifice properly. Cold en-
veloped him as the reapers drew closer, and he could sense the raw
hatred that was their essence; it took all his strength to shut them out
of his mind so he could concentrate.

Then Sebastian yelled, "No!" Startled, Isaac whipped around, and
saw that Jesse had moved away from her protector. Her face was white

with terror but she spread her arms wide, as if to embrace the reapers. "Brothers!" she cried. "Dreamwalkers! I know you! I know what was done to you! Let us help you!"

Heart pounding, Isaac somehow managed to turn back to his work and make the final blood offering, praying that when it was complete there would be some effect. But nothing happened. If anything, the reapers were becoming more agitated, and the unnatural cold of their presence was more intense with each passing moment. Shivering, he tried not to lose faith in his own efforts, but doubt was beginning to erode his spirit. He took a moment to steady himself, then picked up the framework the simulacra were lying on, moving oh-so-carefully toward the fire. The final phase of his ritual was intended as a gesture of respect to the seven murdered Dreamwalkers, and if he dropped one of them on the ground that gesture would lose all its power. Out of the corner of his eye he saw one of the black shapes plummet toward Sebastian, but it pulled up at the last minute, just before reaching the tip of his spear. Like a shark testing its prey, Isaac thought. He longed to keep watching but forced himself to turn away, to focus on the task at hand. As long as the reapers weren't attacking him, his job was to complete their funeral.

They do have physical bodies, he thought as he approached the fire. *It wouldn't have turned aside otherwise.* Slowly, carefully, he lowered his wooden frame down over the fire, positioning it so that the simulacra were directly over the flames. "Find your peace," he whispered. The dried herbs and paper talismans flared brilliantly as the fire claimed them, driving away the cold for a moment. "Rest as the dead were meant to rest."

Now it was done. He turned back to his companions, hoping to see the reapers withdraw—or at least change tactics—but it was as if his ritual had never been performed. One of them dove suddenly toward Jesse, and he knew with terrifying instinct that this time it was not a test: The reaper meant to kill her. Sebastian must have sensed it also, because he grabbed her and shoved her behind him, getting his hand back on the spear just in time to meet the downward charge fully braced. The reaper impaled itself on the obsidian blade with a spine-chilling shriek, slowing to a stop just inches short of being able to reach him. Isaac forced his eyes away from the scene long enough to grab the spear he'd prepared, then ran toward his companions. And he did so he realized to his horror that the reaper wasn't trying to escape, but to work its way down the shaft to reach Sebastian.

As soon as he was close enough to strike he thrust his own spear into the creature, and his blade bit into . . . something. It didn't feel like flesh, but at least it was solid. Jesse was on her feet now, *azteca* blade drawn, ready to join the battle as soon as the reaper got within reach. But then, with a final convulsive heave, the reaper slid down and closed the distance between it and Sebastian. Isaac tried to angle his spear to force the creature back, but he lacked either the strength or the angle needed to succeed. Darkness whipped around Sebastian like strands of a horrific cocoon, and an unearthly scream pierced the air; whether it was his scream or the reaper's was anyone's guess. With a cry of anguish Jesse ran forward and thrust her blade deep in the reaper's substance. Again and again she stabbed it, her blade sinking deep into whatever body it had, but if she was trying to draw its attention away from Sebastian it wasn't working.

Then suddenly Isaac's spear lurched forward; surprised, he went stumbling toward the reaper. But the dark creature dissipated before he made contact with it, and with nothing to resist his thrust he fell heavily to the ground, his spear clattering several feet away as it hit the earth. Quickly he rolled over to see what the other reapers were doing, and he saw—

Nothing.

The reaper that had attacked Sebastian was gone. So were all the others. The swirling black clouds were gone as well, and the sky was a natural blue. It was as if the monsters had never existed.

"No!" Jesse screamed. "No!"

Sebastian was lying limp on the ground, with Jesse holding his face in her hands. "No," she cried. "You can't die now! Come back!" But Sebastian's body had been raked across the torso as if by a

massive claw, with such force that the ends of shattered ribs were visible in the gashes. The largest gash cut so deeply across his chest that
it must surely have reached his heart, which was probably the intent.
All his wounds were edged in frost, and where the surrounding flesh
was visible it was blackened, as if by frostbite.

Stunned, Isaac stared down at his fallen companion, trying to absorb what had just happened. Jesse was weeping now, and she hugged
Sebastian's ravaged body in her arms, rocking him rhythmically as one
would a child. "I'm sorry," she sobbed to him. "I'm so sorry. You should
have let me face them alone. I was the one they wanted, not you."

Though Isaac had no clue what he should say or do to help her—life
among the Shadows didn't prepare one for comforting the bereaved—
he started to move forward, feeling like he should do something. A gentle hand on his arm stopped him. Redwind shook her head slightly,
looked at Jesse, then looked back at him. After a moment Isaac relented,
and he watched as Jesse poured out her grief, telling Sebastian that she
should have been the one to die, not him.

"What happened?" He whispered the question, not wanting to
disturb her. "Why did they leave when they did? I thought the ritual
had failed."

She nodded toward the fire. Looking that way, he saw that his funeral frame had collapsed, and the seven simulacra were nothing but
ash. Understanding dawned slowly. "When they were fully burned,"
he murmured. "That's when the ritual took effect."

One of the *azteca* said something. Redwind turned to him and
responded curtly.

"What did he say?" Isaac asked.

She didn't answer. Jesse was sobbing more softly now, the first
wave of hysteria exhausted, a quieter grief taking its place. He knelt
down beside her and put a hand on her shoulder. When she didn't
draw away he took her gently into his arms, holding her against his
chest as she cried. He buried his face in her hair so that no one could
see the tears pouring down his own face. He should have performed
the ritual faster. Or better. Or . . . something.

"Come," Redwind said at last. "Let's leave this place." She waved to the two *azteca*, who started to lift Sebastian's body from the ground. Jesse jerked herself free from Isaac and threw herself on top of it. "Shhh," Dr. Redwind said, gently pulling her back. "They're just going to bring him back to camp, so you can honor his passing properly. This place isn't appropriate."

"I won't leave him," she said. "Don't ask me to leave him."

"That's fine. You can go with them. Isaac and I will stay behind to clean up, then join you." After a pause she said, very gently, "I'm so very sorry for your loss."

Jesse nodded weakly, and after a moment allowed Dr. Redwind to draw her back from the body. The *azteca* carried Sebastian toward the place where they'd left the horses, which was a safe distance away from the ritual site. Jesse turned a tear-streaked face back to Isaac, a question in her eyes.

"It's okay," he said softly. "Go with them."

She nodded and went after them, trotting a few steps to catch up. He watched for a few minutes as she followed them, heading north.

Sorry, Jacob whispered in his mind.

He nodded then looked at Dr. Redwind. "What exactly are we cleaning up?"

"Table and tools. And you should erase your patterns. Rain will take care of the rest." She looked at the horizon, now cloudless except for El Malo. "When it comes."

She started to move toward the ritual table, but he put a hand on her arm to stop her. "What did the *azteca* say?"

"He said, 'The gods demand sacrifice. Now they are satisfied.'" Gently she removed his hand from her arm. "Now go erase your circle. I'll collect our tools."

27

BADLANDS
TERRA PRIME

JESSE

IT'S TIME."

The words filtered down through my sorrow slowly, and for a moment it was hard to give them context. Memories from the last few hours were all jumbled up in my head: reapers attacking, Sebastian dying, me riding across a scorched wasteland between skull-clad warriors, mourning the fact that someone I cared about had to be dragged on a makeshift frame behind a horse, jostled by every bump and crack in the desert. But what option was there? If they draped the body over a horse it might be frozen in that position by the time we got back to camp. That was too gruesome to even think about. I also had a vague memory of arguing with Isaac and Dr. Redwind over who was going to prepare the body for its final viewing, but I wasn't sure when that argument took place. In the end they prevailed, leaving me to nurse my sorrow as the two *azteca* carried Sebastian away.

"Jessica."

I opened my eyes and saw Isaac seated on the edge of the cot, as he had been for hours, a loyal but exhausted sentinel. Standing

behind him was Dr. Redwind. When she saw I was awake she said
gently, "There's something here I want you two to see."

"Is it what you were waiting for?" I asked.

"Not yet. Something else."

Redwind had told us earlier that someone was on their way to join
us for the funeral, and we should wait until she arrived before we
started. She wouldn't give us any more information, but I trusted her
judgment more than I trusted my own at that point, so I just nodded
and agreed. Now, as she led Isaac and me to the site she had chosen
for Sebastian's funeral pyre, I wondered who in the outside world
could possibly have a role to play in all this.

We walked maybe a quarter of a mile, to a place where the canyon took a sharp turn to the left. Past that was an expanse of shallow
water with a peninsula of rock extending into it, and on that peninsula
was Sebastian. He was lying on a frame of tree limbs lashed together,
not unlike the one Isaac had built in miniature for his ritual. The
frame was raised above a bed of kindling. We followed Dr. Redwind
in silence around the side of the lake and down the peninsula, until
we stood before the body.

How peaceful he looked, lying there as if asleep! Someone had
dressed him in a fresh shirt so that his wounds were hidden, and his
long white hair had been washed clean of blood and neatly braided.
The spear he had fought with was by his side, only now it had feathers
bound to the shaft. I looked at Dr. Redwind, a question in my eyes.

"It's a gift from the *azteca* who were with us. As is this whole
structure. They said to tell you that they offer it as a sign of respect to
one who lived bravely and died well."

I shut my eyes for a moment. "Thank them for me." I looked at
Sebastian. "For us."

"That's not all I wanted to show you."

Curious, I watched as she walked to the end of the frame, where
Sebastian's feet rested. They were bare of shoes, though one ankle
was still swathed in bandages. Gently she loosened the strips of white

fabric, easing them enough to slide them down his ankle and show us his wound.

I gasped.

Where the thorn had pierced him, his flesh was black. Not organic black, like you might see with blood poisoning or frostbite, but pure black, the color of coal and tar and onyx. And not just on the surface. The hole in his ankle hadn't closed completely, and you could see that the flesh inside was the same impossible color.

"What is it?" I asked.

"I don't know. I've never seen anything like it. Apparently those thorns you ran into were more deadly than you realized." She moved the bandages back into place, smoothing them over the wound. "It was spreading up his leg, slowly but surely. And there was nothing I knew of that could stop it. The night we spent in the supply cave, he told me that the blackened part of his flesh had lost all sensation. When the infection got as far as his ankle joint, he would be crippled."

"He knew," I whispered. "When he chose to die for me, he knew that." I turned to Isaac. "Where is he now?"

"What do you mean?"

"His spirit. You can see spirits, right? So you must have seen his."

He hesitated. "It takes conscious effort to do that, Jesse. And I was focused on the ritual at the time."

"But Jacob—Jacob must have seen him. Ask him." Something about the way he and Redwind looked at each other made my stomach lurch. "Is something wrong? You said the manner of a man's death affected what form his spirit would take. So tell me he's all right, Isaac, because that death was not a good way to die."

"I didn't see his spirit," Isaac said quietly. "Neither did Jacob."

I stepped back, feeling as if I'd been struck. "So . . . the reaper destroyed his soul? Or ate it?"

"No. Not that. Jesse . . . sometimes when a man dies, a wraith comes into existence. It may have intact memories, or only broken fragments of recall. And sometimes—sometimes we don't see anything. It doesn't mean his spirit was destroyed. It just means it's not *here*."

"Where else would it be? Why would it leave?"

"Jesse." Dr. Redwind's tone was gentle. "The dead don't belong in this world. The ones that stay here are the ones that have a reason to. Unfinished business, perhaps, or a strong bond to one of the living. And those who are traumatized by death—the ones Isaac calls *soul shards*—can be trapped in this realm until such time as they are able to find peace. But many souls simply move on to another world—what we call the realm of the dead—and cannot be seen or heard by living men."

I looked at Isaac. "That's what you believe?"

He hesitated. "Our theories about it are a little different, but yes. Some deaths don't generate a visible wraith."

"You think that's what happened to him?" I looked at the body on the platform.

"I know he didn't become a soul shard," Isaac said, "because Jacob would have seen that. And since the reapers are essentially Dreamwalkers, there's no reason to think they would have the power to either eat or destroy a human soul." He paused. "His spirit is somewhere, Jesse. I promise you that."

"All right." I lowered my head. "All right."

"And he didn't die badly," Dr. Redwind said.

"What do you mean? He was torn to pieces by a corrupted spirit."

"He died protecting someone he loved. That doesn't destroy a soul, Jesse. It strengthens it."

It took me a moment to find my voice. "He . . . he loved me?"

"Jesus, girl." Isaac shook his head in mock astonishment. "Even I figured that one out."

I remembered the haunting sadness in Sebastian's eyes the night he'd told us how he lost his family. Sometimes it seemed like there was a hint of that same sadness when he looked at me. *He loved his daughter,* I thought. *He protected me as he would have protected her.*

A figure came around the bend and signaled to Redwind. It was one of the *azteca*.

"The last of our number is here," she said. "Let's go back so you can see what's arrived."

||||||||||||||

The person who Dr. Redwind had been waiting for was the Native American girl from the hotel, who Redwind introduced as Charisa. She was carrying Sebastian's musket. The sight of it brought a lump to my throat.

"I made sure it had no powder in it," she said as she handed it to me. "He kept it very clean."

I ran my hand down the barrel, remembering the first day I saw it, displayed on a shelf in the Green Man's hideout. Having it here would have pleased Sebastian, so it brought me comfort. "Thank you," I murmured.

We all walked back to the peninsula together: Isaac, Dr. Redwind, the *azteca*, Charisa, and me with the musket resting on my shoulder. I laid it down by Sebastian's side and kissed him gently on the cheek. "I loved you, too," I whispered. Then I reached into my pocket and took out the small pouch that contained his fetters. Isaac had tried to talk me into keeping them, and I had said I would think about it, but now that I was standing beside Sebastian's body, I didn't want to profit from his death in any way. I placed the pouch on his chest and nodded to Dr. Redwind, who stepped forward and set fire to the kindling. The flames spread quickly, and soon the entire structure was ablaze. One of the *azteca* began to chant, and though I didn't know the words, its purpose was clear, so it was comforting.

As the funeral flames rose to lick the sky I turned to Isaac and asked, "Didn't you tell me once that ghosts can travel freely between the worlds?"

He hesitated a moment. "They can, but they can't go anywhere in particular unless they know the way."

"By which you mean the path that connects two worlds. The design you call a codex."

"Yes."

"Sebastian's the one who gave me the codex for Terra Colonna," I said quietly. "He knew the way."

I looked back at the pyre. A strange peace filled me.

"That's why we can't find him," I murmured. "He's gone home."

28

BADLANDS
TERRA PRIME

JESSE

THE STREET OUTSIDE MY HOUSE is peaceful. The trees are lush and green. The sky is blue. How strange it feels, not to worry that at any moment a reaper might appear! Despite the pall of sorrow that hangs over me, I can't deny how wonderful that sense of freedom is. There may still be enemies who seek my death, but if they aren't Dreamwalkers, they can't reach me here. After so many weeks of constant fear, the feeling of safety is almost surreal.

My mother steps out of the house and sees me. Her first response is simply a casual greeting, as though her real daughter is standing in the street waiting for her. Then I see lucidity dawn in her eyes. "Jesse!" She runs across the street to me, arms opened wide, and when she hugs me it is with such desperate strength that I can barely breathe. "You're all right!" There are tears in her voice. "Oh my God, is it all over? Is everything okay? Can you come home to us now?"

I thought I would be strong enough to handle this meeting with dignity, but I was wrong. It takes all my self-control not to start crying again. "I'm fine, Mom. I'm fine." I pull back from her, just far enough to look into her eyes. There's so much love there that it warms my soul just to look at her. "The reapers are gone. You and Tommy are safe."

"You killed them?"

I hesitate. "Not sure, exactly. Isaac performed a ritual and they disappeared. They may still exist somewhere, but if so, they no longer have any reason to hurt us."

"So it's all over? You're free to come home now?"

The yearning in her voice makes my heart ache. "Soon, Mom. I have one more thing to do first."

Her eyes narrow slightly. "Something dangerous?"

I sigh. "Everything in my life is dangerous these days. I just wanted you to know that I made it this far, and that regardless of what happens from here on out, the two of you will be safe."

She gathers me into her arms again, and I rest my head against her shoulder, eyes closed, the pain in my heart eased by her love. "I have faith in you," she whispers. "Always. You know that, right?"

"I know. And I'll come back to you soon, I promise."

"Are you going to visit your brother?"

"Probably not tonight. I can only do so much dreamwalking in one night, and I've still got a few stops to make. I'll talk to him later if I can. Meanwhile, you tell him I'll all right, okay?"

"He'll be pissed as hell that you didn't come see him yourself."

"I know, Mom. But it's hard to handle any emotional scenes now, even good ones." I force a smile to my face as I push myself gently back from her. "Let's see, murderous Shadows need to be killed, annoyed younger brother wants a visit. Which gets priority?" I make a weighing gesture with my hands. "So hard to decide."

"Smartass. Go." She blows me a kiss.

"I'll come home soon," I promise.

"We'll have donuts waiting," she promises back.

|||||||||||||||

The dream that I find Morgana in is peaceful. That doesn't strike me as appropriate, so I change it: darkening the clouds, increasing the speed of the wind, filling the air with the smells of a coming storm. Yeah, changing someone else's dreamscape on that scale will cost me, but it's viscerally pleasing to disturb this woman's dreams. God knows she's disturbed mine often enough.

I decide to change clothes before I reveal myself to her, trading in my normal tank top and jeans for an outfit that speaks more to my current mood. Black leather with black fittings, mystical symbols inscribed across every inch of it: I am the warrior in mourning, the mystic who belongs to no world and to every world. Briefly I toy with the idea of creating a dragon to ride, but that seems like overkill. Besides, I really can't afford to tire myself out over set dressing.

I see her standing a short distance away, gazing up at the storm clouds, probably wondering where they came from so suddenly. With her white Grecian gown, bare arms encircled with golden bracelets, and golden hair studded with pearls, she looks like a goddess. But of course. What other image would she choose for herself?

She senses my approach and turns toward me. There is a flicker of surprise when she realizes what's happening, but only a flicker. I'm strangely disappointed; I wanted to shock her more. Maybe I should have gone with the dragon. "Sebastian said you wanted to talk to me."

"So the ancient legends are true." There is a sense of wonder in her voice that softens my heart a bit. This woman has spent the last sixteen years trying to bring a Dreamwalker into the world. For her, this moment is a kind of birth.

"Some legends. I've decided to reject the ones where we go crazy and destroy the world."

A slight smile appears. "I never believed those anyway."

"No?" I can't keep the edge from my voice. "You believed in them enough to keep me in the dark all these years. So that if God forbid I suddenly went rabid I wouldn't infect you with my madness."

The smile fades. "I kept you in the dark because there are people on Terra Prime who could pluck secrets from your mind like fruit from a tree. Domitors who could force you to confide in them. Farseers and Soulriders and Shadows who could watch your every move. Seers other than me who could sense what you truly are. Keeping secrets in my world is a little more complicated than in yours. Sometimes it requires extreme measures."

"You were afraid," I challenge her. "You didn't know what form my Gift would take, or how it might threaten you. You thought the ancient legends of madness might be true. You hedged your bets."

For a seemingly endless moment she says nothing. That surprises me. I had expected an immediate denial, or at least evasion. "I was afraid," she agrees, "not only of what you might become, but of what your Gift might awaken in others. And I needed to know who you were, and what you were capable of, before I entrusted you with the truth."

Whatever I had expected from her, honesty wasn't part of it. "And now what? You're satisfied?"

There's a nanosecond's hesitation. "Yes."

I can tell she's not being completely honest with me, but I also know she's adept enough to fool me, so if I notice the hesitation, it's because she wants me to. Games within games within games; dealing with her makes my head hurt. "Tell me, Jesse . . . I see that you can enter my dream and control it; can you do that with more than one person at a time? Draw numerous people into the same setting, all at once?"

Suddenly I'm on my guard. "Why do you ask?"

"Because that's what the first Dreamwalkers did. Or so my sources suggest. Granted, I don't have many details, but it's said they created a location where such a thing was possible. In the words of one source, 'a land poised between the worlds, answering to none.'"

"That still doesn't answer my question about why you're asking."

A smile flickers briefly on those perfectly painted lips. "They used it as a battlefield, summoning all their enemies to it. That was long after the Guilds turned against them. But the Dreamwalkers thought that if they could destroy the Shadows involved, perhaps they could negotiate with the rest. The Shadows were the driving force behind the whole effort, so maybe that would have worked. And what better place to fight your enemy than on a battlefield of your own design? It is said they all gathered in that one place, armed with weapons from a hundred different worlds, and summoned the Shadowlords to them—or so I read in fragments of ancient journals. Who can say how accurate such testimonies are?"

I realize she's probably talking about the battle I saw in the fetter vision, but I'm not going to give her the pleasure of confirming her story. "What do they say happened?"

"The Shadows survived. The Dreamwalkers disappeared. Few witnesses were left, and those who did survive were mentally damaged. Hence the reason I have so few details to offer you. But I do have a theory about why the Dreamwalkers lost that fight."

Now I'm interested, though still wary of her motives. "Which is?"

"They fought as the unGifted would fight. True, they could

control the battlefield itself and create any weapon that the human mind could imagine, but those were still just physical weapons, meant for traditional warfare. Their goal was simply to kill their enemies in the dream world, believing that it would cause them to die in this one."

I reach up reflexively to rub the scar on my arm, souvenir of my first encounter with a reaper. I often wondered what would have happened had it killed me in that dream; now I know. "So what do you think they should have done instead?"

"Fought like Dreamwalkers. Leveraged their unique Gift to advantage. Used weapons that the Shadows could not defend against."

"That's sounds pretty vague. Got anything more specific?"

Smiling enigmatically, she offers me a small book. After eyeing it suspiciously for a moment I take it. The binding is leather with a gilt design around the edges, the kind of blank journal you might buy in an upscale gift shop. I open it to a random page and see a man's name at the top. Beneath it is an odd list:

Sunlight
Claustrophobia
Physical abuse. Uncle?
Political embarrassment. Something in Richmond. No records.

I flip to another page to find a similar list. And another. The whole book is full of them. "What are these?"

"The fears of Luray's Shadowlords. And a few from other cities."

I look up in astonishment. "How did you get this information?"

She laughs softly. "I've spent the last sixteen years sensing and recording every weakness my Gift could detect. Other Seers helped with the project, though they had no idea of its true purpose. They thought it was for political manipulation.

Every Shadowlord who appeared in public was studied. I even arranged meetings with some, under cover of Guild business, to get them into the presence of the right Seers. Only our most gifted Masters can draw that kind of information from a man's mind without his knowledge."

I turn the small book over in my hand, awed by its potential. What might my foray into Virilian's dream have been like if I'd had this kind of information then? What might my current conflict with the Shadows become, with this in hand?

"These are the fears of your enemies, Jessica. These are the nightmares that eat at their souls. All Shadowlords are afraid of strong emotion, because they believe it disturbs the balance of spirit that keeps them both alive and dead. Awaken fear in them—or any strong emotion—and it will cut them more deeply than a sword ever could."

I turn the book over my hand, still struggling to absorb the significance of what I've been given. "You've been working on this for sixteen years?"

"I have."

"Since the day I was born?"

"Give or take a few weeks."

"Because you knew that I would go to war with the Shadows someday."

"Given that they consider it their duty to kill all Dreamwalkers, it seemed likely you'd wind up in conflict with them, so yes."

I raise my head up slowly and meet her gaze head-on. "And you only wanted to protect me. Was that it?"

She smiles slightly. "I wouldn't say only, but yes. I wanted to protect you."

All her manipulations of me have been toward this end. All the spying, all the tests she's put me through, the torment she's imposed upon my family . . . it was all to bring me to this point, so I would take up the sword and win the battle that the first

Dreamwalkers lost. Maybe she even had a hand in inspiring the Shadows to kidnap Tommy as part of the training program; her mind is so twisted I wouldn't put it past her. I have a sudden urge to throw the book in her face, to tell her that she has no right to play with my life that way, preparing me for a destiny I neither understand nor want. But I can't bring myself to do it. Because this time we want the same thing. Oh, I'm sure her reasons for wanting it are completely different from mine, and maybe someday I'll regret having helped her, but right now, in this brief window of time, fate has made us allies. Only a fool would deny that.

"The physical book is in my study," she says. "You understand I can't entrust a messenger with it. When you come back to Luray I'll give it to you."

I shake my head. "I'm not coming back to Luray yet." *And I sure as hell don't want to meet with you in person.* "You'll need to produce a copy here so that I can read it. Which unfortunately means you'll need to go back and memorize the information in it, so that your mind can produce an accurate copy. I'll come to you later tonight and memorize whatever you bring me, so I can reproduce it when I wake up. If you can't remember it all at once, that's okay. We'll just have to do this several times. Whatever it takes."

She looks at me for a long time. I wonder how many people have ever dared to give her instructions. But it really is the only logical way to transfer the information, if we can't meet in person. At last she nods. "Very well."

"Is there other business you want to discuss?"

A corner of her mouth twitches slightly. "That depends on whether you still want to learn who your mother is."

It's bait, pure and simple, and much as I would like to hear her speak the name aloud, I don't want her to enjoy the kind of power that would come of my begging her for information. Thank God Sebastian shared his suspicions with me so that I'd be prepared for this moment. "I know who my mother is. She lives on Terra Colonna, and she's devoted her entire life to keeping me safe. Not because there's some grand scheme she wants me to be part of, but because that's just what a mother does. As for the person who gave birth to me . . ." I hesitate. Bitter words are poised on my tongue, but Morgana deserves better than that. She spared my life and protected me for sixteen years, at risk to her own reputation. And she's just handed me a weapon that may enable me to live for another sixteen. I might not be pleased by her motives or her methods, but she deserves something better than summary rejection. "We can talk about that when all this is over."

She nods—a bit sadly, it seems. Or maybe sadness is just part of her game. "Tell Sebastian he's free from his debt to me."

"Sebastian is free from all his debts," I answer.

I banish the dream before she can ask me what that means.

<hr />

The black plain is still. Peaceful. The instability it has exhibited in recent visits is gone now; apparently that was just a reflection of my fear. Sorrow seems to have no such effect on it.

"We need to talk!" I call out. The words themselves won't be heard, I know, but they help me focus my thoughts. Closing my eyes, I cast my desire out into the darkness, letting it filter into all the dreams that surround me. It seems easier now than the first time I tried to find her, perhaps because this time I know what I'm doing. Or maybe dreamwalking is just easier when you're not afraid that monsters may emerge from the darkness at any moment and devour you.

When I open my eyes she's there, wearing the body that Dr. Redwind described to me: red skin and long black hair, with a garment of shimmering patterns that change as I look at them. I recognize those patterns now, and I can hear a subtle music that ebbs and flows as they transform. The great web that binds all the worlds together is reflected in her garment. "They're gone," I tell her. "The reapers. We freed them from bondage and they left the physical world. We're safe now." I pause. "All of us."

As always she is silent, but I can see how deeply my words affect her. A golden tear shimmers in one eye, and the sight of it fills me with vast sorrow. I realize in that moment that all the things I have speculated about her nature must be right, and I say, very softly, "You died in that battle, didn't you? Probably by your own hand, because if the Shadows had killed you they would have bound your spirit. You wanted to escape them, and suicide was the only way to do it." I pause. "Is that right? You've been around too long for any other explanation to make sense."

Her eyes are filled with a terrible sadness.

"Show me who you really are," I beg her. "Please."

She hesitates, then nods, and the body she is wearing begins to transform. Her red skin changes color to medium brown, with tiger-streaks of black banding her arms and legs. Her hair becomes shorter and takes on a tightly curled texture. Her body becomes smaller and leaner, until she is little larger than a child, with arms that are slightly too long in proportion to the rest of her body. As I realize what she is becoming, a sense of wonder fills me . . . and excitement, for what it implies.

The girl who stands before me now is smaller and darker than I am, and while her features are not exactly those of an abbie, her kinship with them is undeniable. Whatever cluster of worlds produced the abbies is clearly her home as well.

"They're so arrogantly human." I shake my head slowly as I speak. "They hunted down all the Dreamwalkers in their own species, but never imagined that the Gift might have manifested in others. Especially human variants that they regard as little more than animal. That's why you were afraid to show yourself to me, wasn't it? You feared that if a Terran Dreamwalker learned the truth, *they* might find out."

She nods.

"Are there others among your people who have this Gift? Or something like it?"

She hesitates, then nods.

"Can you communicate with them?"

She's more wary now, probably wondering why I'm asking. But she nods.

I draw in a deep breath. It's all or nothing now. "You know that the Shadows were the ones who called for our slaughter. The other Guilds acted at their urging." That much I had seen clearly in the fetter visions.

She nods.

"And the Dreamwalkers who fell . . . you know what was done to them. We may have freed the reapers, but many others are still bound."

A golden tear trickles down her cheek. She nods.

"If I said that there was a way we might be able to free some of those Dreamwalkers, but we would have to confront the Shadows to do it, do you think the others might be willing to help?"

This time there is no nod. No response at all.

"It'll be different than last time, I promise. A whole different kind of battle, one that we can really win. But there will still be risk. I won't lie to you about that." When there's still no response I press, "If I explain my idea to you and you see merit in it, will you at least bring it to your people? We would need strong numbers to succeed, and I . . . I have no way of contacting them myself." Still no response. "Please."

Still there's no answer. I'm frustrated, but I understand the cause. How many centuries has she wandered the dream worlds in search of hope—any hope—praying that things would change for our kind? Guarding the passageway to the Dreamwalker's haven, so that when it was finally needed it could be accessed? But it's hard to accept a call to arms that asks her to fight alongside the humans she has feared for so long. I may be a sister to her in spirit, but in my blood I am kin to slavers and murderers. Nothing I say can ever change that.

But finally she nods. Relief washes over me. "All right." My mind is racing now, a thousand possibilities unfolding before me. No—before *us*. "Let me tell you what I'm thinking . . ."

⸻

When I awoke, the stars overhead were so numerous and bright that the sky looked like a Christmas tree. I lay still for a few minutes, expecting a wave of sickness, but all I felt was an ache in my muscles and a vague nausea. Either my Gift was getting stronger or I was learning to pace myself.

I rolled up onto one elbow and saw our hostess sitting on the steps of her wagon, smoking a long clay pipe. The smell of it wafted over to me as I got to my feet, moving quietly so as not to wake Isaac. Spice and musk. She moved over on the step so that I could sit down beside her. "Did you tell your family you were well?" she asked.

I nodded. "And found the shallow's guardian. She confirmed that there are a lot of other Dreamwalkers. They're from a different branch of humanity, so no one ever thought to look for them."

"Ah, yes. The arrogance of the conqueror, triumphant over the obvious. I could make a comment about Anglo incompetence, too, but I'll spare you that." She drew on her pipe, took a moment to savor the smoke, then said, "You're going to confront the Shadows?"

I sighed. "I don't see that I have much choice."

"Nor I, quite frankly. Do you have a plan?"

"I think so. It depends on some allies coming through for me, so we'll see where that goes." I hesitated. "I would need permission to use the shallow."

Her eyes narrowed as she lowered her pipe. "You want to stage a battle here? Draw the attention of Shadows to this place?"

"I need it to get back to the Dreamwalker haven. Nothing will come in the other direction, I promise."

"I refused your friend when he asked the same thing, you know."

"That was different. He was summoning spirits to your home. I just need a place where my body can rest while my mind goes elsewhere."

"And what if you die in this Dreamwalker haven of yours?"

My smile faded. "Then you have my mother's address, don't you?"

She looked at me for a long moment. "I'll want to know more about your plan. In case something does—as you so succinctly put it—come in the other direction."

"As soon as I get confirmation that the other Dreamwalkers will help me, I'll fill you in on everything. If they won't . . ." I sighed. "Then it's back to square one, I guess." I looked back at the campfire. "I suppose I should go back and start memorizing data."

She raised an eyebrow.

"Long story," I said. "Sort of like cramming for a test. I'll explain everything in the morning, I promise."

"I look forward to it."

I got up, nodded a respectful leavetaking, and started back toward my bedding.

"Ahota," she said quietly.

I turned back to her. "What?"

"Ahota. The name my people know me by."

I was silent for a moment. It was as if I'd just been handed a precious, fragile artifact, and moving wrong might shatter it. "I don't have a special name to give you. Just the two."

She tapped some ashes out of the bowl of her pipe. "It's a shame. Names are meaningful. Your parents gave you one, but now you should choose one for yourself. Something that speaks to the recent transformation of your soul."

The transformation of my soul. I remembered looking at my reflection in the water, how surprised I had been when I saw it hadn't changed. Dr. Redwind was right; I was a different person now than when I first came to Terra Prime. That deserved some kind of acknowledgement. "Did your soul transform?" I asked.

"All souls transform. Some more dramatically than others."

"I guess I'm in the *heavy drama* category."

Her aged eyes sparkled in the starlight as she chuckled softly. "I don't think there's any arguing that, my dear."

As I headed back to my bedroll to see if Morgana was ready to deliver her data, I wondered what kind of name you gave to someone who was about to face off against the undead.

29

SHADOWCREST
VIRGINIA PRIME

SHEKARCHIYANDAR

THE SCREAMS OF THE DEAD are music to Shekarchiyandar's ears. He shuts his eyes, letting the sounds of wraithly suffering refresh his resurrected spirit. Some of his slave spirits still remember a time when screaming had a purpose, when a cry of pain might have brought help running—or at least inspired sympathy—and their voices are the loudest, the most desperate. But here there is no help and no sympathy. Eventually they will learn that. Eventually they will tire of defiance, and their cries will subside to mere whispers of misery, background music to the terror of new arrivals.

All those notes—loud and soft, desperate and despairing—are testaments to Shekarchiyandar's power. Yet even they pale beside his greatest accomplishment, the creation of the *ruuhbal*. The fact that seven of his hunters are still functioning after so many centuries is a monument to his skill as a necromancer, and the fact that they are as obedient to his will now, when he is acting through Virilian, as they were on the night he created them, strikes fear and wonder into the hearts of his fellow Shadowlords. How many could manage such a feat?

He does prefer their original name to what they are called now. *Devourer of souls.* Much more poetic than *reaper.*

As he walks down the halls of the *Bayt al-Hikma*—the House of Wisdom—he knows that he is in a dream, but he lets the illusion play out. One of his greatest shocks upon his return to the living world was learning that the great Persian library had been destroyed, sacked by Mongols after his last death. In his first lifetime the place had seemed eternal, yet it had fallen like so many political monuments, its priceless books and scrolls cast into the Euphrates until the river ran black from all the ink. Or so Virilian's history books claim. How anyone could destroy such a storehouse of knowledge is beyond him. Wars might be writ in human blood, but it is knowledge that determines the course of human history. That was the weapon he used to bring the Dreamwalkers down, casting them as monsters whose existence threatened all of humankind. Once the historical records were altered to reflect his fiction, and enough generations had passed that the truth was forgotten, the Dreamwalkers' fates were sealed forever.

Now there is a new Dreamwalker in town. He is perversely pleased by that, as a dog trainer might be pleased by the appearance of a fox. Even a leashed predator needs to be blooded now and then, and his reapers have little prey these days. But though he is using the reapers to find her, he doesn't want them to kill her. Not yet.

He will do that himself.

That is assuming she manages to escape from the Badlands alive. If she does, and he is able to capture her . . . ah, what pleasure it will be to bind a young new Dreamwalker, her senses crisp and clear, her talent fresh and strong! How many centuries has it been since he last experienced the heady rush that comes of devouring an enemy's soul? Even remembering such things sends a shiver of anticipation through his undead flesh. And once she is dead there will be the challenge of breaking her spirit, as one must break a wild stallion. Perhaps he will even mold her into a new reaper, and command her to join the others and hunt her own kind. So many possibilities! But first he must capture her.

He reaches for a book—and suddenly is aware that he is not alone. Virilian might not have recognized the source of the sensation, but Shekarchiyandar is more knowledgeable about such things. A Dreamwalker has entered the scene. Might it be his quarry? Would she really dare to come here, to this mental landscape which he controls? The first time she invaded Virilian's dreams she had done so stealthily, hoping to avoid detection, but with Shekarchiyandar in the picture such stealth was no longer possible. He had dealt with her kind during the Dream Wars, and knew the signs.

But she has no way to know that, he reminds himself. *She has no idea what she is facing in me.*

As he turns toward his visitor he transforms his Shadowlord robe into a gown of Persian silk, setting a turban of twisted gold cloth on his head like a crown. It is the kind of outfit he wore during his first lifetime, when kings and priests feared him. Let her see him as he was in the days of his living glory.

The girl who stands before him is younger than expected, but she bears herself with dignity and confidence—or at least the illusion of those things. She's dressed in clothing made from a type of cloth that Virilian identifies as *camo*, the hallmark of modern warriors, but she wears no protective armor, and the only weapon visible is a long knife clipped to her belt. It doesn't mean much, of course. She can create any weapon or armor she needs in the space of a heartbeat. As can he.

When she sees that his attention is fixed on her she asks, "Do you know who I am?"

"Jennifer Dolan, I assume. Since there are no other Dreamwalkers around these days, it seems the logical conclusion."

"No other Dreamwalkers that you know about."

He ignores the obvious bait. "Do you know who I am?"

For a moment she doesn't respond. She came here to see Virilian, but obviously he doesn't look like Virilian, so she's probably trying to apply her limited knowledge of the Shadows to make sense of that. "I know whose dream I entered," she says at last. "I also know that the man standing in front of me took part in the Dream Wars, and those ended centuries before Augustus Virilian was born."

"I am Guildmaster Virilian. I am also Shekarchiyandar, called the Lord of Hunters, who helped bring about the defeat of the Dreamwalkers." He folds his arms across his chest. "So, what brings you into my dream? If I find your story interesting I may hold my reapers at bay long enough for you to finish the telling of it."

If his mention of the reapers stirs fear in her, it doesn't show. "I've come here to parley."

He raises an eyebrow. "For what purpose?"

"To end an ancient war."

"The one between your people and mine?"

"Is there another one we should be discussing?"

He chuckles disdainfully. "That war ended long ago, child."

Anger flashes in her eyes. "You're still hunting my kind. So no, sorry, it's not ended."

"Cleanup." He shrugs. "Nothing more."

"The people you took captive back then are still your captives today, Does that sound like 'the war is over' to you? Because it doesn't to me."

"You speak of the souls of Dreamwalkers."

She nods.

"You want them freed?"

"Yes."

"*All* of them?"

"Yes."

"And you are . . ." he smiles indulgently, ". . . *demanding* this?"

"Let's say I'm asking it. For now."

Her audacity amuses him. Impresses him, even. He wonders what it will feel like to drain her of her memories and dissect that defiant spirit. "Even if such a thing were possible, do you imagine I speak for every Shadowlord on earth? Or can give them all orders?" He shakes his head mockingly. "Would that I had such power!"

"I know it's possible. I've met a spirit who was bound by the Shadows and then released, and if it can be done for him it can be done for others. So let's not waste time pretending I don't know that, okay? Second, you may not be able to give orders to every Shadowlord on earth, but you can set things in motion. Bear witness to the other Guilds that war with us is no longer necessary. Order the freeing of Dreamwalker souls within your domain, and encourage neighboring Shadows to do the same. After that, if I must repeat my message to others Shadowlords, city by city, so be it. At least there will be precedent."

"That would take considerable time."

"The Dreamwalkers you enslaved have suffered for centuries. What's another year or two, added to that?"

"And what do you offer in return for all this?" His tone is scornful. "Your eternal gratitude? Undying friendship?"

"How about, we won't tell everyone how you enslaved the Dreamwalkers to claim their Gift? I doubt the other Guilds would be pleased by that." Her gaze is defiant. "And we won't tell the other Guilds how you fed them lies to get them to help you, or how you falsified historical records later so they would never find out the truth."

Anger stirs inside him. "You *dare* to threaten me?"

"I'm offering you peace. An end to secrets. Release my people and the past will be forgotten. No one need ever know the truth. Surely that's best for everyone."

"I could kill you here and now, you know. In this very dream. I could summon my reapers and have them tear your soul to bits—"

"Your reapers are gone, as is the great Shadow army that once destroyed our tower. So who will you fight us with this time? Shadows to whom we're no more than legend?"

His reapers are gone? She is bluffing. She must be bluffing. He reaches out with his mind to contact his *ruuh-bal*, to summon them to his side . . . but there is no response. He tries again. Nothing. *It's not possible*, he thinks. *She lacks the Gift required to do such a thing.* "Your tower is gone," he tells her. "We knew it served as a focus for the Dreamwalkers' Gift, so we destroyed it. The information stored in it was likewise destroyed. I know, because I set that fire myself. So what will you show to the other Guilds, as proof that your accusations are true? Everyone knows that your Gift brings madness. Tell whatever stories you like; it will only be further proof of your insanity." He smiles coldly. "Didn't you think that I planned for this from the beginning? Only a fool trusts that mere silence will guard his secrets forever."

"We made mistakes when we fought you before." Her voice is quiet now, but in the way the stillness before a storm is quiet. "If we have to fight again, you won't have that advantage."

"And who will *your* army be composed of? What Dreamwalkers have survived our purge? Madmen perhaps, who evaded us because their Gift was mistaken for mental illness? Children so young they haven't yet manifested their Gift? We've been hunting your kind for centuries, Dreamwalker. A few might have slipped through our fingers, but I'll wager there aren't enough of you left to stage a street brawl, much less a war."

"Don't underestimate our numbers," she warns. "Or our capacity. Open conflict wouldn't be good for either Shadows or Dreamwalkers. That's why I've come to you, to seek a solution that will allow us to avoid further bloodshed. Release your captives, and all the rest will be forgotten. On this you have my word."

"You speak for all the Dreamwalkers, then? All—what?— two of them? Three? Perhaps as many as a dozen?" He chuckles scornfully.

"Enough." There is ice in her voice. "Don't test us, Guildmaster. You won't like where that leads."

His smile fades. "Your threats are empty. I didn't fear bloodshed in my mortal life, and I don't fear it now. So summon your dozen great dream-warriors. Do your worst. When the dust has settled and all the spilled blood has dried, I will take pleasure in binding your soul myself. You will spend the rest of eternity hunting your own kind."

A muscle at the side of her jaw twitches. "That's your final word?"

"It is."

"Then I'm sorry, Shadowlord. For all the people whose blood you would spill. If you ever change your mind . . ." She pauses. "I'm sure you know how to dream up a white flag."

I know how to turn one into a shroud, he thinks as she disappears.

30

BADLANDS
TERRA PRIME

JESSE

"DID YOU FIND HIM?" Isaac asked.

I opened my eyes. Overhead the canopy at the Grand Portal was a black void against a starlit sky, its carved supports nearly invisible in the darkness. Though the sun had already risen on the east coast—hopefully prompting most of the Shadowlords to retire for the day—we still had an hour or two before the sky would lighten here. Even after that, the full heat of the day would take a while to build. Call it five comfortable hours.

When you're planning to abandon your body for an indefinite period of time, things like that matter.

"I found him. He didn't go for my offer."

"Did you expect him to?" Dr. Redwind—Ahota—was setting out the supplies I would need for my journey. Bags of colored sand, an assortment of weapons, and of course the small notebook I had recorded Morgana's observations in. Hopefully I'd transcribed all that information correctly. Ritual herbs were being placed in the appropriate braziers, waiting to be ignited. Things were nearly ready.

The sheer magnitude of what I was about to attempt was just

starting to sink in, and with it a kind of fear I had never felt before. The last confrontation between the Dreamwalkers and the Shadows had resulted in a field of dead bodies, followed by the genocide of my kind. Did I really think I could do better than that? Up until now, death had been an abstract concept to me. Now, I felt as if the real Reaper—the Grim one, with black robes and scythe—was in the corner of this ritual space, watching me. Waiting for me to make a mistake.

"No." I forced my tone to sound casual; nothing would be gained by letting the others see how overwhelmed I felt. "But it never hurts to try, right?"

Isaac helped me to my feet. "A different Shadow might have listened. They're not all the same, you know. Virilian, he's obsessed with power and not likely to do anything that could be viewed as surrender." There was bitterness in his voice. That was certainly understandable, since Virilian was the one who had banished him. "Arrogant bastard," he muttered.

I already knew the Guildmaster's weaknesses from Morgana's book of fear. *Sunlight. Submission. Condescension.* That kind of man wasn't going to let a sixteen-year-old girl tell him what to do, unless he believed there was no other choice. And maybe even then he would refuse. "I'm not sure it was Virilian I was talking to."

Ahota stopped what she was doing and looked at me. "Wasn't he the one whose dream you went to visit?"

I hesitated. How was I supposed to explain to them that the dreams of a Shadowlord were ten times more complex than those of a normal person? That the uniquely layered consciousness of the undead meant that each dream might reflect a different personality? I remembered the man I had talked to in Virilian's dream: tall, aristocratic, striking in his features, but with a black gaze as empty as the Abyss and a presence as cold as the arctic wind. In my dream I'd been able to control my appearance, so it wasn't hard for me to hide my instinctive response to him; I just created an avatar who didn't look repelled. But there was something wrong with that version of

Virilian, in a way, that hadn't been true of his other personalities. Something I couldn't give a name to, but I could sense it, and it terrified me. "He called himself Shekarchiyandar."

"Whoa." Isaac's eyes widened. "Are you *sure* that was the name?"

"I might be a little off in the pronunciation—he had a bit of an accent—but yeah, that's pretty much it. Why?"

"That's the Shadowlord who created the reapers. All the information I gave you about them was from his biography. Virilian must have Communed with him to gain control over them, which means . . . Shit."

"Why 'shit'?"

"He was crazy, Jesse. And all the people who've tried to Commune with him—" Suddenly he winced in pain.

"It's all right," I said quickly, putting a hand on his arm. "Don't worry about it." Sebastian had told me in private that he thought something had been done to Isaac to keep him from revealing Guild secrets, and it certainly looked that way now. Though I wondered how they were defining 'Guild secrets.'

"It's not all right," he choked out. "I want to be able to help you."

"You've helped me already. And you just warned me that I'll be dealing with a madman. That's a pretty important piece of information, considering he's central to this whole operation.

"He shouldn't have an accent, Jesse. And he shouldn't be using the name of an earlier incarnation. Communion's not supposed to work like—" Again I saw him stiffen in pain, then he doubled over. He seemed to be struggling for breath.

"Hey." I squeezed his arm. "It's okay. I got the picture."

"Let me go with you," he gasped. "I can help you."

My hand fell away from his arm. "You know that's not possible."

"You brought me with you last time."

"Last time I didn't have allies who hated the Shadows so much that if they even suspected I had one with me, they'd leave and never come back. I just can't risk that, Isaac." *Not to mention I don't want to pit you in battle against your own father. That's the kind of thing that could scar you for a lifetime.* "To be honest, they're not that thrilled with me either. I'm trying not to push my luck."

Ahota asked, "You still won't tell us who they are?"

I chose my words carefully, not wanting to betray the trust of my allies by revealing their true nature to anyone. "They're Dreamwalkers from less travelled worlds, places the Shadows didn't really focus on. I mean, it isn't possible to inspect every infant on every human world, right? A few must have slipped through their net now and then, and those who learned to keep their heads down survived to adulthood. The tower enabled me to find them." That seemed to satisfy Isaac, but Ahota looked like she understood what I wasn't saying. As usual.

I took some weapons from her and started arranging them around the edge of the circular platform, leaving room for the sand painting I would have to create to access the tower again. Knives, swords, spears, a bow with arrows, a pistol, a shotgun . . . I had no clue what I might need in the other world, but I was setting out everything I could think of, just in case. The less energy it cost me to create a weapon in the dream world, the more I would have free to invest in other things. God knows, I was going to need a shitload of energy for what I had in mind.

"You shouldn't have talked to Virilian," Isaac said in a strained voice. "Now you've lost the element of surprise."

I sighed. "This battle can't be won just by killing people, Isaac. We could never do enough of that to make a difference. What we have to do is convince Virilian that the Shadows' hunting methods have failed—that there are so many Dreamwalkers he could never hunt us all down—and we're capable of hurting his people in ways they can't afford. And only if they end their crusade against us, and free the Dreamwalker souls they've enslaved will we stop hurting them. If I don't explain all that to Virilian, so he doesn't know what our end game is—if he doesn't understand how to tap out—what can we accomplish here, besides meaningless bloodshed? He has to know the rules."

Ahota nodded. "Not to mention, by offering him a choice, you've placed the responsibility for this confrontation squarely on his head. He called for this conflict; he has the power to end it."

So if people do die, I thought, *the guilt will not be all mine to bear.* Her words didn't banish my fear, but they took a bit of the edge off it.

At last everything was ready. I knelt beside the bags of colored sand and shut my eyes while Ahota walked around the circle setting fire to the herb bundles. Breathing deeply, I tried to prepare myself for what was to come. But there was no way to prepare for something like this. Once more I was going to trust myself to the unknown, only this time all my enemies would be present. What if Morgana's information wasn't good enough? What if using it didn't have the effect I was hoping for? I was painfully aware that I had no plan B. If my strategy didn't work, I would probably not be coming home.

Familiar scents filled the air, marking each cardinal direction: North, South, East, West. I closed my eyes and focused on them. *Breathe deeply. Try to relax.* The smells permeated my spirit, soothing the edge of my fear, consecrating me for my journey. Or for sacrifice.

Then I opened my eyes, took a handful of sand, and began to draw.

〰〰〰〰〰〰

The Dreamwalker's world is empty.

I stand on the ridge between the tower and the red grasslands, alone. Overhead the sky is a sullen purple, like a bruise, with a swollen red sun in its center. The colors seem appropriate to today's business, as if the world itself were bleeding.

I look around me, but there's no one else visible. What if the others don't show up? The guardian promised to carry my message to them, but she'd offered no guarantees about how it would be received. What if the abbie Dreamwalkers decided they were better off staying under the Shadows' radar, as they

had done for centuries, and weren't willing to confront their enemies openly? If so, I can hardly blame them. The last open confrontation didn't exactly go well.

The black thorn bushes have taken over much of the grasslands. I feel a visceral hatred toward them that isn't wholly rational. They hurt someone I cared about and I hunger to destroy them. But I can't allow myself such a luxury. I'm going to need all the energy I have to summon Shadowlords to this place, and then use whatever is left to deal with them. I can't afford to waste any of it.

Suddenly I sense a presence behind me. I turn to see the guardian of the Dreamwalker haven standing there, the spirit I once called the avatar. She's wearing the same body as when I first met her, but this time, instead of being wrapped in mystical patterns, she's armored like an ancient Japanese warrior. I open my mouth to ask her if the others will be coming, but the words catch in my throat; I'm so afraid of being told that they won't, and that all my planning was in vain.

But then another presence takes shape beside her: a thin, pale-skinned *Homo sapiens* female with short golden hair. I feel a rush of relief so powerful it's dizzying. Next a male shows up, this one with skin the color of charcoal and geometric scars decorating his chest. And then another female, tall and lanky, her face painted with streaks of red, black, and yellow, in fearsome patterns. War paint.

Now they're appearing in twos and threes, each one wearing a body that reflects some variant of my own species. There are as many types of armor and war paint and tattoos visible as there are Dreamwalkers. Ancient and modern, primitive and sophisticated, details randomly intermingled, as if someone flipped through the pages of a book on Terra Colonna history and chose images at random. Which is possibly what happened. Most of these people have probably never seen my world in person.

After believing for so long that I was the only Dream-walker left, the sight of the others is overwhelming. I'd esti-mate at least three dozen are present, maybe four, more than I'd dared hope for. I want to say something to welcome them, but will they understand me if I do? The guardian spirit has been interacting with people on Terra Prime for centuries and clearly understands some of our languages, but to the rest of these visitors the Terran cluster is no more than a fearsome legend: the birthplace of monsters, a realm to be avoided at all costs. What are the odds they would have bothered to learn the monsters' language?

I look at the guardian. She's waiting. They're all waiting. "Can they understand me?" I ask.

She shakes her head slightly. Damn.

"Can you translate?"

She nods.

How the hell did I get to this point, when the fate of so many people is riding on my shoulders? I take a moment to steady my nerves before speaking. "Thank you for coming." The words seem insufficient in this fantastic setting, but they're the best I can come up with. I wait for the guardian to trans-late them, but she says nothing aloud. Suddenly I realize that I've never heard an abbie speak. Do they communicate on fre-quencies I can't hear, maybe, or have a means of psychic com-munication, like Farspeakers do? Or is she using the special power of this place to insert knowledge into their brains with-out words, as sometimes happens in a dream? She's not signal-ing me to stop, so I must assume she's communicating with them somehow. "We're here to force the Shadows to abandon their hunt of the Dreamwalkers, and to release the souls of the dreamers they've enslaved. We can't do that just by killing. Even if we could get all the ones who came here, there would still be thousands left in the world, and they would want re-venge for their losses. We need to try a different strategy."

Dozens of faces are staring at me, their features stylized in the same way that the guardian's are. "We need to accomplish two things. First, demonstrate by sheer numbers that their hunt has failed. They've spent centuries trying to kill us off, and it obviously didn't work." That is a lie, of course. The Shadows' genocidal efforts was frighteningly efficient within the Terran Cluster, and if they ever learned there were Dreamwalkers in other clusters they would start slaughtering those as well. But since my new allies had all disguised themselves as *Homo sapiens* to prevent that, it would look like dozens of dreamers on the Shadows' own world had survived the holocaust. There was power in such fiction.

"Second, we need to show them we have the knowledge and the power to hurt them. Really hurt them, in a way no one else has ever done before. They need to know that if this state of war continues, their people will be in danger every time they sleep. Then they'll have no choice but to negotiate." Or so I hope. What is the saying about mice and men?

I create a copy of my book of notes and hold it up to show to them. "I have here a list of their fears. Strong emotion interferes with how their talent works, so if we can inspire that emotion, we can turn their own Gift against them. Unfortunately, we can't target Shadowlords individually when we don't know who is who, so we're going to need a more general strategy. I think each of us should take one of these fears and apply it to multiple Shadows. See who responds to it most strongly, and then focus on them. Unless someone has a better idea?" I look at the guardian. She is silent for a moment—listening to something, perhaps?—then looks at me and nods her approval. "Okay. I'll read through these and we can divvy them up . . . somehow.

"Sunlight is at the top of nearly everyone's list. I don't know if they're actually harmed by it, or if the phobia is just a side effect of being undead, but either way, it gives us control over something that can hurt all of them." I point to the swollen red sun overhead. "We need to brighten that. And bring the lake back, for its reflective properties. Extend it as far as we can."

I read the rest of the data to them. Some of the Shadows' fears are surprisingly mundane, a reminder that each Shadowlord was once a normal human being, with normal human weaknesses: claustrophobia, arachnophobia, herpetophobia. Others are deeply personal in nature, rooted in traumas that they must still be struggling to forget: abuse, abandonment, humiliation. As I read each fear aloud, a Dreamwalker gestures acceptance of that one as his or her personal project. So my translator is clearly doing her job.

By the time I'm done reading there are three times as many Dreamwalkers crowded around me as before, but I sense through my Gift that the real number hasn't changed. One of the abbies must have bolstered our small army with dream constructs, so that we'll appear to be a larger force than we actually are. Good move. The sun has doubled in size and now blazes white in a cloudless blue sky, so someone took care of that, too; I have to create a pair of sunglasses so I can see comfortably. The lake is back, looking just like it did in the avatar's dream, a gleaming mirror that reflects the sunlight with painful intensity. The whole world is awash in light.

It's time.

Shutting my eyes, I focus my mind on the mystical pattern that will lead me back to Virilian's dream. This time I can't simply follow it to him, but I need to use it to draw him into my dreamscape. I'm honestly not sure how to do that, but my fetter visions suggested that the tower once channeled such knowledge to those who dreamwalked here, so I cross my fingers and hope that the building is still intact enough to help me. If not, then this is going to be a very short campaign.

But as I envision the pattern in my mind, I can indeed see

where changes will be needed. A few alterations in one place will shift the flow of energy between myself and Virilian, so that it runs against its natural current; a few extra connections in another will bind his fate to that of the tower, so that he is naturally drawn to it. I craft a new pattern to reflect these changes, weaving it strand by strand, with delicacy, like a spider creating its web. As I do so the music of the dream world resonates around me, echoing my creation back at me. I allow it to draw me into a half-trance of concentration, so that all things fade from my mind except the codex and its music. It feels good. It feels right. This is what I was born to do.

But binding Virilian to my web is only the first step. A single witness wouldn't be enough to carry our message to the Shadows, especially if he was someone the Shadows considered mentally unstable. If Virilian told the others about a nightmare confrontation with militant Dreamwalkers, it might be judged nothing more than a delusion. No, we need enough Shadows to attend that the truth of the event can't be denied later—but not so many that we lose control of the confrontation. It's a delicate balancing act.

The last time I visited Virilian's dream, I used his personal relics to find him. Now I'm using him as a relic to find those who are connected to him. One by one, I reach out to the people who are part of his fate-pattern, following mental paths of authority, loyalty, rivalry, duty, and even hatred, back to their sources. I'm able to get a solid fix on eleven Shadowlords that way, which seems a good number for our purposes. I weave them into my web, trapping them in its pattern like helpless flies.

At last my creation is complete, and I begin to draw my flies to me. Virilian is the first to arrive, manifesting so suddenly that it startles me out of my trance. He flinches in pain and raises up an arm to protect his face from the sunlight, a welcome validation of our strategy, but an instant later he recovers his composure and straightens up. Now he's raising both arms to the sky and chanting in a foreign language. Dark clouds appear overhead, and for a moment I'm afraid that he's trying to summon the reapers back. Am I really sure they're gone for good? But it's only storm clouds that he wants, thick grey ones that congeal in front of the sun's blazing face, casting the landscape into shadow. Rain begins to fall, not so heavily as to be a threat in its own right, but as it strikes the lake it breaks up the surface into a million shivering ripples, destroying its mirror-like perfection. Our most powerful weapon has been negated.

Shit.

Much as I want to counter his efforts, my immediate duty is to complete my summoning. I shut my eyes and try to focus again, trusting the other Dreamwalkers will deal with Virilian. But can they? This man has bound the souls of Dreamwalkers and claimed their Gift for his own; he may have as much power over this dreamscape as we do.

More Shadowlords are beginning to manifest now, some with ghostly attendants trailing behind them like wisps of silk. The new arrivals seem confused by their surroundings, and I wonder if they even know that they're dreaming. If not, that's good; they won't think to take control of the landscape. Now the clouds are starting to thin out and the rain begins to falter; I see that one black-skinned abbie is staring upward, doubtless trying to restore the sunlight. But Virilian overrides his efforts easily. As he does so he sees me looking at him and smiles. There is hunger in his eyes, black and boundless, so nakedly cannibalistic that it makes me shudder.

It's time for our assault to begin.

The ground beneath the Shadows starts to buck and heave, then liquefy. Spiders rise up from cracks in the ground in swarms so thick the earth can no longer be seen, and rabid rats claw at the grey fabric of the Shadowlords' robes as they scramble to climb up toward their faces. Walls of stone appear around some of the invaders, sealing them into tomb-like enclosures; those who have not yet realized that they are dreaming have to break free by brute physical force, while others concentrate to banish the stone. Flames spurt from the ground, and the air is filled with the smell of burning flesh, while faceless, nameless corpses litter the earth as far as the eye can see. Each of these things is an emotional trigger for one of the Shadows, but which one? I must leave it to my companions to figure that out, because right now my attention is fixed on Virilian.

Infinitely confident, maddeningly arrogant, he stands in the midst of the chaos, brushing our constructs aside with the power of his mind as casually as one might swat a fly. The ground beneath his feet is stable, and neither snakes nor spiders nor rats nor any other noxious beasts come near him. A wall of stone that begins to take shape around him crumbles at his touch. Wildfire streaks across the ground in his direction, but it divides as it reaches him, leaving him unscathed. I hear others cry out as they are burned, but his clothing isn't even singed.

Shekarchiyandar has been to this world before, and he knows how to control it.

His black eyes fixed on me, he mutters another incantation. Suddenly I can see all the ghosts that surround him—horrific creatures, starved and bruised and bleeding, forever looking like they did when they were tortured to death. One of them looks at me, and I see a desperate plea in its eyes: *Destroy us! End this!* When Virilian summons lightning to cast at the abbies, the ghosts twitch in pain, and several cry out; in that moment I understand what they are, and why he wants me to see them.

Dreamwalkers.

He's drawing on them for power, draining them of energy

to fuel his dream creations, so that his own vitality isn't diminished. Can all the Shadowlords do that? If so, then we are sorely outnumbered. There may be three times as many Dreamwalkers in the field as Shadows, but the latter have ten times our ability to alter dreams. Long after we collapse from exhaustion, the Shadows will still be going strong.

I feel sick.

The battle is beginning in earnest now, two nightmare forces meeting on the field of the human imagination, unrestricted by the laws of science. Black fire roars across the landscape, rain turns to scalding steam, and monsters appear, strike, and then vanish. I see a small Asian-looking abbie summon a scarlet dragon from the clouds, flames licking forth from its mouth, as it heads straight toward the Shadows. But then a flock of bats meets it in mid-air, and they tear at its wing membranes until it, too, vanishes. It's impossible to tell which nightmare images are being controlled by which side. Some even seem to change sides, as a Dreamwalker or Shadow takes control of an enemy's creation. I see a swarm of venomous insects heading directly toward a group of Dreamwalkers, so I counter that attack myself, creating a cloud of insecticide that the insects must fly through to get to them. The gambit is successful, but it costs me dearly. Sickness wells up in my throat, and for a moment I am so dizzy I can barely stay on my feet. Summoning so many Shadowlords must have drained me of nearly all my vital energy; I'm running on empty now. And unlike the Shadows, I have no wraiths to devour for fuel.

Suddenly a Shadowlord screams. I look over and see that one of them has been encased in a concrete cylinder, whose sides are steadily contracting. From inside we can hear terrified screams and the frenzied pounding of fists against stone. Apparently someone figured out which of the Shadowlords is claustrophobic. Virilian notices as well, and he takes control of the cylinder, forcing the concrete to crumble to dust, freeing its occupant. But it's too late. The man's skin no longer bears the chalky pallor of the undead, but is a sickly yellow streaked with blood; his eyes are no longer featureless black orbs, but reddened whites with pinpoint pupils. As he falls senseless to the ground I am struck with wonder and fear at what I am seeing and what it implies.

He is alive. Truly alive.

Virilian looks back at me, and this time there is no arrogance in him, nor laughter, only a black and terrible hatred. His eyes remain fixed on me as he begins to incant again, and something about his tone warns me that it's a summoning. Reflexively, I step back a few feet, as ghosts begin to appear on both sides of him. I see men and women, old and young, and even small children, each one ritually lacerated like Jacob was in Isaac's dream. Their eyes are empty and their faces are slack; it's as if someone has surgically removed their souls. More and more of them appear as I watch: a dozen, two dozen, three: soldiers in an army that now outnumbers mine by vast numbers. Distantly I am aware that the fighting has stopped, both sides now focused upon this frightening panorama, albeit with different motives.

"Kill them," Virilian commands, and he points to the Dreamwalkers.

A red-skinned abbie conjures a wall of flame to block their path, but Virilian banishes the fire with a gesture so casual it is insulting. Then the army of wraiths is rushing toward us and we're all scrambling to create weapons and armor in time, but what do you use to attack a ghost? They reach the front lines and I see one of them assault a fake Dreamwalker, which causes the construct to dissolve like mist. Virilian starts laughing, because now he knows that not all the Dreamwalkers on the field of battle are real. He barks out another command and his ghosts begin striking out wildly, not worrying about doing any real damage, just trying to hit as many of us as they can in order to banish the fakes. Each moment our ranks are revealed to be smaller and smaller, while our best efforts to strike down the ghosts or take control of them all are proven futile. Soon there will be only real Dreamwalkers left to target.

A black shadow suddenly appears overhead. I look up and see that the clouds are beginning to move in an all-too-familiar pattern. *No*, I think desperately. *No. It can't be. We dealt with the reapers! They can't show up now.* Several of the Dreamwalkers disappear from the ridge, retreating to their own worlds just in time, but once the first reaper manifests overhead it is too late for the rest of us. With a loud cracking sound the lake freezes over, fingers of ice exploding across its surface. Even the ghosts seem stunned by what is going on, and for a moment there is no fighting, only fear.

I create a long spear like the ones we were given for Isaac's ritual, and I brace myself for what may well be my final battle. If I'm going to die, I'm damn well going to go down fighting.

But though all seven reapers manifest, they don't attack us. They don't do anything. I have the impression they are taking stock of the situation, much as they did with Isaac's ritual.

"Do what you were meant to do!" Virilian commands them. There is triumph in his voice; his servants have returned to him, and surely this piddling force of Dreamwalkers cannot hope to stand against them! But I can sense hate in those servants, and a terrible, all-consuming anger, and maybe I'm wrong, but it doesn't seem like those emotions are directed at us.

They dive down from the sky to attack. But we are not their targets. I see the look on Virilian's face as he realizes what is happening. Then he is surrounded by reapers, engulfed in their unearthly darkness. I hear a human scream and then a howling sound that is anything but human, a cry filled with agony and hatred and loneliness—terrible loneliness—but there is triumph in it, too, and when it finally fades the reapers withdraw just far enough for us to see the mound of broken bones and shredded flesh that Virilian has become.

For a moment the entire world seems frozen, and my heart pounds wildly as I wait to see what the reapers will do next. I get the sense that they, too, are considering that question. Are they going to go after the other Shadowlords, to wreak vengeance upon the entire Guild that enslaved them? If all the Shadowlords here are killed, there will be no witnesses left to tell the others what happened. That would defeat our purpose.

Suddenly one of the Shadowlords steps forward. The others have all retreated in fear, but he walks right up to where the reapers are hovering, holds up a hand, and cries out, "Enough!"

The reapers seem agitated, and for a moment it looks like they're going to attack him, but they don't. "Enough!" He repeats. The force of his presence is a palpable thing, and for the moment it seems to be holding them back. "I, Leonid Antonin, elder and Secundus, acting Guildmaster of the Shadows, give you my word that none will attempt to bind you again. If you go in peace now, you will have peace from us in return."

It's Isaac's father, I think. The reapers seem to shudder as he speaks, and I remember back to Isaac's ritual, how he gave his own family name to the reapers, adopting them into his line. Is that affecting how they view this man now? On some level of consciousness, do they recognize him as family? Or are they actually bound by Isaac's ritual not to harm him? Whatever the cause, the reapers slowly begin to move away, withdrawing into the sky. A moment later they are gone. The army of wraiths, meanwhile, seems frozen, as if in the absence of Virilian they don't know what they are supposed to do.

Antonin looks at the assembled Dreamwalkers. "I imagine you have done what you came here for." He nods toward what is left of Virilian, then looks at the transformed Shadowlord who is moaning on the ground. "And you have proven what you came here to prove. Enough blood. Enough dying. It is over."

"There are terms that need to be discussed," I tell him.

He gestures toward the field of battle; Virilian's ghosts vanish from sight. "Gather your wounded and your dead, and return to the world of the living. Then send word to Shadowcrest, and we will arrange for a proper meeting. This is not a suitable place for such a discussion."

"What about the people hunting me?"

"By evening all will know that you are granted safe passage to speak to me. That order will be honored by the Shadows, and by all who answer to us." He pauses. "If you've made enemies outside our ranks, I can't help you with that."

"I want safe passage for those who travel with me."

He nods. "Agreed. Now . . ." He glances back at the other Shadowlords. "Release us from this place."

There's nothing I want less right than to use my Gift again, but it has to be done. Wincing from exhaustion, I shut my eyes, envision my web, and mentally sever the strands that I used to bind Virilian to the tower. By the time I open my eyes, the Shadowlords are gone.

I look at the Dreamwalkers. Most of the ones who fell in battle are moving or moaning, so they're still alive. Thank God.

"We did it," I say hoarsely. The reality of it is just starting to sink in. "They know we can screw up their Gift. We *won*."

The guardian spirit looks at me. Though she doesn't speak aloud, I can hear her words clearly in my mind. *It is not over yet.*

"I know. I know. I'll send word back to you when I know what the resolution is." I draw in a deep breath. "Thank you. Thank you all."

Thank you, the voice in my head responds. *Sister.*

The exhaustion of battle takes over then, and I have no reserves left to deal with it. Sinking to my knees, I let the dream world fade from my mind, focusing on the sounds and scents that will guide me home. It's easy this time. My body wants me back.

"Did it work?" Isaac asked as soon as my eyes opened.

"Yes," I murmured weakly. "And by the way, your father is Guildmaster."

The rest of the story had to wait until I was finished vomiting.

31

GUILD COUNCIL

Contamination Assessment for the Cleansing of Terra Colonna:
Summary of Findings

Our preliminary assessment of the feasibility of Cleansing Terra Colonna (hereafter TC) has determined that it is within acceptable risk parameters for the Terran Cluster, provided the social model is followed.

Implementation:

The effort required to initiate a fully self-destructive pattern through manipulation of key leadership figures, with the ultimate goal of creating a state of global chaos, is within reasonable practical and budgetary constraints, and could be launched within the year.

Effectiveness:

While complete societal collapse would take 5-10 years to manifest, we believe there would be sufficient disruption in the early stages to safeguard the interests of Terra Prime, as resources and personnel currently dedicated to investigating the Gates would be assigned elsewhere.

Effect:

While some contamination is unavoidable in any Cleansing, we believe that the Terran Cluster as a whole is well positioned to maintain its integrity, and to resist the pressure toward chaos that will result from TC's breakdown.

Alternative models:

The negative effect of biological and/or technological Cleansing on the Terran Cluster would exceed acceptable parameters for contamination, hence those methods are not recommended.

For further details, see attached report.

32

BADLANDS
TERRA PRIME

JESSE

LEAVING THE BADLANDS felt strangely like leaving home. Not because I had developed such great affection for the place, but when you've survived a life-and-death trial and been transformed by it, you feel a natural connection to the place where it occurred. Also, I was leaving behind someone I loved, which was hard for me to accept. I kept turning around, expecting to see Sebastian coming up behind me, his white hair blowing in the desert wind, fetters glittering in the sun.

Our farewells were moving but minimal. Ahota returned Mom's rings to me, then hugged me briefly in a formal, ritualized sort of way, which left the smell of sage and tobacco clinging to my clothes. She told Isaac that he would always be welcome to return, which, in a roundabout way, communicated that he had earned the right to leave. I think if his brand of necromancy had been at all compatible with local practices he might have asked if he could stay, but it clearly wasn't, so the subject never came up.

It was painful having to making a new latex patch for his forehead. He handled it bravely, but I could see in his eyes that he dreaded returning to a world where his Guild stigma would define his existence.

Charisa led us to a tunnel a few miles north of Ahota's camp. It allowed us to pass safely under the sands of El Malo, but not beyond its psychic influence. We passed by several skeletons, probably the remains of explorers who had entered the tunnel only to drown in El Malo's nightmares. Whereas we had already been tested and approved during our first passage, so outside of a vague sense of foreboding, we suffered no ill effects this time.

I half expected the Soulriders to be waiting for us when we got back to Rouelle, but apparently Antonin had made good on his word, and no one bothered us. We bought tickets for the next train heading east, then collapsed onto one of the benches in the station, too tired to find a hotel. I was numb by that point, my mind dazed by sorrow and exhaustion, and when it was finally time to board the train, Isaac had to help me up the stairs.

By the time we transferred to a train on the main eastbound line, and were able to secure a private cabin, I felt a little better. I took out the com fetter that Sebastian had given me, ran a finger over its crystal surface, then closed my palm over it and willed it to activate. Though it warmed immediately in my hand, a few minutes passed before the image of Morgana appeared. Evidently she was busy.

"It's over," I said.

"May I ask the outcome?"

"We won. Thanks to the information you gave us. The Shadows saw that we could hurt them and called for a truce. We still have to work out terms." As an afterthought I added, "Virilian's dead. Killed by his own creations."

She raised an eyebrow. "Do you know who's taking his place?"

"Leonid Antonin." I glanced at Isaac, who was out of range of the fetter's field of vision. "I'm told he's one of their elders."

"I know the man. Fiercely prideful. As I recall, his fears were pride-related."

I nodded. "I'll be meeting with him in Luray to discuss . . . well, I guess you'd call them terms of surrender."

She chuckled. "I doubt he'll agree to call them that."

"I also have some information that might get the ban on Dream-walkers lifted. I hope. We'll see how it goes."

There was silence for a moment. "If the ban was lifted, you could stay here."

"You mean, for good? Not go back to Terra Colonna?" I laughed. "Thanks, but no thanks."

She said it quietly: "It might be safer here, Jessica."

"What do you mean?" Now I was getting anxious. "What's happening?"

She sighed. "There's been a contamination assessment for Terra Colonna. It just came back positive."

"Which means . . . what? That they want to Cleanse my home world?"

"It's been proposed. Authorities on Terra Colonna are close to dis-covering our Gates, and the threat is too widespread to deal with on a local basis. We'll be voting on a global strategy later this week. I'm honestly not sure how that will go."

"Shit." I fell back in my seat. "Seriously?"

"I know how much your family means to you. If we can get the ban lifted, so you can stay here, I'll see they're brought across."

"To Terra Prime? To live on Terra Prime?" I shook my head. "No. That's not a solution."

"Unless you have another way to neutralize the threat your world now poses to us, I'm afraid there's no other option."

"Threat?" Now I was pissed. "What kind of threat? That someone on my world will find a Gate and try to go through it? The way your people do every day of the week?" I forced myself to take a few deep breaths before demanding. "What gives you the right to make that kind of decision for us?"

"I'm sorry, Jesse." The sympathy in her voice was maddening. *So sorry that I'm planning to destroy your home world. Please bring your family for a visit, so they miss the holocaust.* "There are numerous agencies on your world that are close to learning the truth. Unless another solution is found . . ." She spreads her hands. "There's nothing I can do."

"There's got to be a better way. Damn it, it's my world. I know how it works better than your people do. I'll come up with something."

She said nothing.

"When is this vote taking place?"

"Soon. But that'll just be for Luray's stand on the matter. Condemning a world is a long process. This is just the first step."

"If I do come up with another option, will anyone listen?"

She hesitated. "The Shadows know what you are now. If the ban on Dreamwalkers is still in place—"

"Assume it won't be."

She hesitated. "Then, yes. It's a bit unorthodox, but I don't see why you could not present your ideas."

Yeah, you usually don't give condemned worlds a chance to defend themselves. "I'll get in touch with you after I settle things with Antonin. A lot will be dictated by how that goes."

"I look forward to us talking again. In person, perhaps." She sighed. "Though I do wish the circumstances could be better."

"Yeah. You and me both."

I opened my hand. The image faded.

"Crap," I muttered.

"You have an idea?" Isaac asked.

"Not a clue," I muttered. "Not a friggin' clue."

33

GRAND GUILDHALL IN LURAY
VIRGINIA PRIME

LEONID ANTONIN

ANTONIN COULDN'T STOP THINKING ABOUT Shadowlord Hawkins.

He sat at the end of a conference table in one of the guildhall's meeting rooms, trying to banish the image of the fallen Shadow from his brain. Why was Hawkins' collapse after his concrete prison was banished so much more disturbing to him than Virilian's demise at the hands of the reapers? When the Shadowlords had awakened after their Dreamwalker confrontation to find nothing but a mass of mangled flesh in Virilian's bed, that should have outweighed all else in his mind. Yet it was Hawkins' last moments as *umbra maja* that he kept seeing: the concrete cocoon shrinking—Virilian banishing it—the man inside collapsing to the ground, not a Shadowlord any longer. So what was Hawkins now? Truly alive, or something else?

All Shadows were taught that the *umbrae majae* must rein in their living emotions. That was included in their elementary education, a fact as basic as learning the times tables or studying the history of the British Empire. If one of the undead surrendered to living emotion, they were taught, he might lose the balance of spirit which enabled him to remain undead. Yet as far as Antonin knew, that had never actually happened. The warning alone had been enough to keep the *umbrae majae* from straying too far.

Until now.

The Dreamwalkers had turned Hawkins' own mind against him, using his emotions to force him back into a living state. Whether he would survive the transformation was still up in the air. Oh, his flesh would recover—the doctors said no permanent damage had been done—but his mind? The journey back to life had thoroughly unhinged him, and since the Guild of Shadows had no experience dealing with this kind of trauma, it was ill-equipped to help.

Antonin had suffered his own nightmare during that battle. Suddenly he'd found himself surrounded by dead Shadowlords, and he was filled with the knowledge that all of them had died because of him. The illusion that he had failed his Guild and sullied his family's honor was a more subtle torment than being trapped in a concrete tomb, perhaps, but for him it was no less unnerving. If Virilian's dramatic demise hadn't distracted him right when the nightmare started, causing the illusion to shatter, Antonin might have wound up in the same state of mind Hawkins was in now.

They all could wind up that way, if this conflict went on.

A servant appeared in the doorway. "She's here, your Grace."

He stood. "Escort her in."

The man hesitated. "She's with someone—"

"I know who she's with," he said sharply. "The dead have already informed me. Show them both in."

Isaac was here. That infuriated Antonin, but he had to admit that he had opened the door for it himself. When he'd given the Dolan girl permission to bring someone with her, promising safe passage, he hadn't set any restrictions. Honor now required that he make good on his word, even if the last person he wanted to see right now was his failed progeny.

When they entered together, Antonin got his first good look at the girl who had orchestrated the tower battle. She looked young, defiant, and very tired. The last was hardly a surprise, given her recent events. Any sane man would be exhausted in her place. As for Isaac, the sight of him standing next to her, the mark of shame emblazoned on his forehead, awakened an anger that was not easily dismissed. Only the memory of what happened to Hawkins enabled Antonin to keep his emotions in check. "Jennifer Dolan, I assume."

"Yes. You are Guildmaster now?"

He nodded and gestured for her to take a seat, then resumed his own. Coldly he asked, "Do you understand the status of your companion?"

"He's here as a translator, nothing more. I thought that if you and I needed to discuss something that involved sensitive Guild information, he could represent me. That way your secrets wouldn't be threatened." She glanced as Isaac. "He was the only one I knew who could play such a role, so I asked him. He wasn't present at the tower battle, and he hasn't acted against your Guild in any way."

Except by shaming us with his presence. "Very well. You wished to discuss our situation."

She nodded. "As you know, centuries ago your Guild fought a genocidal war against my people. The world may have forgotten your motives—or perhaps it never really knew them—but records were left behind. I found them. There are fetters which contain witness testimony from the Dream Wars, revealing what really went on. From them I learned that the Shadows never believed we were mad, but spread that rumor to turn the other Guilds against us. I learned that your Guild bound the spirits of Dreamwalkers in order to steal their Gift, and that those spirits are still bound. And I saw Virilian with some of them at the tower battle, so I know how they're being used." Her eyes narrowed. "How they're being *devoured*." She leaned forward on the conference table. "*End* it, Guildmaster Antonin. End it all. Allow us to return to the light of day and free our captured people, and we'll forget that those fetters ever existed. History will be a clean slate between us, and the other Guilds will never know how you manipulated them, or why." She leaned back in her chair. "Those are my terms."

He considered her words in silence for a moment. If her story about the fetters was true, and there really was hard proof that the Shadows had lied to the other Guilds to convince them to participate in genocide, she had the ability to destroy his Guild's reputation. True, she couldn't diminish its actual power—the Shadows would still control passage through the Gates—but socially, politically, they'd be finished. He couldn't even argue that the Shadowlords who had overseen that genocide were dead and gone, because anyone who knew about Communion would understand that their memories and motives had since been absorbed by others. In the eyes of the outside world those ancient offenders were still alive, and in many cases running the Guild. Every act of Communion from now until doomsday would be read as support for their crimes.

There would be no recovering from that. Ever.

"Even if it were possible to release such spirits," he said evenly, "I doubt it would accomplish what you're seeking. The mind of a wraith is destroyed when it's bound. And with these in particular, passed from master to master down through the centuries, there'd be nothing left but vague fragments of human awareness. I doubt they even know who they originally were."

Anger flashed in her eyes. "Virilian made a point of showing me what you use them for. Do I have to explain why that needs to stop? I'm sure if you know how to bind ghosts, you can figure out how to unbind them." She paused. "I'm not asking you to restore them to their former state, or take any kind of responsibility for their finding peace. Just let them go free. They can search for peace on their own."

"So those are your *terms*, then. Anything else?"

Her expression hardened. "Yes. Cease to use our Gift. I realize there are Shadowlords who've learned how to see the dream realm as we do, and that can't be changed, but no new ones should be taught our ways." She paused. "Respect that our Gift is not yours to steal or imitate, and we'll show equal respect for yours."

For a long moment he looked at her. Then he turned to Isaac. "I believe we have come to the moment when your services are needed."

He looked at Dolan. "There are some things I cannot discuss with an outsider."

She nodded and rose. "As I said, we anticipated that might happen." She touched Isaac gently on the shoulder. "Let me know when you're done."

When the door shut behind her Antonin looked at his son. Isaac was thinner and more haggard than when he'd left home, and his skin was blistered and peeling in several places. Still, there was a strength about him that had not been there before. "She's talking about Communion," Antonin said.

Isaac nodded. "I know."

"To give that up would be to give up the method by which we transfer knowledge from one generation to the next. It's not going to happen."

"But what kind of knowledge are you transferring? You told me once that after Communion an *umbra maja* could hear the music of the spheres. That's a Dreamwalker talent. Being able to see the patterns that bind the worlds together is also a Dreamwalker talent. Shadows can't do any of that on their own. So what's really being transferred?"

"The echo of their Gift, most likely. But it's part of our Guild identity now, and I tell you bluntly, no arguments from me or threats from the Dreamwalkers will convince the Shadows to give it up. Especially when that would require abandoning the method by which so much of our other knowledge is transferred."

"Father, there's a force in the Badlands that sometimes allows a person to glimpse hidden truths. I had a vision there. I saw that the ancient Shadowlords not only bound Dreamwalkers to them, but were bound by them in turn. When we stole their Gift, we corrupted our own. Now, I don't have enough education to know what the Shadows were like before the Dream Wars, so I can't tell you how we changed, but I'm sure there are historical records a Guildmaster can access. So check out what we were before that, and then ask yourself what we lost. And ask if it's really in the Shadows' best interest to continue on this path . . . especially when it may cost us so much with the Dream-walkers now." He paused. "Will you do that?"

How strong his son seemed now—how unlike the fearful child who had once struggled so hard not to offend his father! Exile had tempered Isaac's soul. "I'll research the matter," he promised. "But will that be enough for your Dreamwalker friend?"

"What she wants is freedom. Lift the ban that has driven her kind into hiding. Free the Dreamwalkers that our ancestors enslaved. Give her those two things and I think she'll be reasonable about the rest."

"And what do you think will happen to our Guild if the Dream-walkers return? Right now we're the only ones who can cross between worlds freely. It gives us control of the portals. What role do you imag-ine we will play when another Guild can do those same things?"

"Dreamwalkers see the paths between the worlds, but they can only travel them in dreams. And they're visionaries, not bureaucrats; I doubt they have any interest in controlling transportation hubs. They might serve some role in interworld communication, but they can't cross back and forth between worlds like the dead can. Shadows would still be needed as messengers, scouts, explorers, and guides. Not to mention, we'd still be necromancers. That's what we were orig-inally, right? Very little would need to change. Other than the fact that there would be people with greater vision than yours to help de-velop proper codexes."

"And if we don't agree to this path?"

"Then I believe she will indeed lay the past sins of this Guild bare. And she has patrons powerful enough that her accusations will be taken seriously. Not to mention the fetters."

"Those are real? You can vouch for that?"

He nodded.

With a heavy sigh Antonin sank back in his chair. "So is this how you think the Antonin story should end. We are the ones who must declare defeat, sue for terms, and dictate submission for our people. After centuries of leading this Guild, our family will be responsible for its downfall. Because that's what this would lead to, don't mistake that. The Dreamwalkers were condemned because people believed their madness made them dangerous. In order for them to return, we would have to reveal it was never true. That we condemned an entire people with a lie. How do you think that will play out in the political arena?"

"If you don't agree to her terms it will happen anyway," Isaac warned him. "So what's the alternative?"

Slowly Antonin steepled his fingers before him. *Maybe it's a good thing the boy is here,* he thought. *She'll listen to his counsel.* "We weave a story between us that gives her what she wants, without doing harm to our interests."

Isaac looked surprised. "A fictional history?"

He shrugged. "We've done it before."

He shook his head. "Lies to cancel out lies—"

"The truth is a tool, nothing more. Sometimes lies are a better tool. Do you think she would be willing to go along such a plan?"

He hesitated. "I think she would probably go along with anything that gave her what she wants. Terra Prime politics mean nothing to her."

"Excellent." He nodded toward the door. "Then perhaps you should fetch her back now. Do take your time, though. You two might want to discuss a few things along the way."

Isaac stared at him for moment, and then, without further word, rose and left the chamber.

In his absence, Antonin shut his eyes. As always, he could hear the sounds of ghostly suffering around him. Normal wraiths were simple servants, freed when their masters died. Their suffering was moderate, and they rarely complained. So if the Dreamwalker wraiths went away, would the sounds of misery leave with them?

It darkens the human soul to hear such suffering, he thought. *There can be no denying that.*

Footsteps approached the door. He opened his eyes again, nodding to the two as they entered and resumed their seats. "Let me make one thing clear," he said. "I do not rule over the Shadows. No one person does. If we make an agreement here today, I can guarantee that the Shadows of Luray will honor it, and I have enough influence in neighboring regions to expect support from them as well—especially as you drew Shadowlords from Front Royal and Richmond into your battle. Beyond that, I can only promise to do my best to present our treaty to the others and convince them to honor it. There are no guarantees. That said, I am the head of a powerful family, with members in key cities throughout the Empire. If I order them all to support your cause, that's no small thing."

"Understood," the girl said. "And I likewise have no official authority over the Dreamwalkers. I expect those who stood with me at the tower will honor my word, but it's the next generation, raised in freedom, that will shape our politics. I'll do what I can to make sure they understand the importance of peace between us, and honor the terms of that peace, but I, too, can make no guarantees." She folded her hands on the table in front of her. "I understand you have a proposition."

"Virilian was preparing an army of the dead to send against you. You saw them on the field of battle. I believe his intent was to muster thousands, enough to scour all the human worlds for any Dreamwalkers who might still be in hiding. The elders of my Guild were aware of this plan. Some were asked to help with it.

"So let us say . . . this had been going on for some time. Virilian's first crop of war wraiths proved a serious enough threat that your people felt it had to be dealt with. The battle at the tower was your response to that threat. There you showed us that you had weapons of your own, equally lethal, and that a continued war between our peoples would involve losses on both sides. And so we negotiate peace today, equal partners in ending a conflict that has grown too costly for both of us."

"I see your interests in this more than mine," she said. "But go on."

"To seal that peace, the Guild of Shadows offers the release of all Dreamwalker spirits in our custody. Understand, it will take time to get all Shadows to comply, but we will work steadily toward that goal. The Dreamwalkers, in turn, offer to leave control of the Gates to us. That doesn't mean you can't communicate freely between worlds, but the *business* of interworld commerce will remain in our hands. Dreamwalkers will not challenge us for it. If you have information we need, or we have services you need, we will handle that as an exchange between equals."

Her eyes narrowed slightly. "And our legitimacy?"

"It seems the Shadows have uncovered evidence of an ancient division within the ranks of Dreamwalkers. Only one strain was prone to madness. It's a terrible tragedy that we didn't know this at the time, so our efforts to eradicate that strain cost many innocent lives. But now that the mad ones are gone, such extremes are no longer necessary." He smiled slightly. "With this new evidence in hand, and the reputation of my Guild behind it, there should be no problem getting the other Guilds to accept your return—and no need for us to admit that our old reports were mistaken."

She raised an eyebrow. "Evidence?"

He shrugged. "I can have something convincing forged by morning."

She was silent, considering his offer. At one point she glanced at Isaac, which was a good sign; his son must have argued in favor of accepting it. "If we do this," she said at last, "that will be the official explanation for why you claimed we were all insane. The fetters won't be a threat to you anymore."

"That is indeed the case," he agreed. "Anything else?"

For a long moment she just looked at him. "No." She shook her head. "There's nothing else." She held out her hand to him. "I believe we have a deal."

He wasn't accustomed to the living seeking contact with him, so it felt strange to take her hand. He saw her shudder slightly as she felt the unnatural cold of his flesh, but for the most part she did a good job of hiding her response. He knew Guildmasters who might not do as well.

The three of them rose then, and Dolan and his son headed toward the door. But as they reached the threshold Antonin said, "Isaac. A moment alone."

Startled, the boy looked back at him. Then at Dolan. "I'll wait for you," she said, and she left the two of them alone together in the room.

Isaac turned to his father. "Sir?"

"It was Virilian who banished you," Antonin said.

Isaac nodded.

"I'm Guildmaster now. I could undo that banishment. I could remove the mark of shame from your forehead. I could even have Virilian's Domitor undo his work, as a gesture of the Guild's faith in you. Yet you don't ask for any of these things. Why?"

Isaac looked away. "We both know what my situation is. We both know what you could do to make it better. My father . . ." His voice caught for a moment. "He taught me to bear myself with dignity at all times. I can't say I've always managed that, but I do recognize the wisdom in his words. So I won't beg. No matter what that costs me." He met his father's eyes. "You'll do what you think is best for the Guild. As always."

Antonin watched in thoughtful silence as his son left the room.

34

SEER GUILDHOUSE IN LURAY
VIRGINIA PRIME

JESSE

THE FOYER OF THE SEERS' GUILDHOUSE was much as I remembered it: cavernous, full of echoes, and refreshingly cool. I walked to the center of the inlaid marble floor and gazed down at the pattern in its center, a sigil that echoed the pyramid-and-eye design on US dollar bills. I remembered that when I first saw it I'd wondered about the connection. Had someone from the Seers Guild influenced the design of American currency? But now I understood how such things worked. Somewhere near a shallow, a sleeping human mind on one world had dreamed about that symbol; somewhere on another world, a sleeping human mind had sensed it. Thus it was with designs, philosophies, passions, traumas: they seeped from one reality to the next through dreams, with no one aware it was happening. No world was truly independent. No human civilization could escape being influenced by those that surrounded it. The universe was one vast ecosystem.

"She'll see you now," a servant said.

Morgana and Seyer were waiting for me in the study. Now that I knew what their relationship was, I was struck by the deliberate visual contrast between them: one draped in pure white and crowned in golden curls, the other all in gothic black. Seyer's appearance was a statement of rebellion, a reminder that though she was bound in service to her mother, she was also an independent human being with tastes and desires of her own. Morgana could not look at her without being reminded of that.

I respected such a statement.

Morgana greeted me and gestured toward the sitting area. I still didn't trust the woman, but as I took a seat opposite her I discovered that my hostility had lost a bit of its edge. I was furious with her for manipulating my life the way she had, putting my safety and that of my family at risk as she ran experiments on me, trying to mold me into a proper tool for her purpose. But it was her notes on the Shadows that made it possible for me to defeat them. And to be honest, she had never actually forced me to do anything. My choices had always been my own. If I chose to go back to Terra Colonna now, and demanded that she stay out of my life forever, she would probably respect that.

There was a tea set on the table, and she poured three cups full as she said, "You've been granted safe passage to address this afternoon's Council session."

"Thank you."

She handed a cup to me and another to Seyer. "Now tell me about your meeting with Antonin."

"He said he'll support the lifting of the death sentence on Dreamwalkers, in return for us not challenging his Guild for control of the Gates. There won't be any restriction on communication, which is more of what our Gift is about anyway, so for us it's a good deal," I dropped a sugar cube into my tea, "though maybe not as much as his enemies would hope for."

"If we can set up a method of communication between the worlds that the Shadows don't control, many things become possible. You did well."

I shrugged. "It's all just theoretical until the ban is lifted. No Dreamwalker is going to help with communication—or anything else—while there's still a death sentence hanging over all our heads."

She nodded. "Antonin raised that issue in Council this morning. He said that his Guild had discovered evidence that suggested only a small fraction of Dreamwalkers ever suffered from madness, and those were all killed in the Dream Wars. So, the ones who are alive today should be no threat to anyone."

So Antonin had come through for me. "Good to know. How was his statement received?"

"Discussion is ongoing. We'll be resuming this afternoon." She paused. "It was certainly convenient. Imagine discovering such evidence on the very day you were scheduled to address the Council."

"That is indeed a remarkable coincidence," I agreed carefully.

"They asked me to verify it."

My heart skipped a beat. "And?"

She smiled slightly. "It has the proper appearance for its age. And Antonin seemed to be telling the truth about it."

"Also good to know." I sipped my tea, letting the cup mask my expression. "So what's left before you all make a decision?"

"The Council wants to hear your petition on Terra Colonna before they vote on the Dreamwalker ban. Remember, most of them have never seen a Dreamwalker. You are a creature of legend to them, and a frightening legend at that. Since the entire argument about your status hinges on the question of mental stability, they no doubt want to get a feel for yours."

"So now I'm the poster child for my Gift."

"A colorful way of putting it, but yes, that seems to be the case." She sipped her tea. "When you asked me to speak to the Council about Terra Colonna, you didn't yet have a plan to offer them. Do you now?"

"I think so. It's a bit out of the box, but if it wasn't, they would already have considered it." I hesitated. "If I fail, and a Cleansing is approved . . ." I couldn't finish the thought.

"Your family will be welcome here," she said quietly. "We'll bring across the ones you love. They'll be safe on Terra Prime."

Yes, but seven billion other people won't be. "Your Grace . . . may I ask you something?"

"Of course."

I put my cup down. "Why are you doing this? I mean, I understand the Guild politics involved. But it seems to me there's more going on than that. You seem way too invested in this for it to be only about politics."

She smiled slightly. "Are you playing the Seer now?"

"I'm *playing* someone who's about to make her first public appearance as a Dreamwalker. People are normally put to death for that. Don't I deserve to know what the real game is?"

A corner of her mouth twitched. "Fair enough." She sipped again from her cup and then lowered it. "Your Gift is very similar to ours. Seers sense the secrets that are in a man's waking mind, while you sense the secrets that are in his dreams. Because of that similarity, Dreamwalker births are much more common among Seers than they are in the general population. Not a year passes without some member of my Guild giving birth to a child who has the potential to develop your Gift . . . and who must be put down for it."

"Jesus," I whispered.

"When you were born to me, when I held you in my arms, when I sensed the seed of the forbidden Gift in you, I thought: Enough. It's time for our sacrifices to end." She paused for a moment, maybe waiting for me to respond to this new revelation, but thanks to Sebastian I'd been prepared for it, and my expression revealed nothing. "I had long suspected that the tales of Dreamwalker madness were false, but I had no proof. I believed you could test that for me. And so I hid you away, and when you were old enough for your Gift to manifest, I placed challenges in your path. I tested your mettle. I gave you reason to seek out others of your kind, because only someone with your Gift could find them. And I'm sorry I couldn't tell you the truth until now, but first I had to know you were strong enough to handle such a secret." She paused. "You are, without question."

I stared at her in disbelief for a moment. Then turned away. "Crap," I muttered.

A delicate eyebrow arched upward. "Why 'crap'?"

"Because all this time I've resented you for how you used me. I thought you were nothing but a cold-hearted manipulative bitch. Now you tell me it was all about saving babies." I shook my head.

A faint smile. "Well, one can be a cold-hearted manipulative bitch and also a mother. The roles aren't mutually exclusive. And it wasn't *all* about saving babies." She put her empty cup aside. "I've laid out some clothes for you upstairs, which should fit. Go choose something appropriate for the Council meeting. We need to start getting ready; the afternoon session will begin soon."

"Why can't I wear the clothes I've got on?"

"They look like you've slept in them for a week. Probably because you *have* slept in them for a week. You need to present yourself to the Guildmasters as a peer, Jessica. If the ban is lifted, that's how they'll see you: a Guildmaster in function, if not in name."

"*No*," I said. "Not a Guildmaster. I am *not* going to become part of your—"

"Miriam," she said sweetly, "take your sister upstairs and help her choose something to wear, won't you?"

Seyer put down her own cup and stood. I stared at her for a minute, then shook my head in exasperation and followed her lead.

"Something nice," Morgana called out, as we left the room. "And be timely about it. We need to leave soon."

In the hallway I muttered to Seyer, "Something black, please."

She smiled. "Already laid out."

⁜

Morgana told me that the Guildmasters of Luray normally met around a large circular table, but when I was led into the meeting room I saw that part of it had been removed so that a small podium could be placed there instead. The arrangement put me between the arms of a large curved crescent, with thirteen of the most powerful people in Luray seated around it. Far more intimidating than anything I'd ever had to face.

The attendant who led me in guided me to the podium, where I saw that a glass of water and a copy of the contamination assessment had been provided. As I took my place, he announced, "Jessica Drake, Master Dreamwalker of Terra Colonna." Apparently I'd gotten a promotion.

And then there I was, facing the thirteen people who would decide not only my fate but the fate of my entire world. I had chosen a pair of slim black denim pants for the occasion, with a matching silk tank and a wine-colored vest, but now I was regretting that choice. In theory it had seemed the perfect outfit for a midsummer Council presentation, but now I was afraid that one of these people would see the goosebumps that were forming on my bare arms. Around my neck I wore Mom's two rings on a chain, for luck, and I'd tucked my fake wren feather into the upswept hairdo that Miriam had insisted I adopt; I took a moment to draw strength from those things. *These people are not all strangers to me,* I reminded myself. Directly across from me sat the head Fleshcrafter, his six golden arms arranged symmetrically, like the limbs of a Hindu god. He smiled at me ever so slightly, a subtle gesture of encouragement, and I remembered how he had received me when I'd presented information to him in his own guildhall, to convince him to help my mother. So, at least one person here viewed me in a positive light. Then there was Morgana two seats over from him, with Antonin seated at one end of a pincer. He'd come through on the forged evidence, so it was likely he'd support me now, which made two more on my side—unless I totally screwed up—for a total of three. I only needed seven supporters to carry the day. Suddenly my task didn't seem quite so impossible.

I drank some water, cleared my throat, silently voiced a prayer to any god who was listening, and began.

"Guildmasters and mistresses of Luray. I thank you for giving me this opportunity to address you. My name is Jessica Drake, and I come here today to address the issue of Terra Colonna. Recently my home world was declared a threat to Terra Prime's interests, because various factions on my world had caught wind of the changeling program. As they compared notes and launched an investigation into the matter, it was feared they would discover the truth about Terra Colonna's portals and gain access to them.

"I agree that this would be a disaster. My world has many violent factions, some armed with weapons that could wreak havoc here. And the fragmented nature of Terra Colonna's society means that it would be difficult—if not impossible—to impose any kind of global restrictions on my world, or establish a treaty that all would respect. Hence, it was decided that the best way to deal with the threat was to Cleanse Terra Colonna, so that it was no longer a threat to anyone."

I paused. "I've come here today to present a third option. One which will protect not only Terra Colonna, but other worlds as well. Yes, the contamination assessment assures us that any damage would be within acceptable parameters . . . but there would still be damage. The destruction of a world by any means, anywhere, impacts all the spheres in its cluster." I paused. "If that weren't the case, no contamination study would be necessary."

I took another drink of water, not because I was thirsty so much as to buy me a second to settle my nerves. "My proposal is simple. Withdraw all your people from Terra Colonna. Dismantle the Gates. Remove from my world every physical sign of your presence, from the stockpiles of carefully labeled bodies to the high tech archways, down to the piles of travel waivers. All of it. Then . . . shut down the portals. Quarantine my world for a set period of time and leave my people to their own devices. Let them investigate the changelings as much as they want—even inspect the locations where portals once existed. There will be nothing there to find. It won't even matter if their investigation does turn up evidence that other worlds exist. They could stumble over a guidebook explaining the operations of the Gates and describing Terra Prime in detail, and it still wouldn't help them. Without the portals, it's all just paranoid fiction.

"All your solutions thus far have focused on keeping my people from learning the truth. I say, let them learn it, if they can. And after years of banging their heads against a wall in an attempt to verify it, they will declare it fictional of their own accord and move on to other things. Oh, a few conspiracy nuts will persist, but those types are easily discredited . . . at least as far as the authorities are concerned. Then the blockade can be lifted and normalcy restored." I paused. "Meanwhile, the dying cries of a murdered civilization will not have poisoned a thousand other worlds. Including yours."

Silence.

"That's all I came to say," I told them. "Please consider it as an option."

A Guildmaster sitting across from me said harshly, "This plan assumes we have the power to shut down all the portals on a given world."

"You do. You did it on Terra Fuentes when the plastic plague hit. I don't know enough about your science to speak to the details of the process, but obviously when the need is judged great enough, quarantine is possible."

The Fleshcrafter said, "How long would you recommend such a blockade be maintained?"

"I'd suggest ten years. It shouldn't require more than that, especially since the governments of many countries of my world have rapid turnover. Leaders of today who might consider the search for interworld portals a priority would give way to those who see it only as a pointless drain on their budgets. Oh, conspiracy theorists might persist, but they wouldn't have the backing they'd need to get around your normal precautions. The Greys are masters of misdirection." I nodded respectfully toward the Grey at the table; he seemed pleased by the compliment. "Aliens and demons are so much easier to blame for this kind of thing than invisible worlds."

Antonin said, "If we do this, how can you be sure we will not cut off your world permanently?"

Ah, that was the question, wasn't it? Permanent quarantine would indeed solve all our problems with Terra Prime. But it would also condemn Terra Colonna to permanent isolation. Shut off from all outside contact, my world would soon be forgotten, a mere footnote to history. And if someday the Guilds came to accept the enlightenment of other worlds—as I believed they eventually must—Terra Colonna would likely remain forgotten, an island of ignorance isolated from the thriving multiverse surrounding it. Forever.

I, Jessica Drake, did not have the right to impose that sentence upon my world.

I braced myself to look directly into Antonin's black, empty eyes. "First, because Terra Colonna's gene pool produces many Gifted children, and you would lose access to them. Isn't that why you were so involved with our world in the first place? Because so many Gifted children are born there? And second, because there are Gifts that allow for communication between worlds, independent of physical passage. People with those Gifts might not appreciate being cut off from others of their own kind forever."

Jeez. Had he just manipulated me into threatening them? Or had he simply voiced what everyone was thinking anyway—that Dreamwalkers on Terra Colonna could never be cut off completely, and if our world was not treated fairly, those of my Gift who lived elsewhere might be displeased.

"Look," I said, "Terra Colonna may be the first world to offer this kind of threat, but it won't be the last. Numerous worlds are in the process of developing advanced DNA technology. Are you going to destroy every civilization that catches a glimpse of the truth? The universe is going to become a very small place if you do that. So . . . consider Terra Colonna an experiment of sorts. See if this is a viable solution. If so, you can apply elsewhere. If not . . ." I shrugged. "The nuclear option will still be on the table in ten years. All you'd be agreeing to do is try something else first."

The Fleshcrafter folded two of his hands on the table. "I assume you're volunteering to report on the progress of your world? Because a quarantine would make our normal methods impossible."

So much for getting away from these people, I thought. But he was right; they would need some way to evaluate Terra Colonna before a quarantine could be lifted, and unless they wanted to exile someone to my world for ten years, I was the obvious choice. And this would establish a unique service that Dreamwalkers could provide to the other Guilds, which might play favorably in the debate about our legitimacy. "Of course."

There was silence again. "Any more questions?" I asked.

A Guildmaster whose name I didn't know said, "Thank you for sharing your thoughts with us, Miss Drake. We'll discuss the points you've raised in private Council."

It was clearly a dismissal, so I bowed my head with what I hoped was appropriate grace and somehow managed to walk out. My legs were shaking so badly that as soon as I got outside the room I had to lean against a wall to steady myself.

"This way." An attendant outside the chamber was pointing to a nearby door. "You can wait in here."

I let him guide me to a waiting room outfitted with comfortable chairs and coffee. I couldn't sit still, and I didn't think caffeine was a good idea, so I paced. And waited. And paced. And waited.

Just about the time when I started wondering if I might not go crazy after all, the door opened. It was Morgana.

"Yes?" I asked. My voice was shaking. "Please say yes."

She nodded. "Yes."

"Which one?'"

"Both. Ten years of isolation for your home world will be proposed to the National Council, after which the situation will be assessed. More time will be added if necessary, with periodic reassessment." She paused. "I expect soon we'll have to consider bringing the more advanced worlds into our circle, as opposed to trying to keep them perpetually in the dark. As you so eloquently pointed out, the latter isn't likely to work much longer. Once the need for secrecy disappears, so will the need for your quarantine."

"And the Dreamwalkers?"

"Your suggestion regarding the sort of service they might provide was well received. There was some concern that without a proper Guild structure, your first generation would have little guidance.

We're assuming your hidden allies would want to stay hidden, so there would be no one other than yourself to train new Dreamwalkers, or teach them how the Gifted are expected to behave. I volunteered the Seers for that purpose, until such time as there are enough adult Dreamwalkers to take over." She smiled at me. "Is this acceptable?"

I found myself speechless. *You just took control of all the Dream-walkers. You get to train an entire generation of them, indoctrinating them into the Seer's culture, molding them into your pawns. Could this be what you really wanted all along? 'Saving the babies,' my ass.* But what was the alternative? The Council was right. You couldn't have children manifesting a Gift and not offer them some kind of support.

Maybe I would have to come back and play Guildmaster in ten years after all.

"You understand," she said, "This is only in Luray. The ban must be lifted region by region, and ultimately country by country. But I have no doubt that when Antonin's evidence is presented, demonstrating that Dreamwalker insanity is no longer an issue, the Guilds of other cities will have no objection to your return." She smiled slightly. "His 'documentation' was very cleverly designed. And of course the Seers will verify it, when asked." Her eyes sparkled. "You must have put quite the fear of God into him."

"I'm sure I don't know what you're talking about."

She chuckled. "Come. You deserve a celebratory dinner. No reapers, no Hunters, no magistrates questioning your status. Just family." She stressed the last word slightly.

"With all due respect to you and Miriam . . . I just want to go home now." *After I tell Isaac what happened. He's like family, too.*

Her expression softened. "All right. I'll make the arrangements. But only if you promise me an update later."

After I'm home, I thought. *I can contact anyone I want to, even with the quarantine in place. But how much involvement do I want with you? With this world?*

Don't worry about that now. One step at a time.

I shut my eyes and breathed deeply. So this was what it felt like to have the weight of the world lifted from your shoulders. It was good. I liked it.

Mom, Tommy, Manassas . . . I'm coming home.

35

MANASSAS
VIRGINIA

JESSE

I TOLD TOMMY AND MOM that I was on my way back to Terra Colonna, but not exactly when I would arrive. I wanted to surprise them.

When Tommy opened the apartment door and saw me standing there in the hallway, his mouth dropped open. "MOM! JESSE'S BACK!"

She came running, and I was dragged into the apartment by both of them with hurricane force, and hugged until I could hardly breathe.

"My God," Mom said, when she finally allowed me to take a breath. "Why didn't you let us know you were coming? We would have picked you up."

I grinned. "I wanted to surprise you."

There were tears of joy in her eyes. "That's one hell of a surprise. I haven't slept for days . . . I was so afraid you would never come home."

"I wasn't that sure myself." Her tears were making me want to cry.

"So are the reapers all dead?" Tommy asked. "Are the Shadows going to leave you alone now? What about the government guys here?

They're going down into Mystic Caverns. What if they find what's left of the Gate? Is someone going to do anything about that? Other than destroy the whole world to get rid of everything? Because that would really, really suck."

I couldn't help but smile. "Yes, Yes, and it's all taken care of." God, I had missed my annoying little brother. His rapid-fire questions were a beacon of normalcy. "Our world's going to be quarantined for ten years at least. All the portals are being shut down, so no one can come in or out. I was one of the last people allowed through."

I watched comprehension dawn in Mom's eyes. "So . . . it doesn't matter what investigators find in the caverns? If none of the portals work, no one can ever learn the truth?"

"Exactly. It was my idea."

"Jeez." Tommy grinned. "My sister saved the world. How cool is that?"

"Not that you can ever brag about it," I said sternly.

"Of course not!"

"Or write gaming modules based on it."

His face fell a bit.

"Hey, cheer up." I reached out and mussed his hair, just the way he hates. "I promised I'd bring you back something from Terra Prime, right? Something special?"

He brightened up again. "You brought me a souvenir?"

"Well . . . no, not exactly."

I leaned back into the hall and signaled. A moment later Isaac appeared in the doorway.

"Holy crap." Tommy muttered.

Now that Isaac was clean, well groomed, and dressed in a T-shirt and jeans that I'd bought for him on the way home, he looked pretty normal. His sunburn was mostly done peeling, and his forehead was clear of any disfiguring marks. I felt a pang in my heart every time I looked at him, knowing what it meant to him that his father had freed him from that burden. A parting gift.

I waved him into the apartment. "Mom, this is Isaac Antonin.

He's the one who helped Tommy and me escape from Shadowcrest. Without his help I wouldn't be here today. Isaac, this is my mom, Evelyn Drake. And of course you've met my brother, Tommy." *And by the way there's a ghost present, but none of you can see him.*

"We met briefly," Isaac said, a spark of amusement in his eyes.

Tommy was still in shock.

"Thank you," my mother said. "For all you've done. Thank you so much. But . . ." She looked at me, confused. "Didn't you say the portals were all shut down?"

"They are," I said quietly. "We were the last ones through."

Isaac reached back and shut the door. "Jesse told me that her brother was having issues with hearing ghosts. I thought I might be able to help."

Tommy's eyes grew wide. "You mean, like, necromancy lessons?"

Before Mom could protest, Isaac told her, "I can't teach him to do anything but hear spirits more clearly . . . or stop hearing them whenever he wants to. The latter is actually far more important. No summoning, no commanding, no binding—the Gift needed for all that isn't in his blood. But I can help him control what's happening to him, so it doesn't disrupt his life."

"Oh, *please*, Mom." Tommy grabbed her arm and shook her gently. "Can I have necromancy lessons? Please?" When she didn't answer right away he added, "I promise when school starts I'll do all my other homework first."

Her expression softened. She looked at Isaac. "Do you have somewhere to stay?"

I said quickly, "I was hoping we could put him up for a little while. Just until he got settled in." I'd intended to broach that subject more privately, but what the hell.

"I'll be fine on my own," Isaac told me. "Don't forget, I lived independently for quite a while."

Mom bit her lip as she considered. I figured she was listing pros and cons in her mind, but if so, it was just a motherly ritual. Isaac had saved our lives, and there was no way she was going to turn him out on the street. Finally she sighed. "Well, he'll need ID. And some kind of cover story. With all the attention this family has had recently, we can't just have him appearing out of nowhere."

I nodded. "I'm thinking Rita probably knows how to get a fake ID." *Assuming she's still on Terra Colonna, which I'll have to check.* "She understands how the foster system works, so she can help him set up a convincing background story, one that would explain why there are no parents for anyone to check on. She owes me that much."

"I can teach him about computers and cars," Tommy said, "and how to speak regular English so no one asks questions about where he's from. Please?"

Mom looked at Isaac again. I found myself holding my breath. He'd left everything behind for a chance to make a new life here. It would be magnitudes harder without our help. "The apartment's pretty small," she said at last. "Not exactly luxurious accommodations."

He nodded gratefully. "Any day you decide I'm crowding you too much, I'll leave."

Tommy grinned. "You and I can share the bedroom. Since there are two guys here now, that seems fair." He looked at me defiantly.

"Sorry." I shook my head. "I just saved the world, I get the comfortable bed."

Mom chuckled softly. "You can share my room, Jesse. Let the boys have the other one. Maybe it'll help keep the ghosts out of the living room."

Tommy grinned. "C'mon!" He waved Isaac toward the bedroom. "I'll show you where everything is."

Isaac started to follow him, but when they reached the bedroom door he paused for a moment, looking back at my mother. "Thank you," he said softly.

As he disappeared into the bedroom, Mom and I looked at each other. Suddenly I found myself at a loss for words. How did a person even start to tell a story as dark and complicated as the one I'd just lived through? Or express the incredible gratitude I felt, for her taking Isaac in like that? There were things in my head I didn't know if I'd ever find the right words for.

Silently she came over to me and took me in her arms. And that was enough for the moment. No words were needed.

"Welcome home," she whispered.

EPILOGUE

RICHMOND
VIRGINIA

JESSE

THE FIELD OUTSIDE RICHMOND was lush and green, with only a hint of brown on the tips of the grass to testify to summer's heat. In the distance some horses were grazing, and beyond that a small house and stables were visible. Both looked like they had been built recently. Nothing else was in sight, other than a small stand of trees about a hundred yards away. "You sure this is the place?" Tommy asked.

I took out the map of Richmond that I'd annotated, and he and Mom and Isaac moved closer so they could see it. The rectangular shape I'd drawn just northeast of the city was labeled *Hayes 1771*, and it had GPS coordinates at all four corners. I took out my cell phone and checked the coordinates for where we were standing. "According to county records this is it." I looked at the house again, wanting it to be the building we'd come to find. But it was just too modern. The original house on this property had probably been demolished long ago.

Two figures appeared in the west, heading our way, and I shielded my eyes from the glare of the afternoon sun to watch them approach. Devon was wearing his usual impeccable T-shirt and jeans, with Rita in a white tank top and denim shorts. They were walking side by side, so Devon must have made his peace with her betrayal, but I felt a twinge of bitterness as I watched her walk across the field. It would be a while before I fully forgave her for spying on me.

But there was no one to spy for now. No Gates, no Guilds, no Morgana. And in a world where there were only five people I could talk to about my recent experiences, I had to preserve those relationships.

"Hey." Devon nodded to Mom and Tommy and then came over and gave me a big hug. "How are you doing?"

I hugged him back, basking in the comfort of the contact. "Better. It's amazing what a good night's sleep will do for the spirit." I saw out of the corner of my eye that Isaac was frowning slightly. Was he jealous? The thought brought a blush of guilty pleasure to my cheeks. "How'd you get permission to come down here, anyway?"

"Dad thinks I'm touring VCU. Actually, I *will* be touring VCU, but only after this is done." He and I had been chatting in furtive texts about using a demonstration of dreamwalking to convince his father that our stories about other worlds were true, but things had been so busy since my return that we hadn't gotten to it yet. Until that happened, Devon still wasn't allowed to hang out with me.

Rita had stayed back a few yards during all this, probably not sure about how she would be received. I nodded to her and said—perhaps a bit too sternly—"Rita."

Taking that as permission to approach, she nodded back to me, took a large manila envelope out of her purse, and walked over to Isaac. "I didn't know your age, so I made you eighteen on everything. Much less hassle that way. Couldn't get the birth certificate into the hospital database, but the rest is good to go." She handed him the envelope. "Be warned, street forgeries like this won't get you through a police investigation. You'll want to get a social security number and start accumulating real paperwork as soon as possible."

He opened the envelope and peered at the documents inside. "Not sure I understand most of these, but thank you."

"And don't try to drive until you learn how. The license is just for ID."

Tommy rolled his eyes. "Duh."

Devon offered, "My dad can probably get all that entered into hospital records, once he's on board with everything."

Rita turned to me. Her smile faded. "I'm sorry, Jesse." The regret in her voice sounded genuine. "For everything."

I sighed. "You did what you thought you had to. I will say I was surprised to find you were still here, though. I would have thought you'd want to be on the other side when the Gates shut down."

"It was tempting," she agreed. "But having a long-distance patron who occasionally asks you for favors isn't the same thing as being on call 24/7. Given the choice between settling in as a house servant or continuing on in glorious cash-strapped freedom, I decided to go with door number two. Though probably sometime in the next ten years I'll regret that decision." She looked out over the field. "So where are we doing this?"

I checked my map again to make sure I knew exactly where Sebastian's former property ended, then pointed to the stand of trees. A huge oak whose spreading branches dominated the grouping seemed the perfect location for our needs, so we headed over there. The grass rustled as small animals scurried out of our way, and I relished not having to worry about them. For the next ten years I would be living on a planet where birds and raccoons were nothing more than birds and raccoons, and if a pair of eyes peered at me from the shadows I didn't have to wonder if there was a human spy behind them. There were some Gifts I wouldn't miss.

Amidst the twisted, half-buried roots of the oak I found an open spot the right size, and gestured for Isaac to dig there. The hole didn't need to be large, so it only took him a few minutes to dig down the depth of his forearm. When he was done he laid the shovel off to the side, and everyone looked at me.

I took the small bundle from my pocket and for a moment just held it in my hands, gently stroking its white cloth wrapping. Though

I'd done pretty well up to now in holding back my emotions, the feel of the bundle invoked a wave of memory so intense that for a moment it took all my self-control not to cry. Then, very gently—like I was handling a child—I parted the fabric, revealing a portion of Sebastian's ashes. Kneeling beside the hole, I poured them down into the tiny makeshift grave. I hadn't been able to recover all of him from the remains of Redwind's fire, but at least this token bit could rest in the place where he had once been happy. He would have wanted that.

By the time I was done there were tears running down my cheeks. I wiped them away as I stood. "Should we pray now, or something?"

My mother put a gentle hand on my shoulder. "Whatever you want."

I folded the cloth and stuck it in my back pocket, then looked down at the grave. "God . . ." Words stuck in my throat. "Give him peace," I whispered. "Wherever he is. He was a good man and he deserves peace." I paused. "That's all."

Isaac and Devon both reached out to comfort me, but it was Mom who drew me into her arms first, in whose embrace all the pain and sorrow of recent events finally overwhelmed me. Everyone stood silently by while I wept, but I could feel their sympathy radiating like sunlight, soothing my sorrow. Finally my tears slowed enough for me to take up the shovel and push a bit of dirt into the tiny grave. Isaac then did the same, and then Tommy, and Rita, and Devon, and finally Mom. Isaac then shoveled the remaining dirt into place, and I smoothed the top of the grave and placed a single blank stone at its head, like a tiny tombstone.

We stood there for a while longer before leaving, just listening to the birds and the wind and the rustling grass, savoring the echoes of memory.

Rest in peace, Private Hayes.

Celia Friedman teaches an online class in science fiction and fantasy writing. For more information, go to http://www.writer.org.